MIDWINTER

MIDWINTER

MATTHEW STURGES

an imprint of **Prometheus Books**
Amherst, NY

Published 2009 by Pyr®, an imprint of Prometheus Books

Inquiries should be addressed to
Pyr
59 John Glenn Drive
Amherst, New York 14228–2119
VOICE: 716–691–0133, ext. 210
FAX: 716–691–0137
WWW.PYRSF.COM

13 12 11 10 09   5 4 3 2 1

Library of Congress Cataloging-in-Publication Data

Sturges, Matthew.
    Midwinter / Matthew Sturges.
        p. cm.
    ISBN 978–1–59102–734–8 (pbk. : alk. paper)
    A revised and expanded edition of a work originally published by Clockwork Storybook
(Austin, TX), 2002.
    I. Title.

PS3569.T876M53 2009
813'.54—dc22

                                                            2008054565

Printed in the United States on acid-free paper

This book is dedicated to

SHERRY HARPER,

a teacher to whom more than one person has dedicated a first novel,
and with good reason.

acknowledgments

This book was created with the support of the Clockwork Storybook writer's collective, so thanks to those guys: Mark Finn, Chris Roberson, and Bill Willingham. Roberson deserves extra credit for having more faith in the book than I did, as does Willingham for the loan of a couple of his clever ideas. A wonderful gent named Shane Guy proofread the original manuscript, as did my wife, Stacy. Many thanks also to Lou Anders, my editor at Pyr Books, who resurrected the book.

And of course, my parents.

Part One

Winter comes to the land only once in a hundred years.

When it comes, the always-blossoming cherry trees close their petals and turn away from the chill wind. The animals of the forest come down from their trees and rocks and burrow deep into the ground for warmth. The Channel Sea grows angry and gray. The sun shines less brightly, hiding its face behind clouds rough as granite. When the River Ebe freezes over and a man can walk from Colthorn to Miday over the ice, then Midwinter has officially begun.

Midwinter is the darkest season. It is a time of repentance and of somber reflection during which even the Queen will wear black. In the mountain temples of the Arcadians, the icons are covered with dark cloth and the ancient censers are unwrapped and burned; they swing dangling from the fingers of silent monks who walk the frigid stone floors of their temples barefoot. Around lakeside villages and in certain city shops where gaiety is the order of business, signs are hung reading simply, "Closed for Midwinter."

There is a rumor in the court of the City Emerald that during Midwinter even Regina Titania's powers ebb, that the Queen herself becomes pale and cold to the touch. But this is only a rumor, and a treasonous one at that.

It lasts until the ice cracks and the first new fish is caught in the Ebe. The lucky fisherman who catches it becomes Lord of Colthorn for the day, and so for months before they have any chance of succeeding, the peasantry bring their poles and lines to the water's edge, waiting for Firstcome to return.

Firstcome is the time of rebirth. Every city in the land, from the tiniest hamlet to the City Emerald herself, has its own centuries-old tradition for celebrating the coming of the new summer and the greens and yellows and blues that accompany it.

But until then, the trees will wear a wreath of white around their heads and the hills will be capped with reflective ice. From the farthest north expanse of the land, the snow will creep southward, stirring hurricanes in the Emerald Bay to lash at the city folk. Even the desert gnomes will feel a chill in their mud homes in the far south, but the snow will melt over the swamp-lands and its inhabitants will suffer a year or more of icy rain before First-come rescues them.

Until then, it is Midwinter.

the prison of crere sulace and certain of its inhabitants

Dumesne, huge and crazy, took a step toward Raieve and flashed his ugly teeth. He showed her the blade of a thin knife in his belt and smiled at her.

Raieve spared a glance for the Low Guard of Watch and found him nowhere in evidence. She planted her foot and stood firm in the freezing narrow courtyard that separated the towers of Crere Sulace, facing Dumesne. A new fall of snow twisted in the windy courtyard, settling on clothing and hair and dusting the courtyard walls with white. Many of the assembled prisoners, in their ragged furs and cheap boots, clapped their bare hands against the cold and urged Dumesne on. Some of the others, the pretty folk, hung back and watched with feigned disinterest from afar. Mauritane, the strong quiet one, stared directly at her. She felt his eyes watching her movements, appraising her.

Raieve glared at her attacker. "See these?" she said, pulling three of her braids from the left side of her head and holding them before her. "I earned each one of them facing an armed opponent with my bare hands."

Dumesne ran his gloved fingers over his recently shaved head, the tips of his ears rising just above the top of his skull. "I once had more braids than you could count, foreigner. Don't make me cut your tongue out before I kill you."

Raieve whirled her metal-tipped braids like whipcords and flashed them out. One of them caught Dumesne in the eye and he staggered back, clutching his face. He went for the knife then, but it was already gone. When he managed both eyes open again, she was holding it in his face.

There was courteous applause from the pretty section. From the corner of her eye, she watched some of them pass coins back and forth. They were betting on her. Mauritane, though, did not move.

"You fight like a woman," said Dumesne, sneering.

Raieve planted the knife in his thigh and dragged it out at an angle. Dumesne pinwheeled backward and she advanced on him. "Where I come from," she said, "there is no higher compliment." She swept with her left leg, and Dumesne fell to the ground, clutching his wound. "Must I kill you now," shouted Raieve over the yells of the crowd, "or do I have your oath of respect?"

"I would rather be dead than swear oath to a woman and a foreigner."

"That is your option," she said. She raised the knife.

"Halt!" came a voice from the side. Mauritane rose and approached them. Raieve held the knife still, waiting.

"This is no concern of yours," said Raieve.

Mauritane approached her and took the knife from her hand. He made her feel like a child; it never occurred to her to defend against him.

"I don't need rescuing from you, *Captain*," Dumesne sneered the title.

"Give me your oath," said Mauritane, "and you can suffer your humiliation and live. Otherwise, I'll leave the two of you to your business." He glared at Dumesne.

Dumesne looked back and forth between them. He hung his head. "I swear it. By oak and thorn I swear it. No harm will come to the woman by my hand."

"Wise choice," said Mauritane. He helped Dumesne to his feet. "Go," he said, "or I'll fillet you myself." He handed Dumesne the knife, handle first.

"You made me look small," Raieve said, once Mauritane had led her back to the fire. The crowd was dispersing, and the ragged onlookers gave Mauritane a wide berth.

"No, I saved your life," Mauritane answered. "Dumesne has blood oaths sworn with twenty other inmates. Any of them would be honor bound to kill you if you'd slain him."

"I would face them all," said Raieve, her pride making her face glow red.

"No doubt," said Mauritane, sweeping his braids back from his face as he leaned over the fire. "But that would be a poor strategy for survival here. You're new. You need to learn patience."

"Why did he call you Captain?" asked Raieve after a brief pause. "Are you an officer of the Unseelie Army?"

"No," said Mauritane.

"What then?"

"The honorific no longer applies to me, so it doesn't matter. You may call me Mauritane, if you wish."

He was quiet then. He pulled out a pipe and lit it, squinting at the sky. Raieve looked up as well but saw only gray. Around the cornice of the East Tower, a few crows flitted through the swirling snowflakes.

She looked at Mauritane, and he allowed her the look, studying the contents of his pipe. He was not young, but far from old. The thin creases in his face stood out, ruddy in the freezing air. His braids were long and precise, done in the military style of the Kingdom, unlike Raieve's, which she'd tied herself without the aid of a mirror, standing over the men she'd killed to earn them. Built compactly, Mauritane was only a finger taller than she, but he carried himself the way a taller man stands, and his shoulders were wide and strong.

"Do I meet with your approval?" Mauritane asked, not looking at her.

She scowled and turned away, breathing a curse only when she knew he could not hear it.

The prison was once the summer home of Prince Crere Sulace, the Faerie lord of Twin Birch Torn, but the Queen appropriated it in the distant past over some forgotten sin, and its lord was incarcerated there. Over the years, Crere Sulace became the Queen's favorite dumping ground, home to those not fated for the hangman's noose or the executioner's ax. It was a gulag for lords who no longer found favor at court, ranking officials in the polity who were caught with their hands in the coffers, and visiting dignitaries from worlds who managed to earn the Queen's spite. Those prisoners of the lower classes were lumped in with them, it was rumored, simply out of spite.

The setting for Crere Sulace, among the granite cliffs and the weeping heather of the Channel Sea lands, is dreary enough in the fair years, but in Midwinter the snow-clad peaks and ashen parapets sing of gloom and frustration. In Midwinter the prisoners can see their own breath; they must wear scavenged heavy furs out in the courtyard; they linger by the braziers at the guardhouse gates, swapping stories with the grizzled deputy wardens and guards.

The South Tower was once the primary residence of the Prince Crere Sulace in the time of the Unseelie Wars. Old prisoners believed that the Prince could still be found there, wandering the spellturned halls of the tower, singing spirit songs of death and decay. The towers had been turned dozens, if not hundreds, of times in years past, and now it was no easy thing to say which room was next to which other or what distance separated any two places in the tower. In recent years, the ghostly apparitions and vertiginous twisting hallways finally caused enough harm that the Chief Warden was forced to take notice. He shut down the tower for all but bulk storage and the maintenance of the sea lamp in the cupola.

In the highest floor of the tower, Jem Alan, the Vice Warden, checked the lamp oil for the sea lamp and tilted the reflector out a bit in case some fishermen from Hawthorne were north this evening, hunting the dark northern lanes for sturgeon and salmon. The hour was approaching sunset, or what passed for it in this icy hell of a season, and he didn't want to get caught in the South Tower after dark. Buttoning his fur cloak, he edged his way carefully down the slick steps along the tower's inner wall. Tired green witchlight cast multiple shadows over the steps, and as there was no rail, Jem Alan hugged the wall, holding his torch before him like a ward. He tried to ignore the heaving, moaning sounds that came from the barred doors at each landing.

He closed the tower's inner door and sealed it with its rune before opening the outer door. Across the main yard he saw a cluster of inmates singing shanties with Gray Mave, the Low Chief of Watch. Mave was a local, one of the Hawthorne natives who eschewed fishing in the cold Channel Sea waters for lighter duty at Crere Sulace.

"Enough, Low Chief," called Jem Alan from across the yard. He marched to the guardhouse and leaned on the cord for the Evening Watch bell. The snow that had begun earlier in the day was erratic now, coming in fits and starts, visible only in the slowly growing halo around the fire. "Get up and relieve Drinkwater; the Evening Watch is upon us."

Mave reached slowly into his pockets for a pair of gloves, his heavy frame causing his own cloak to billow around him comically.

"And have someone brought in to recharge the witchlight on the tower steps," added Jem Alan. "I nearly killed myself coming down just now." Jem Alan removed his own gloves, tired brown things with holes cut for the fingers, and held them over the fire.

"Riders will come tonight," said Mave suddenly, his eyes pondering the firelight around the grill. "It will be the beginning of bad things."

"Don't be superstitious," said Jem Alan. "Are you a witch woman, that you can see things in fire?"

Gray Mave shrugged. "I only know it, is all."

Jem Alan rolled his eyes. "Get to your post."

Night had nearly fallen on the mountains when the riders appeared in the Longmont Pass. Even from a distance it was clear that this was a royal emissary, sporting the blue and gold griffon standard of the Seelie Court. Gray Mave, keeping the Evening Watch, sent up the spot flare and rang the visitors' bell in the guard tower.

Chief Warden Crenyllice summoned Jem Alan to his office, which comprised the entire second floor of the North Tower.

"Vice Warden, did I just hear the visitors' bell?"

"Aye, sir." Jem Alan struggled to fasten the straps of his dress tunic around his barrel chest.

"This is unexpected."

"Aye, sir. The supply train isn't due for a fortnight. This party flies royal colors, sir." Jem Alan chose to omit his hearing of Mave's prediction earlier in the evening.

The Chief Warden ran his fingers through his hair, drawing his single braid forward so that it brushed against the medals on his chest.

"If they're here out of turn then it'll be a special prisoner or a pardon. Have the guards come to line in the yard, and be quick about it. And by the Queen's tits, have the men in uniform."

Five riders in formation approached the crest of the pass, which was a knife's edge crevice that received snow year-round during Midwinter. Framed neatly between the nearly vertical rock faces that composed the pass, the Prison Crere Sulace rose from its plateau of rough basalt and granite like an embedded snowflake, its spellturned towers and crumbling spires forming a ghostlike symmetry against the darker rock face from which it projected.

The lead rider was the color point, carrying two standards cross-armed. One was the blue and gold griffon of the Queen. The other, smaller flag was the purple sign of the Royal Guard, the Queen's personal army. Flanking the center rider was a pair of Standard Guards, bearing the insignia of their companies on their capes, their lances slung at their backs. The post rider was the junior officer, a lieutenant by rank.

In the center of the formation, riding an armored mount, was the party's leader, wearing the cape of a commander in the Royal Guard. He rode in the chill wind with the hood of his cloak pushed back, his nine victory braids whipping behind him in the wind. He stood his mount with perfect poise, even over the slick terrain of the rocky pass, his eyes fixed on Crere Sulace.

The commander, whose name was Purane-Es, motioned the party to stop just past the summit of the pass. The road dipped gently here down to the flat plateau abreast of the ocean. At the far end of the plateau, the road led up a steep incline to the gates of Crere Sulace and ended there.

From Purane-Es's vantage point, it was clear that Crere Sulace was no longer the summer estate of a grand lord of Faerie, nor had been for many, many years. The walls showed signs of age and disrepair. The balconies along the rooftop of the structure's South Tower had been replaced with rough crenellations and archery nests. Around the main wall, a coil of iron wire angled down toward the palace; a measure meant to keep people in rather than out.

Originating in the South Tower, a spot flare sparked in the sky, reaching an altitude that brought it over the ocean. It crackled three times in a welcome of tenacious recognition. It was now Purane-Es's turn. He nodded to his lieutenant, who retrieved a signaling flare from his saddlebags and sent it into the air. Three more cracks signaled the party's friendly intentions. Purane-Es dug in his spurs and urged the party forward.

A trio of mounted guards, including Jem Alan, rode out from the gates to meet them. They quickly exchanged formal courtesies (a process much accelerated due to the cold) and rode through the gates together.

Chief Warden Crenyllice stood at attention in the loggia that lined the main yard's south wall. When Purane-Es dismounted, Crenyllice bowed deeply to him and quickly waved to the grooms to fetch the party's horses.

"Welcome to Crere Sulace, Commander," said Crenyllice, bowing again. "It is indeed an honor for us to receive a guest of your rank. May your children meet you in Arcadia."

Purane-Es nodded. "Take me to your office," he said. "I'm here on important business." His silver braids fell around his face.

Crenyllice frowned at the lack of etiquette but had no room to show his displeasure. The commander outranked him by orders of magnitude, and his impropriety would have to pass without comment.

Once in Crenyllice's office, Purane-Es removed his gloves and brushed snow from his shoulders and hair. He seated himself without being asked.

"May I offer you a drink?" said Crenyllice hopefully.

Purane-Es's face softened. "Aye, a brandy will do."

Crenyllice squirmed against the vague insult of "will do," but said nothing as he fixed the drink himself, waving the guards back, and handed it to the commander.

"We are a remote outpost of the Queen's Army, sire, doing our best with what we receive," said Crenyllice. "I'm afraid this brandy is the best I can offer, you see."

"Please spare me your homespun attempts at courtesy," said Purane-Es, bored. "It embarrasses both of us. In my presence you will simply do as I say and leave the formalities for your betters."

Crenyllice's face reddened, but he said nothing.

"I come with a letter from the Chamberlain Marcuse," said Purane-Es, finishing his drink. "The letter instructs you to release several inmates on my recognizance, to perform an errand for Her Majesty."

Crenyllice sputtered. "But sire. Surely the guard . . ."

Purane-Es waved his hand. "Even in this darkened corner of the world, I presume things do not always follow the straight path. It is not yours to question. You will do as you are instructed."

"Which prisoners?" Crenyllice managed.

"There is only one I have in mind: Mauritane. Do you know of him?"

"Aye, sir. He's been mine for two years now."

"Now he's mine. I want him brought to me, and I will allow him to choose the remainder of his party."

"What is the task for which he is summoned, sire?"

Purane-Es laughed. "I'm sure that's none of your concern. Only see that Mauritane is brought to me quickly."

Gray Mave knocked quietly on the door to Mauritane's cell. Once a grand bedroom, the space had been spellturned so many times that it seemed an echo of itself. Not even Gray Mave, who'd been a guard at Crere Sulace for twenty years, knew how many of it existed in the tower.

"Come," said Mauritane. He lay on his bunk, fully dressed, as though he were expecting to be disturbed. Around him, the gilt-edged walls angled blankly to the ceiling, the original wall coverings and paintings having been removed ages ago, light shapes on the tattered wallpaper their only legacy.

Gray Mave fitted his key into the lock and opened the door outward. "You're to come to the warden's office right away." Mave's fat face heaved as he strained to catch his breath.

"What is it?" Mauritane sat up warily.

"A lord from the City Emerald, sir. Rode in flying royal colors. Wanted to see you personally."

Mauritane rose and pulled on his fur cloak. "You don't have to call me 'sir,' you know," he said.

Gray Mave bowed his head. "I know, sir. But considering your history, it doesn't seem right to call you by name."

"Much lower men than you have called me worse," Mauritane said. "I don't see that it matters much these days, anyhow." He joined Gray Mave in the hall, accepting the manacles Mave placed on him without question.

"I should tell you," said Mave, as they walked the darkened hallway. "Since you've given me no trouble during your stay here and all."

"What?"

"I've had a premonition. Bad omen. The riders that have come."

"I see," said Mauritane. "Is Premonition a Gift of yours?"

"Aye," said Mave. "But you're having me on, aren't you? You don't believe that one such as me could have the Gifts. Jem Alan doesn't."

"I'm built from coarser clay than you, Gray Mave," said Mauritane. "And I've got more Gifts than do me any good. I wouldn't put too much stock into what Jem Alan says."

Gray Mave smiled, then frowned. "This sign was very dark. I fear for you to be caught in it."

"If I am," said Mauritane, "then at least I've been forewarned."

Gray Mave led Mauritane, shackled, into Crenyllice's office. The glow from the fire and the lamps in the warden's elaborate wall sconces were bright after the dim hallway, and Mauritane squinted against them briefly.

"Hello, Mauritane," said a familiar voice. "I see that imprisonment agrees with you."

When Mauritane looked up, it was into the eyes of Purane-Es, seated at the warden's desk across the room. For a moment, Mauritane stood completely still. No emotion showed on his face.

With a single fluid movement, Mauritane twisted around Gray Mave and ducked behind him, pulling the larger man down to his knees. Dislodging his arms, he planted his leg on Mave's back and then drew the guard's sword with both hands. "Your premonition was correct," he whispered in Mave's ear.

He turned the sword in his hands as he leaped, directing the blade's gleaming point at the throat of Purane-Es.

the chamberlain's letter

Purane-Es flinched and fell backward into his chair, raising his hands to his face. Mauritane's leap was carrying him far enough to compensate, but he was tackled before he reached the desk. The commander's Color Guard, who had flanked Purane-Es silently since Mauritane entered the room, moved with an impressive swiftness. One went for the body while the other went for his sword arm. Their attack was precise, calculated, seemingly rehearsed, though Mauritane had seen no signal pass between them. He wondered about it until his head made contact with the floor, and then he stopped wondering.

It was less a loss of consciousness than a temporary withdrawal of the senses that quickly subsided, leaving Mauritane seated in a wooden chair across the warden's desk from Purane-Es, his still-manacled arms now restrained by means of a ring set into the stone floor. His chains did not allow him length enough to sit up straight, so he was forced into a bow that made his shoulders ache and his ears redden. His head throbbed from its blow, sending bright pulses of pain down into his left eye socket.

Purane-Es was seated calmly at the warden's desk, while the warden himself, Jem Alan, and the Color Guard stood in a rough line behind him.

"Well met, Mauritane," said Purane-Es, as though nothing had happened. "It seems I've made an impression on you after all."

Mauritane spat on the floor. "I vowed I would kill you the next time we met."

"And yet, you haven't."

Mauritane said nothing.

Purane-Es opened an ornate leather satchel, inset with colored metal studs, and withdrew an envelope sealed with bright blue wax. "But I say, 'He who forgives shall be forgiven.' Isn't that how the Arcadians put it?" He held the envelope aloft for Mauritane's eyes. "Do you recognize this? It's the seal of the Chamberlain," he said, breaking it.

Mauritane nodded.

"This is an ironic situation," said Purane-Es, tapping the letter on the desk. "You despise me, have even made an attempt on my life, and yet I am here to offer you deliverance from your current downcast state. I, for my part, have no love for you either, but I have been employed as a messenger from Her Majesty to you. I do not claim to understand the mind of Our Sovereign Lady, but I think, and this is merely my opinion you understand, that she appreciates ironies such as these. Perhaps she even orchestrates them. What do you think?"

Mauritane only spat again, running his tongue over a bruised lip.

"Here's what I think," Purane-Es continued. "I think you're very fortunate that you did not slay me just now, since the Queen herein orders you to receive instructions from me personally, and that would have been difficult with the Low Chief's blade in my throat, would it not?"

"Read the letter," said Mauritane.

"I will," said Purane-Es. "But we must clear up something first. You will get your opportunity against me, you have my word, for I've long awaited it myself. Until then, your errand requires that you refrain from assaulting me. Understood?"

"If Her Majesty requires me, I am hers."

"I'll take that as a yes. Guard," he said to Crenyllice, who grimaced at the insult, "remove the prisoner's manacles."

Crenyllice waved at Jem Alan, who took a heavy ring of keys from his belt and removed the chains from Mauritane's hands and feet. Mauritane spat one last time, then sat up straight, stretching his shoulders and arching his back.

Purane-Es took the letter from its envelope and unfolded it gracefully. He read:

To Mauritane, Erstwhile Captain of Her Majesty's Royal Guard:

Though you languish at Crere Sulace, your Queen is merciful; she has not forgotten your many years in Her Service. She regrets the unfortunate circumstances leading to your imprisonment there and wishes to offer an opportunity wherein you may earn parole.

Your Queen requires that you perform an errand of the utmost importance and of the utmost delicacy. This task can be given to no one in Her Majesty's court yet must be undertaken by one whose trustworthiness is unquestioned. The Queen appreciates your loyalty to her State and to her Person and is certain that you will treat your assigned task with the dedication and discretion that has distinguished your efforts in the past. Upon successful completion of this errand, your imprisonment will cease, and your name shall be restored. You may then pursue any occupation within the realm with the exception of public service, from which you shall be permanently barred. The same offer is made to those whom you choose to assist you in your endeavor.

Time is critical, Mauritane. You must make the City Emerald before the Sun enters the Lamb. Failure is death.

You will receive your assignment from Commander Purane-Es. His instructions are to be obeyed to the letter.

Her Majesty's wishes go with you.

In the name of She whose word is law, She whose breath is the wind, She whose heart is that of Her kingdom, I am

Marcuse, Lord Chamberlain of Faerie

Purane-Es refolded the letter and slid it across the desk to Mauritane, who picked it up and stared at it.

"I am shocked," he finally said.

"And well you should be, Mauritane. Well you should be. That the Queen should choose you, a traitor and a liar, for such an important assignment proves only that Her ways are mysterious indeed. I trust you accept the assignment?"

Mauritane saluted slowly, deliberately. "I await your command, sir."

Purane-Es grinned. "Prison has eroded none of your natural charm, Mauritane." He turned to Crenyllice. "Leave us. What I have to say to Mauritane is for his ears only."

Crenyllice moved to protest, but Purane-Es stared him down, and the warden allowed himself to be escorted from the room by Purane-Es's guards.

"I haven't forgotten Beleriand or what happened there," Purane-Es said, when they were alone, his smile vanishing. "I'll have my vengeance on you, and soon."

"It's good that you haven't forgotten, only a pity that you take no lesson from it," Mauritane said. He stretched his arms and stood. "But that's not relevant right now. Our feud can wait; Her Majesty, apparently, cannot. What is my task?"

Purane-Es rose as well, pacing as he spoke. "Your task is to retrieve an article of utmost importance to the security of the land and bring it to the City Emerald before the first day of Lamb. You are to form a party of four or five of your fellow inmates. Who you choose is irrelevant, but let it be known that any word breathed of this operation is suicide, swift and painful. You are to receive mounts and supplies from Crere Sulace, with provisions for three days. From Crere Sulace you will leave at sunrise tomorrow and proceed with all due haste to Sylvan, where you will rendezvous with Commander Kallmer in the Rye Grove, at highsun on Fourth Stag. You will travel without papers and without identification. If you are detained by the Seelie Army, or by local constabulary, all knowledge of you and of your mission will be disavowed and you will be eliminated. Are these orders understood?"

"What am I to retrieve?" said Mauritane.

The grin returned. "I have no idea. None of us knows the whole of it. Presumably Kallmer knows."

"Does Kallmer know that it is I who will be meeting him?"

"He does," Purane-Es said. "One assumes he is as eager to kill you as I am, although he must forswear it until your task is complete."

"Most important, how am I to make Sylvan in so short a time? Traveling without papers will force us to skirt the border crossings at Obore and Reyns. Even at top speed it would be at least twenty days, and that's without this weather."

"It should be no trouble for an accomplished strategist such as you. Don't you have the Gift of Leadership? I might remind you that since you will not be an official platoon of the Guard, there is no reason you cannot travel directly west."

"You expect me to lead a group of untrained prisoners through the Contested Lands and survive? You overestimate my skills."

"Your group's survival is not a requirement. Only the completion of your objective."

"I see."

Purane-Es sat. "I recommend you begin your preparations. In Midwinter, dawn comes all too quickly." Purane-Es took a pipe from his leathern satchel and lit it contemplatively. "I'd wish you luck, but of course I won't shed a tear if you fail." He smiled.

"Of course you won't," said Mauritane, turning on him. "Your predisposition to place personal grudges over matters of state is what brought me here."

"Spite is a luxury you cannot afford right now, Mauritane. You have work to do."

"Fine. Tell the warden to give me two men and then get the hell out of my way."

Mauritane saluted again, turned on his heel, and left the room. Purane-Es smoked his pipe and swore every curse he could think of.

Outside, Mauritane nearly stumbled over Crenyllice and Jem Alan, who hovered by the door. Catching himself, he drew his shoulders high and spoke to Crenyllice for the first time not as a prisoner but as a commander. "Go inside. Purane-Es has orders for you," Mauritane told the warden. He took Jem Alan's shoulder. "You're coming with me. Time is short." Neither of them questioned him. The Gift of Leadership, he realized, had not fled him.

Within an hour, Mauritane had two guards, as well as a number of prisoners, helping him make preparations. The overnight kitchen detail loaded dried meat and biscuits into folds of waxed paper, then into the saddlebags Mauritane requested. They filled skins with water and hung them alongside. In the prison armory, Jem Alan helped Mauritane select arms, all the while complaining in his rough voice about the breach of protocol it entailed. He did, however, compliment Mauritane's choice of sword: a long, curved saber with no adornments, but a wicked blade.

"What is its lineage?" said Mauritane, swinging the sword gently, thrusting into the air. "It spoke to me."

"None as I know of," said Jem Alan. "Perhaps you'll give it a start in life."

"I rode into many battles with my Guard blade," said Mauritane. "Purane-Es's father wears it now. Perhaps it's time for a new one." He handed the sword to Jem Alan. "Give that to Gray Mave and have him sharpen it."

Jem Alan took the blade. "Haven't you heard, Mauritane? Mave's been fired. They sent him packing after you took his sword. Worthless lump of dung, he was, anyway."

Mauritane took the sword back, his eyes cast downward. "I'll sharpen it myself," he said.

He paced the prison stables, asking the head groom about each beast in turn, ordering that his selections be spellwarmed and saddled by dawn.

"Which of these horses is touched?" he asked the groom.

"None, sir. We've no call for smart horses around here."

Mauritane approached Purane-Es in the warden's office.

"Give me your horse," he said.

Purane-Es laughed out loud. "You're dreaming if you think . . ."

"If I'm going through Contested Lands with four undrilled prisoners at my back, I'm doing it with a touched mount, or I may as well slit my own throat here and now and save some buggane the trouble."

"Fine," said Purane-Es. "Take the horse. Just one more debt to collect on when you're through."

Mauritane left the warden's office and found Jem Alan at the guard station, drinking chicory with the other guards. Mauritane took a page from the logbook and dipped a quill, writing out ten names. "Bring me these ten," he said, pushing the page into Jem Alan's hand without bothering to blot it.

Jem Alan held up his fingers, black with ink and swore. "I much preferred him as a prisoner," he said.

silverdun

The cell was empty save for a cot, a chest of drawers, and a few personal items on the windowsill: a hairbrush, an opal ring, a long pipe and tobacco pouch. Moonlight, filtered through clouds, dusted the floor of the chamber in pale gray. The cell's occupant, Perrin Alt, Lord Silverdun, Master of Oarsbridge and Connaugh manors, knelt at the edge of his prison cot, his head bowed as if to pray. He often knelt this way, thinking of nothing, coming close to mouthing the words of his mother's Arcadian prayers, but he always stopped short, disbelieving, scowling. At times he wept bitterly for his wasted future, for his sisters and the ignominy they must face, for the loss of his title and deeds to his lands, those things that identified him as a peer and a nobleman. Other nights, such as tonight, he simply watched the moonbeams grow across the rough wooden floor until his knees ached and he stumbled into bed, his mind racing, but his sleep, when it came, was black and dreamless.

When he heard the key sound in the lock of his door, he bolted upright, smoothing his tunic and running his hands through the waves of black hair that fell around his face as he stood.

"Do you require something of me?" Silverdun asked, referring to the guard who stood in the doorway, a bright lamp in hand. The lamp cast long flickering shadows across the floor that evaporated the pools of moonlight there.

"You're wanted in Jem Alan's office."

Silverdun studiously avoided meeting the guard's gaze. "I didn't hear a 'milord' in there anywhere," he corrected. "You are not permitted to speak evenly with me."

"Fine," said the guard. "You lordship is wanted. Now move your lordship's ass or I'll move it for you."

Silverdun locked eyes with the guard. "Much better," he said.

The guard frowned.

"What does the old fool want with me at this hour? Am I about to be engaged in one of his drunken reveries? How much has he had to drink?"

"I'm to say nothing about it."

"Ah, intrigue! And here I was just moaning about how dull my life has become."

The guard's frown intensified. "This way, *milord.*"

Silverdun followed the guard across the empty courtyard to the North Tower, wind from the sea catching his braids and lashing his face with them. The night air had a frozen tang to it that Silverdun could taste. It was not a wholesome flavor.

"This is the last night I will spend at Crere Sulace," he suddenly said, and knew that he meant it, although he had no idea why. It was not uncommon, however, for his mouth to know things before his mind could consider them.

When they reached Jem Alan's rooms in the North Tower, Silverdun pushed ahead and flung the double doors open with a shove.

"By the Queen's tits, Jem Alan, do you never sleep?" he shouted. "One drink and one drink only." Silverdun drew up short when he realized it was Mauritane and not the Vice Warden, at the desk in Jem Alan's sitting room.

"Promoted from prisoner to Vice Warden all of an evening? I'd say you've been busy tonight, Mauritane. Tell me, is it really all about who you know?"

Mauritane waved the guard away. "Sit down," he said to Silverdun. "I'll be with you in a moment." Before him on the desk was a set of charts and maps and a compass, arranged neatly over the surface of the desk. In the center, Mauritane took notes with a long, black quill on a wide sheet of paper.

Silverdun dropped into a chair opposite Mauritane and took a cigarette from the carved wooden box on the table, lighting it with a bit of witchlight from his fingertips. He glanced around the room with a disconcerting sense of finality still lingering from his moment of lightheadedness in the courtyard.

Jem Alan's rooms were once those of the Prince himself, or at least a spellturned version of those rooms; it was impossible to tell. The fire burning in the enormous stone hearth seemed solid enough. The same moonlight that had quietly played in Silverdun's cell erupted here through the enormous floor-to-ceiling windows on the far wall, their arched tops casting looming, rounded shadows on the double doors through which Silverdun had entered. The only other light came from the lamps Mauritane had on the desk, serving the dual purpose of illumination and of weighing down the scrolling maps.

Mauritane circled a sum with his quill and looked up, catching Silverdun's eye for the first time.

"I need your help," said Mauritane.

Silverdun leaned in. "Any assistance I can render, sir." He saluted.

"You still find it amusing that I once outranked you."

"Only in the military sense, Captain."

"You heard that a party of riders came tonight, flying royal colors? They delivered this." Mauritane held out the letter.

Silverdun scanned the page quickly, its charmed ink already fading from exposure to light. "Fascinating," he said after a moment's reflection. "What instructions were you given?"

Mauritane recounted his conversation with Purane-Es and Silverdun listened intently. His ears perked at the name of the commander.

"Purane-Es. That bastard," said Silverdun.

"You know him?"

"I know of him. I flirted briefly with his sister when she was at court a dozen years ago. Pretentious brat, from what I gathered, deeply buried in the combined shadows of his father and elder brother."

"You know that his father now commands the Royal Guard, and that he is the likely replacement?"

"Yes. The Elder Purane and my father had business with each other on occasion. But what became of the elder brother? Surely he would be in direct succession for the captaincy?"

"No. He's dead."

"You're certain of this?"

"I killed him."

Silverdun nodded. "Well, then, I suppose you're certain. Hardly a trustworthy messenger, this Purane-Es, it seems."

"The Chamberlain's seal was genuine. And I recognize the handwriting."

Silverdun shrugged. "I don't doubt the veracity of the letter. But if what you've told me is true, and not even Purane-Es knows the full extent of the Queen's plan, you can be sure that you won't survive to tell the tale once this game is complete."

Mauritane leaned back in the leather chair and sighed, the creases in his forehead darkening. "It would appear so, though I have doubts of that. If the Crown simply needed a patsy, why travel so great a distance to find one? There are any number of able soldiers in the City Emerald who earn the Queen's disfavor on a given day. And the Chamberlain's word, even printed in invisible ink, still carries with it some honor."

"You're a dangerous optimist," said Silverdun.

"I have to be. I have no choice in the matter." Mauritane held up his hands.

Silverdun clucked his tongue. "Well," he said, looking around the room. "I wish you luck, then."

Mauritane's eyes narrowed. "Wish yourself luck. You're coming with me."

"I? I'm no soldier. And I value my life."

"I need you, Silverdun. You possess valuable Gifts. I know you have Glamour and Elements, and I suspect you have Insight as well. And . . ."

"Yes?" Silverdun leaned forward.

"You're the only person I trust."

Silverdun bit his lip, then burst out laughing. "Ah, dear Mauritane. If that's the case, then you haven't a chance."

Mauritane smiled, but the smile was brief. "I'm serious, Silverdun."

"Even if your optimism is well founded, there is a reason that the Queen hasn't bothered to conquer the Contested Lands. There are shifting places there, and vast untamed fields of wild essence, not to mention Unseelie excursionary forces. It's a death march, Mauritane."

"Would you rather die here?"

Silverdun stared into the fire.

"Silverdun, I know you think I'm naïve, but consider this: what if this task is as crucial to the Kingdom as it purports to be? Would you rather die in defense of the Crown or cowering in a cell on a frozen mountain?"

Silverdun gripped the arms of his chair and leaned farther forward.

"Don't talk to me about loyalty, Mauritane. I'm stuck here because of my own misguided loyalties. If it's love for Queen and country you're trying to inspire, you can forget it. I've none to spare."

Mauritane looked away. They both watched the fire dance for a time.

"Who manages Oarsbridge and Connaugh in your absence?" Mauritane finally asked.

Silverdun sat back. "An uncle of mine, a fatuous cretin with a tenuous claim and deep pockets."

"Your estates are near the border with Beleriand, aren't they?"

"What are you getting at, Mauritane?"

"I am owed favors in Beleriand," Mauritane said. "I'll leave you to draw your own conclusions as to what that might mean."

Silverdun's eyes widened. "You know, Mauritane, you may not be as naïve as I thought."

"Then you're with me?"

"I . . . I suppose."

"That's a relief," said Mauritane, returning to his charts. "Because I would have been forced to kill you otherwise."

"Very funny," said Silverdun.

Mauritane caught his eye again, and there was no trace of mirth there.

"Damn you, Mauritane. You are a bizarre creature."

Mauritane consulted the hourglass on the desk. "Summon the guard," he said. "I want to start interviewing the others."

science/spiders

After Silverdun, Mauritane's next two choices were deemed unsuitable. Dol was a mixed breed of elf, troll, and something neither of them could identify. He was strong but evasive, uncommunicative. Mauritane and Silverdun agreed that he could not be trusted. The second choice, Gerraca, was a wiry elf with fighting experience, but he and Silverdun had dueled indeterminately a few months prior, and he was avowed to slay Silverdun in a second duel to which Silverdun had never agreed.

As they waited for the next prisoner, Mauritane leaned back in Jem Alan's leather chair, perusing the files of his fellow inmates. They were hastily scribbled, barely literate documents, written in poor hand, some accompanied by judicial decisions from Royal Courts, others nearly blank. Prison recordkeepers had attempted to make notes on the status of inmates as addenda, but these were spare, not uniform, and probably not very reliable. Mauritane found his own file in the stack, a loose sheaf of documents bound in a large paper envelope. One was from the Areopagus in the City Emerald, whose verdict was stamped in red ink above his name: Traitor. The word stung him as though he were seeing it for the first time.

Silverdun, on the other hand, had no file that Mauritane could find, nor even a proper cell assignment. "My imprisonment is of a solely political nature," was all he'd said, shrugging. "It amounts to the same thing. I'm guilty of enough sins to deserve this fate regardless."

While waiting for the fourth choice, Mauritane happened to look down at his feet. A spider was crawling beneath the desk, its legs moving fluidly over the coarse rug that covered the obsidian floor. He watched the spider traverse the rough surface of the rug to Silverdun's feet, wondering at its natural elegance. Silverdun looked down, noticed the spider, and stepped casually on it.

"Who's next?" he said. Mauritane handed him the file as the door opened and Brian Satterly was led into the room.

"Beriane Sattarelay?" said Silverdun. "What sort of name is . . ." he looked up and saw the man in front of him. "What in the world are you?"

Satterly shrugged, nervous. "Human," he said.

"Really?" Silverdun said, leaning forward. "I've never seen one before. Do all of you have ears like that?"

"Yes, round at the tops," said Satterly, smiling weakly.

"Fascinating," Silverdun said. "Why is he here? Do we need a squire or a stableboy?"

"Actually," said Satterly. "I'd like to know as well." He nodded at Mauritane and Silverdun.

Mauritane said, "I've been charged with a task for the Queen, and my orders are to recruit a unit from among the prisoners here. Upon successful completion of this assignment, you are to be paroled."

Satterly looked between them. "I don't get it. Why prisoners? Is this a fancy way of saying work detail?"

Silverdun shook his head. "No, although it occurs to me that that would make an excellent cover story for the other inmates, after we've left."

"Yes, we'll have the guards spread the rumor that we've been sent down the Ebe to plow roads or something," said Mauritane.

"What is this, then?" said Satterly

"It is the means by which you may achieve parole," said Mauritane. "According to your file, you're here for the remainder of your life. Is it true that humans live only sixty or seventy years?"

"Some longer than that," said Satterly. "But that's about right."

"Sparse time to be wasting it here," said Silverdun.

"What would I have to do?" said Satterly.

"Yes, Mauritane," said Silverdun. "What is he for?"

"He," said Mauritane, "is a scientist."

"Really?" said Silverdun, eyebrow raised. "That *is* interesting."

Satterly chuckled. "Well, I am a scientist, but I'm afraid we don't really deserve the reputation we've developed in Faerie."

"Don't be shy. Do some science for us!" said Silverdun, raising his glass.

Mauritane leaned forward, mirroring Silverdun. "I'm not sure if one can simply 'do' science, at least not without the proper equipment. Perhaps Satterly can explain this."

Satterly pursed his lips. "Mauritane is at least partly right. Many scientific displays require equipment of one kind or another. But it's not the sorcery that the Fae seem to think it is; it's really just a method of inquiry. To the layman, it's often fairly uninteresting."

Silverdun shook his head. "That's not what I've heard. I once met a man who'd been to your world; he said you have houses that fly and boxes that transmit images and sounds from place to place. If that's uninteresting, I'd love to know what intrigues you."

"I may have one thing to show you," said Satterly. "If you'll let me return to my cell, I can get it."

"Go," said Mauritane.

When Satterly returned, he carried with him an item forged of black metal; a rounded base with a thick cylinder above connected to it by a rounded arm of the same material.

"This is a microscope," he said. "One of the few things they let me keep. I told them it was a religious statuette."

"What is it?" asked Silverdun.

"In your language you'd call it a Tiny-Thing-Appears-Itself-Large-For-You-With-It or something equally silly."

"Does it work?" said Mauritane.

"Yes, I'll show you." Looking down, he noticed the dead spider curled into a tight ball at Silverdun's feet. "If I may," he said, reaching for it. He took the spider and wedged it between two differently shaped pieces of glass. These he slipped into a pair of silver guides on the base of the microscope. He placed the instrument gently on the desk and twisted the thick cylinder, which Mauritane could see possessed a number of protrusions on its bottom. Satisfied with his choice, Satterly manipulated a knob on the side of the device and peered into the top.

"Not enough light," he muttered.

Silverdun suffused the air around them with green witchlight.

"Okay," said Satterly. "Take a look."

Mauritane peered into the top of the microscope, at first seeing nothing. Then his eye adjusted, and he discovered a circle of light. There, beneath his eye, was the visage of a hideous creature, with eight stalked eyes and pinching mouthparts, like something out of the Mere Swamps.

"What is this?" he asked.

"That's the spider, only much, much larger. This magnification is fifty times how it appears with the naked eye."

Silverdun looked down into the eyepiece, frowning. "Does the spider itself actually become extremely large at some point? Because I could see where that would be useful."

"Well, no. It's just how you're seeing it that changes. The lenses inside the microscope refract the light coming from the spider to make it appear much larger than it is."

"Hm," said Silverdun, reaching for a jug of watered wine, "You're right, Satterly. Science *is* boring."

Satterly smiled, whether at Silverdun or at some internal joke it was difficult to tell.

"Silverdun," said Mauritane, dismissing him, "if you knew how much of our existing war magic was based on human scientific knowledge, you'd be less glib. The development of explosives, field glasses, and some others I can't mention have their base in the science of his people."

"You think his knowledge will be useful on our journey."

"I do."

Satterly raised his hand. "I'm still not sure exactly what you're asking," he said.

"I will tell you what I have been told," said Mauritane. He recounted the contents of the Chamberlain's letter, the original having already faded to white. He explained as best he could the dangers of the Contested Lands and even reiterated Silverdun's concerns about the legitimacy of the deal the Chamberlain offered.

"Now you know as much as we know," said Mauritane. "If I'm going to ask you to risk your neck, you should understand the danger as well as the potential reward."

"Thank you, and I'm sold, if you'll have me. I've always wanted to visit the Contested Lands. If half of what I've heard of them is true, it should be quite an adventure."

Silverdun snorted. "What a bizarre race of creatures you come from!"

"A few more questions," said Mauritane. "Are you a skilled rider?"

"I don't know how skilled I am, but I've ridden before."

"Can you defend yourself? If we engage a threat, every soldier fights."

"I'm a pretty good shot with a rifle, but I don't guess that's what you mean. If you're talking blades, I'm useless."

"Let's see," said Mauritane. "Take this." He took a scabbarded cavalry sword from its place on the desk and pushed it over to Satterly.

Satterly pulled the blade from its cloth sheath and eyed it warily. "What do you want me to do?"

"We'll be on horseback, so I'll be training everyone in mounted swordplay over the next few days. First, though, I want to see how fast you learn at basic engagement. Stand over there."

Satterly stood where Mauritane pointed and held the blade loosely in his grasp.

"Hold it like this," said Mauritane, drawing his own blade. "Put your thumb on the hilt and your next finger out toward the blade. Now lower your arm and hold the blade upright."

Satterly did as he was instructed, following Mauritane's lead.

"Keep your left foot back," said Mauritane, crossing behind him and tapping his hamstring with the flat of his sword. "All of your weight goes here. When you thrust, thrust with your right arm and foot in concordance."

"Okay," said Satterly, positioning himself.

Mauritane came around and faced him, nodding. "Come at me," he said.

"I'll try." Satterly lunged with his right arm and leg extended outward, thrusting the point of his sword at Mauritane's chest. With a flick of his wrist, Mauritane disarmed him, sending the blade clattering across the floor.

"Let me try it again," said Satterly. "I think I see what you're doing there."

Mauritane nodded. "I've definitely seen worse."

"I have one last question for you," said Silverdun. "How did you come to be here?"

Satterly frowned. "In Crere Sulace? Or in Faerie?"

"Either."

"I came here with some others of my world. There's an organization that finds and rescues human changelings. I came with them."

Silverdun winced. "A dangerous occupation," he said. "I assume you 'rescued' the wrong human."

"Something like that." Satterly looked away.

Mauritane stood. "We leave at dawn. Find Orrel at the main guardhouse. He'll fit you for clothes and a mount. Then report back here."

Satterly turned to leave, then stopped and turned back. "Wait a minute. How do you guys know that I won't just desert you a mile from the prison and go on my merry way?"

Mauritane smiled. "If you try to desert, I'll find you and kill you."

"Ah."

Satterly left the room, closing the doors behind him.

"Can we trust him?" said Silverdun.

"I don't know. His manners are so different from ours; he's extremely difficult to read. He'd be a fool to ride off by himself in the Contested Lands, which is where I believe his skills will be useful. If he deserts later, I won't feel as bad about slaying him."

"Will you stop talking about killing people?" said Silverdun. "I'm beginning to wonder if it's all you think about."

"If you want to survive out there," said Mauritane, "you should think of it more."

Silverdun grunted.

In the walls, between the blocks, floating in the chipped mortar, something stirred and flitted away. A cool breeze passed through the chamber then, and Mauritane shivered. He stopped short, thinking for a moment that he detected a young girl's scream at the edge of his hearing. But when he motioned Silverdun for silence, there was nothing more.

the complete party/
the lord of twin birch torn

The remaining candidates were each called in and had the situation explained to them. During the second or third of them, snow began to fall outside, illuminated from above by witchlit security lamps around the walls of the castle. The monotonous pattern of flakes, angling sharply to the southeast, refused to admit any alteration while Mauritane watched. He and Silverdun dismissed Caeona, Adfelae, and Sybaic Id after brief discussions.

"There are only three names left," said Silverdun, his fatigue beginning to show around his eyes. "I hope you saved the best for last."

"We can be certain of Honeywell," said Mauritane, surveying the remaining names on the list. "Ce'Thabar I included because I believe he possesses Resistance. Raieve is a mystery, but an intriguing one."

"Not bad to look at, either," observed Silverdun.

"Not even a hint of impropriety, Silverdun. In the Guard we had strict rules about such things."

"Who is more proper than I?" asked Silverdun. "Besides, I freely admit that she intimidates me."

The doors opened, but rather than Ce'Thabar, it was Purane-Es who entered.

"Your time grows near," he said, striding to the desk and peering over the documents spread out there.

"Yes, we have a clock in this room as well," said Mauritane, not looking up.

"Will you be ready? I'm not to leave this place until you do. And I'd like to be in the City Emerald by Stag."

"'It is often better to want than to have,'" quoted Silverdun gaily.

Purane-Es ignored him. "See that you are prepared to leave by sunup."

"As you wish," Mauritane said. He held up his provision list. "The prison is not stocked with the supplies I need. I'll require several hundred silvers to purchase these things in Hawthorne."

Purane-Es laughed. "You're enjoying this, aren't you Mauritane? I know how you love barking orders at your troops; you must have missed that these past two years."

Mauritane looked him in the eye and said nothing.

"Forget it," said Purane-Es, handing over his sabretache. "Here's more than five hundred, in gold and gray. Now you've got my horse and a month's pay. Will there be anything else?"

"Only your head when the time comes." Mauritane took the satchel and placed it on the desk. "Anything else, sir?"

"Don't push it, Mauritane. If you were simply to disappear between here and Hawthorne, no one would ever know."

"If I were to disappear between here and Hawthorne, you would no doubt be cursed by your own father as a fool and likely lose your commission. I won't be looking over my shoulder."

"You overestimate your own importance."

"I don't think so."

Purane-Es swept out of the room, slamming the double doors behind him, nearly knocking over Ce'Thabar, who was led in handcuffed by a guard.

"What is this?" said the lanky Ce'Thabar, looking over the two Fae seated at the desk. "Where's Jem Alan?"

"Ce'Thabar, we would like a word with you," said Mauritane, rising. "There is an offer you should consider."

"I can take no offer from you," said Ce'Thabar. "I'm sworn against you on behalf of Dumesne. He's covenanted against you for what you did in the courtyard today."

Mauritane and Silverdun looked at each other. Mauritane sighed. "Fine. You are excused."

After Ce'Thabar was led away, Silverdun said, "That leaves only two."

"I'm certain of Honeywell. If Raieve doesn't work out, we can take Adfelae as a last resort. He wasn't so bad."

"I hope for all of our sakes that Raieve works out. Adfelae is an idiot."

Silverdun fell silent, and Mauritane heard the odd sound again, this time a bit louder, coming from the south side of the room. A girl's scream.

"Do you hear that?" he asked.

"I don't hear anything. What?"

"It sounded like a girl screaming."

"Probably one of the cats in the courtyard. They're all freezing to death out there. Someone should put them out of their misery."

"You're probably right."

Geuna Eled, called Honeywell, saluted when he was presented. "Sir," he said, his voice strong and firm in a way that his body was not. Prison life had not been kind to Honeywell. Without exercise his weight had increased over the past two years, and his face was puffy and red.

"Honeywell, you served me ably as lieutenant when I was Captain of the Guard. Will you ride with me again?"

Honeywell bowed deeply. "I would be honored, sir."

Mauritane recounted the Chamberlain's offer for the eighth time that night, barely listening to himself speak. Honeywell's mouth was an "O" of wonder throughout.

"This is such an honor, sir," said Honeywell. "I don't know how to thank you enough."

"You can thank me by surviving until we reach the City Emerald. I was responsible for your imprisonment; I'd hate to be responsible for your death as well." Mauritane rubbed his chin.

"I know we've agreed to disagree on that one point, sir. But for Lord Silverdun's benefit, I must say that I am here by my own leave, and it wasn't anyone convinced me to be here other than me."

Silverdun forced a smile. "It is . . . good of you to say so."

"Thank you, milord."

"Just cut the 'milord' crap. I only require it of the guards because it annoys them so. You may call me Silverdun."

Honeywell bowed low, his outstretched wrist nearly scraping the floor.

Though it was still hours from First Watch, the sounds of prison morning life were beginning to seep in from all directions. Somewhere nearby the kitchen staff were lighting their fires, clattering their heavy skillets and pots. Elsewhere the laundry vats rumbled to life, their gears turned by the pale white slaves from Edan.

"Only one more, then Arcadia," said Silverdun, resting his chin in his cupped hands, once Honeywell had managed to bow his way out of the room.

"We ride for Hawthorne in three hours," said Mauritane. "Don't tell me you're going to fail me before we reach the gates."

Silverdun smiled ruefully. "No, I'll have a witch in Hawthorne spell me some awake time. That'll keep me until we camp tonight. Which reminds me. Should we stop in Colthorn," he asked, turning to the maps. "Or do we press on and make camp in the hills to the south?"

"We'll bed at inns until we cross the border. No reason to deplete ourselves before then."

"You'll get no argument from me."

They passed the next few moments in silence, then Raieve was brought in.

She was less enthusiastic than Honeywell.

"Do you think me mad?" she laughed. "It's not enough that I rot in your prisons, but you want me to follow you on some twisted errand of fealty to your bitch queen?"

Mauritane held his tongue so he would not speak without thinking. Her words made him furious, but Silverdun was right. She was beautiful. Her long, metal-tipped braids framed an angular face, blue eyes inlaid over high cheekbones, arched eyebrows in a permanent slant of anger. There was something wild about her.

"You may hold what opinions you wish," he said. "But in my presence you will refer to the Queen as Her Majesty or Regina Titania. If not out of respect for her, then out of respect for me."

Raieve had been standing, pacing across the floor as Mauritane delivered his pitch. Now she sat, pulling her braids forward and peering down at them. "As you wish."

"You have the offer, parole in exchange for your services. How do you answer?"

Raieve pursed her lips. "The only thing you could offer me is guaranteed transport back to Avalon when this is finished and the arms that I came here to purchase. Then I might accept."

"I can probably guarantee your return to Avalon, but beyond that I make no promises," said Mauritane.

"You can promise to do your level best. I would accept that." She glared at him.

"I've watched you since your arrival here," said Mauritane. "I believe you can be of great value to me. I'll do what I can to help you when our task is complete, but it may not be possible."

"You said it yourself," she said. "The alternative is dying here. I don't hate your queen enough to punish myself for spite. You have my word; I will fight by your side. I'll take what you can offer."

"I'm pleased," said Mauritane. "Perhaps when this is done you will not think so badly of us."

"I hardly see how it matters either way," she said.

Mauritane started to say something else but stopped. "Fine. The guard at the door will take you for provisions. Move quickly; we leave in an hour."

Mauritane watched her leave, feeling the curve of her legs with his eyes as she left. He forced himself to remember his wife, the Lady Anne, and put Raieve out of his mind for the moment.

He opened his mouth to speak to Silverdun and heard the scream again, even louder this time, definitely from the south. Could it be one of the Edani? They usually had lower voices and did not often allow their young to be taken captive. Raieve was one of four female inmates. The other three were locked in their cells on the other side of the prison.

"I'll be right back," said Mauritane. Silverdun nodded wearily, reviewing the list of provisions for the fourth time in an hour.

He picked up one of the guards at the door. "Where are we going, sir?" the guard said.

"Do you hear that sound?" said Mauritane. The girl's cries were insistent, pleading. Mauritane wondered for a moment that a woman's cries of pleasure and pain could sound so similar. Raieve's face flashed unbidden across his mind. He frowned.

"I don't hear anything," said the guard.

"Come with me," Mauritane said.

They passed from the North Tower into the main yard, where a trio from the night watch warmed their hands in the guardhouse. Snow continued to fall in its angled sweep, casting irregular diagonal lines across the faces of the guards.

"No!" the girl's voice cried. The sound emanated from the South Tower.

"Come," said Mauritane, taking his guard by the shoulder. "Don't you hear this?" They approached the tower's interior gate. Here, the wind caught the falling snow in an updraft and it swirled in tight ovals in the portico.

"Can you unlock this door?" said Mauritane.

"Um, sir, we're not to go in there. Only Jem Alan goes to monitor the sealamps."

"Do you have the rune or don't you?"

"Yes, but . . ."

"But nothing!" Mauritane gripped the guard at both shoulders. "Did Jem Alan tell you to give me full run of the place, or didn't he?"

"Uh, yes, but . . ."

"But nothing! Don't say 'but' again. You have your orders. Open the door."

Cowering, the guard took a set of runes from his belt and fitted one into the enormous metal door's latch with a shaky hand.

"I'll wait here," he said.

"Fine." Mauritane took a torch from the inside wall and lit it from the grate that burned there.

The door opened onto a wide hall with a curved stairway on the left, or east, side and a number of doors on the north wall. A dusty iron chandelier hung overhead, its candles burnt to tiny stumps, blackened and sooty. Besides the torch, the only other illumination was the dim green witchlight from irregularly placed globes along the stairwell. Their light glimmered on the damp gray stones of the walls.

"No! No! Father, help me!" It was the girl's voice again, coming from above. Mauritane leapt for the stairs, noticing the curious antiquity of the girl's accent, similar to that of the oldest men and women in his village, those who'd been raised centuries before his own time.

Darting up the stairs, Mauritane reflected that it could not have been possible for the girl's voice, not much louder now than it had been in Jem

Alan's office, to have been audible at all from the North Tower. He grew more wary with each step, and by the time he reached the first landing, he was walking, his blade drawn and held at the ready.

At the first landing, the spellturning of the structure became noticeable. The stairs above were faintly doubled, one set of steps was superimposed on the other, as though seen through thick glass. From the landing, a pair of boarded-up doors let onto the second floor, their locks rusted and worn with age.

"Father! Somebody! Help me!" The girl's cries became shrieks, still coming from farther up the stairs. Mauritane began to run again, taking the stairs two at a time, his eyes moving in every direction for potential threats. He stopped again at the second landing and listened again. The shrieks were muffled here, but they were not from above this time. Two more doors faced Mauritane, identical to the ones below. They, too, were boarded up, though Mauritane could see that the boards on the nearer one were fairly loose. Pulling a dagger, he wedged the blade beneath the board and strained against it, feeling the homemade nails slowly give way.

Mauritane's muscles hummed from the exertion, and it felt strangely good to be in action again, regardless of the circumstances. His face reddening, he pried first one board, then another from the door and examined the lock. It was a simple keyed affair, one easily picked with the tools he'd liberated from the prison armory. As he knelt, the screams grew more and more muffled and eventually faded.

"Damn," he said, finally managing the lock. The door swung open with effort, hanging from hinges that were nearly rusted shut. The passage beyond was dark, but there was a light some distance away. Before Mauritane's eyes, the light became two lights, then four, then eight, then one light again, depending on how he turned his head. It was a disorienting sensation.

He stepped lightly over the transom and into chaos. The floor gave way beneath him and he stumbled forward to right himself, only to discover that he was suddenly sitting up on the frame of the door through which he'd just passed. When he'd crossed into the hallway, his sense of direction had pinwheeled backward over his head in a quarter circle, so now the wall had become the floor, and the floor was now the wall in front of him. The light source was now above his head.

Mauritane began to feel queasy. Looking back through the doorway, he saw the stairway exactly where it had been, only now the stairs appeared to be sideways, their steps clinging to the wall beneath him.

"Salutations," said a voice above him. Mauritane jumped and looked up. Standing on the ceiling was a man in ancient costume, wearing a long white wig and a frock coat that hung upwards to fall at his feet.

"I am the Prince Crere Sulace, Lord of Twin Birch Torn," said the man, speaking in an ancient dialect Mauritane struggled to comprehend. "And you are trespassing in my home."

an abduction

Mauritane attempted to stand, but the room shifted again around him, and he landed at the other man's feet, his thigh resting painfully on his sword hilt.

"Perhaps I should leave the way I came," said Mauritane.

"That would be unwise," said the man, drawing his rapier and holding the point to Mauritane's neck. "You are an intruder in my home and I intend to know your business before I have you flogged."

Mauritane sat up slowly, feeling the pressure at his neck give a bit. "If you are indeed the Prince Crere Sulace," said Mauritane, speaking in Elvish, "then I am more surprised than you. For your home has been a prison these many years and you have been thought dead for centuries."

"Centuries! You are mad!" said the man. "Perhaps you are better off on a Foolship than in my dungeon." He jerked Mauritane roughly to his feet with a strength not suggested by his narrow frame. "Now come out of this room before we both drop out of it. It's been spellturned recently and, I fear, quite badly."

Mauritane let himself be guided from the room by Crere Sulace's sword. He was led down the dark hallway's wall and around a bend where, without warning, his orientation shifted again and he found himself propelled toward the stone floor. Twisting his body, he managed to land on his back without much pain, but the continual shifts in perspective were nauseating.

Crere Sulace stood above him, having anticipated the shift. "Get up," he ordered. He led Mauritane farther along the hallway until it widened into a large sitting room with floor-to-ceiling windows across the south wall. The windows were open to let in the full light of day, despite the fact that daylight, by Mauritane's reckoning, was still at least two hours away. Deep green velvet curtains hung partly drawn over the casements, casting the room in an odd emerald hue. A stunningly beautiful woman, of roughly the same age as Crere Sulace, sat knitting on a divan by the window. She looked up quizzically as Mauritane was marched into the room.

When Mauritane saw her there was a brief flash of recognition, although he could not say from where. Her ears were long and delicately pointed, and a gem-encrusted tiara nestled in her tightly woven blonde hair.

"Husband," she said, looking back at her knitting. "You should clean your blade. You appear to have something on it."

Crere Sulace chuckled. "It is an intruder I found in the courtyard passageway. I was just leading it to the dungeon."

Sulace's wife looked up again. "An intruder? How delightful. Do you suppose he's come to ravish me?"

"Again you overestimate your charms, wife. No, this one is a madman; he claims to have come from the future." He tickled Mauritane's neck with the point of his blade.

"Ah, an intruder from the future! Now, that is novel. Must you dispose of him so readily, husband? Perhaps he can tell us who will win the Unseelie war or what the price of tulips shall be in Firstcome!"

"To which Unseelie war do you refer?" asked Mauritane.

"You mean there will have been more than one? Those nasty devils! One ought to teach them their place." The Lady of Twin Birch Torn smiled affably.

"If you're referring to the first Unseelie War, from the fortieth year of Hornet in Ram, it is the Unseelie who will claim victory, having defeated the Queen's forces at Selafae and Unel."

Crere Sulace wheeled Mauritane around. "The Unseelie prevail at Selafae? Hardly likely, since the Seelie Army numbers in the thousands there and is well reinforced. You *are* mad."

Mauritane lifted an eyebrow. "The Unseelie will take Selafae in a sneak attack at midnight on the first of Swan. It will be revealed that a colonel in the Seelie army is a traitor and has given away the position of Seelie forces across the length of the Ebe."

"He speaks well for a madman," said the Princess. "But he begins to bore me. Please escort him away."

"Come along," said Crere Sulace. "I've a rack that's become lonely of late."

Mauritane stood firm. "I appreciate your position, sire, but I am committed to an errand. I must refuse."

"Then I must slay you where you stand."

"If that is your will, you may attempt it."

"I've no wish to kill an unarmed man. Draw your blade and have at you." The Prince lowered his rapier and stepped back, en garde.

Mauritane reached for his sword and drew it in a smooth, silent motion. The two men faced off, but before either could proceed, they heard a scream from elsewhere in the tower.

"No! Father! Help me!" called the now-familiar voice.

"Laura!" shouted Crere Sulace. He shoved Mauritane into a column and ran from the room, his blade drawn and ready. Mauritane followed, sparing a look back for the Princess, who still sat at her knitting, a bemused expression on her face.

Crere Sulace led the way up a flight of stairs and across a wide gallery that overlooked a library. Bright yellow witchlit sconces filled the room with their warm glow. From the gallery, Sulace took another flight of steps and stopped at a narrow landing. Mauritane rounded the curve of the stairs just in time to see the Prince stride through a doorway, shouting, his face red.

"Who goes there?" shouted Crere Sulace. "Unhand my daughter!"

Mauritane hurried up the steps and entered a large bedroom, many floors above the castle grounds. From the windows, Mauritane saw the courtyard and the buildings he'd come to know all too well over the past two years. From here, though, the courtyard appeared as a carefully manicured hedge maze, evenly coated with a pure white glaze of snow. That was all Mauritane could take in from the windows before turning to evaluate the scene before him. Crere Sulace stood with his back to the near wall, to defend against both Mauritane's entrance and the men who occupied the center of the room. There were four of them, dressed in what Mauritane recognized as the uniform of the Royal Guard from the age of the Unseelie Wars, roughly six hundred years before his own time. They were armed and appeared to be in the process of apprehending a teenage girl, clad only in a silk dressing gown. Her long, girlish legs hung kicking beneath her, supported as she was by her elbows. She appeared to have just woken and was only now beginning to struggle.

"Father, what is happening?" she asked, eyes wide.

"Princess Laura of Twin Birch Torn, you are hereby placed under the custody of the Royal Guard by order of Her Majesty Regina Titania," said one of the men, who wore the colors of a lieutenant. The others, two of whom held the Princess, wore the stripes of sergeants-at-arms.

"Leave this place, rogues!" shouted the Prince. "My own guards will be along shortly, and they are loyal to me, not the Queen."

"Our orders are clear, sire," said the lieutenant. He was a seasoned officer, with a craggy face and a deep scar running along his left ear. "We are to take the Princess to the City Emerald."

"Over my corpse shall you take her," said the Prince.

"If necessary, yes," said the lieutenant. "But there's no need for that."

"Are you with them?" the Prince said, pointing his sword at Mauritane. Mauritane shook his head, baffled.

"Then use your blade on them or begone!" cried the Prince, lunging at the lieutenant.

The trio of sergeants fell back, one of them securing the Princess's hands behind her back, while the others covered him. These two stepped toward Crere Sulace just as his own guards' footsteps sounded on the stairs.

Mauritane, forced into the room by the onslaught of the Prince's men, sidled along the far wall from the Prince, his sword still at the ready.

Crere Sulace turned out to be a fair swordsman. He hacked away at the lieutenant's blade without much success, the military man parrying his blows but making little headway himself. He pressed the Prince back against the wall, leaving his own men to protect his flank against the oncoming guards.

Crere Sulace's men, upon entering the room, appeared as confused as Mauritane felt. Their collective gaze went from the Prince, to the Princess, to Mauritane, apparently unsure whom to attack first.

"Save the Princess," shouted Crere Sulace from behind the lieutenant. His men advanced on the Royal Guardsmen, who leapt at them preemptively. Though Crere Sulace's retainers outnumbered them, they found themselves blocked by the heavy oaken furniture that filled the room, so the rear two stood useless.

The lieutenant twirled around Crere Sulace and struck him with the flat of his blade's forte. The Prince pitched and fell forward, slumping against an ottoman.

The lieutenant turned and regarded Mauritane. "You! What is your role in this? You wear the braids of an officer of the Guard."

Mauritane swallowed. "I . . . I am no longer with the Guard, sir."

"You're recommissioned. To arms!"

Mauritane shrugged and joined in the fray, slashing at the nearest of Crere Sulace's men. Caught unaware, the man took a deep cut in the shoulder and fell back, leaving the next open to attack from the rear. Quicker than the first, he whirled and caught Mauritane's blade with his own. Mauritane riposted, whipping his blade around his opponent's weak side and catching the man's side with the point of his weapon. The injury caught the man off balance, and Mauritane pulled him down onto his knees and clubbed him with the hilt of his sword.

The lieutenant and his men held their own against the remaining three. When they saw Mauritane coming, they were forced to spread their defense, and the middle one went down with a swift attack from the lieutenant. The other two, seeing their comrade fallen, dropped their swords and surrendered.

Mauritane wiped his blade on his tunic and sheathed it, saluting to the lieutenant out of long practiced habit.

"What is your name?" said the lieutenant, returning Mauritane's salute. "Your help was much appreciated. I'll see that you receive a special commendation from the captain."

"Bersoen," said Mauritane, giving the name of an ancestor from the time of the Unseelie Wars.

"We must go," said the lieutenant. "There will be other guards behind these. Bersoen, will you ride with us?"

Mauritane shook his head. "No sir. I am tasked with an errand as well."

The lieutenant looked him up and down. "There's something odd about you. It is a shame I won't have the opportunity to know what." He nodded to his men, and they dragged the girl out the door and down the stairs, having rapidly secured the remaining of Crere Sulace's men. The Princess made no sound as they carried her off.

Mauritane ran out of the room, retracing his steps through the gallery and back to the sitting room, where the Lady still sat at her knitting.

"What news, future intruder?" she asked. Mauritane did not stop to answer her.

Crossing back into the spellturned hallway, Mauritane caught the stem of a brass sconce and heaved himself up into the skewed portion of the passage. His senses reeled again, and he walked unsteadily back toward the door through which he'd entered. There were two more twists of balance, and Mauritane dropped heavily through the once-boarded door into the dark stair, where his prison guard still waited.

"What happened in there?" said the guard, noticing the blood on Mauritane's tunic.

"I don't know," said Mauritane. "Let's get out of here."

When they emerged from the tower, it was night again, and Silverdun was waiting for them, locked in a heated discussion with Purane-Es about the equipment they'd taken from the stables.

"Where have you been?" said Silverdun, annoyed. "It's almost time to go!"

"Hand me a silver khoum," said Mauritane, holding out his hand.

Silverdun knit his brow in confusion but produced the coin from his purse anyway, handing it over.

Mauritane studied the impression on the worn old coin. There, surrounded by a wreath of silver holly leaves, was the familiar face of the Lady of Twin Birch Torn, missing only her knitting to make the image complete.

"Hmph," said Mauritane, handing the coin back to Silverdun. "Take whatever Purane-Es deigns to give you and let's get the hell out of this place. We ride in one hour."

three pounds of gold

The prison stables were outside the inner wall, in a part of Crere Sulace that Brian Satterly had never visited. It was a low stone building that might have been a thousand years old for all Satterly knew. Guards and servants hurried across the snow-covered ground between the tower and the stables, stealing clandestine glances at Mauritane and his companions, their curiosity poorly hidden. The stables smelled of melting snow and wet horses and dung and straw.

Satterly stood just inside the stable doors, next to a brazier, watching Mauritane direct the final preparations for their journey. Satterly had heard the phrase "natural born leader" before but had never met anyone who truly fit the description until now. The prison staff who'd directed Mauritane's life since Satterly had arrived at Crere Sulace eighteen months ago now took orders from him as if they'd been doing so all their lives.

As he often had since his arrival in this world, Satterly felt useless and uncomfortable. With the Fae there were any number of social traps you could fall into. The wrong word at the wrong time could enter you into a blood feud; for a commoner (a group into which Satterly fell by default), looking a noble in the eye while he was eating was a justifiable grounds for murder. Accepting a gift from a Fae, under the appropriate circumstances, could make you beholden to the giver for the rest of your life. Of course, nobody could explain to Satterly what the appropriate circumstances were. It was something so basic to Fae culture that it was rendered inexplicable.

As a result, Satterly kept mostly to himself and tried to speak as little as possible. Saying nothing was almost always the right answer for someone in his position. Though the Fae were sometimes curious about the human world and its customs, most simply treated him as an outsider and ignored him completely.

Humans weren't unknown in the Fae world they way that the Fae were in his. Despite the ban on travel between the two worlds, a few managed to make it through from time to time for various illegal ends. It was one of those illegal ends that had landed Satterly here in Faerie.

There were a number of known worlds; Satterly wasn't sure how many. Earth was one of them, Faerie was another. The woman Raieve was from a place called Avalon, which Satterly had heard of but knew little about other than that the Unseelie had unsuccessfully attempted to conquer it a few years back. He'd heard the names of others but they were scarcely more than names: Annwn, Mag Mell, Nibiru, Pathi. Nobody Satterly had met knew anything about them. "Filled with monsters and that," Gray Mave had once opined when Satterly asked him.

In the past, there had been free commerce between Faerie and the human world, known to the Fae as Nymaen—literally the "place of men"—but a treaty between the Seelie and Unseelie had made such travel illegal hundreds of years ago. It was one of the few treaties, Satterly had been told, that had never officially been broken by either party, though Satterly had never learned why or what the purpose of the treaty had been in the first place.

It was difficult for him to believe that two years ago he'd never heard of this place or the Fae people. He now spoke Common every day and had even begun to dream in it. Sometimes lately he'd started to forget the English words for things. With a start, he realized that he was thinking in Common even now.

"Human," said Mauritane, breaking Satterly from his reverie. "Come saddle your horse in the manner you prefer."

Satterly started forward and looked at Mauritane, wincing. "I've never saddled a horse before."

Mauritane's glare said, *don't they teach you humans anything?* It was a look Satterly had received more times than he could count. But Mauritane only said, "Then have one of the stableboys do it for you. But watch closely, because I don't intend to do it for you on our journey. Every man carries his own weight."

Satterly followed the stableboy into his horse's stall sullenly. He tried to keep up with the boy's motions, but this was clearly a task the young Fae had been doing his entire life and his hands moved more quickly than Satterly could take in. "Can you slow down a little?" Satterly asked, feeling ridiculous. "Show me again how you hold the bridle before you put it on."

The boy looked at him a bit incredulously. "You've really never done this before, have you?"

No, Satterly thought. No, I've never saddled a horse. No, humans don't possess the Gifts. No, humans can't feel *re*. No, humans don't know the hundred million goddamn rules of propriety that every single Fae takes for granted.

"No, I haven't," he said.

"Well, it's not so hard once you get the hang of it," the boy said, chuckling under his breath.

"Fuck you," Satterly said, but in English.

Could anyone blame him for not knowing this stuff? Satterly was a physicist, and a theoretical physicist at that—he barely knew how to use the microscope he'd borrowed to bring with him to Faerie, let alone something as outré as saddling a horse. If he'd been born a hundred years ago, maybe.

"All done," said the stable boy, grinning. "Do you know which direction to face in the saddle, or can I help you with that as well?"

"Thanks," said Satterly. "I think I can figure that one out on my own."

Satterly's unexpected acquaintance with the world of Faerie had begun the night that his two-year-old niece set his sister's house on fire. Satterly had been in his office at Caltech, grading undergraduate physics papers, when Angela called. Since her husband had left, Satterly was used to getting upset calls from Angela at all hours, but this was something altogether different.

"Brian! I need you. Come quick!"

"What happened?"

"It's Leila. Just come, okay?" Angela had sounded petrified; he'd never heard anyone sound so frightened.

The drive to Irvine seemed to take hours. Satterly spent most of the time imagining his sister's little girl dead or hospitalized or kidnapped. He tried a dozen times to call her on his cell but she never picked up.

When he arrived, the inside of the house was a shambles. It looked like a tornado had hit. Angela led him into Leila's room, where Leila was sitting on her bed, playing with a doll. The blue curtains on the wall—the ones with ducks, Satterly recalled—were now singed and black. The dresser was charred, the plastic piggy bank on top of it melted; coins were scattered on the floor. There was white foam everywhere from the now-empty fire extinguisher that lay on the floor amid the chaos.

"What happened?" said Brian.

Angela took him out to the hall. "I was in her room. We were playing with dolls, just like any other day. Then she told me she wanted to show me something, something wonderful."

Angela started crying. "She started singing, Brian. She started singing in some weird language and then there was this wind and suddenly there was a fire and Leila got scared. She said, 'Stop it, mommy! Stop it!' but I didn't know what to do. So I ran and got the fire extinguisher and sprayed it all over.

"Leila was crying, I was crying. None of it made any sense. And then it just stopped."

"What happened then?" said Satterly, holding her tight.

"Then she said, 'I'm sorry, mommy. I won't do it again.' And she went right back to playing with her dolls."

Five minutes later, Evelyn Yeoh appeared on Angela's doorstep. She was a petite Asian woman with a serious face dressed in jeans and a sweater. She was carrying an odd little device that looked something like a compass but glowed with a hazy blue light. She explained about Leila, but it wasn't anything that Angela or Brian were ready to hear.

"Don't worry," said Evelyn. "When it happens again, you'll call me." She left her card. Angela wanted to throw the card away, but for some reason Satterly kept it.

The next time it happened, Angela ended up in the hospital with second-degree burns. Standing in her hospital room, with Leila asleep in his arms, he called Evelyn Yeoh.

The scene at Satterly's apartment a few days later hadn't been pretty. Evelyn arrived, in jeans and a different sweater, this time carrying a black jewelry box. Angela was still in pain and was furious that Satterly had allowed this strange woman into their lives with her little devices and her ludicrous claims. Satterly was skeptical too, but if there were even a chance that Evelyn could help them, what could it hurt? They were way off the map already.

"Get ready," said Evelyn. "This will be the worst part. Removing the glamour, that is." She sat Angela down at the kitchen table with Leila in her arms. Then she took a small metal bracelet from the box and slipped it over Leila's wrist before Angela could object.

The instant the bracelet touched her skin, Leila shrieked. "Get it off! Get it off!"

Angela reeled backward, almost tipping backward in her chair, but before she could reach the bracelet there was a bright white flash and Leila suddenly *changed* in her arms. Satterly was awestruck; one instant his niece had been there, and the next she was replaced by a rail-thin girl with palest white skin and long, pointed ears. The little girl, who looked *nothing* like Leila, was pleading now, tears falling from her crystalline blue eyes.

"Don't send me back," said the little girl. Her voice was nothing like Leila's now; her words were stilted and strange, as though she were reading words in a foreign language from a script. "Please, please! They'll send a wolf to eat me if I get sent back. They promised!"

Evelyn reached out for Leila, and Angela pushed the little Fae girl away, horrified. "What . . . did you do to my Leila?" Angela whispered.

"I'm sorry," said Evelyn, picking up the girl. "But as I tried to explain earlier, this isn't your daughter." The little changeling wailed and buried her face in Evelyn's shoulder.

Angela refused to believe at first, threatening, then begging. Satterly sat and watched, his mind a whirl, unable to understand what was happening. What finally convinced him was the patient, sympathetic look on Evelyn Yeoh's face. This woman, he realized, had done this hundreds of times.

Angela, however, remained unconvinced, until Evelyn finally persuaded "Leila" to tell the truth. "They told me if I was good," the girl whimpered, her face still half buried in Evelyn's breast, "and never let on, that I'd be loved and taken care of in the Nymaen world. I never had no mama 'til now."

"How long?" said Satterly. "How long since they were switched?"

"Probably not very," said Evelyn. "It usually only takes them a couple of days to manifest."

"You mean," began Angela, "my little girl is . . . out there somewhere?" Angela waved her hand in no particular direction.

"Yes," said Evelyn. "But we can get her back. That's what I do."

The next night, Satterly found himself on a hill in Topanga Canyon, several miles away from anywhere. In one hand he held the changeling girl, and in the other he carried a gym bag containing three pounds of South African gold Krugerrands, forty-eight in all. Together they were worth about thirty-eight thousand dollars. He'd cleaned out his savings account to buy them. Evelyn had insisted on gold coins.

As he stood waiting, he slowly became certain that he and his sister had just fallen for the most bizarre con ever practiced. Any second now, a big guy with a gun was going to step out from behind a tree, take the gold coins, and leave Satterly with this strange little girl on a hill somewhere inland of Malibu.

What happened instead was that a pair of men in gray and gold robes appeared in front of him with a low snapping sound but no other fanfare. These, he learned later, were Masters of the Gates, a brotherhood whose members were the only ones able to travel between worlds without the assistance of a gate.

The two men both had shaved heads and the same pointed ears as the child in his arms. They were both tall, but one was burly and the other was thin, almost emaciated. The burly one looked Satterly in the eye, but the other one only looked down, kicking his feet sullenly in the dirt.

"My name is Pilest," the stout Fae said, his eyes sparkling. "You are the human named Brian Satterly, I hope?" Then he reached out and patted Satterly's shoulder. "I'm kidding, of course. My partner Jindo is never wrong." Pilest held up his hand and Satterly realized that the two men were joined together with manacles made of what appeared to be silver.

"Okay," Satterly said.

Jindo roughly took the gym bag from Satterly's hands and hefted it a few times, then unzipped it. He took one of the Krugerrands and held it up to the moonlight, bit it, then replaced it in the bag.

Jindo said nothing, but Pilest said, "Good. Then let's be on our way."

Instantly, Satterly was somewhere else. A meadow in broad daylight. The air was sweet, almost perfumed, but clear and fresh. It was as though he'd never breathed before. A feeling of deep joy rushed through him and then he remembered where he was and what he was doing and the warm feeling became a chill.

"Welcome to Faerie," said Pilest. "It's been a pleasure doing business with you."

With that, Pilest kicked Jindo harshly and the two of them disappeared.

The rest of it had been like a dream. Traveling to Sylvan, meeting up with Evelyn. The real Leila had already been rescued by the time Satterly arrived at Evelyn's house in the Fae city. Leila ran to him, squeezed him tight, sobbing. The changeling girl was whisked away by one of Evelyn's assistants, her eyes blank.

"What will happen to her?" asked Satterly, after Leila had fallen asleep in his arms. "The little Fae girl?"

"We'll try to find her a good home," said Evelyn. "Adoption isn't common here, but it's not unheard of, either."

"You're very lucky, you know," she said. "We got to her in time."

"In time for what?" said Satterly, pulling Leila close to his chest.

Evelyn gave him a measured stare. "You don't want to know."

Back in the meadow a few hours later, Pilest and Jindo reappeared. Pilest reached out his hands for Leila.

"Can't we go together?" said Satterly. "My sister's meeting us on the other side, but I don't know if she managed to find the place."

"Oh, no. One at a time. My partner here is no grand magus, you know."

"Stop there!" cried a voice behind him. Satterly turned to see a pair of guardsmen at the edge of the meadow, both of them holding crossbows aimed at his chest. Behind them stood a gaunt man with a flowing gray beard.

"We will see that the girl gets where she needs to go," said Pilest. He and Jindo vanished, Leila struggling in Pilest's arms.

Satterly shouted, "Wait!"

The guardsmen approached slowly. One of them spoke to the bearded man. "Is this the one?"

"That's him!" the man shouted. "That's the man who stole my little girl!"

"You are under arrest," the soldier said. He spat. "Changeling trader."

Needless to say, he'd never seen Pilest, Jindo, or his home world again. The thought of little Leila on her own out there in the wilderness had haunted him for two years.

Satterly felt a rough kick. He opened his eyes and looked around wildly. Mauritane was standing over him. "Sleep on your own time," Mauritane said. "We're leaving."

Satterly sat up; he'd dozed off next to the brazier in the stables. Silverdun, Honeywell, and Raieve were all mounted. Everyone was waiting for him.

"Great," he said, pulling himself to his feet. "The human comes up short yet again."

ruminations upon freedom/ a stool and a sturdy roof beam

Mauritane's party picked its way down the steep road to Hawthorne in the early morning light. The sky was a dozen shades of blue and pink, with a gold polish in the east, where the riders were headed, fading to indigo in the west. Purane-Es stood on a bluff overlooking the Hawthorne Road, his eyes tracing Mauritane's route across the switchbacks, through the winter-shorn trees that rose like clawed hands from the snow-bound earth.

The bridle on Purane-Es's borrowed mare was loose, and one of his men was seeing to it. The delay gave Purane-Es a moment to watch Mauritane go, and he allowed himself to hope, despite his threat, that it would be the last he saw of the man. If the Queen's errand were to fail due to Mauritane's death, he would not shed a tear. If, for that matter, the Royal Guard were disbanded tomorrow, he wouldn't even frown.

It had never been his intention to join the Guard, certainly never to rise to such a prominent position there. As second son of the Lord Purane, nothing had been expected of him but to carouse with the other courtiers in the sumptuous playgrounds of the City Emerald, writing poetry and singing lays accompanied by the mandolin and balalaika. The palace grounds were majestic swirls of intrigue and artistry, each day promising new adventures. His only real worry in those days had been the nagging task of someday selecting a bride. He longed for the willowy ladies in waiting who cooed at the sound of his voice and clapped appreciatively when he sat with them by a fountain and played them tunes he'd written for someone else.

Building strong families, that was what second sons were for. Marriage to wealthy daughters, beautiful, silly Fae daughters whose only purpose in life was to smile delicate smiles and bear a *first* son. If a second son came out of the arrangement, it was looked upon as an insurance policy.

Some of these second, third, even fourth sons were despondent over their lot in life. They joined the priesthood, arranged sorties against the Unseelie across the Contested Lands, looking for honor and value in their fathers' eyes. Not so Purane-Es. He'd never been happier than when his father was ignoring him, never felt freer than when his elder brother had been held up again and again to his father's standards instead of him. It had been Purane-La's place to stand out in their parents' garden, practicing at rapier and dagger from dawn until dusk, feeling the flat of Father's blade against his thigh if he slipped or let down his guard. And Purane-La had wanted it. He'd lived for Father's approval, ached and bled and led entire campaigns against the Unseelie and the rebels in Beleriand in order to make Father proud.

And look where it had gotten both of them.

Purane-Es turned at his lieutenant's signal and rechecked his bridle.

"Now it's too tight, you idiot," he said. "Get down here and fix it or I'll saddle *you* and ride *you* back to the City Emerald."

On the slope below, Mauritane let the others ride ahead while he became acquainted with his mount, a touched Arion stallion named Streak.

"You are not the leader," said Streak in Elvish, his horse-voice strained and high pitched.

"I am the new leader," said Mauritane, putting as much authority in his voice as possible. "You will do as I say."

Streak pulled against the reins, testing him. "I want to believe you," he said.

Mauritane reined the horse in, patting his neck with his left hand. "I won't disappoint you," he said. "But you must mind me in all things."

"I shall," said Streak. "If you do prove worthy of it."

"Have no fear, beast," Mauritane said, stroking the creature's mane. "I am your master now."

"It is good to be a member of the herd once more," said Streak, shaking his mane.

Mauritane breathed deep and let the icy morning air sting his lungs. Overhead, stray seagulls and cormorants plied the winds from the ocean, beating their wings and screeching into the morning sun. As the day settled in, the scarlets and purples of the sunrise coalesced into daylight, the risen sun warm on Mauritane's face despite the dimming of winter.

Mauritane nudged Streak and came flush with Honeywell and Satterly, who rode double file behind Raieve and Silverdun. Honeywell, ever the guardsman, rode with perfect posture, his borrowed clothing from the prison laundry providing him with a trim that nearly became an officer. He rode with pride, his gray eyes glinting in the morning sun. Though his expression was impassive, Mauritane knew from his many years in the Guard how to read the frank joy behind it. The freedom of someone who expected never to be free again.

Satterly rode poorly, but he improved with every mile. His expression was a human one, something akin to curiosity but more so. It was as though Satterly lived each waking moment in rapt fascination. His eyes followed everything, from the gulls overhead to the elk that capered back and forth in the wooded hills to the north.

Mauritane pulled forward to lead the group, casting a glance at Silverdun and Raieve as he passed. They were like bookends, both stone-faced, both unreadable. Silverdun had years at court to train him to look continually unimpressed. Raieve must have had her own history among dangerous people, or she was very well trained. Either way, the two of them revealed nothing of their individual moods, and Mauritane noted that he would need some other yardstick of their emotional condition if he were to lead them properly.

They were approaching the bottom of the slope that angled down from the mountains to a plateau that skirted the water's edge. Here the road widened and straightened so that they were able to ride in a line, with Mauritane a few yards ahead.

Wanting to lead, Streak strained against his bit. "It is good to lead the herd. I want to run!"

Mauritane turned back and made a forward motion with his free hand. "Let's give the horses their heads. We can be at Hawthorne by midday!"

At that, even Silverdun cracked a brief smile. He dug in his heels and urged his roan mare forward, following Mauritane's lead.

Streak fell into a smooth, flowing canter, his long head dipping into the wind with each stride. Despite the dark forebodings of the previous night, even Mauritane let the breeze and the sunlight work their way into him. As he leaned forward into the saddle, feeling the strong legs of the stallion pulse beneath him, he allowed himself a brief, broad smile that no one else could see.

The Hawthorne Road followed the base of the Olive Mountains to the southeast, eventually approaching the coastline and turning directly south toward the fishing port of Hawthorne that was the largest town in the region. The road opened onto a high bluff overlooking a rocky beach where black seals darted among the rocks a few yards out to sea. The languorous sigh of the ocean rode in on the wind, drenching them in noise and the smell of salt and the fine spray of seawater. Here the road narrowed again, and Mauritane slowed Streak to a trot in order to find his way across the now rocky trail.

After a minute of riding in silence, the human Satterly rode up beside him, standing poorly in his stirrups but, to his credit, not complaining about what must have been a very uncomfortable seat.

"Satterly," said Mauritane, in his best approximation of the human name.

"I'm just curious," said Satterly, trying to adjust his posture. "What can you tell me about these Contested Lands? All I know is that it's some kind of demilitarized zone between the Seelie and Unseelie kingdoms."

Mauritane nodded. "True, but it's more than that. Some jokingly refer to them as the UnContested Lands. If the Queen wanted them, the Contested Lands could be hers in a fortnight. Mab and the Unseelie could no doubt achieve the same goal, although neither would attempt it." Mauritane reached into his sabretache for a pipe and filled it methodically.

"Why not? What's so undesirable about them?"

Mauritane lit the pipe, and they both watched the smoke from it leap and catch in a gust of briny air. "There are shifting places there, for one," he said.

"Shifting places."

"Yes. They're areas that have come sort of unfastened from the world. Time and distance don't work properly there. It's easy to ride into one and never ride out again."

"How do we navigate around them?" asked Satterly, concerned.

"They're difficult to detect, although I believe with Silverdun's Insight and Elements we can avoid most of them."

"So that's why no one goes there—these shifting places."

"That's part of it." Mauritane dragged on his pipe. "You see, because the Seelie Court does not enforce its rule in the Contested Lands, those criminal elements and monstrous creatures who can't abide Fairy law tend to congregate there. We're sure to encounter some of them, though it's hard to say exactly who or what we'll run into."

Satterly screwed up his face. "Wow, I'm sorry I asked."

They rode another moment in silence, then Satterly said, "Mauritane?"

"Hm."

"How do you know the rest of us won't make a break for it as soon as you turn your back on us in Hawthorne?"

Mauritane blew out a thin stream of smoke. "Are you planning it?"

Satterly flushed. "No! No, I'm just curious."

Mauritane waved at the others. "Honeywell, Silverdun, and Raieve are Fae. Whatever their faults, their honor remains intact. And if honor proves insufficient, I have the fastest horse and the quickest blade."

"What about me?" said Satterly. "You don't think I have honor?"

"I don't know," Mauritane said coolly. "Do you?"

After an hour the sun rose, bringing light but no warmth. Satterly's hindquarters were already beginning to feel sore from the steady trot they maintained down the increasing slope of the Hawthorne road. Mauritane called a stop for breakfast and they dismounted by a bridge over a sluggish stream that was nearly icebound. On the seaward side of the road, the steam tumbled over the bluff and vanished in a spray of mist.

Satterly walked gingerly back and forth near the road, stretching his legs. Noticing his discomfort, Raieve joined him, handing him a cold sausage wrapped in greasy paper. "You must remember to move your hips in the saddle when you're sitting a trot," she said. "It's hell on the thighs but if you keep bouncing up and down like that you're going to hurt the horse's back." She cracked a thin smile. "It also doesn't hurt your ass as much."

Satterly made a halfhearted attempt to smile back. "I'll keep that in mind," he said.

"So," said Silverdun, leading his horse back from the stream, Honeywell at his side. "Your first time in the Contested Lands, eh, human?"

"That's right," said Satterly.

"Lots to be wary of in that forsaken place," Silverdun said.

"Aye," Honeywell agreed. "The shifting places, for one."

"True," said Silverdun. "Bugganes as well. Unseelie raids are always a fear. And of course," he paused, looking at Satterly with a frown, "there's the Thule Man."

"What's the Thule Man?" Satterly asked, skeptical.

"He's forty feet high," Honeywell said, "with eyes of flame. Fists like boulders, capable of crushing a man's head." Honeywell slowly closed his own fist around an imaginary victim."

Satterly felt his stomach sink. "But that's just a superstition, right?"

Honeywell and Silverdun looked at each other, then back at Satterly. "No," said Silverdun, looking confused. "Why would you say that?"

"Because it sounds like something out of a fairy tale or something. A big monster with eyes of flame. Come on."

"Perhaps in your world," said Silverdun. "But in ours, such creatures are quite common. Remnants of the Great Reshaping."

"Aye," said Honeywell. "I once had a teacher who claimed that it was beasts such as that who gave rise to the fairy stories in the human world, so closely joined were the two worlds in the past."

"Jesus Christ," said Satterly, running his hands through his hair. Why had he agreed to this? This world was insane; there was no telling what they might encounter on this trip. He didn't know anything about violence! He'd never killed anything more threatening than a cockroach.

Honeywell's serious expression began to melt, then he burst out laughing. "I'm sorry, Silverdun. I can't help myself!"

Silverdun caught Honeywell's eye, then he too began to laugh. He doubled over, clutching his stomach.

"What's so funny?" said Satterly, feeling his face and ears grow hot despite the cold.

"Oh, you poor bastard," Honeywell managed through his chuckles.

Silverdun tried to contain himself. "Did you see the look on his face?" he cackled. "I thought he was going to piss himself!"

"There's no such thing as the Thule Man," said Satterly. "You guys are assholes."

Honeywell slapped Satterly on the back. "The Thule Man's just an old tale that mothers tell their misbehaving children. A fairy tale, as you put it."

Silverdun's laughter ceased and his smile began to fade. "Yes," he said. Then he shrugged. "Probably."

"That's enough, you two," said Mauritane, mounting Streak. "You're clearly finished eating, so let's be on our way."

Raieve, who'd remained silent during the conversation, muttered, "I hate this world," and went to fetch her own horse.

The fishing port of Hawthorne nestled around a natural harbor, surrounded on three sides by rock formations jutting from the foot of the Olive Mountains. Perhaps the oldest city east of the Ebe, Hawthorne sported the white stucco walls and blue tiled roofs of the antebellum east, from an era before the southern architecture of rounded spires and granite walls rendered such places quaint. The Hawthorne Road cut a gently curved path between the hills and into the city, ending at the docks themselves.

From above Hawthorne, Mauritane watched the fishing boats coming in from their morning runs, blowing their horns. He could just make out the shouts of the fishermen calling out their catches to the vendors on the docks, their cries mixed in with those of the gulls and the crash of the waves from beyond the harbor. There was something enviable about that life, Mauritane thought. He'd been told by the guards at Crere Sulace that the Channel Sea was a harsh mistress, but she couldn't be any harsher than Regina Titania, nor half as cold.

"What's the matter?" said Silverdun, coming up next to him on the bluff. "You've stopped."

Mauritane looked around. The others were waiting for him on the road, their horses shifting back and forth on eager legs.

"Sorry," he said. "The only faces I've seen in years are those of my jailers and my fellow inmates. It's not an easy thing."

"No more easy for any of us," Silverdun whispered, leaning in. "But you're their leader. You can't let them see that it bothers you."

Mauritane smiled. "You're right. It's unseemly of me. I suppose I'm out of practice in a few things."

Silverdun chuckled. "You've got the Gift, Mauritane. Just let it flow and go where it points you. Our Gifts are not ours."

"An Arcadian sentiment."

"A true one."

Mauritane pulled Streak's head back toward the road. "Let's go," he said.

Gray Mave, who had served as Low Chief of Watch at Crere Sulace for twenty years, sat in a darkened, nearly empty cottage near the edge of Hawthorne. He was perched at the edge of a peasant bed, which was a wooden frame filled with straw and covered with a goose down mat. In his hands was a length of rope that he tied and untied into a hangman's noose without looking. In his years at Crere Sulace, he'd been trained to tie a noose that would never slip and that would always snap the neck when the gallows dropped. Mave had no gallows, but he had a stool and a sturdy roof beam. They would have to suffice.

hawthorne by the sea

Mauritane rode to the gate and stopped, waiting for the lone guard at the gatehouse to rise and amble out to meet him.

"State your name and your business," he said, in a voice heavy with the accent of the East.

"My name is Mauritane; I'm a merchant from Miday. I've come to arrange for a shipment of eel."

The guard looked past him at the remainder of the party. "It takes four retainers to pay for a shipment of eel?"

"These are dangerous times," said Mauritane.

The guard shrugged. "You may enter. And ah," he said, leaning up toward Mauritane, "if you need any companionship during your stay, I can probably point you in the right direction."

Mauritane lifted an eyebrow. "That won't be necessary."

"Suit yourself." The guard waved the party forward and retreated to his perch.

Inside its walls, Hawthorne came alive with sights and sounds, the colorful flags of the fishmongers and their calls across the wide market just inside the gate: "Smelt, two coppers! Eel fifteen coppers!" The smell of cooking fish and sawdust and the ever-present seawater mingled in a way that Mauritane found comforting.

Mauritane motioned Silverdun to him and dismounted. "Silverdun, take the horses and have them freshly shod. Send Honeywell to get the supplies on the list. We'll meet back here in three hours."

"Aye, Mauritane."

"Give me some of the money we got from Purane-Es," said Mauritane. "A few silvers and some copper."

Silverdun measured out the coins from the purse at his belt and Mauritane pocketed them.

"Take the signal flare from my saddlebag. If anything happens, use it."

"Where will you be, o captain?" said Silverdun, shaking the dust from his hair.

"I need to see about some maps and charts of the land west of here. And there's another errand I'll tell you about if it's successful." He handed Silverdun his reins and strode off into the throng of the marketplace.

Silverdun leapt from his mount, trying to shut out the fatigue of the long night and the soreness of muscles long unused to riding. "Honeywell, our great captain has spoken. We're to fetch and carry like porters while he peruses the cartographer's."

Honeywell smiled uneasily.

"Oh, don't fret, Honeywell," said Silverdun. "I don't have a mutinous streak; I just have a healthy sense of humor."

"There's some as might not find that sort of humor funny, sir," said Honeywell. He too dismounted. "What are my orders?"

Silverdun rolled his eyes. "Take the list of supplies and fetch whatever you can. I'm to take the horses to the farrier's. Would you rather have the human or the woman?"

"I'll take Satterly," said Honeywell. He whispered, "He says he knows about horses, but I don't think he really does."

Silverdun glanced at Satterly, who sat rigid in the saddle, peering off into the market. "Humans are just that way. They lie like boggarts. If I were you, I'd keep an eye on that one."

"Aye, sir." Honeywell turned, then turned back. "That last bit, about humans, was that also your sense of humor, sir?"

Silverdun sighed. "Trust me, Honeywell. There's nothing amusing about them; not in my brief experience."

Silverdun and Raieve led the horses down the steep, narrow cobblestones of Hawthorne, past the market.

"Why don't you just ask where the farrier is?" said Raieve, frustrated.

"I'm sure there are a dozen of them in a town this size," said Silverdun, leading three of the horses beside him. "And a gentleman never asks directions."

Raieve rolled her eyes. "Gentlemen must spend a lot of time wandering around, then. You just passed it."

Silverdun turned and looked up. A simple wooden sign above a shop showed a horseshoe turned upward.

"And here we are," he said. The farrier's shop was an open-berthed storefront, with a fire and bellows in the back and a set of makeshift stables running the length of the side wall. Shoes, bridles, bits, and other pieces of tack hung from pegs on every vertical surface.

The farrier, a short, red-faced elf wearing a heavy leather apron, approached them from the back of the shop, wiping his hands on a rag.

"How can I help you today, sir?" he said, bowing to Silverdun.

"I need all five of these reshod and all their saddlery checked and rehardened."

"Of course, sir. I can have them ready for you in two days." The farrier smiled.

"That won't work. I want them in two hours."

The farrier frowned deeply, scratching his beard. "Hm," he said. "I don't know. That's a tall order and there are others ahead of you."

"What if I added thirty in silver? Would that speed things up?"

The farrier struggled to contain himself. "Ah, thirty, sir? I suppose I could rearrange my schedule a bit. Three hours, then? I can't do much better than that if you want your silver rehardened."

"Fine," said Silverdun. "I'll be back then."

The farrier took the reins of Silverdun's roan and examined the silver bridle. "Excuse me, sir," he said, just as Silverdun turned to leave. "Where did this bridle come from?"

Silverdun, without missing a beat, said, "I'm sure I don't know. It was a gift from a relative. Why do you ask?"

The farrier fingered the bridle gently. "No reason. I'll see you in two hours, sir."

Silverdun placed ten silver coins on a nearby workbench. "Here's ten for your discretion, my good man."

The farrier nodded, saying nothing.

Silverdun strode regally out of the shop and took Raieve by the elbow. "The farrier suspects something," he said. "We should be prepared."

"For what?" said Raieve, easing him into an alley.

"I don't know. Just be prepared. If anyone finds us out, we're in a difficult situation. We have no papers and we're here under false pretenses."

Raieve had pulled him close for privacy, and now Silverdun found himself with her practically in his arms. "I . . . you're a very lovely woman," Silverdun said.

She pulled away. "Not bad looking for a half-breed, right?" she spat. "Thinking of me as a pincushion is unwise, Lord Silverdun."

Silverdun forced his best smile. "My apologies." Raieve turned away, storming from the alley.

Mauritane examined the charts laid out for him on the cartographer's table. Each of the thick sheets was held in place by a number of ornately carved stones.

"Is this the farthest west you have?" said Mauritane, pointing at the regional map.

"Aye," said the cartographer, an elderly bespectacled man with a trimmed beard. "We don't get much call for farther west than the Ebe. And if it's the Contested Lands you're thinking of, there are no charts of those." He tugged at his beard. "I've got a royal map that shows some of the details to the west."

"I'll take it," said Mauritane. "I'll take all of them."

The cartographer began rolling the charts. "I've got a scribe in house; I can have them for you in a day."

"No," said Mauritane. "I need them from a copyist. Is there one in town?"

"Aye, but he's expensive. Eighty coppers per sheet."

"That's not a problem. Have it done."

"This is one hell of a hunting expedition you're going on, sir, if I may be so bold."

Mauritane looked him in the eye, his face cold. "No, you may not."

The cartographer looked away, laughing nervously. "Of course. Will an hour be enough time?"

"That's fine. I've some other business in town. You don't happen to know a man by the name of Gray Mave, do you?"

Gray Mave's home was at the end of an unpaved street on the edge of

Hawthorne. The roadway straddled the coastline beneath a sheer granite cliff that formed the southern wall of the city. Mave's house nestled in a row of similar structures, anonymous and aging, a sagging willow tree before it.

Mauritane knocked on the heavy oak door and waited. There was no response. Then, from inside, there was a sharp crack of wood against wood and a brief, choked cry. Mauritane threw his shoulder against the door and broke it down, splintering the wood around the latch.

In the middle of the front room, hanging from the rafter by his neck, was Gray Mave. He swung slowly from side to side, facing toward the ocean. A toppled stool lay beside his twisting legs.

Mauritane rushed into the room, pulling his blade from its sheath. He struck the rope above Gray Mave's head, severing it almost completely, but not quite. The body recoiled at the blow and swung in the other direction, nearly knocking Mauritane off of his feet. He swiped again with the cutlass, and Gray Mave fell to the floor.

Mauritane knelt beside the man and listened at his chest for breathing, loosening the coil of rope from around his neck and throwing it on the floor. There was no breath in the man. He felt for a pulse—nothing. Or was there? He reached out again and detected a heartbeat, weak and uneven, but evident. As Mauritane held his fingers against Mave's neck, he felt the man's pulse grow stronger and stronger until it beat normally.

Mave's body shuddered and he took a deep rasping breath, then coughed, choking. His body came to life then, all at once. He twisted onto his stomach, his large frame moving more quickly than Mauritane would have imagined. With a fierce spasm, Mave vomited on the floor, then pushed himself backward and sat up. His eyes were wide open and crosshatched with red.

"Where have I gone?" said Gray Mave after a moment, his voice thick and hoarse.

"You're alive. Barely," said Mauritane. There was a pitcher of water on the sideboard. Mauritane poured Mave a cup and sat down next to him.

Mave felt around his neck. "My throat hurts."

"You're fortunate that you're a poor executioner."

Mave looked at him for the first time. "You. What are you doing here? Were you pardoned?"

"Not exactly. My reason for coming was to apologize for last night. While I do not regret that I made the attempt on Purane-Es, I deeply regret that it was you that suffered as a result. I am responsible for this." Mauritane held up the remnants of the noose.

Mave looked at him for a long moment, the focus steadily returning to his eyes. "You should have let me hang there," he finally said. "When the town finds out what I've done, I'll be a laughingstock. I'll never get on one of the boats."

"Why does anyone need to find out?" said Mauritane. He toyed with the pommel of his sword idly.

"It's no good, Mauritane. I can't face these folk anymore. I can't go back onto the fishing boats; I'm too old and out of practice with the nets. I scan my future for something bright, sir, and I see nothing but blackness."

Mauritane stood and faced the window that looked out upon the sea. "If that's so then you have nothing to lose by coming with me."

Gray Mave took a sip of water and choked but managed to keep it down. He chuckled. "Come with you? Where are you going that I would be useful to you?"

"I've been charged with a task for the Queen," said Mauritane. "I need to be in Sylvan by Fourth Stag. That means riding through the Contested Lands."

"A suicide mission," said Gray Mave, taking the noose from Mauritane and throwing it on the floor.

"Not on my watch it won't be," said Mauritane. "Anyway, at least come as far as the Ebe. If you don't care to join us crossing the Contested Lands, you can find work as a guard somewhere."

"I don't know, sir. This is too much for me. I just . . . yesterday everything was so simple!" Mave pounded the floor with meaty fists.

"Come on," said Mauritane. "Bring your horse around front and saddle her. We need to be off quickly."

Gray Mave let a few tears fall onto the dusty wooden floor of his nearly empty home. "All right," he said. "Let me get my things."

They had just retrieved the maps from the cartographer when Gray Mave took Mauritane's arm and pointed into the sky over the market. "Look," he said.

It was Mauritane's signal flare, bursting into glistening trails of red fire.

"Are your men in trouble?" said Mave.

"They'd better be," answered Mauritane. "That was my only flare."

life is fragile

"**Y**ou are under arrest! Dismount and lay down your weapons."

Gestana, the leader of the Hawthorne City Guard, was a young man, with thin, oily hair that sported two limp victory braids which hung down his back. He led twenty-two of the Hawthorne Guardsmen, including the gatekeeper, as well as a few dozen of the city's militia. The guardsmen, armed with poleaxes, had Silverdun, Raieve, Honeywell, and Satterly surrounded in the center of the fish market, while the militiamen, most of whom were fishermen, stood ready to leap into a melee with their long, serrated fish knives.

Silverdun remained in the saddle of his roan, a sour expression on his face. He still held the spent flare cartridge in his hand. Looking over his shoulder, he could see Raieve and Honeywell sizing up their opponents with the same pessimism he currently felt. Satterly was trying his best to remain calm but still cast furtive glances at the gate from which they were now separated by two layers of armed men.

"You heard me," said Gestana. "I said dismount. And no tricks."

"What crime have we committed?" asked Silverdun.

"What crime?" Gestana chuckled. "You want to do it this way? Fine. We have reason to believe that you are escaped convicts from Crere Sulace."

"By what evidence? I won't lay down my arms without evidence." Silverdun dropped the spent flare and touched his sword.

Gestana sighed. "Appeals to legality will only delay the inevitable," he said. "And they won't improve your treatment in our cells one bit."

"I only ask what is mine by right." Silverdun narrowed his eyes.

"Fine," huffed Gestana. "Milon, come forward."

Silverdun recognized the farrier, who stepped forward and pointed at Honeywell's horse. "The bridle on that mare," he said, "belongs to Jem Alan. He's the Vice Warden at Crere Sulace and my wife's brother. I fashioned the bridle myself as a birthday gift for him two years ago."

The farrier nudged Gestana's shoulder. "And those boots. Those are prison issue."

Gestana thanked the farrier and turned to Silverdun. "Such is our evidence."

"That means nothing," said Silverdun. "Perhaps Jem Alan loathes this man and rues the day his sister married so far beneath her station. He probably threw the bridle in the trash the day he received it. I myself received it as a gift from a notoriously cheap uncle." He shrugged.

"Hold your glib tongue, or I'll have it cut," said Gestana. "Dismount. Now."

Mauritane entered the market from a side street and strode to the center of the market, a scroll tube under his arm, with Gray Mave a few paces behind him. "He'll do no such thing," Mauritane said. He walked past Gestana and took Streak's reins from Honeywell. "Now step aside. We're leaving."

"I think not!" shouted Gestana, his face reddening. "I don't know who you people think you are, but you'll dismount and surrender right now!"

"Or what?" said Mauritane, casually stowing the long cylinder containing his charts behind his saddle. He looked Gestana in the eye. "What will you do?"

Gestana's eyes widened. "We'll cut you down where you stand! Is that clear?"

"No, you won't," said Mauritane, busying himself with the straps of his saddle.

When it became clear that Mauritane was not going to elaborate, Gestana laughed. "You're mad! Pray tell me, why not?"

Mauritane turned on Gestana and marched toward him, his sword still scabbarded. "You won't kill us. You won't even try. For two simple reasons: you lack the skill and you lack the desire."

"That's enough," said Gestana. "Men! Take . . ."

"Be quiet," said Mauritane, holding up his hand for silence.

"You don't tell me . . ." Gestana began.

Mauritane raised his voice. "I said be quiet." Mauritane's stare was fierce and unmoving. Gestana fell silent beneath it, the weight of Leadership bearing down upon him.

"First of all," said Mauritane, "my men are well trained and well armed, whereas yours have been poorly trained and armed even worse. The weapons your guardsmen are carrying are appropriate only against mounted opponents. As soon as you order an attack, my men will dismount and close with them before they have a chance to take a swing. Regardless, half of your men are handling them incorrectly." Mauritane waved his hands around the market, which had grown silent.

Mauritane turned his back on Gestana and addressed the guardsmen. "Second, each of my men is prepared to die here attempting an escape. We have been charged with a mission of critical importance to this land, and we will stop at nothing to achieve our goal. You, on the other hand, have nothing to gain by killing us and very little to lose by allowing us safe passage. Certainly you outnumber us, but how many of you do you think we can kill before you take us? Twenty? Thirty? Which of you wants to be the first to die? Which of you wants to make his wife a widow? His child an orphan? Anyone?"

Mauritane drew his sword and swung it over his head. "Life is fragile, friends," he said. "Once we're gone, you can make this story out to be whatever suits you. But if we fight, you will never be able to glamour over the loss of your brothers and sons."

He wheeled on Gestana and pointed the tip of his sword at the man. "The decision is yours."

"Take them!" shouted Gestana. "Now!"

About half of the guardsmen, including Gestana, came forward. The others hesitated, only briefly, but it was enough. Silverdun leapt from the saddle and drew his weapon, swirling it in the air. Raieve and Honeywell followed suit. Satterly remained mounted, looking frightened.

Gestana raced at Mauritane, sword and dagger drawn. He led with a clumsy attack, lunging low at Mauritane's belly, dagger up to parry an overhead blow. Mauritane riposted, pushing Gestana's blade out of the way with an ugly scraping sound and thrusting at his midsection. Gestana's sword lodged in the cobblestones at Mauritane's feet and he stumbled. Mauritane lodged his sword in Gestana's belly and dragged upward, putting all his strength into the effort. An artery in the guardsman's chest burst, gushing a fountain of blood onto Mauritane's fur cloak. Gestana grunted and choked. He waved his hands, trying to rear back. A thin trickle of blood escaped his mouth and Mauritane dropped him.

Only a few of the other guardsman made it into the fray. Some of the remaining men were stuck in place, watching Mauritane disembowel their leader. The rest of them, overcome with fear, took a few steps back, then ran. The militiamen, apparently rethinking the efficacy of their knives, followed them.

When only five of the guardsmen remained, desperately trying to wield their cumbersome poleaxes against Raieve, Honeywell, and Silverdun, who had closed with them as promised, Mauritane stepped into their sightline and waved his sword.

"Enough!" he shouted. "Drop your weapons and go home. You're not soldiers and you don't deserve to die like soldiers."

The fighting stopped and the guardsmen noticed their fallen leader as a unit. The fight went out of them and they ran, saying nothing.

"Come on," said Mauritane to his people. "Get mounted and go. Don't give them time to think about it." He dropped his cloak on the ground, exchanging it for Gestana's. "I grieve at your death," he whispered into Gestana's ear. "You were a worthy adversary." Using Gestana's dagger, he cut a length of the man's hair from the back of his head and tied it in a loose knot, stowing it in his sabretache.

"What's Mave doing here?" said Silverdun, pointing at the former guard, who retrieved his horse from the alley and joined them.

"Coming with us," said Mauritane. "That's the errand I mentioned earlier."

Mauritane climbed onto Streak with a sigh and led the way toward the gate. No one stood in their path, and the gate was already open when they got there.

They took the Hawthorne Road at a gallop, heading toward Crere Sulace. "They'll be expecting us to turn south toward Colthorn," Mauritane shouted. "So we'll take the Longmont Pass instead. They'll assume we're avoiding the prison."

They made Crere Sulace by nightfall. From the road they could just make out the torches moving along the perimeter walls; Mauritane imagined he could hear the bell for the Night Watch ringing over the wind that sighed through the hills and bent the thinnest branches of the gnarled trees in a ghost dance. In the sky, a waxy moon lit the ground with an almost witchlit glow. There were no other riders on the trail. They were not being followed.

Mauritane slowed to a trot and fell back among the others. "We'll keep going for another few hours. Once we're through the pass, we can cut south and camp in the foothills there."

Satterly groaned. "I thought we were staying at an inn tonight."

"Not anymore," said Silverdun. "When the good folk of Hawthorne recovered their wits, they no doubt sent message sprites to Colthorn and Miday. We'll have to cross the river on the other side of the Longmont Pass and continue south around Miday. That means sleeping on the ground."

Satterly furrowed his brow. "Can't you just glamour us into a caravan of desert gnomes or something? Then we could go wherever we want."

"A glamour would be detected around here," said Mauritane.

"In these parts," said Silverdun, "only criminals wear glamours. They'll have deglamouring wards at every guard post. Better to just avoid cities altogether for a few days."

"Looking forward to a comfortable bed, Satterly?" laughed Raieve. "A few nights on the ground will do you some good."

"Ah," said Silverdun. "There's something else." He looked at Mauritane with a scowl on his face.

"What is it?" said Mauritane.

"In all the excitement I forgot to mention it. When we were arrested by the constabulary, the first thing that odious man did was take my purse."

"How much of our traveling money was in that purse?" said Mauritane.

"All of it," Silverdun sighed. "In addition to being fugitives, we are now destitute as well."

The wind tore at them as they crested Longmont Pass. It had shifted as they'd climbed toward the narrow opening and now pressed at their faces, feeling its way into their clothing and their ears, noses, mouths. They clutched at their cloaks and bowed their heads. The horses fought every step of the way. Mauritane led them single file, taking the worst of it on himself.

Beyond the pass, the land flattened and gently descended toward the River Ebe, a silver strand glowing gently in the distance. The road wound downward toward the river through a dense clutter of scrub brush, bent trees, and smooth rock formations that were twisted and warped in impossible shapes. Beyond the Ebe, past the horizon, lay the Contested Lands and, somewhere past them, the walled city of Sylvan.

Mauritane rode a bit down the trail until the wind calmed enough for conversation. "Did any of you get spellrested while we were in Hawthorne?" he asked.

They all shook their heads. "We were busy being apprehended," said Raieve.

Gray Mave raised his hand, the gesture barely visible in the darkness. "I had a few hours of sleep last night. I don't mind taking the first watch."

"Well, you are Low Chief of Watch," said Silverdun, sounding tired. "I suppose it's fitting."

They rode off the trail and followed a rocky declivity that paralleled a shallow stream. The stream rounded a short outcropping that would protect well enough from the wind and would hide the light of a small fire from the road.

With the horses watered in the stream and tied, Honeywell broke out rations of dried meat and flower petals and passed them around while Mauritane built a fire. "I picked these daisies up in Hawthorne," Honeywell said.

Satterly passed on the daisies, contenting himself with the dried venison that had served as the basis for any number of meals at Crere Sulace. After a day of painful riding and the scene in Hawthorne, he found himself ravenous, if a bit queasy.

After a few minutes, Honeywell, Silverdun, and Raieve lay beneath their cloaks and turned their backs to the fire. Eventually, Honeywell began to snore. Gray Mave took his sword and climbed to the top of the ledge above them to keep watch.

Satterly looked at Mauritane over the fire. Mauritane was staring into the flames, pulling strands of his long hair out before him and twisting them into a braid.

"I'm sorry," Satterly said after a long pause.

"For what?" asked Mauritane, not looking up.

"For freezing today, in Hawthorne. I just sat on my horse like an idiot while you guys did everything."

Mauritane looked briefly at him. "I didn't recruit you for your fierceness in battle," he answered after a breath.

"Well, that's just the thing," said Satterly, wringing his hands. "I felt totally useless back there. I just hope that's not an indication of things to come."

"You'll prove useful yet, I've no doubt," said Mauritane, returning to his task.

Satterly watched Mauritane create his victory braid, taking the knot of Gestana's hair from his sabretache and weaving it carefully in with his own in an intricate pattern. "How many braids do you have?" Satterly said.

"It's my fifty-first kill," said Mauritane, without altering his expression. "Each of these," he said, holding out a row of braids on the left side of his head, "counts for five."

"You just . . . killed him," said Satterly.

"What?"

"You just ran him through. That guard in Hawthorne. You didn't even think about it. Doesn't it bother you?"

Mauritane looked at him quizzically. "What did you expect me to do?"

"I don't know. I mean, couldn't we have talked our way out of it or something?"

"Would you rather be sitting in a cell in Hawthorne right now, awaiting your execution?"

"They wouldn't have. I mean, they would have contacted the prison and . . ."

Mauritane raised an eyebrow. "And Crenyllice would have told them that we were escaped prisoners, just as they suspected. They hang escaped prisoners in the courtyard by the South Tower."

"I just can't believe that you killed that guy. Don't you wonder about who he was? What kind of person he was? What his life was like? Don't you ever feel bad for their families or anything?"

"Life is fragile," said Mauritane. He returned to his braiding.

Satterly sat and thought for a while, watching individual fingers of flame merge and separate in the fire.

"I don't know if I can do that," said Satterly. "I don't know if I can just kill someone like you can."

Mauritane tied the braid off with a length of silky black thread that shone in the firelight. "Then pray to your god that you never have to," he said.

an empty jarl the danger of talking trees

The next day dawned gray and cold, smelling of dissipating smoke and old ice. Mauritane rose at the first dim light and climbed the embankment to the bluff where Raieve kept watch. She sat perfectly still, staring into the distance beyond the River Ebe. In the growing light the valley was barren and inhospitable, gray and white slopes marked with evergreen stands and the bizarre rock formations that sprang irrationally from the otherwise even ground. Far beneath them the river seemed frozen in time, its green ice dull and somber.

Mauritane sat next to her and looked out over the valley, following her gaze. "You fight well," he said, for lack of anything better.

Raieve turned her head slowly and eyed him sharply. Years in the sun had dusted freckles over the bridge of her nose and drawn thin lines from the corners of her crystalline blue eyes. Her hair moved in the morning breeze, wanting to take flight but refraining.

"For a woman?" she countered, eyebrow cocked, daring him.

Mauritane shrugged. "A dead man isn't any less dead if it was a woman who ran him through," he said.

Raieve thought this over, then laughed out loud, a short husky laugh. "True," she said.

"How many women, then, do you have in the Royal Guard?" she asked.

"None."

There was the eyebrow again. "Aha. Why not?"

"None have applied. It's considered unladylike."

Raieve gestured to herself with mock courtliness. "Am I not the very picture of a noble lady?"

Mauritane grinned, the first time he could remember doing so in months. "Would you want to be?"

Raieve leaned in toward him but kept her eyes fixed on the valley below. "I do not think you are a man who has much truck with noble ladies."

Mauritane winced. His wife the Lady Anne—a noble lady if ever there was one—waited for him back in the City Emerald while he sat flirting with a woman he barely knew. It was wrong.

He stood, clapping his hands together against the cold. Raieve stood as well, sensing something amiss but saying nothing.

"How did you come to be at Crere Sulace?" Mauritane asked, regarding her with what he hoped was a professional distance.

"You read my file, certainly," she said, glaring. "You know why."

"Reports contain facts, not motivations. I know what you did, but I don't know why you did it."

Raieve picked up a handful of rocks and hurled one over the edge of the bluff. "I was chosen by my clan as an emissary to your government. In the wake of the Unseelie invasion, the Concordat crumbled, leaving the clans to fend for themselves. Many of the clans were left with nothing after the war and turned to raiding for survival. Others have taken advantage of the chaos to settle old grievances."

She hurled another stone, watching it fall before she continued. "The Heavy Sky Clan wishes to reform the Concordat, but without weapons and battle thaumatics we don't stand much of a chance. We believed," she paused to chuckle ruefully, "that the Seelie government would see the value in supporting a unified Avalon. Trade between the two worlds has slowed to a trickle, and more than one Fae merchant has been slaughtered within a day's ride of the Gates."

"Did you speak to the Fae ambassador at Tiripali?"

Raieve laughed. "Oh, yes. In one of his rare moments of sobriety. He intimated that the Seelie government did not take sides in foreign disputes but that I was free to discuss the matter with the Foreign Office in the City Emerald. But only after taking any number of bribes.

"The Travel Office, however, refuses to take Avalona currency as payment; they require their fee in gold. I sold a portion of my ancestral lands in order to raise the money.

"In the City Emerald I waited for three weeks for an appointment with an Assistant Minister of the Foreign Office, a conniving bastard named Olifen. That appointment required even further bribes."

Mauritane sighed. "I knew Olifen, though not very well. He is a political appointee, a nephew of some lord or another. A nobleman's son dallying in governance. A fool."

"You don't seem to think much of noblemen."

"Not the incompetent ones. What transpired between you and Olifen?"

"He sympathized. He made a show of raising money for arms and claimed to have contacted the Seelie Army for the loan of a detachment of battle mages. Then one evening he invited me to his private apartments. There was a bright red dress laid out, a bottle of rose wine. He told me that all would be arranged, but that I—how did he put it—might "show my gratitude" first."

"And you refused."

Raieve bristled. "Of course! Politely, at first, with all the decorum I could muster. I was the emissary of my people. Lives were at stake. For a moment I even considered it. Given a bit more time to consider his proposal I might even have accepted it. But he forced himself on me and I . . . reacted."

"You slit his throat," said Mauritane, without emotion.

"I did," she said, hurling the last of her stones, this one farther than the others. "A detachment of the guard arrested me. I was tried in the Aeropagus, if you can call it a trial, and within two days I was in Crere Sulace, sentenced to live out my natural life there."

"It could have been worse. Had you not been a foreign emissary they would have had you drawn and quartered."

"Small comfort," she said.

She looked at Mauritane, her eyes searching him. "You're a queer one," she said. "Not much like the other Seelie I've met."

"Yes," he said, looking back. "And you see where it's gotten me."

They stood there, silently, for a long moment. Mauritane felt a sudden, unexpected desire to reach out for her and draw her close to him.

"It's getting light," she said, finally breaking the spell that was of an older kind of magic than is taught in universities. "We should be on our way."

Silverdun was stirring, not yet awake. The others were still asleep, huddled beneath the thick cloaks they'd purchased in Hawthorne. Streak stood tied near the tiny stream, nodding and chuffing at Mauritane urgently.

Mauritane took a handful of oats from a saddlebag and held them beneath the horse's nose. Streak's thick tongue darted expertly and took the entire handful in a swallow.

"Many thanks, master. Oats are delicious."

"You're welcome." Mauritane patted the horse's neck.

"Master, a man came to me last night. He put his forelegs in my saddlebag. It was not you, master. His smell was not yours."

Mauritane stopped cold. "Was it one of the men traveling with me?"

"Master, there are many smells. I do not know them all. It was not the female smell."

Mauritane looked at the two bags on Streak's left side, casting a glance at the camp, where no one had yet to rise. He quickly inventoried their contents. Everything was in place: fish hooks, whetstone, flint, and silver. The extra dagger remained in its sheath.

He crossed in front of the horse to the right side, realizing there was only one thing he had that the others did not, only one thing worth taking. He opened the front leather pouch and counted his message sprite jars. One of them was missing.

Quietly, Mauritane circled the camp, searching for the empty jar. He whispered an old finding spell his mother had taught him, a little rhyming cantrip in Elvish that would have made him chuckle under other circumstances. After a few moments he felt a slight tug that drew him across the stream and down a steep slope to one of the strange rock formations, this one vaguely shaped like a woman's body, her arms stretched above her. At the foot of the formation was the missing sprite jar, its lid lying on the ground near it, the sprite long gone, its message and recipient unknown. Mauritane collected the jar and screwed on the lid, placing it in the pocket of his cloak.

He made his way back to camp to find Silverdun awake and washing his face in the stream. "Where did you get off to?" he said, stretching and groaning from a night's sleep on cold ground.

Mauritane looked up and saw Raieve still perched above the camp, her face like chiseled stone.

"Just getting some air," said Mauritane.

It was not a pleasant morning. Neither Mauritane nor anyone else had slept well and the cold which had at first been a nuisance was now becoming a serious problem for all but Gray Mave, who seemed immune to it. The horses were slow to move and stubborn, reacting against their exposure to the elements and their rationed foodstuffs. Keeping enough food on hand for six working horses traveling over frozen soil was an irritating reminder of troop movement tactics from Mauritane and Honeywell's Academy days. Little was said as they mounted and began their descent into the Ebe River valley.

The river always seemed near to hand, but through some trick of geographical perspective, it appeared to grow no nearer, even after a full morning's ride. Regardless, Mauritane's spirits began to lift as the sun rose, taking some of the chill from the air. The wind shifted to their backs. Mauritane began to relax in his saddle, letting Streak find his own way, and the others fell in line behind him. For several hours they simply rode, without speaking, letting Streak guide them toward the ever-distant Ebe.

Honeywell was the first to hear the trees. As the road descended into the valley, groves of pine and spruce became more and more frequent, until eventually the path was lined on both sides by dusty green branches, some tall enough to block out the sun.

"Did you say something?" asked Honeywell, pulling forward to pose the question to Mauritane.

"No," said Mauritane.

Honeywell pricked his long, pointed ears. "That. Do you hear it?"

Mauritane cocked his head to the side and listened. There were soft voices speaking, but they were coming from the side of the road and not any of the travelers. Mauritane squinted into the trees and frowned. "It's just the trees," he said.

Satterly rode up alongside them. "What are those voices?" he said. "It sounds like there's a whole crowd out there, but I can't see anyone."

"It's the trees," said Honeywell. "They're talking."

"Are you serious?" said Satterly, a wide grin appearing on his face.

"Yes," said Mauritane, "but don't talk to them."

Satterly slowed his horse to a walk and peered at some branches that hung over the road.

"Hello," said the tree. "Isn't it a nice day?"

"It *is* a nice day, isn't it?" said Satterly. "What's your name?"

He felt Mauritane's hand on his wrist. "Didn't I just say not to speak to the trees?"

"Yes, but they're . . . trees. What's the problem?"

Mauritane sighed. "You'll see."

"My name is Tree!" said the tree. "Isn't that a nice name? Isn't the sun pretty?"

"Good morning!" said another tree. "So nice to see you!"

"Have a wonderful day!" the first tree said, waving a branch. "Lovely to meet you!"

"The air is fantastic this morning," observed a third.

Other trees joined in, wishing Satterly well, offering kind words of support, inquiring after his family. Soon the entire forest was a cacophony of arboreal babbling and branch fluttering, loud enough to drown out any conversation the travelers might have had. Their one-sided conversations followed the six riders the full length of the forest, their volume never decreasing until the pines and spruce gave way to more rocks and the voices faded into the wind.

"See you another time!" offered a fir on the tree line. "It was so nice to meet you!"

"I am so sorry," muttered Satterly once they were out of range.

"You should be sorry," said Mauritane. "When I give an order, you follow it. The next time you blithely disregard a direct order from me, I'll drag you the rest of the way to the City Emerald. Are we clear?"

"Yes," said Satterly. "Understood. I just . . . I mean, they're talking trees!"

"I loathe talking trees," said Silverdun. "I absolutely loathe them. I should call you out for doing that." He scowled at Satterly and rode ahead.

"You ought to be more kind to the human," Raieve said. "He finally got the opportunity to interact with his peers."

Even Mauritane smiled at that.

"Very funny," said Satterly. "But I have to ask. Why are there talking trees?"

"What do you mean?" said Mauritane.

"What possible biological justification could there be for talking trees? They have no need to communicate with each other; they don't eat, so they don't need mouths, or tongues, or teeth, or any of the other body parts involved in speech. They never go anywhere or do anything, so they couldn't have anything worthwhile to talk about. So why do they talk at all? It doesn't make any sense."

"The trees do not talk in your world?" said Gray Mave, joining the discussion. "How strange!"

"No. We don't have sentient wildlife in my world hanging around making small talk. That would be considered extremely unusual where I come from."

"Have you done much traveling in Faerie?" said Mauritane.

"No," said Satterly. "Most of my time here's been spent at Crere Sulace."

Mauritane nodded. "Faerie is an old place," he said. "A very old place that was once overflowing with magical essence. There's still magic today, of course, but in the earliest times, the essence was everywhere, freely available.

"The earliest of the Seelie Fae were a capricious race. Once they mastered the art of shaping, anything they could imagine was theirs for the having. They had banquets at every meal, the finest wine, the fairest slave girls, everything they could possibly dream of. There are volumes and volumes written about them in the City Emerald; their histories would take a lifetime to read.

"These exploits sufficed for centuries, but eventually they became bored. Simply living well was not enough. They began experimenting, making changes in the fabric of the world itself; it was called the Great Reshaping. It went on for years, and over time fads and fashions came and went. One year it might be changing the color of the sky, the next year might be building islands in the clouds, the year after that might be creating talking trees."

"What they didn't realize, though," said Raieve, joining in, "was that their creations drained the source essence of the land. They were the stewards of the most powerful magic the universe has ever known, and they squandered it on talking trees."

"It was a more innocent time," said Mauritane.

"It was a stupid time," said Raieve. "It's legends like that that make me glad I'm not from this foolish world."

Mauritane fell silent, letting the others continue to bicker genially, as long as it kept their spirits up. He rode silently, his eyes focused on the Ebe, thinking about the empty spirit jar in his cloak and what it might represent.

Part Two

Once, at the dawn of memory, the two great Faerie kingdoms were one: a massive empire that stretched from the Northern Islands to the desert wastes of the south, from the Eastern Sea to the mountains in the West where the great dragons ruled from their rocky keeps. The emperor Uvenchaud united the wild Fae clans under his iron rule, ushering in the Rauane Envedun-e, the Age of Purest Silver. It was during the Rauane that the Fae philosopher Alpaurle wrote his Magus, the first book of magic. It was during the Rauane that the Great Reshaping took place, when the mountains spoke and the sky rained wine and the flowers sang odes of tender longing to the morning sun. And it was during the Rauane that the Stone Queen, Regina Titania, was born, and it was she that brought that thousand-year reign of peace to an end.

Now Titania was the daughter of a simple farmer from the high country, in a small town called Nyera. Beautiful and poised, wise beyond her years, she brought suitors from all over the Faerie lands to bid for her hand, and she would have none of them.

"I will take the hand," she said, "of the one who will give the very land to me, and no less." At this, her many suitors flushed and scoffed, rolling their eyes. But one man did not. His name was Auberon, and he was a son of the great god, Aba. Aba had many sons and all were forbidden to interfere in the affairs of mortals, but Auberon was smitten with Titania from his first glance. He vowed upon hearing her proclamation that he would present the Faerie land itself to her as a wedding gift.

Auberon went to his father's great palace in the sky; far, far above the land and he knelt, saying, "Great father, all things and all lands are yours, and many are your strengths. I wish but one small land in all the many worlds at your feet. Give it to me and I will ask nothing further for all my days."

Aba, the wise one, looked his son in the eye and a great sadness filled him. "You are my son," he said, "and for that I will always love you, but what you ask, I cannot give."

Auberon stood his ground. "I know, father, that you think me immature and unworthy, but whatever you ask in return, I will give you."

Aba did not turn. "My son, if I give you what you ask, a mighty kingdom will fall, and another will spring up in its place that will cease to know me. They will toil for a thousand years times a thousand under the rule of a usurper, and her rule will be hard, indeed."

Auberon said, "I will bear their wrath."

"Your love is that strong?" said Aba.

"It is, my lord."

"Then take the land, but know that you will be a plague to my people and they will curse your name through the centuries, and you will be known as their Adversary, even though they forget the name of him who fathered you."

"So be it," said Auberon.

"And so it is," said Aba, and his face became dark.

Auberon returned to the land from the castle of his father and found that he could now hear the voice of each sparrow, that in his fingers rippled the tides and winds, and that his feet were rooted deep within the earth. These things he laid at the feet of the fair Titania and she accepted him, saying, "All this time I have waited for the one who would bring the land and lay it at my feet, and now I find the son of Aba has done this thing. I will marry you."

They were married in the Seelie Grove under the full moon, and when the vows were spoken and the wreath tied, Titania took the power of the land and wrested it from her husband, saying, "Auberon, you were unwise to grant me such power, for now your father's people will curse your name and call you Adversary. And you will be my slave down through the ages, for I will not suffer fools gladly." And when she spoke, Auberon was struck blind and dumb, and a veil fell over his eyes. Titania then caused the Great Seelie Keep to be erected, ordering the stones themselves to bend to her will, and she led Auberon to the throne room, which is like a cavern, and placed him upon the first throne and herself upon the other.

When Aba's people heard the news, some of them said, "Aba is our father and would not lead us astray. Let us stay within this land and toil for the Arcadia our father has promised us if we remain." And they stayed.

But some of the others said, "Look, over there to the north, there is a land that does not bow to the will of the Usurper and the Adversary. Let us go there and make for ourselves a home." And they left. And when they reached their new home, they passed out of the Stone Queen's influence and were free of her. But when Aba saw what they had done, he became angry and said, "Look how little faith my people have in me! I will lay a curse upon those that have gone, that the ground will not remain still beneath their feet, and they will not be able to raise up stones to shelter themselves."

And Aba looked at those who remained to suffer under the Stone Queen, and he said, "These are my people, and I am pleased by them. For them I will increase their Gifts, and they shall use those Gifts to glorify me, even though they are prisoners in their own land. And one day they will rise up as a people and the Stone Queen shall be cast out, and that will be my reward to them."

Everything that Aba had promised came to pass. Those who remained, they forgot the name of Aba, though their Gifts were made strong by him, and those who went away were given many hardships, and nothing they built would stand.

And then it was that those two peoples, the Fae of the Seelie Queen Titania and the Fae who called themselves Unseelie, went to war, and there could never be an agreement between them. Mighty magicks were wrought and cast from each land until the air between them split and shifting places sprung from the rift, and this also was the will of Aba. And those lands that contained the shifting places became known as the Contested Lands, for neither side would release claim to them . . .

Vircest-Ana Aba-e, Book II ("Rauad Faehar"), Canto 1

the city of mab

Along a ridge overlooking a purple mountain range, the floating city of Mab prepared to cut stakes and sail. Far to the south, the Seelie lands were in the grip of Midwinter, but here in the highlands the eternal desert heat baked the earth to a cracked brown, the harsh wind kicking up swirls of dust and bending the scattered trees to brush the ground. Throughout the city, the shouts of water bearers and hunters returned from their labors filled the market tents and the stalls along the outer rim.

From the rigging high above the poised tents of the royal spire, the city's crew called out the ancient magic language of motion amid the steady flapping of the sheets. The sails, multicolored and embroidered with the bright crests of the Unseelie families, unfurled from their masts and climbed the spars, crewmen heaving against the lines of thick brown rope. The wind caught the sails and filled them; they strained against the weight of the city beneath with an anxious groan. Finally, the crewmaster hoisted the pennant of Queen Mab, and from the rigging they called down below to cut the stakes. With a mighty roar, a thousand knives fell to the sound of the chorus "Forever Mab!" and the Queen's city left her earthly moorings and embraced the dusty currents, beginning her slow journey south. On the ground, the nomadic creatures of the desert scattered, leaving the remains of their camp-fires to be swallowed by the dust.

Outside the city, the sailing tent of Hy Pezho jumped into motion as its moorings grew taut against the city's thrust and began to pull the tent forward. Inside, Hy Pezho barely noticed.

Her name was Moonwind, or so she claimed. Hy Pezho didn't know and didn't care. He removed her clothing with calculated motions, running his fingers over her exquisite skin. She lay back among his pillows, moaning softly, whispering in his ear. His tongue found hers and he lowered himself gently on top of her, tracing the contours of her body with a practiced touch. She helped him out of his tunic and into her, and he groaned with pleasure. In the tent, the perfume of spice incense wafted up from a censer on the low teak table by his pallet. The gauzy drapes wove in and out, drawn by the wind.

The sounds of urgent lovemaking were soon replaced with heavy sighs and Hy Pezho rolled off of Moonwind with a faraway look in his eye.

"What are you thinking?" said Moonwind.

"What am I what?" Hy Pezho was confused. "Oh. What do you care?"

"I was just making conversation." She reached for her robe and shrugged into it, taking an apple from the bowl above the bed. She bit into the apple and the juice ran down her chin.

"I didn't bring you here to make conversation." Hy Pezho turned his back on her and reached for his own clothing.

"It's always fun when it's fun, and then it's always over when it's over, eh?" she laughed. She rolled over onto her stomach. "Here. Have an apple and we'll try again. What do you say?"

"No," said Hy Pezho, distracted. "I've lost the feeling for it."

"You're strange," she said. "I sort of like you."

"Well, don't get too attached." Hy Pezho stood and turned his head toward the door. There was a quiet buzzing sound coming from beyond it. He opened the tent flap, allowing in the afternoon sunlight and, with it, a tiny flying thing that darted into the room and lighted on the fruit bowl. The thing took flight again and buzzed around Moonwind's head, then spotted Hy Pezho and circled him.

"Hy Pezho! Hy Pezho!" the creature whispered.

"I am he," said Hy Pezho. He held out his palm and the message sprite glided into it, tucking its wings behind its back.

"Message for you! Message for you! A message from the far south." The tiny sprite cupped its hands over its mouth and whispered, "It's a secret. *Big* secret!" It jerked its thumb at Moonwind.

"Don't worry about her," said Hy Pezho. "She's irrelevant."

Moonwind leapt to her feet. "What do you mean by that?"

"I mean that you won't speak if I tell you not to," said Hy Pezho. He jumped on Moonwind, pinning her on the bed. The sprite still remained standing in his palm. He placed the creature gently on his shoulder, where it sat patiently.

"Be still!" he commanded Moonwind, with the tone of the black art in his voice. Moonwind froze, splayed over the pillows.

"Ooh, scary!" said the sprite, shouting in his ear. "Can I give you my message now?"

Hy Pezho placed the sprite on the counter. "Speak," he said.

"Your message is from the one who calls himself the Awakened One. Very poetic! I thought so, anyway."

"Please spare me your comments, sprite."

"Okay!" The sprite stamped its foot. "I am a sprite. I must needs be sprightly."

"Get on with it."

"The Awakened One says, 'I am with them.'"

"Anything else?"

"Nothing else."

Hy Pezho clapped his hands together, grinning. "I knew it!" He turned to his wardrobe and examined its contents, searching for his most formal robes.

"Ahem," said the sprite. "I'm sleepy and I need a nice jar to lie down in. And a firefly! And a sprig of parsley! But a jar would do." The sprite looked petulantly up at Hy Pezho.

Moonwind made a muffled sound from the bed, her eyes wide. Hy Pezho sighed and drew a knife from his robes. He waved his fingers at her and she fell splayed onto the bed. Finding herself able to move, she crawled awkwardly backward, away from Hy Pezho.

Hy Pezho strode quickly across the tent's floor and took her roughly by the throat, holding her easily. "Can you read or write?" he asked.

Moonwind shook her head violently back and forth.

"I can tell if you're lying, you know."

"No," she choked. "There's no school for girls like me, you know that. Please!"

"Fine then," he said. "Hold still a moment longer." Hy Pezho pried her mouth open and gently extended her tongue. Her eyes widened, but she remained motionless.

"Sorry," he said. He drew the knife between his fingers and Moonwind's tongue came off in his hand, along with a spray of blood.

"Now go," he said. He yanked her off the pallet and pushed her toward the door. Free to move, she sank to her knees, her hands pressed to her face. She tried to scream and a sick, wet sound came from her mouth.

"Go!" Hy Pezho kicked her in the stomach. She rolled onto her side, then stood, unsteadily, and crawled through the open doorway. He threw the tongue after her.

Hy Pezho turned to the counter along the far wall and washed in the bowl there, pouring warm water from a pitcher over his bloodied hands.

"Come, Bacamar," he said. "We've business in Mab's tent."

A transparent shape uncoiled itself from the bamboo rafters of the tent, its smooth edges glistening in the sunlight. "Did you receive a message while I slept?" the familiar asked drowsily.

"Yes. Your errand was a success."

"I am pleased." Bacamar flowed toward the tent's floor, gently flapping her diaphanous wings.

"Something for you," said Hy Pezho, indicating the sprite.

The sprite looked from Hy Pezho to the familiar on the floor baring her tiny, sharp fangs. "Uh, I was just kidding about the parsley!" it said, backing slowly toward the thick canvas wall. "It was a joke, honest!"

Bacamar advanced, a delicate tongue appearing from her mouth, licking gently over her teeth.

"Can't we reconsider?" the sprite said.

The Royal Complex stood at the center of the city of Mab, its violet hangings and golden tassels setting it apart from the rest of the inner court. Gossamer banners of blue and yellow fluttered in the breeze, hung from struts high above the wooden floor of the court. Hy Pezho's boots made a gratifying sound on the wide floor; the rest of the courtyard was silent save for the quiet titters of the robed ladies-in-waiting who clustered in groups of three and four around the potted palms and the stone fountains. A pair of the Queen's Guard stood at the entrance to the Royal Complex, allowing him access based on his sigil of rank.

Inside the complex, Hy Pezho climbed a wide stair, passing more of the youthful ladies of the Queen's cortege. He stopped to admire them. "Very soon, I will be the one about whom you whisper," he said to himself, catching the eye of one of them, a waif in blue silk who passed over his gaze without notice. Hy Pezho smiled. "Soon."

He approached the clerk's desk in the main antechamber of the palace, ignoring the guards who leaned in as he approached, waiting for him to do or say something questionable.

"I am Hy Pezho. I request an audience with Her Majesty," said Hy Pezho, in his best gentrific manner.

The clerk examined his sigil. "Do you have a grant of petition?" said the clerk, looking up at him from beneath smoked glasses.

"I do." Hy Pezho withdrew the scroll from his cloak and unfolded it on the clerk's desk.

The clerk glanced at it and snorted. "This petition is over thirty years old!"

Hy Pezho leaned in close and hissed, with just a touch of the black art, "I do not see an expiration date."

The clerk stiffened. "Wait there," he said, indicating a low wooden bench.

Hy Pezho waited for an hour, then another, then another. The clerk studiously ignored him. It would be unseemly to do anything but wait, as though waiting were the sole purpose of his existence.

Finally, as the daylight began to fade through the open windows in the gallery above, the clerk called him forward. "You will have five minutes. At the end of your five minutes, a bell will ring and you will leave." The clerk eyed Bacamar, coiled lightly around Hy Pezho's arm, nearly invisible. "Your pet must remain outside."

"Sorry, Bacamar," said Hy Pezho. The familiar undulated upward into the gallery above and wrapped herself around a balustrade, sulking.

A pair of burly guards ushered Hy Pezho into a dim parlor and searched him for weapons, poisons and hexes. The search was embarrassingly thorough. Finally the guards sat him in a chair and placed a loose binding charm on him that made his arms heavy and his legs numb. He waited there for another hour, feeling his nose itch, unable to raise his arm to scratch.

Finally, the curtain on the room's far wall drew back and Her Royal Majesty, Queen Mab, entered the room, her entrance preceded by a stream of butterflies and a gentle drift of incense and rose petals. She was taller than Hy Pezho expected, an ancient woman of impressively regal bearing, dressed in a tightly bodiced gown of pure scarlet, the Unseelie Crown woven perfectly into her silver hair. She seated herself on a cushion, drawing the curtain closed behind her.

"Royal Highness. It is a great honor indeed," said Hy Pezho, bowing his head toward her.

"Your petition is an old one, granted to your father. It is in his memory that I allow it for a son."

"You are most kind, Majesty."

"No, I am curious. I want to know what the son of the Black Artist has done with his life. Have you followed in your father's footsteps?" Her voice was high and nasal, clipped, precise.

"Aye, Majesty. That is why I have come."

"When your Queen asks a yes or no question, son of Pezho, only a 'yes' or a 'no' is required."

"My apologies, Majesty."

"The black arts are most dangerous. They consumed your father. Do they not consume you as well? Elaborate."

"The art may be controlled, Majesty, by one with sufficient will."

"Ah," said Mab. "And I suppose you possess such a will."

"I do, Majesty."

"Have you not heard the expression that love may not be ridden, only grasped by the reins? The same is true for hatred."

"That is the saying, Majesty." Hy Pezho attempted a smile.

"State your business, son of Pezho. Then begone and do not trouble me again."

"Majesty, I bear news of great import to the Unseelie." With a supreme effort, Hy Pezho reached for the locket at his breast and forced it open, spilling the desiccated body of the message sprite onto the divan before him.

"What is that?" said the Queen, nudging it with her finger.

"Right now, there is Midwinter in the Seelie land," said Hy Pezho, "and Titania has sent out her emissary."

The Queen frowned. "How do you know of such things?"

"My father had a loose tongue, especially near the time of his death." Hy Pezho smiled.

"What of it?" Mab frowned.

"I have tracked the party of the emissary," he said. "And what's more, I have placed an operative among them."

Now the Queen smiled. "Hy Pezho, perhaps you are your father's son after all."

"No," said Hy Pezho. "I am better."

A moment later, a tiny bell rang overhead. The Queen reached up her hand and silenced it.

the city emerald

I t is called the Jewel of Faerie and the Dragon's Heart. It is the oldest place in the known world, the beginning of history and the source of all power in the Seelie Kingdom. It is thousands of centuries old, its cobbled stones worn from the treads of millions, its buildings moaning with the sighs of countless generations. It is the setting of legend and myth. It is the City Emerald, the eternal city, the capital of the Faerie Kingdom and the self-proclaimed center of the world.

At its heart is the Seelie Grove, Her Majesty Regina Titania's ancient pleasure garden, the perfectly landscaped, verdantly green center that gives the city its name. It is accessible only to the Queen and to her groundskeepers, handpicked eunuchs from across the Channel Sea. Each morning the Queen can be seen there, her head bowed in meditation.

The Royal Palace borders the Seelie Grove to the east and south; opposite the palace the Boulevard Laurwelana runs the length of the grove's wall, its sidewalks glowing with high silver witchlights. Rising above the Boulevard are the town homes of Fae lords and the Aldermen of the prominent guilds, their wide windows overlooking the Seelie Grove and the palace beyond. It is the most exclusive street in the most exclusive city in all the known world.

During Midwinter, it is customary for the Forthel, the Guild of the Magi, to decorate Laurwelana with streamers of illusory fire and spiraling glamoured hawks that circle overhead and sing, in harmony, praises to Her Majesty

Regina Titania. The Lady Anne watched them idly from her window three stories up, waiting for the mail. It was her daily ritual; she curled in the window seat of the parlor, watching the snow fall and waiting. She longed for the gaily-decorated invitations that no longer came, the letters from her friends at court that slowed to a trickle when Mauritane was arrested and stopped completely when he was sentenced to life at Crere Sulace. It was as though she had vanished; it was as though she'd become a ghost haunting her own home, invisible to the outside world.

Though no one came to call on her, she was dressed and glamoured for visitors, her hair delicately balanced in a fashionable scooped bun, her makeup and jewelry perfect. Though there was no one but her to drink it, she had the servants prepare tea in the kitchen every afternoon at teatime. The furniture in the parlor was dusted and polished to a shine, the pillows plumped and fluffed, the flowers arranged artfully in crystal vases throughout the room. When night fell, the servants would pour the tea down the drain, drape the tête-à-tête in its silk cover, and throw the flowers in the trash. It had become almost normal, happening as it had every day for the past two years, without exception. Almost.

The postman appeared on the street walking from the south as he always did, his bag stuffed with tiny parcels and brightly colored envelopes, his cloak pulled tight against the cold. He entered the first building on the block, number fourteen, and disappeared from her sight.

She sighed and thought of her husband. If the postman brought a letter, it would no doubt be one of his. They were all the same, written in his tightly scripted hand on cheap paper borrowed from the prison office, filled with awkward, distant affirmations of love and hope. She had stopped reading them months ago; they only depressed her. When maid brought them to her on her silver tray, she simply picked them up between gloved thumb and forefinger and dropped them in the fire, watching them burn with a dim satisfaction.

The postman reappeared at the door of number fourteen, his bag only slightly less full. Despite herself, she eyed the bright envelopes he carried and felt a pang of desire that one of them might be hers. He checked his inventory, skipped number twelve altogether, and went for number ten instead.

How had things gone so wrong?

When her father had insisted that she marry a man whose only rank was military, she'd balked. Mauritane came to Nyfaesa to court her and she'd run away from home in the middle of the night, not knowing where she was going, only away. Mauritane had ridden after her on his white stallion, finding her at dawn at the edge of a stream, her feet in the water. It was a warm summer morning and it felt good standing there with him watching over her. She'd realized with a start that he was handsome, that he was not crude or base, and that he truly desired her company. In those days there had been a gentleness in his eyes, a smile that he carried with him wherever he went. She'd fallen in love with him then. After a fashion.

It was his marriage to her that catapulted him to the captaincy of the Royal Guard. Well liked and well regarded by the Queen's cabinet, he'd lacked only noble blood to bring him so high, and he'd found it in her. For a short time, things were happy for them. They'd moved here to Laurwelana, and Mauritane had presented her with the gift of a great mahogany four-poster bed. He'd carved it himself at his father's home in distant Nest Ce'Ana. They'd made love on the bed that night; it was the last time she remembered being happy.

When the Beleriand uprisings began, Mauritane was called away more and more often to lead peacekeeping forays into the Western Valley. Mauritane called them "buggane hunts," scowling every time the Seelie Army asked him to provide troops and weapons to assist in the fighting.

"These people have done nothing wrong," he said, again and again. "They wish only to be left alone."

She responded the only way a lady could, by making a joke and scolding him for bringing his work home with him. The first time he laughed with her, shaking his head and holding her tight. The second time he laughed *at* her, then asked her to be serious. He stopped laughing after that. With each mission he grew more distant, and for the six months leading up to his arrest, they hardly spoke at all. He came in late, if at all, and spent his suppers poring over charts and ship manifests and all sorts of dreary things. The Lady Anne was not accustomed to being ignored, and she let him know in no uncertain terms over a late dinner that had grown cold in his absence. Her mother had told her years before that men need to be whipped sometimes, like horses, and that afterward they would show respect, however fleeting. But mother's advice did not apply to Mauritane. He simply stopped coming home at night, sleeping instead on a cot in his palace office.

Then everything had gone wrong. He killed the other officer, the son of some powerful and well-connected lord. The crown had spared no time, nor any of the Lady Anne's dignity, in bringing Mauritane down. The trial had been long, sensational, and worst of all, public. She'd hidden from it all as much as she'd been able. She shuddered now to think of those days.

The postman appeared again and walked to the door of the Lady Anne's building, passing beneath the veranda. A few seconds later, she heard the bell ring downstairs. Like it did each time the postman rang, Anne's heart leapt into her throat. It was best not to hope, because hope only bred disappointment. This would be another of her husband's letters, and she would drop it in the fire like all the others. Perhaps she would tear this one up first. Yes, that would be the thing for it.

Maid entered, carrying the silver tray. Anne blinked and looked again. Could she be imagining things?

No, it was no illusion. Resting there on the silver tray was a bright blue party invitation, handmade paper folded in the shape of a swan, perfectly preserved by the postman, who'd no doubt been bribed heavily to keep these works of art intact. With trembling fingers she reached for the invitation and snatched it off the tray as though it might disappear if she were not quick enough.

She unfolded the swan gently, careful not to rip the paper or dislodge one of the bright ribbons affixed to its wings. The invitation fell neatly into a flat shape and, somehow, the unfolded paper was still swan shaped.

She read aloud. "The presence of the honorable Lady Anne is requested at the homecoming fete of a commander returned home from the far northeast. The gracious lady shall be serenaded by musicians and delighted by glamourists from parts east. The location shall be the city home of Commander Purane-Es, of Her Majesty's Royal Guard. The date shall be Third Stag. Dress and glamour shall be formal."

An answer to a prayer. She read it to herself three more times.

Who, though, was this Purane-Es? The name sounded familiar. Perhaps he was an old friend of her father's? Yes, that was it. The gala had been arranged as her reintroduction to Fae society, signaling her return to life at court and the end of her mourning and exile. It was everything she could have hoped for.

The Lady Anne held the invitation to her breast, caressing it beneath her fingers.

"Maid," she said, biting down a smile. "Have driver make ready my carriage. I'm going to need a new dress and a fresh glamour. And bring my stationery at once; I must write my reply!"

honeywell

After nearly another full day of riding, the River Ebe gave itself up to them and began to grow nearer. The road wound down a broad slope and terminated at an abandoned ferry landing, its icebound wooden struts overgrown with brown, dead weeds. Another half hour's ride would bring them there, giving them a few hours of daylight beyond.

Mauritane cautioned them about riding across the river. "These shoes are designed for footing on rock and snow, not ice. When we cross the river, ride no faster than a trot if you value your neck. I'll take the lead and let Streak find the safest path across the ice."

The others nodded, but none of them spoke. The tedious downhill ride had given them all the opportunity to consider the larger purpose of their errand and their possible fate upon its successful completion.

"Mauritane," said Honeywell, pulling alongside him. "I would never question your leadership, but you've always said that a soldier's best weapon is knowledge."

"Yes," said Mauritane. "I've said that." He looked askance at Honeywell, smiling. "What is it you want to know, Lieutenant?"

"Well," Honeywell began, searching carefully for his words, "in my Guard career, my judgments and opinions were rarely sought. I didn't mind it; I even appreciated it. I'm not a great decision maker. I always trusted you, and I always trusted the Crown. It never occurred to me to think otherwise."

"And now you're not sure," said Mauritane. He kept his eyes forward.

"Yes . . . I mean, I trust you yet, Captain, and I know you would never lead me astray." Honeywell's wide brow was furrowed in confusion.

"But you're having doubts about the trustworthiness of the Crown."

"I . . . yes, I suppose I am. What should I do?"

Mauritane thought for a moment. "Honeywell, do you remember Commander Baede'ed from Selafae?"

"Yes, he was the Guard detachment commander there."

Mauritane nodded. "He was my first commanding officer. He used to do a training exercise at the barracks. He would have a recruit scale the climbing wall, then he would stand beneath them with his arms outstretched and shout, 'Jump down, and I'll catch you.' The first one would jump, and he'd step out of the way at the last second. He'd laugh and say, 'That is to teach you never to take things at face value." He'd order the next recruit up the wall, while the first was carried away, and give the same order. Invariably, the second recruit would jump, and Baede'ed would step away at the last moment. 'That is to teach you that continuing unsuccessful tactics is the surest path to defeat,' he'd say."

Honeywell chuckled at the notion.

"The third soldier up the wall was always carefully chosen by Baede'ed as the most loyal man in the company. When he jumped, Baede'ed would catch him and give him a day's leave. I watched him do it at least ten times. It always made an impression."

Honeywell scowled. "What was the lesson of the third recruit?"

"That loyalty and trust are two different things."

Honeywell pondered for a long moment. "So you're saying that I should be loyal to the Crown, regardless of my personal feelings?"

Mauritane shook his head. "No, I'm not saying that. I'm just saying that loyalty and trust are two different things."

They rode a little farther, Honeywell looking out over the trees.

"But if none of us trusts the Crown entirely, why are we even here?"

Mauritane smiled again, and this smile had an edge to it. "Perhaps because we are soldiers, and loyalty is all we know."

Honeywell opened his mouth to respond, but no sound came out. Eventually he drifted back to join the others, who'd remained silent through the entire exchange.

As they neared the river, Mauritane suddenly brought the company to a stop, holding up his hand for silence. "Do you hear that?" he whispered to Silverdun.

Silverdun focused on his hearing and nodded slowly. "There are riders coming. More than a few, from what I can tell."

"From which direction?" said Honeywell drawing his sword.

"Over there." Silverdun pointed at a low rise to the south, downriver, where a narrow trail ran parallel to the water's edge. The rise was high enough that whatever lay beyond it was completely hidden from view.

"Who'd be riding out here during Midwinter?" asked Gray Mave, drawing his own weapon.

Mauritane set his jaw. "I can think of two possibilities. Either a band of highwaymen or a Guard detachment searching for escaped prisoners."

Silverdun listened harder. "They're riding in step," he said, frowning.

"Then it's a detachment."

"Could they really be looking for us?" said Mave.

"It's safe to assume so," said Mauritane. "There's no other reason for them to be patrolling this far from the city."

A line of riders appeared over the rise, at least twenty in number, some in the blue-spangled colors of the Hawthorne Guard, some in the red of Colthorn. Their leader was an officer of the Colthorn Guard, wearing the long mustache popular with men in that city.

"Wonderful," said Silverdun.

The riders stopped upon seeing them. Their leader raised his hand and waved it twice overhead.

Honeywell gawked. "He wants to parlay? Why? They outnumber us four to one!"

"You know these country folk," said Silverdun, examining his blade. "They hate dying. Avoid it at all costs."

Mauritane cut him off with a glance. "I'll ride out to parlay with them. The rest of you wait for my signal and make for the river when I give it."

"But sir!" said Honeywell.

"Honeywell," warned Mauritane.

"Yes sir," said Honeywell.

"You know what to do," said Mauritane. "I'll . . ."

He stopped short. Without speaking, Honeywell had ridden ahead without him.

"Lieutenant!" Mauritane barked.

Honeywell turned to face him. "Don't follow me, Mauritane. It will make us look weak." The riders on the hilltop, outside of hearing range, watched their leader intently.

"What are you doing?" Mauritane's face was red.

"We both know that capture is not an option, and we both know that whoever rides up there isn't riding down again. If you're to make it across the river under pursuit, you'll need that touched horse. And if you're to make the City Emerald," he said, "you're going to need a captain. I've decided that if I'm going to jump from a wall, I'm doing it on my own terms for once." With that, he turned again and rode to meet the Colthornan.

Mauritane's knuckles whitened from his grip on Streak's reins.

"What are we going to do?" said Mave, his voice shaking.

Mauritane said nothing for a long minute, watching Honeywell ride up the hillside. Finally he said, "You heard the man. Let us respect his wishes."

"What will he do?" said Silverdun.

"He'll wait until his opponent raises his hand to begin the parlay and then he'll run the man through. Then he'll ride directly for the first man who comes after him. It will buy us some time to escape."

"How do you know all that?" asked Silverdun.

"Because that's what I would do," Mauritane said. "And Honeywell knows it. When you see the Colthornan raise his hand, break for the river at top speed. When we hit the ice, drop your reins. Streak will guide the horses across." Mauritane bent down and whispered to the beast, his eyes never leaving Honeywell.

They watched the two riders approach each other warily, the Guard leader suspicious of Honeywell's every move. The Colthornan stopped his mount a few paces from Honeywell and said something none of them could hear. Honeywell raised his arm in the salutation of parlay, his unsheathed sword hidden behind his back.

The Colthornan raised his hand in answer and Honeywell dug in his spurs, his horse rearing beneath him. The horse leapt at the Colthornan, and before the man could lower his arm, Honeywell's sword had already pierced his chest. Honeywell rode past him, pulling his weapon from the Colthornan's body without looking back.

"Go! Now!" shouted Mauritane. As one, they spurred their mounts and raced for the water's edge.

Mauritane spared a glance back toward Honeywell. The guardsmen had responded admirably; some of them already had their blades drawn when Honeywell engaged them. The first to gain his wits was one of the Hawthorne Guard. Honeywell rode straight for him and managed to unseat him with a bold thrust. Unsure what to do next, the other riders forgot about Mauritane and his companions and concentrated on the more immediate problem in their midst.

Mauritane reached the river first. Streak hit the ice at a run but slid quickly to a stop and resumed with a tall, prancing gait that resembled the trot of a parade pony. "Drop your reins!" shouted Mauritane.

Streak called out in the language of horses to the other mounts, instructing them to follow his lead. With some difficulty, they copied his gait, and they began to make progress across the slick ice.

Mauritane looked back again. At some point in the intervening seconds, Honeywell had fallen. He lay on his back at the top of the hill, a spear in his chest, his mount bolting for the hills above. His maneuver had bought them even more time than Mauritane would have expected; they would be halfway across the river before the guardsmen reached its banks. Only now were they resuming the chase. Without a leader, they had little hope of mounting an effective pursuit. Mauritane urged Streak faster anyhow.

The guardsmen took the slope at a gallop, jumping their horses onto the ice and spurring them on. It was a critical error. The running horses lost their footing on the frozen surface of the Ebe and most of them went down, throwing their riders. They few that remained standing slowed to a walk and began to pick their way carefully. The rest would eventually recover, but by then it would be too late.

Mauritane led them to the far side, prodding Streak up the steep western bank. They stood on the bank briefly, looking across the river, all of them hoping for a glimpse of Honeywell. But he was too far away, and the snow was beginning to fall again.

"Let's ride north for a few minutes," said Mauritane. "Then double back through the trees and rejoin the road a few miles south. "It'll confuse them."

As they rode off, Gray Mave remained in the rear, hiding his eyes, hoping that no one would catch him crying.

mortal creatures/
the bittersweet wayward mestina

Deep into the night and through the forests near Miday they rode, skirting the few towns and villages they came across, running the horses to the point of exhaustion. The trees swept by in a blur of white, gray, and brown, sometimes whipping their faces with tiny branches and dead leaves. The bitter southern wind reddened their faces and hands and stung their eyes. Fortunately, their flight left no opportunity for conversation; no one felt much like talking.

Finally, Streak begged to be allowed to rest. The other horses, he said, were dangerously fatigued and desperate for water. Mauritane ordered a stop and saw to the horses himself, anything to further delay speech. While Silverdun started the fire and Raieve and Satterly began cooking, Mauritane took the horses two at a time and walked them. Just downhill from the campsite, a trickle of a stream ran past some brown grass, and Mauritane left the horses there to feed and water themselves, ordering Streak to keep them nearby.

Mauritane returned slowly to camp, his limbs aching and his head low, unable to put it off any longer. "All of you sit," he said. "It is time to remember our friend."

They gathered around the growing campfire. Gray Mave took five white tapers from his pack and passed them out. Confused, but not wishing to tread on anyone's feelings by asking, Satterly simply did what the others did, lowering the wick of his candle to the fire until it lit, holding it out before him.

"We are mortal creatures," Mauritane began, reciting from memory, "and our time of living is brief. As children we gather our light and as children we release it, each of us, when we give up the flame of self and return it to the fire of creation. The candles we bear are a symbol of the man Geuna Eled, called Honeywell. We hold them to remember the light that was his, and to take his mark upon us, that we may remember."

Mauritane held his candle up. "Honeywell was, to me, a loyal friend and officer. I will remember him as the man who stood up in the Seelie Court to defend me when everyone else turned away. He paid for that choice with his life."

Mauritane pulled up the sleeve of his tunic. His arm was covered with dozens of perfectly arranged circular red scars. He lowered the flame of Honeywell's candle to his flesh, let it burn there for a moment, the briefest instant, then the candle went out, leaving its impression on Mauritane's skin.

Raieve was next. "He was kind to me. I will remember him as the man who brought me food when I was ill, the week after I arrived at Crere Sulace. I didn't even know his name." She, too, raised her sleeve and stubbed out a candle on her arm.

Silverdun took his turn. "I regret that I hardly knew him," he said. "I will remember him as one well loved by others."

Gray Mave muttered something gently to himself and burned his arm quickly, his head bowed.

Satterly stammered. "I, uh, Honeywell was a decent guy. I'll remember him as the only guileless person I ever met." When he brought the candle to his arm, his hand shaking, he was surprised at how much it hurt.

The next day dawned warmer than usual, and the wind was low and at their backs. Mauritane ordered a casual pace to give the horses a rest from their ordeal the day before. At midday they crossed a series of low hills and found themselves on a dirt road that ran relatively straight toward the south. In the distance, a pair of brightly colored wagons, traveling southward, rounded a corner and disappeared from view.

"What do you think, Mauritane?" said Silverdun. "Are we far enough south to strike west into the Contested Lands?"

Mauritane consulted his charts. "No, I believe if we went west now, we'd come dangerously close to Unseelie lands. Better to take another day's ride to be certain." He pointed to a line on one of the charts. "If this is the road we're on," he said, "then Sylvan is another day's ride to the south of our current latitude anyway, so we lose nothing by hedging that bet."

"What do you make of that caravan?" said Satterly, pointing down the road to where the wagons had been.

"Most likely merchants trading between Saurdest and Estacana. They don't seem a likely threat. But keep your eyes open, just in case; we'll ride past them quickly."

They started down the road, and Mauritane was glad to be back on level ground again. Streak's constant protestations about the quality of the terrain were beginning to make him question his decision to bring a touched animal.

They rounded the first bend and the road continued on straight, down into a wooded valley. There was no sign of the wagons.

Mauritane came to a halt. "What happened to that caravan?" he said.

Silverdun searched the trees with his eyes. "I don't see them."

"Could they have left the road? Hiding from us, perhaps?"

"It's possible. This area is notorious for its highwaymen. I doubt they saw us, unless they were being cautious to begin with."

"I don't like it," said Mauritane. "There's something about this that bothers me."

"You really think they might have been frightened of us?" said Satterly.

"Listen to him," said Raieve, "he sounds like he enjoys the thought."

"Look at us," said Silverdun. "We certainly have the cut of a group of brigands."

"We sure as hell don't look like soldiers," said Raieve.

"Hm," said Mauritane. "I'll take suggestions. Shall we continue along the road or strike out again into the trees? I fear we may be somewhat too exposed, even this far west."

"I hate to say it," said Silverdun, "but I agree with you. Perhaps we should stay off the roads for a while longer."

A tree by the side of the road rustled, a pine the height of a man. "Perhaps I may offer another suggestion?" the tree said, in a deep booming voice.

"More talking trees," said Silverdun. "Wonderful."

Satterly gulped. "I didn't say anything. I swear to God."

"Nay, young lord," the tree said, its form beginning to shimmer. "No tree am I." The branches of the pine shook and folded in on themselves, merging to form arms and legs. After a moment, a man stood in place of the tree, graying and somewhat overweight but an imposing figure nonetheless.

"I am Nafaeel, of the Bittersweet Wayward Mestina. I am at your service, lords." The man bowed deep, his cap scraping the ground.

"Come out, my precious ones. These are not the highwaymen who attacked us."

Mauritane looked around and saw trees and boulders on each side of the road begin to melt and form into people, horses, and carriages. All of the men and women were brightly dressed and the horses gaily caparisoned. The wagons were filled to overflowing with enormous wooden apparatuses, planks joined with metal struts, pulleys, and hinges and devices Mauritane did not recognize.

"No," said Mauritane, once the transformation was complete. "We are no threat to you. Go in peace."

The men and women of the Bittersweet Wayward Mestina gathered behind Nafaeel.

"Gentles," said Nafaeel, bowing again, slightly. "I was about to offer a suggestion. May I inquire your name, sir?"

"I am called Mauritane. What is your suggestion?"

"You'll forgive me for eavesdropping on your conversation a moment ago. The lovely lady there mentioned that you are soldiers of some stripe?"

Mauritane frowned. "We are eel merchants from Hawthorne."

Nafaeel nodded knowingly. "Of course, of course. Eel merchants." He smiled. "I was not aware that the transportation of eel had become so perilous." He raised an eyebrow, indicating Mauritane's sword.

"These are dangerous times," said Mauritane.

"Just so! Just so, good sir. You treat upon my point precisely. You see, we are but a poor band of traveling entertainers, and the proceeds from our most recent performance were taken from us at knifepoint by a band of ruffians this very morning. I believe we could use a few, er, eel merchants to keep us company and provide a bit of protection for the rest of our journey."

"I see," said Mauritane. "And why would we do such a thing?"

Nafaeel tapped his lips with a finger. "Why, indeed? Hm. Let's say that

I were a captain of the local constabulary and I were searching for five purveyors of eel, four men and a woman on horseback, carrying swords. Just hypothetically, of course. It seems to me that if those eel merchants were, shall we say, commingled in a company of traveling entertainers, they would become much more difficult to spot. Wouldn't you agree?"

Mauritane patted Streak's neck. "I take your point," he said. "But I do not feel it would be a beneficial pairing. I do, however, appreciate the offer." He began to turn away.

"Wait!" said one of the women, coming forward and taking Nafaeel's hand. They were roughly the same age, though her hair and makeup conspired to give her the appearance of youth. "My husband means well, gentlemen, but he's rarely able to speak without orating. The matter is this: we have been stopped by highwaymen twice since Saurdest, and some of the girls have been poorly treated by them. We need help, and while we have no money now, we can pay you well when we reach Estacana. Please."

"Woman!" said Nafaeel angrily.

Gray Mave nudged his horse toward Mauritane and leaned in to him. "We must ride with them," he whispered.

"It wouldn't be wise," whispered Mauritane.

"Please, Captain." Mave's eyes were wide and a single bead of sweat trickled down his forehead despite the cold. "Trouble comes for them."

"You've seen this," Mauritane frowned. "With your Gift."

"Aye, sir." Mave shifted uncomfortably in his saddle. "You believe me, don't you?"

Mauritane sighed. "All right," he said to Nafaeel. "We'll ride with you to Estacana. But we won't accept payment, and you'll ask nothing about us or where we're going. Are we agreed?"

Nafaeel nodded gratefully. Many of the Fae behind them breathed sighs of relief, although some appeared skeptical.

"Um, what's a mestina?" Satterly said to Raieve.

"What is a mestina?" said Nafaeel, overhearing. "My children, this oddly flat-eared gentleman has never heard of a mestina!" That brought smiles and laughter from the troupe.

"They're glamourists," said Mauritane. "Actors."

"Glamourists, yes," said Nafaeel. "Actors, no. We purvey the dewdrops of reality the way others purvey, well, eel. We are the precise opposite of those who strut and preen on the stage pretending, reciting lines written by another; we are the voice of what is true. Only larger."

"Much larger," said one of the women, stepping forward. She was young and beautiful, her features sharp and her body graceful and petite. A sultriness burned in her eyes as they passed over Mauritane's group, finally resting on Silverdun. She peered at him for a moment before speaking again. Then she turned to Nafaeel. "Father, may I offer a demonstration?"

"By all means, Faella."

The girl removed her outer robe and stood in the road wearing only a skintight body suit of a dark, flexible fabric.

"This is called Snowflake," she said, "in honor of the recent weather." Her companions applauded.

Faella lifted her hands above her head and began to sing, a high-pitched lyrical chant that repeated itself with odd variations and harmonics. For a few seconds, nothing happened. Then it began to snow, gently at first, then harder. Soon white flakes were blanketing everything, the horses, the riders, the mestina's wagons.

"Look up," Faella sang, pausing between chants.

Mauritane raised his eyes to the sky and his attention fixed on a single snowflake, swirling in the maelstrom overhead. Something about that single point of white captivated him. It looped and whirled in a pattern that reminded Mauritane of something, something that was made of longing and regret and lost hope. The snowflake moved toward him, growing in size. It was the largest snowflake Mauritane had ever seen. It expanded to fill his vision, then hovered over him, rotating gently in the sunlight. It consisted of six perfect spokes, radiating an endless progression of ever-smaller crystalline lines. Whichever point Mauritane focused his attention on, that section of the structure grew larger, its tiny angled projections expanding, and Mauritane saw that the succession of ever smaller lines never stopped; it continued forever, spiraling down into the darkness of the infinite.

Faella let them watch the snowflake for a minute or so, then closed her hands in front of her and curtsied again, letting the vision disappear gradually.

Mauritane was stunned by the beauty of it. The image remained in his mind, the ever-descending spokes, the brightness of the smooth crystal edges. Those in his company were equally rapt, especially Silverdun, who sat astride his horse with his eyes closed, savoring the experience. Even some of the mestina players were taken aback.

"My darling daughter!" cried Nafaeel. "Your talent grows with each passing day." He took her in his arms and held her. "Someday you will surpass even your mother!"

"Wow," said Satterly, after a pause. "I've never seen anything like that before in my life."

"That, my uninformed friend," said Nafaeel, "is mestina."

the fate of highwaymen on the estacana road

Traveling with the mestina, Silverdun found himself more often than not riding alongside Faella who, unlike many of the performers, had her own horse. They seemed to gravitate toward each other, and they passed the time talking about the weather, or the famous mestina of the past, or the City Emerald. Their banter had no subject, and they spent as much time watching the steam of their breath in the cold air as they did each other. He'd introduced himself simply as Perrin, hoping that none of his companions would slip up and give away his title.

"Do you like these boots?" she asked, lifting her heel out of its stirrup. They were riding a few yards ahead of everyone else.

"They're delightful," he said, admiring them. "The ladies at court are no doubt wearing something similar this winter?"

Faella smiled. "So, you've been at court?"

Silverdun raised an eyebrow. "I've heard about such things," he finally said.

"Aha! I knew it. I can't tell about your friends, but I knew you had noble blood from the moment I laid eyes on you. I have a talent for such things." She tossed her deep red hair, and Silverdun had to concentrate not to stare at her.

"Well, perhaps I do and perhaps I don't, but it's no concern of yours either way. Another topic, if you please, miss?"

"Do you have Glamour yourself?"

"Another talent of yours? Intuiting people's Gifts?"

"Just a guess."

"A lucky one then. My focus at university was in Glamour."

"I thought so. And no, I won't ask which university you attended because I'm certain it was either Estaena or Nycuel."

"If you say so." Silverdun kept the eyebrow raised.

"Will you indulge me with the fruits of your studies? A small illusion to impress a lady?"

Silverdun laughed. "I'm no mestine," he said. "I'm certain I'd disappoint you."

"Oh, don't be coy," she sighed. "I detest coyness. All of the little girls my father has working with us are full of calculated sweetness and false modesty. It makes me ill; no wonder none of them can stand me."

"Perhaps they're jealous," said Silverdun.

"Perhaps," she said. "But no changing the subject. I want to see what you're capable of."

Silverdun cleared his throat. "All right," he said. "But I'm very much out of practice."

"Understood."

Silverdun watched her breathing, the flaring of her nostrils as she inhaled, the twin puffs of steam as she exhaled. He whispered a few syllables of the language of change and on her next exhalation, the vapor of her breath became a pair of small silver dragons that twirled around each other in flight, producing tiny jets of blue flame from their own noses. They twisted around each other and dissolved again into mist.

Faella clapped her hands. "Not bad at all, Perrin Alt. With a few lessons, you could be a mestine." She pouted at his laughter. "I'm serious. Why are you laughing?"

"Because that's the best I could do after three years at . . . an unnamed university."

"Ah," she said, raising a finger. "Unnamed universities are the worst of all. They seldom attract the finest instructors."

"You raise an excellent point."

"If you wanted, perhaps I could provide some . . . private instruction."

Silverdun whistled. "I'm not certain I could afford the tuition."

She looked at him. "My rates are very reasonable. All you have to do is whatever I want."

"Something tells me," said Silverdun, "that could be quite a lot."

"Yes, but," she said, "like the Aba of the Arcadians I never ask for more than my subjects are prepared to give."

They were interrupted by a pair of mounted men who rode from opposite sides of the path, blocking the road with their horses. The men were ragged from time spent outdoors, their beards long and unkempt, their clothes dirty and worn.

"Stand and deliver!" said the larger of the two, who wore his dark hair at shoulder length, free of braids. He carried a loaded crossbow and had it aimed at Silverdun's head. The other was blond and similarly braidless, equally menacing, sword in hand.

"Why look," said the blond, "it's the same mestina we visited yesterday!"

"I don't suppose they've turned a profit since last we met?" said the dark-haired man.

"Doubtful," said the blond. "But there are other forms of payment." He cast a long look at Faella, an ugly grin smeared across his face.

"Just so," said the dark-haired thief. "Just so."

One of the women aboard the front wagon screamed abruptly, a brief cry that stuttered and faded. Raieve, sitting beside her on the bench seat of the wagon, squeezed her hand gently and slipped off the vehicle's far side.

Mauritane nudged Streak forward from his position alongside the caravan and began riding at a walk toward the highwaymen.

"You just stay where you are, mestine," said the leader, bringing the crossbow around. "I don't want to have to use this."

Mauritane continued riding toward him. His expression was like stone, and there was no weapon in his hand.

"Stop. I'm not kidding!"

At a distance of about twenty paces, the leader steadied his wrist and fired the crossbow directly into Mauritane's face with a sharp snapping sound. At the same instant, Mauritane's hand flashed out in front of him and returned just as quickly to his side. Someone shrieked; several gasped. Silverdun, who was now alongside Mauritane, flinched and recoiled. When he turned his eyes back toward Mauritane, his friend was neither dead nor injured; he was, in fact, totally unharmed.

"That," said Mauritane, his expression unaltered, "was a mistake." He opened his hand, and the spent crossbow quarrel fell to the ground.

Mauritane drew his sword and advanced on the dark-haired man, who had become ill at ease.

"I . . ." he began, jerking backward on his reins.

The leader's mount began to rear but stopped when Mauritane grabbed its bridle and pulled downward with a sharp tug. The horse leaned forward, nearly throwing the thief. When the man leaned forward as well, Mauritane swung his sword in an arc and brought it down on the highwayman's neck, severing his head with a single blow. Both head and rider fell to the ground, a dying word curtailed.

"Oh dear," said Faella. Silverdun turned just in time to see her slide from her saddle into his arms, her face pale.

The blond, his fight taken out of him, began to turn his horse. As he turned, a hand reached from behind him and grabbed his cloak. Raieve appeared at the man's side, her lip curled upward in a snarl, almost feral. She dragged him from the saddle, his legs kicking out uselessly in front of him.

"Wait!" he shouted. "Wait!"

He fell to the ground on his back, his sword tumbling to the ground out of his reach. He made a quick fist and lashed out, catching Raieve in the lip. She caught his arm before he could retract it and pinned it, bringing it down over her knee with a dull cracking sound. He screamed, rolling onto his side.

With the flat of her sword, she smashed the wrist on the other hand, breaking the bone so badly that it tore the skin. Blood began to pour from her lip.

"Stop!" the man shouted. Raieve could not hear him.

She rolled him again onto his back.

"Raieve," said Mauritane.

"I don't like men like him," Raieve muttered.

"I believe you've subdued him."

"It's not my intent to subdue him. It's my intent to castrate him."

"No!" the highwayman shouted. "Please don't!" He tried to lift his arms and was unable.

Raieve leaned in to him, spitting blood on his face. "You should have thought of that before you raped the girl on the wagon."

The man started to cry. "I didn't mean to . . . it was a mistake! Please!"

Raieve took a thin dagger from beneath her cloak. "Lie still and it won't hurt as much," she said.

She raised her dagger arm and held it aloft, reading the fear in the man's eyes. But when she moved to bring it down she found Mauritane's hand gripping her wrist.

"No, Raieve," he said.

"This is my business," she said.

"No, Raieve. You are under my command, so this is my business."

"Thank you. Oh, thank you," said the highwayman, crossing his legs.

"Under my command, you kill who you must kill, and the rest you only disarm."

"That's exactly what I was about to do," said Raieve, her bitter smile showing bloody teeth.

"If you require vengeance for the girl, then kill him," said Mauritane. "Otherwise, leave him and let's be on our way."

Raieve stood and looked back at the wagon. "This is the man?" she said to the girl who sat rocking on the bench, tears streaming down her face. The girl nodded slowly.

"Shall I kill him?"

The girl thought, and then shook her head just as slowly.

Raieve nodded. "Let's go."

She and Mauritane rolled both of the men into a ditch at the side of the road.

"We'll send the Estacana Guard after you," said Mauritane to the blond man, who crouched in a fetal position in the ditch. "If you eat snow and keep your cloak dry you should survive until then."

Mauritane turned and faced Nafaeel, who drove the lead cart. "I've upheld my end of the bargain," he said. "I trust you'll uphold yours."

Nafaeel bowed low. "I am in your debt, sir."

Mauritane frowned. "You should take those horses," he said. "They look healthy enough."

Later, when they stopped to rest the horses and eat, Mauritane took Raieve aside. They stood on a low ridge overlooking a stand of snow-clad spruce. Below them, the Estacana road stretched to the south, a brown line in a field of white. The walls of the city were barely visible in the distance.

"Would you care to explain your outburst?" said Mauritane. "I thought you were more professional than that."

"Oh, come on, Mauritane!" she shouted. "Are you really that stupid? Do I have to spell it out for you?"

Mauritane hung his head. "You were raped yourself, I suppose."

She spun on him. "A brilliant deduction, Captain. Of course I was raped! Of course I was." She clenched her lips, tears beginning to form in her eyelids. She fought them.

"During the war, half the women in my village were raped at some time or another, and some of the boys as well. And now that the Unseelie have left, some of the less honorable clans have begun to follow their example."

Mauritane's eyes softened. "And that was why you became so upset. You were just reacting to . . ."

Raieve turned away, her hands on her ears. "Don't try to interpret me! Don't try to interpret me like a dream or a bad omen! I'm not a product of my environment like a beaten dog that bites. Everything I do is a conscious choice."

Mauritane watched her silently. He gazed out over the trees, pretending not to hear her crying. "I apologize," he said. "Let's just forget it."

"Yes," she said. "Let's."

To Silverdun, traveling with the mestina was a fair bargain; they had extra tents, which meant they were, for the time being, no longer forced to sleep on the cold ground. When he came to his tent after taking the first watch, he found Faella there, naked, lying beneath his blanket and skins.

"I thought you'd never get here," she said, lifting the covers for him.

Silverdun overcame his shock gracefully. "If I'd known you were coming," he said, "I'd have had the maid clean up a little."

"Come to me," said Faella, "Come to me, Lord Silverdun."

Silverdun was taken aback. "How do you know that name?" he said.

She held out a paper. "I'm an avid reader," she said.

Silverdun took the sheet. It was a copy of the *Annals of the Court*, a cheap publication distributed to the merchant class in bulk by the City Emerald's Copyist Guild. This edition was from several years previous; on the front of the page was a spelled engraving of nobles dancing at a court function. Silverdun was there, in his best black suit, dancing with the Lady Lelnest. A caption underneath bore his name.

"I was right about you," she said. "I knew it."

Silverdun smiled weakly. "Let's keep this just between the two of us," he said. "No one can know. It's very important."

She nodded. "It'll be our little secret," she said, smiling innocently. "Now come here."

He lay next to her and her skin was hot. He found her mouth with his own and they kissed, her arms around his neck as he removed his clothing.

She proved to be as able a lover as she was a mestine; Silverdun wondered briefly if they amounted to the same thing. Her body was lithe and supple, her breasts small and firm. She made love willingly, forcefully, matching each of his thrusts with one of her own. When she climaxed, she bit down on his shoulder to stifle a scream.

They lay together, a tangle of arms and legs, and finally slept.

Silverdun awoke with an icy hand on his shoulder. He opened his eyes and looked up into the face of Nafaeel. "Perrin Alt," said Nafaeel coldly. "Would you mind explaining what you're doing with my daughter?"

impropriety

Dawn filtered through the clouds that hung low over the hills north of Esta-cana. Away from the tents, Mauritane led Raieve and Satterly through a set of fencing drills. Raieve simply wanted the practice, and Satterly struggled to achieve some kind of fighting ability. What he lacked in experience, Mauritane noted, he made up for in ambition; he refused to rest until he displayed enough prowess to survive an actual battle. Mauritane was impressed with his progress but still not ready to hurl him toward an enemy.

Silverdun approached from Nafaeel's tent, his face red, his head held low.

"Mauritane," he said quietly. "We need to talk."

"All right," said Mauritane. He motioned for Satterly to repeat a difficult lunging drill focused on estimating attack distance. As he spoke, Mauritane walked forward a few paces and stood en garde. "What is it?"

"I'm afraid I've gotten myself involved in an impropriety."

Mauritane lowered the sword, his brows furrowing. "What have you done?"

"Nafaeel caught me in bed with his daughter."

"I see," said Mauritane. He nudged Satterly's blade. "Keep coming, Satterly."

Satterly renewed his attack, but with less force, straining to overhear the conversation.

"I'm sorry, Mauritane. Need I remind you that I haven't been with a woman in close to three years? When I came in last night, there she was, willing and able. What was I to do?"

"So you were outmaneuvered by your own cock?" said Mauritane, brushing away Satterly's thrust. Satterly chuckled.

Mauritane brought the tip of his blade down across Satterly's bare chest, leaving a scratch. "There," he said. "I just killed you."

"Why did you do that?" said Satterly. He touched his chest and winced.

"Never laugh with a sword in your hand," Mauritane answered. He dropped his blade, turning to Silverdun and looking him in the eye. "Now what? Am I to be your second in a duel?"

"Ah, not exactly," said Silverdun. He held up a poster, rendered hurriedly in ink.

Mauritane read aloud, "The Enigmatic Nafaeel presents an evening with the Bittersweet Wayward Mestina, featuring the talents of the lovely Faella and a special appearance by His Lordship Perrin Alt of Silverdun. Silverdun!" Mauritane snatched the poster from Silverdun's hand. "How do they know who you are?"

Silverdun scowled. "Faella found my picture in one of those Seelie Court papers. But listen, Mauritane. This may work out for the best."

"And how might that be?" Mauritane said.

"Nafaeel has promised us half of the proceeds of the mestina in return for my participation. He's received a message sprite from his agent in Estacana saying that the City Guard is looking for five escaped prisoners and that they're stopping everyone who tries to cross the western border into the Contested Lands."

"Meaning we'll have to bribe our way out of Estacana."

"Exactly."

Mauritane sighed. "Is there no other way to satisfy Nafaeel?"

"None that would generate such a large profit for him. Apparently the locals are infatuated with anyone related to the Seelie Court."

Mauritane handed Satterly his sword. "I wish I could say the same right now. Let's go speak with Nafaeel." He pointed at Raieve. "You and Satterly keep practicing. Try not to kill him."

When they'd gone, Raieve and Satterly took turns at Mauritane's favorite parrying drill.

"I have to admit," said Satterly between thrusts, "even after two years in this world I really don't understand Fae propriety at all."

"Most humans don't," said Raieve, easily blocking his attacks.

"What I don't get," Satterly continued, ignoring her, "is why Silverdun and Mauritane take this situation so seriously. Why don't we just ride off and leave the mestina behind? If Silverdun agrees to appear in some show, won't that jeopardize our mission?"

"It could get us killed," said Raieve. "But that doesn't matter."

"So you're saying that Silverdun has no choice?"

"That's correct. Let's switch." Raieve waited for Satterly to set himself, then leapt at him, thrusting low.

"Ow!" said Satterly. "You're not trying to kill me!"

Raieve smirked.

"Can you just explain to me *why* Silverdun has no choice?"

Raieve finished her thrust. "Let me make an analogy," she said. "Imagine that you were at a wedding and you had to urinate. Would you raise your tunic and piss on the bridal party?"

"Well, no," said Satterly smiling.

"Neither can Silverdun ignore his obligation to Nafaeel. As much as he'd like to do otherwise, if he is to retain any honor he must answer his impropriety."

"And that doesn't bother you?"

She lunged again, hard. "Of course it bothers me. I find Silverdun odious. But now my honor is tied with his, as is Mauritane's, as is yours."

"But I'm not Fae. I don't have any honor to wound," said Satterly.

"Truer words were never spoken," Raieve said, preparing for her next leap. "Now shut up and defend yourself!"

Estacana boasted the distinction of being the only city in all of Faerie never to have been built by Fae hands. Rather it materialized, fully formed, from the halated mists of a Midwinter a thousand years gone, its mammoth spires and wide archways perfectly constructed from granite and marble, untouched by wear or weather. Shepherds out watering their flocks along the banks of the upper Ebe stumbled across the glittering walls and named the city Estacana ("by the water's source"), because it overlooked the headwaters of the river.

Frightened to enter, the shepherds led a garrison of the Royal Guard to the site; the garrison entered the city, found its buildings uninhabited, its streets and rooms empty. The city was built for giants; the doorways soared twenty feet high in places, with stair steps that reached a man's knee. In the center of the abandoned metropolis stood a massive, terraced spire that towered over the rest of the city. Like the other buildings—vacant storefronts, apartment blocks, and town homes—the spire was deserted, but there was a message scrawled in the stone floor in Elvish. The message said simply, "We concede," and nothing else.

No giants ever came to claim the city. The City Emerald was silent on the matter, returning all correspondence from the nearby lords with variations on "It is no concern of ours." Eventually, despite their fears of bad omens and witchcraft, the shepherds of the surrounding valleys moved in to Estacana and fashioned it into a Fae city. Over the years, many of the buildings were torn down to make way for progress, and the walls lost their sheen, but the spire remained unoccupied (for no one would live or work there) and the scrawled message remained to be puzzled over for eternity.

The Bittersweet Wayward Mestina performed before a capacity crowd in the Amphitheater Estacanal. As promised, Lord Silverdun made an appearance, however bashful. He stumbled over his lines, glamoured some purple trout that swam up the aisles and out the great open gates, then took a deep bow and was met with a standing ovation. Waiting in the wings by the stage, Raieve muttered noises of disgust while Mauritane and Satterly looked idly on. Gray Mave, unaccustomed to city life, chose to remain with the horses in the public stable.

After the show, all of the mestina's players and their entourage were invited to a fete at the home of a city Alderman. Backstage, Silverdun removed his costume, trading it for his silk and fur attire, and caught Faella as she passed carrying a pair of dresses used in the show.

"How was I?" he said.

"You were adequate, I suppose," she giggled. "You were wonderful. I told you that you would be."

"And your father? Is he satisfied?"

"He's thrilled. He's back in the wagon counting the receipts. If I were you I'd send Mauritane over to get his money now, before father makes off with it."

Silverdun took her in his arms. "If he's in the wagon, then he can't see us." He kissed her, pulling her close.

"Not so fast, your lordship," said Faella, waving a finger. "We have a date."

"Yes," said Silverdun. "I wonder if the Alderman's ever hosted a Seelie lord? What do you think?"

She whispered in his ear. "If he hasn't, he's going to get an eyeful tonight, and I'm not going to let go of your arm even for a moment."

"I trust you'll let me off to visit the latrine, at least."

"Pig. Watch your mouth or I'll take this room at the Sable Inn all for myself." She held out a silver key with a numbered tag dangling by a chain.

Silverdun took the key. "I'll be the perfect gentleman," he said.

The Alderman's party was a gay affair. A pair of doormen waited in the home's spacious foyer, taking the guests' snow-dusted cloaks and sprinkling them with flower petals. Music drifted out from somewhere deeper in the house, lutes and violins and other instruments Mauritane couldn't recognize. He stood outside in the courtyard, leaning against a tree, smoking his pipe. He watched the guests arrive in twos and threes. Estacana was not the City Emerald, and its nobility were not that of the capital, but their finery was impressive enough, he decided. Such things had never interested Mauritane in the slightest, despite the Lady Anne's protestations. It was to Mauritane's great relief that custom allowed for soldiers to attend such affairs in their dress uniforms—had it been otherwise, Mauritane would have refused outright.

Mauritane had arrived in a coach with Silverdun and Faella, the two of them as cozy as lovers in a court ballad. If Silverdun wasn't careful, he could jeopardize everything. He'd assured Mauritane that nobody at this party could possibly recognize him; that they were much too far from the City Emerald for anyone to make the connection, but Mauritane was unconvinced. The only reason he allowed it at all was that Nafaeel refused to pay them their share of the mestina proceeds unless Silverdun put in an appearance. So he waited, his saber comfortably heavy under his cloak, and hoped for the best.

Another carriage arrived, and out of it stepped Satterly, dressed in one of

Nafaeel's suits, followed by a woman in a sable cloak. It took Mauritane a moment to realize that the woman was Raieve. Her hair was pulled up, glamoured a reddish gold, and she was wearing makeup as well; her face was powdered white, her lips painted red. She was beautiful.

Satterly looked right past him, but Raieve caught Mauritane's eye and crossed the courtyard toward him, holding up the hem of the cloak to keep it from dragging on the ground.

"How do I look, Captain?" she said, smiling wickedly. She opened the cloak and Mauritane caught his breath. Beneath it was a dress the color of sapphires, its bodice low and bordered with lace. It conformed closely to her figure, gathered at the waist and then cascaded down to the ground. Mauritane realized that until now he had only seen her in her thick wool prison uniform and the traveling cloak she'd been wearing since they left Crere Sulace.

"This all belongs to Faella," she said. "She insisted I wear it. There may have been a bit of wine involved."

"I am . . . impressed," said Mauritane, suddenly finding it difficult to speak to her. "I would not have thought you comfortable in such clothing."

Raieve scowled, but her mood was unspoiled. "We have dresses in Avalon, too, Mauritane. We are not animals."

"I would not have thought otherwise," said Mauritane.

"Even during the worst of the Unseelie occupation, we danced," said Raieve. She moved closer to him. "Do you dance, Mauritane?"

He took a step toward her. "In happier times," he said.

She stepped even closer and he could feel her breath warm on his neck. His blood rose. "They say an Avalona woman is every man's dream: a lion on the battlefield, a swan on the dance floor, and a vixen in the bedroom."

Mauritane finally stepped back. "I can't see you as anything other than a soldier!" he said, a bit too loudly. "You must understand that. This . . ." he gestured toward the party, "this is a bit of playacting so that we can collect the money we need. Nothing more. Keep that in mind, will you?"

"Of course," said Raieve, her eyes blazing and her jaw set. Her voice lowered. "I must have forgotten myself."

"I'm sorry," said Mauritane, as she turned and started back toward Satterly.

"You should be," she hissed over her shoulder.

Inside the home's large banquet hall, the party was well under way when Silverdun arrived with Faella. He winced a bit when his name was announced with fanfare, but a quick scan of the room revealed no one who looked remotely familiar. Surely in a city like Estacana there would be no trouble.

"Keep your head up, love," scolded Faella, rapping his shoulder. "You act as though you've been caught cheating at cards."

"You have no idea the things at which I've been caught cheating," he said, swallowing heavily.

Faella was radiant. All eyes were on her, and Silverdun could see that this was everything she'd ever wanted. A poor girl, the daughter of a commoner, draped across the arm of a nobleman. Silverdun sighed. Despite his worries, he had to admit that he was in a way more comfortable than he'd been in years. He'd always been better with verbal sparring than with a blade. The life of the pretty folk, however shallow it might actually be, was a beautiful thing to behold.

"They're all looking at us," Faella whispered. "Is that what it's like?"

"What *what* is like?"

"To be of the nobility?"

"I suppose," said Silverdun.

"I see a great future for us," she said. "Oh, so much." Silverdun hoped she was talking about their night together at the inn, but he feared that she meant something rather more involved. Still, he reasoned, he'd eluded girls far more skilled in coquetry than Faella. It was only a matter of the right words at the right moments and she'd never even realize that she'd been dumped. If nothing else, he would be gone in the morning; that was the one saving grace of being on a secret mission, wasn't it?

And yet, he'd enjoyed himself as a mestinal. More than he cared to admit. As he and Faella stepped onto the dance floor and began moving with the music, he began thinking about what it might be like traveling with Faella and her mestina, savoring the applause in all the cities of the kingdom.

And the girl moved like a dream. She danced the way she made love, slowly and with great deliberation, with an elegance that belied her youth. Looking across the room, he saw Satterly stumbling along with Raieve in his arms and smiled. The look on Raieve's face was priceless.

For many years, Silverdun had made a career of living in the moment. Before he'd gotten wrapped up in his mother's religion, he'd been one of the most celebrated rakes in the City Emerald. Why had he ever stopped? It seemed that at some point his life at court had become impossibly shallow, but now he could hardly remember why. The music, the dance, the wine, the girl. They were all intoxicating, each in their own way. For the moment, he decided, he would forget Mauritane, forget their bloody mission, forget everything but the girl in his arms and the daydreams of things that could never happen, but might. Oh, they might!

Then he saw a familiar face and his heart leapt into his throat; the daydream vanished like a bad glamour.

"Perrin Alt!" came a booming voice from across the room. "You scoundrel!"

A woman approached, a very fat woman in a bright purple dress draped with pale pink flowers. She held a large goblet of pink rosewine. Silverdun struggled to remember her name.

"Lady Amecu!" he blurted out, having plucked the name from some dim recess of memory. As they always had, the name came to him just as he needed it. "What a pleasant surprise!"

"For a moment I couldn't believe it was your handsome face that I was seeing," Lady Amecu declared, her hand against her breast. "And who is this charming young creature I see on your arm? The daughter of an eastern prince, no doubt?"

"I am Faella," said Faella, curtseying deeply.

"Ah," said Lady Amecu, her eyes darting quickly away from the girl as if she'd just seem something that horrified her.

"I would not have expected to see you so far afield of the City Emerald," said Silverdun, trying to keep his voice even. This woman could ruin everything! The wrong word in the wrong ear and they would all be arrested before dawn.

"I'm only here for my sister's betrothal," said Lady Amecu. She took Silverdun's arm, drawing him away from Faella, careful not to look directly at the girl. It was a great breach of propriety for her to even acknowledge that a girl of Faella's class even existed, and she was in no hurry to repeat her mistake. On the positive side, the same sense of propriety made it impossible for her to ask what Silverdun was doing with her in the first place. "Ila is such a dumpy thing," Lady Amecu confided to Silverdun. "A fat, ugly little troll. Father had to search far and wide to find a husband for her." She took a deep swig from her wineglass, a most unladylike gesture, and Silverdun realized that she was drunk.

"The man is a baron out here," she said, "and with a good reputation. "But still . . ." she began, unable to finish the thought.

"We do what we must," said Silverdun. He glanced over his shoulder and saw Faella glaring at him, standing alone on the dance floor. He smiled his most winning grin and turned back to Lady Amecu. "Why, I once had a cousin who was so ugly, my uncle considered marrying her to a wild boar!"

Lady Amecu laughed heartily, spilling wine down the front of her dress. She gasped, but an attendant hurriedly came and wiped it with a spelled cloth that removed the stain in an instant.

She leaned in even closer and Silverdun could smell the wine on her breath. "Now, you must tell me, Silverdun. If I recall correctly, the last I heard you were . . . indisposed."

There it was. Lady Amecu knew all about him. She was letting him know that she carried his fate in her hands and that he was now completely at her mercy.

"You know how rumors get started," said Silverdun helplessly. "In point of fact I've been here in the East managing some old family lands. I just had to get away from it all, you know. I see that my enemies at court are spreading slander, as I suppose they must."

"So, you mean to say that you were not convicted of treason and shipped off to Crere Sulace?"

It was out on the table now. There was no way to avoid it.

"What do you want?" he said.

"Oh, I think you know what I want," said Lady Amecu. She pressed her more than ample bosom against his arm and Silverdun suppressed a groan.

"I'm drunk and you're handsome and I believe I hold your very life in my hands, do I not? I'm told that can make a woman quite attractive."

Silverdun had to admit she had a point.

"Excuse me for a moment," he said.

"Of course."

Silverdun took Faella by the arm and marched her quickly over to where Satterly and Raieve sat, at a small table in the corner of the room. Raieve was scowling and Satterly looked as though he'd rather be just about anywhere else. "Look after her for a moment," said Silverdun, sitting Faella next to Raieve. "There's a bit of business I must attend to."

"What's going on, Silverdun?" said Faella, her face awash in hurt.

"I won't be but a moment," he said. "Save the next dance for me."

When it was over, Silverdun found his way to the washroom and stripped naked, washing himself from head to toe and then looking at himself in the mirror.

"The things I do for Queen and country," he said.

Ah, well. He'd done worse.

That night Silverdun and Faella made love again, and the unpleasant business with Lady Amecu finally faded from his mind. With a few glasses of wine he found himself able to return to the daydream he'd experienced on the dance floor.

"I had no idea," he said afterward, "how powerful a thing it was to be on a stage. It was intoxicating."

Faella turned to lie on her side and looked at him, tousling his hair in the firelight. "More intoxicating than I?"

"Impossible," he said. He kissed her elbow.

"You're right," Faella said. "There is no feeling like it. I was hoping you'd think so."

"Were you?"

"Of course. Think of it, Perrin. Faella and Lord Silverdun together, on stage. We could ditch the rest of them and continue as a duet. I don't want to perform in these tiny places anymore. I want to perform in Sylvan, Selafae, the City Emerald!" She rolled onto her back. "I would even travel to the city of Mab and perform in the Queen's tent itself. As a goodwill gesture."

"That sounds like a lovely idea," said Silverdun. He held her tight.

"I'm serious, Perrin." Faella rolled back on her side and looked into his eyes. "I want to do this. With you. Now."

Silverdun laughed. "You move quickly, darling! Why don't we worry about tonight and take the rest as it comes?"

Faella sat up. "Forgive me, Lord Silverdun, but I thought this meant something, you and I."

Silverdun's laugh faded. "It does mean something. It's lovely. But it's not something you want to base a career choice on."

Faella's face grew pinched. "But Perrin, it would be so wonderful. Just the two of us. Say you'll come with me."

"I can't, Faella. I have a duty to perform."

"I don't care about that."

"But I do."

She took her dress from the floor and worried at the hem of it. "I thought . . . I thought I would be yours."

Silverdun sighed. "You belong to no one."

Faella stood and began to dress.

"Wait, darling," said Silverdun. "Don't be upset. Not everything is meant to be. I'm sorry if I've misled you. It wasn't my intention."

She sat back down on the edge of the bed. "No, you're right. I was just being silly."

"Good," he said, reaching for her. "Come back to bed and forget all that."

Faella smiled, her eyebrows raised, and crawled beneath the covers next to Silverdun.

When he awoke in the predawn of the following morning, Silverdun found himself alone. He stood and dressed in the pale light, washing his face in the basin. All of Faella's things were gone.

He looked in the mirror and there was something on it, red lines over the silvered surface. Silverdun flared witchlight from his fingers and read it. It was a message from Faella, written in scarlet rouge. "Be as ugly out as in."

Silverdun refocused his eyes on his own reflection. The man staring back at him was not Perrin Alt, Lord Silverdun. His proud chin was now sunken and pitted with scars. His cheeks were pale. His nose, once straight and patrician, had become a short, bent thing that huddled on his face. Scowling, he reached deep within himself to let loose whatever glamour Faella had placed on him. He felt around his face for the loose threads of illusion and could not find them. There was nothing there. It wasn't a glamour.

how silverdun appears

"Why would I believe that you're Silverdun?" said Raieve, frowning from behind her raised sword. She stood at the entrance to the public stable, where inside the others were preparing the horses. "You don't look a thing like him, and you don't sound like him either."

The man in front of her wore a dark scowl that certainly reminded Raieve of Silverdun, even if his unpleasant appearance wasn't a match.

"It's me, Raieve. Lower your blade." The man made a lowering motion with two outstretched hands. "Faella did this to me. We had a disagreement, and I suppose this is her crafty method of punishment."

"If it's a glamour, then remove it."

"I can't. It's not a glamour."

"Then we have a problem."

Satterly, Mauritane, and Gray Mave appeared at the wide stable door, leading all five mounts by the reins. The morning was dawning misty and gray, the sun buried somewhere behind the ash-colored sky. Even so, the temperature had risen above freezing during the night, and the streets were infused with the sound of melting snow and ice dripping onto the cobblestones.

"Who's this?" said Mauritane.

Raieve kept her eyes and her weapon trained on the stranger. "He says he's Silverdun."

"I am Silverdun," the man said. "Faella did this to me."

"How do we know you're Silverdun?" said Satterly, stroking his chin. "Tell me something only Silverdun would know."

"Such as?" said the would-be Silverdun.

"What did I have for breakfast yesterday?" Satterly raised his eyebrows. "How on earth should I know? Watching you eat is too repellant an act to make a habit of it. Besides, I was busy being scolded by Nafaeel for succumbing to his shrew of a daughter."

"Certainly sounds like Silverdun," noted Gray Mave.

"As I was telling Raieve," the stranger said, "Faella did something to me. It's not a glamour. I can't remove it."

"If not a glamour, then what?" said Mauritane. "Some kind of spirit curse or hex?"

"I don't know," said the stranger, "but it's me, and we're in a hurry, so let's be on our way."

"Just a moment," said Mauritane. "I believe that you are who you say you are, but the nature of our mission requires proof."

"What about the horses?" said Satterly, after a moment's thought.

"How do you mean?" said Mauritane.

"Silverdun's horse should recognize his scent. If the curse, or whatever it is, altered his smell along with his appearance, then it's awfully subtle."

"I agree, but let's get away from the stable," said Mauritane. "I think we're beginning to draw attention."

Indeed, a few of the townspeople had stopped to watch the confrontation. Raieve dismissed them with an ugly look and Mauritane led them away from the stable, into a deserted square near the main spire.

Mauritane leaned close and whispered into Streak's ear. The horse shook his mane and nodded, whispering something back that only Mauritane could understand. Streak nuzzled Silverdun's roan, Adequate, and made a series of chuffing sounds.

"Hold out your hand," said Mauritane.

The man raised his hand to Adequate's nose, and the animal sniffed at it, licked it once. Adequate turned to Streak and let out a single low grunt.

"It's him," said Mauritane. "Or an amazing facsimile."

"Oh, please," said Silverdun. "If I were an imposter, why on earth would I do such a terrible job of copying my likeness? I don't even resemble myself!"

"Maybe you're very bad at illusions," said Satterly. "And this is an elaborate ruse."

"Are all humans as annoying as you?" said Silverdun, pulling his hair back and tying it with a bit of ribbon.

"I'm convinced," said Satterly.

"Enough," said Mauritane. "I'm assured that this is Silverdun. If we discover later that he is not, we're four and he is one. Until then, let's return to our mission. There is much to be done this morning."

"Is the deal arranged, Mauritane?" said Silverdun.

"It is. We're to meet a guard named Edi at the tavern."

"And you got the money from Nafaeel?"

"I did," said Mauritane, patting his sabretache. "And a good thing I got it last night, because this morning there's no sign of him. The entire troupe packed up and left town during the night."

"Really?" said Silverdun. "What a surprise."

The guard Edi was a thick-waisted career guardsman with a scruffy beard and not a single braid in his tousled hair. Mauritane was suspicious of him from the first, perhaps because he'd known a few of the guardsmen in Selafae who were willing to take a bribe, and he wouldn't have turned his back to a single one of them. Still, Edi was a necessary evil, and Mauritane had no choice but to deal with him. Thorough checks were being made at all of the city's exits; even the mestina couldn't have helped them leave.

"I can take you as far as the border," he said. "But if we meet any patrols en route, they'll require something in exchange for looking the other way as well." Edi slouched in his seat. A glass of wine sat on the table in front of him even though the morning bell had only just rung.

"We had a deal," said Mauritane. "One hundred in silver for your help. You never mentioned anything beyond that."

"The one hundred *is* for my help. Unfortunately, you'll need more than my help to make it out of Estacana today." He sighed. "But if you don't want to go . . ."

"Fine," said Mauritane. "Just know that if there is any deception, my blade will find you first."

Edi whistled. "You must trust, sire. Without trust, where are we?"

Edi led them out of the city through a wide-open aqueduct, a stone channel that began at the city's central cistern and meandered through the city, elevated on arched pilings, then cut through the city wall and into the farmland beyond. The horses splashed in knee-high frigid water, scared of the echoes that reverberated in the curved space.

A pair of guards stationed by the aqueduct's egress from the city paid them no attention as they passed through the opening in the wall, only nodding at Edi as he rode by. The high stone channel angled downward from the wall until it came even with the ground on a gradual slope. Here, high juniper bushes surrounded the aqueduct, and Mauritane could just make out farms beyond them, empty fields lying useless beneath a blanket of snow.

At a break in the shrubbery, Edi nudged his horse up the slope of the canal and through the juniper branches, motioning for them to follow him. They emerged onto a narrow path that skirted the fence line of the farmland, where the snow was broken by several sets of fresh tracks.

"Morning patrol," said Edi, shrugging. "They're friends of mine. It's not a problem."

The path followed the aqueduct for several miles, broken by irrigation canals that extended from the main canal and ran beneath wooden bridges. The horses' hooves made thick, hollow sounds on the wood. Otherwise, the fields were silent.

Mauritane allowed the others to pull ahead, nodding to Silverdun to hang back with him.

"Silverdun," he said. "Let's talk for a moment."

"Do you still need convincing? Shall I show you a birthmark?"

Mauritane cracked a smile. "No, I believe you. Now that I look at you, I see that you are not so changed as I'd thought. The eyes are the same. I trust eyes."

They rode in silence for a moment.

"What then?" said Silverdun.

"In thinking of our mission a few things trouble me. Things I've been pondering for days on my own. I need a fresh perspective." He sighed. "In the past, I could always count on wise counsel from Honeywell."

Silverdun nodded. "I'll do my best in his absence."

"There is a crucial question of the Queen's motive in all this," Mauritane began. "Her Majesty is often mysterious, but there is usually a method to her. I'm trying to imagine what circumstances could lead to Purane-Es's appearance at Crere Sulace, and I can think of nothing."

"Men have given their careers in pursuit of understanding the Queen's mind on far simpler matters."

"Yes, but our lives may depend on it. You know as well as I the risk that we're taking."

Silverdun ruminated. "I can offer two possibilities. One is misdirection. There is someone the Queen wishes to confound, and our mission is simply a way to divert attention away from something else."

"Perhaps. But what?"

"No way of knowing. But if that is the case, any further speculation is futile."

"A rather elaborate sleight of hand," said Mauritane. "Even for our Queen. Let's proceed on the assumption that it is not the case. What is the other possibility?"

"She's hiding something from a noble in the Seelie Court."

"Whom?"

Silverdun shrugged. "Perhaps Purane-Es himself. His father is influential at court and she may fear him knowing too much of it. Otherwise she'd send Purane-Es or one of the other lackeys in the Guard to do the job. And they all talk."

"Yes, when I was Captain, stopping rumors among my commanders took more of my time than the Unseelie."

"And there's yet a third possibility."

"Mab?"

Silverdun nodded. "She has spies at court. Someone once told me that at any given time easily a third of the Queen's ladies-in-waiting are Unseelie operatives."

"That's only a rumor," said Mauritane. "Remember, it was not that long ago that protecting Her Majesty was my occupation. And I was very good at my job."

"And you can attest that there were no Unseelie spies at court?"

Mauritane scowled. "Next question. The Queen asked for me by name. What do you think that might mean?"

"I've considered that," said Silverdun. "And a thought suggests itself, but not one I think you'll enjoy hearing."

"And that is?"

"She knows you're the only one loyal enough to do the job even knowing that success is probably suicide."

"The thought crossed my mind as well."

"And?"

"It does no good to think such things."

Silverdun leaned toward him. "You'd better start thinking such things, Mauritane. Your life may well depend on it."

"There's something else," said Mauritane, changing the subject. "Do you remember the night before we left Crere Sulace, when I left you and went to the South Tower?"

"Yes," said Silverdun. "I was wondering if you would ever bring it up."

A frown touched Mauritane's lips. "The tower has been turned to excess. There were strange things there."

"I remember you heard something."

"Yes, a girl's voice. You couldn't hear it and neither could anyone else. That makes me think what I saw there was meant for me to see."

"What was it?"

"It was Crere Sulace, as it was when its prince still ruled there. But still Midwinter outside. I met the Prince, spoke with him. He was as surprised to find me there as I was."

"Fascinating. It was as though you'd been spellturned yourself. Back into the past."

"Yes. And to a very specific time. I was not alone in my arrival. A company of the Queen's Men was there to abduct the Prince's daughter. I helped them do it."

"The Prince's daughter? Was her name Laura, perchance?"

Mauritane looked at Silverdun. "You know of her?"

"Yes, I remember something of it from a history class. Crere Sulace mounted a brief insurrection against the crown during the Unseelie Wars. He claimed that the Queen had kidnapped his daughter."

"Your history is better than mine. What happened?"

"No one believed him. He was arrested and tried as a collaborator with the Unseelie. It was Her Majesty's idea to turn the castle into a prison. For years he was its only inmate."

"And they say he wanders the halls even now."

Silverdun chuckled. "Apparently, they're correct."

"I can't help but think that my participation in these events is somehow related to our errand. If so, it's the only information I have that Purane-Es does not, and that is valuable."

"You say you helped the Queen's Men. Did you give your name?"

"No. I gave the name of one of my ancestors. Bersoen. The lieutenant of the company promised me a medal."

"I see," said Silverdun. "When we arrive in Sylvan it may be of some interest to consult the Histories and determine if that medal was delivered."

"So you think there's a connection to our mission?"

Silverdun scoffed. "Mauritane, if you knew the Queen as well as you claim to, you'd know that the question doesn't need to be asked."

Edi brought them to a halt before a patrol of four city guardsmen.

"These gentlemen will each require twenty," he said.

Mauritane grumbled but paid the men from the rapidly dwindling proceeds of the previous evening's mestina.

"You'd better pray that they are the last patrol we encounter," said Mauritane, once they'd ridden on. "Because I'm running out of silver and patience both."

Edi looked around him and, realizing that he was now alone with them, chose to say nothing.

Raieve squinted at Silverdun. "That Faella certainly took care of you," she said. "What on earth did you do to her?"

"Does it matter?" said Silverdun.

"I'm curious." Raieve suppressed her wicked grin.

"She wanted me to leave Estacana with her and become a mestine. She thought we could work as a duet." Silverdun made a face, looking away.

"And you refused her to remain with us? I'm touched," said Raieve.

"Your facetiousness is not appreciated," Silverdun said. "She was serious. And she did not take my refusal well."

Raieve nodded. "Well, you got what you deserved."

Gray Mave cocked his head to one side; he'd been following the conversation. "How do you figure, miss?"

"What?"

"How do you figure he got what he deserved? Sounds to me like the poor girl was touched with the madness."

Raieve's brow furrowed. "Ah, and I suppose you believe Silverdun did nothing to encourage her? A young girl meets a dashing lord and becomes infatuated with him. What would you have her think? Who among us escaped wild fantasies at that age?"

"Yes," said Silverdun. "But it was not I that encouraged her. If you'll recall, it was she that found her way unclothed into my tent."

Raieve laughed. "Oh, and you had no choice but to bed her?"

"Honestly, the thought of resisting never crossed my mind."

"Then you got what you deserved," said Raieve. She spurred her horse and rode forward to watch Edi.

Edi halted them again, but not for another patrol. They'd reached the end of the path. It terminated at a line of dark trees, stretching as far as the eye could see in either direction. A wooden sign affixed to a post protruding from the snow read, "Beware: Here begin some Contested Lands. Beyond this marker, Seelie Law does not pertain."

"*Lasciate ogne speranza, voi c'intrate*," intoned Satterly.

"What's that?" said Mauritane.

"It's from an old story in my world. It says pretty much the same thing."

a choice

Marar Envacoro awoke with a start, his premonitory Gift aching in his head and bones. He raised his head gently and peered at his wife and son, still asleep on the bed beside him, the boy's ash blond hair falling across his wife's face. Marar leaned and kissed them each on the forehead gently, careful not to wake them.

He opened the tent flap to a gentle breeze that meant the city was still in motion and that his water-bearing skills would not be needed today. He'd hoped the premonition was only to underscore a water stop, as it often did, for he needed the extra money. Instead, it would be another day walking the streets. It was Aba's will. So be it.

He dropped the flap and kneeled beneath the window ledge, prying out the false bottom of the cabinet there, removing his worship beads. He counted them off, the prayers of the morning, the prayers of safety, the prayers of thanksgiving, the prayers of repentance. He whispered them, every few moments glancing at his wife to ensure that she still slept. If she were to stir, he knew from experience, he could have the beads in his pocket before she saw them. And Marar would be certain that she never would. Not until the time was right.

It was not easy, leading this double life. It went against everything he believed in and everything he knew to be good. But Aba's will was not a straight line, and he would walk it as best he could.

"Aba protect me from my foes, give me the voice to speak against the oppressor, give me the will to thwart my enemies. Aba, I ask for your protection in the name of She Who Will Come." Marar repeated the words in a murmur, fighting to retain their meaning in his mind despite the number of times he'd spoken the prayer in the past five years.

He replaced the prayer beads and washed himself in the basin, staring at his reflection. This is the face of a tax collector, he thought. This is the face of one who gathers water to make extra money when the city stops. Frowning, Marar took his collection bag from the bed frame and went out to make his rounds.

He stopped at the door to his apartment and pulled himself over the walkway railing to the rigging that ran alongside his home. There, tied up among the similar ships belonging to the wealthier of his neighbors, was the flyer. It was small, room enough for only four or five, but it would come in handy if it came time to flee the city of Mab. The flyer was registered with the city and could be taken out without special permission. The monks at Sylvan had even rigged it to come at his command.

The Gift of Premonition did not feel like a gift today. It urged him to leap into the flyer now and abandon his post, flying as far as he could manage, then running into the desert to live among the wild people. He swore to himself, checking the craft's mooring, then climbed back onto the path.

A sunny day. Dust in the sandals, sweat along the hairline. Marar climbed the steps of the tenements on the city's fringe. The buildings dragged behind the city of Mab on old ropes that had frayed over centuries and were patched and repatched until the bindings became a patchwork of sisal and hemp fibers that stuck out at odd angles, fluttering in the breeze.

He rang the bell of an apartment at the top of a rickety stairwell, the wooden planks swinging nauseatingly on their rope supports. From the top of the stairs, the city's backside was plainly visible, leaving no doubt about this location's undesirability. Like a giant snail, the city left a stinking trail in its wake, a slime made of wastewater and refuse and dirt. The odor was so intense that it survived even at this height, hundreds of feet above the ground.

An elderly gnomish woman answered the bell, a permanent snarl etched on her face. Seeing Marar, she recoiled.

"You tell them!" she shouted. "You tell them I already paid my tax this month!"

Marar sighed. "Woman," he said. "You paid your imperial at the stall. I'm collecting for the city. We've been through this before."

"I shouldn't have to pay," she muttered, fishing in her pocketbook for the coins. "I'm old and the city gives me nothing but trouble."

"It's fourteen in copper," said Marar, consulting his list. "That's seven for this month and seven you owe from last month."

"Seven?" the woman said, clamping the pocketbook shut. "It used to be five!" Behind her, a pair of scrawny gnomish children wandered to the door and tugged at the woman's skirts. Marar felt a deep sadness for them, and his premonition headache throbbed.

"The city raised it four months ago. We've been over this."

"What's your take? I know you pocket the difference."

Marar smiled. "No, woman. I only profit from those who can afford to pay extra. I put no more burden on you than you can withstand."

She fished out fifteen coppers and handed them over. "You can keep the change," she said. "You're not as bad as the last man they had."

"Thank you," he said.

Marar finished his rounds in the tenement district and returned to the Assessor's Office for his break, his bag half full. The two legionnaires standing outside the office gave him pause; he stopped and closed his eyes for longer than a blink. They could not be there for him. No one knew. He'd been too careful. Even so, the premonitory headache refused to go away. It pounded behind his eyes, presaging terrible things.

One of the legionnaires cast a glance backward at the assessor, who nodded slowly in Marar's direction.

The legionnaire approached Marar, and for an instant his vision went gray, and the soldier spoke as if from a great distance.

"Marar Envacoro," he said. "You are under arrest for crimes against Her Imperial Majesty, Queen Mab."

Hy Pezho, seated at the right hand of the Queen, paid close attention to his fingernails while Prefect Laese'am rattled on about taxation. Pezho knew that his inattention to Laese'am would draw disfavor from among the Prefecture, but it was necessary to bolster his position with the Queen. Only one truly close could ignore a Prefect so openly without censure. Mab, for her part, appeared to be ignoring both of them.

A messenger entered the council chambers deep within the heart of the

Royal Complex. He bowed to Mab and held his message toward her, his face to the floor.

Mab read the message and laid it on the table. She rose.

"Gentlemen, there is more pressing business to which We must attend. Let us proceed to Our observation deck that we may witness yet another sign of Our glory."

Mab led the way from the council chambers, creating a frenzy among the attendants and servants both of the Royal Person and of her Prefects. A swarm of valets saw to the robes and tunics, assuring that they hung correctly for walking. A pair of servants dusted the ground before the Queen, lest she tread on dirt. It was a group of over fifty that left the council chambers in a double-file line through the main entrance. A two-story teak door with brass knobs fit for giants opened for them. Hy Pezho stroked the wood as he passed, three paces behind the Queen.

They ascended a wide spiral ramp at the top of which Hy Pezho could see blue sky stippled with cirrus clouds. Along the ramp's path were hung bright scarlet banners bearing slogans in Old Court Fae depicting the past triumphs of Mab.

Hy Pezho drank it all in with a hidden smile. Already heads were beginning to turn when he entered rooms. And, no doubt, the tall, thin ladies-in-waiting were whispering his names from behind their pillows and fans. It was all he could have asked for, and soon it would be more than that.

Queen Mab's observation deck was a generous tiled expanse overlooking the entire city and the lands below. Terraced gardens overflowed with marigolds and chapelbells laced with flowering vinca and begonias. A fountain in the shape of the city sparkled in the afternoon sun, its worn stones scrubbed and polished to a shine. Servants had placed deck chairs near the south-facing railing, and the assembled Prefects jockeyed politely with each other for seats nearer Her Majesty.

Hy Pezho, accepting an iced coffee from a servant, looked out over the railing and saw what the Queen intended them to see: the city of Gefi.

Gefi was smaller than the city of Mab, but what she lacked in size she made up for in architecture. Golden spires pushed up past the city's mainmast, glittering in the sunlight. On the city's main deck, the streets were laid out like the spokes of a wheel, with a great fountain in the center. Even from this distance, Hy Pezho could see the rainbow that hung eternally over the fountain. Streamers of red and gold silk hung from the lower decks, and when the wind gusted, they twisted with the currents of warm air. The city's sails were at full mast, and she was tacking against what appeared to be a strong crosswind.

"Behold the city of Gefi," said Mab. The assembled Prefects slyly checked each other's faces for a sign of the attitude one ought to take toward it. No one seemed certain.

Mab called forth a messenger and dictated a note to the Chambers of Elements and Motion. "Bring the wind at Our back," she said, "and pull Gefi nearer." The messenger bowed and ran from the deck.

The Queen took her seat and, as one, each of the Prefects did so as well. Hy Pezho found himself again at the Queen's right.

"Is Our demonstration ready?" she asked him, beaming broadly.

"Yes, Your Majesty," said Hy Pezho. He sipped his coffee.

Mab waited a few moments, wearing no discernable expression, her attendants hanging with ever-growing suspense on her next motion. Finally, she clapped her hands.

"Have the prisoner brought forth," she called.

A pair of legionnaires dragged a man onto the deck, holding him by a pair of manacles on his wrists. He was dressed in the robes of a tax collector and had been beaten severely. He had difficulty keeping up with the legionnaires and stumbled often.

The legionnaires brought the man before the Queen and pushed him to the ground, then retreated a single pace, at full attention.

The Queen stood, precipitating a mass arising within the rows of deck chairs.

"Your name is Marar Envacoro?" Mab said to the man.

The man lifted his head toward her and took a deep breath. "Your Majesty," he said. His voice was strained.

"You are an Arcadian spy, are you not?" The Queen lifted a single eyebrow, a refined gesture.

Marar shook his head slowly. "No, Your Majesty."

Mab smiled. "Do you know the human tale of the disciple who denies his Lord three times before the cock crows? Will you do the same, Marar Envacoro?"

Marar said nothing.

Mab nodded to the legionnaire. "Are these not your Arcadian prayer beads, Marar Envacoro?" The legionnaire held a string of red beads aloft.

A tear formed in Marar's eyes. "No, Your Majesty, they are not."

Mab smiled again, the grin of a predator. "Turn around, Marar Envacoro." The legionnaires stepped forward and dragged Marar around to face afore the city. "Do you recognize the city of Gefi? Have you not spent many days there with the Arcadians who have infected that place, coordinating their evangelical efforts?" She strode toward him and pushed down on Marar's shoulder, bringing him to the ground. "Are you not, in fact, the chief operative for the Arcadians among Our people?" Her voice was stern, deep. Some of the Prefects cringed.

"No, Your Majesty, I am not." Marar's head hung.

"And sadly there is no cock to crow at your denial. But there is still work for you, Marar Envacoro." Mab knelt before him and took his face in her hands. "You see, We know who you are. And We know that the leaders of the Arcadian conspiracy make their home in Gefi. What We do not know are their names. We want you to tell Us their names, Marar Envacoro."

Marar fixed his jaw. "I cannot tell you that."

"Really?" said Mab. She stood, her skirts swirling about her like a storm in the dust. "Prefect Laese'am. Tell us the crime of Blasphemy."

Laese'am rose to his feet and cleared his throat. "Your Majesty is the law of the earth and its sole ruler. To raise another's words and deeds above Your Majesty is the highest treason. That is the crime of Blasphemy"

"Correct," said Mab. "Bring forward the wife and child."

A second pair of legionnaires led a petite woman onto the deck. The woman carried a small blond boy of two or three years.

"We rarely offer choices to traitors, Marar Envacoro," said Mab. "But We are a merciful ruler and We are not without lenience. There will be crucifixions in the main square tomorrow morning. Either We will have the Arcadians in Gefi, or We will have your wife and child. The choice is yours."

Marar's wife clutched the child to her chest. "Marar, what is happening?" she cried. "What have you done?"

Marar stood, his limbs shaky. He spoke, as if reciting, "The children of Aba will not dwell in fear nor will they suffer the lash of the tyrant, for Aba will protect them."

"Marar!" shouted the wife. "Stop it! Stop, please. What's going on?" Her words broke into deep, throaty sobs. The child, who had been sleeping, awoke and began to cry.

"Well, Marar Envacoro?" said Mab, sternly. "Which will it be?"

"Aba," he prayed, "protect me from my foes, give me the voice to speak against the oppressor, give me the will to thwart my enemies. Aba, I ask for your protection in the name of She Who Will Come."

"Answer me, Marar," snapped the Queen. "If you do not choose, I will choose for you."

Marar began to shout, his eyes shut. "Aba, protect me from my foes! Give me the voice to speak against the oppressor!"

"Marar!" his wife cried again and again.

"So be it," said Mab, and her voice was bitterly cold. "Take the woman and the child and prepare them for keelhauling."

Marar lifted his arms skyward. "Aba, do not forsake me!"

"You are a fool, Marar!" said Mab. "You place your faith in a god who does not answer, a power that cannot be shown. If your god is so great, then have him deliver you from me! I defy your Aba. I spit on him. Let him come and take me!"

She leaned in toward Marar and whispered in his ear. "They'll take your boy, truss him like a pig. Then they'll hang him upside down beneath the city and let him dangle. When the wind blows just right, the garbage and ordure from the aft neighborhoods will bathe your boy as it falls. He'll starve down there and no one will hear his screams and then the crows will eat out his eyes. Tell Us what We wish to know and he will be freed. You have Our word."

Marar looked skyward. "Not my son!" he shouted, his face flush with rage. "My son! My son! Aba!"

"Tell me their names!" The Queen shook Marar by the throat. The Prefects, the legionnaires, the servants, all sat perfectly still. "Tell me their names and your son will live!"

"My son!" Marar whispered through sobs.

"Enough!" the Queen shouted. Her voice took on a supernatural depth; it rang out across the hills.

"If We cannot know their names, then We must assure their destruction another way. Hy Pezho, I give you the floor." The Queen brushed a few stray hairs from about her face, returning to her seat, her face blank.

Hy Pezho rose. "Gentlemen, I have prepared something for this contingency," he said. "Have the catapults brought forward."

One of the guards at the edge of the deck signaled to another below, at a garrison post just outside the Royal Complex. A number of legionnaires there wheeled a great wooden catapult from a bay beneath the post.

"The missile within that catapult," said Hy Pezho, "is of my own devising. I trust you will be impressed."

Hy Pezho looked southward. Gefi was near firing range. Another minute and it would be his.

Marar lay prostrate on the ground, saying prayers into the dirt. The Queen spat. "By failing to decide, you have made your decision, Marar Envacoro. Now you will observe its consequence." She waved at the legionnaires who'd brought Marar in and they lifted him to his feet, facing him directly toward Gefi.

"When you are ready, Hy Pezho, give the word."

Hy Pezho fought a grin. He made a chopping motion with his right hand. The legionnaire at the balcony's edge repeated the motion. Far below, a soldier with an ax hove against the catapult's restraint and the engine's arm whipped forward, sending its package, a blackened globule, skyward.

The projectile fell far short of Gefi. It struck the ground near the city's edge and rolled beneath her sails and planks.

"Hy Pezho!" barked the Queen. "You missed!"

Hy Pezho let the grin come. "I never miss. Your Majesty." He whispered the word of unbinding.

Beneath Gefi, a column of flame erupted from within the projectile, a vertical beam of red and orange and blue. The city's center tore apart as though it were made of paper. A halo of debris, flashing sailcloth, and vaporizing flesh made a corona around the column as it expanded upward. Beneath the city, a colossal black cloud of dirt and ash billowed out, breaking trees like matchsticks and setting the grass aflame.

The sound came soon after, an impossibly low bass rumble; it hit Hy Pezho in the chest, nearly pushing him backward. For a few seconds, the only thing he could hear was the fierce thunder of destruction, as the city's enormous yellow and green sheets caught flame, sending plumes of white smoke skyward.

Marar watched, defeated, as the terrified citizens of Gefi leaped to their deaths in order to escape the flames.

Gefi, riding high at an altitude of over a hundred feet, began to topple. With her chambers of Elements and Motion destroyed, she no longer had the power to remain aloft. The city—burning, scorched, ablaze—toppled and fell to earth, her structures collapsing, her massive floors breaking apart with thick wooden cracking sounds. When she hit, she hit hard. Every remaining building fell into sticks, every spire crumbled and disintegrated. Within seconds, there was nothing left of Gefi but an enormous ember, a smoking hull where a city had been only moments before.

"Most impressive," said Mab, when the sound abated enough to allow speech.

"It pleases me you approve," said Hy Pezho, bowing.

"Marar," said Mab, rising from her seat. "See what you did?" She turned her back, saying, "Cut his throat."

"What of the wife and child?" said Hy Pezho. Everyone on the deck stopped short, including Mab. She turned slowly.

"Let them live," she said to Hy Pezho. "Show them that their Empress is not without mercy."

The legionnaires stepped forward and slit Marar's throat open with their swords. His blood poured onto the immaculate tile of the observation deck, but his eyes remained skyward.

contested a comeuppance

Beyond the boundary, the Contested Lands proved bleak and dry, littered with sharp stones and dust. Dry brush and gnarled trees grew in places, and shadows lay low upon the ground, even at noon, with nothing to cast them. A bitter wind scraped along the floor of the valley in which they rode; it was warmer here than in the Eastern lands they'd just left, but the wind was harsher and it blew dust and sand in their faces. Will o' the wisps darted among the dry branches of the trees and small rodents skittered through the dust. In the sky above, carrion birds waited, circling.

Their progress west had been halted by a mountain range that ran north and south across the Contested Lands. They'd followed it north for most of a day before discovering this valley, and Gray Mave's weak Gift of Premonition indicated that it was passable. So far the valley's bottom had been level enough, following the course of a tiny stream which was frigid but unfrozen. At least they didn't have to melt snow over the fire in order to drink.

Raieve rode in back, tasting dust, keeping watch behind them. That was fine; the steppes of Avalon were dusty as well, and feeling the grit against her teeth almost made her homesick.

Thinking of home made her stomach twist inside her. She'd been gone for three years; anything might have happened during her absence. Had the Tongul warlords conquered the steppes in the Unseelie's absence? Had her own Heavy Sky Clan managed to unite the other clans and reform the Concordat? Or had the Unseelie perhaps returned and begun their predations anew, this time with better leadership and in greater numbers?

There was no way to know, and the not knowing ate at her.

Ahead of her, Mauritane rode point, insisting on silence and stopping often as they progressed through the valley. He'd told her to watch for any sign of an ambush, and she held back a hundred yards or so, eyes searching all around for signs of trouble. For the moment, though, she only watched Mauritane.

Here was another mystery. She'd been brought up to believe that the Fae were capricious, spineless fools. Her experience with the Unseelie in Avalon had gone a long way to confirm the impression. Their strategy had always been to make sloppy attacks with overwhelming numbers, seeming not to care how many of their own soldiers died as long as they achieved their objectives. Their invasion of Raieve's world seemed to progress almost randomly, without any apparent forethought. Granted, their lack of strategy often wreaked havoc on the plans of the insurgence movement, but it was also the Unseelie's ultimate undoing. Five years ago, the attempted occupation had proved a failure in both governance and profitability, and Queen Mab's army simply stopped fighting and left. Cowards. Barbarians. Fools.

Raieve had come to the City Emerald in the hopes that the Seelie Fae would prove to be the opposite of their counterparts to the North, but as yet they'd turned out to be as frivolous and untrustworthy as any Unseelie she'd ever encountered. Until she met Mauritane.

At Crere Sulace, Mauritane had been gloomy and taciturn. He'd never said a single word to her until the day he interposed himself between Raieve and Dumesne, may he be damned to a thousand hells. And yet she'd been drawn to Mauritane even then. He was not charming or easy with words. He wasn't particularly handsome. But he had something, an inner strength—a *solidity*—that had shown through his guarded demeanor at Crere Sulace and practically blazed now that he was back in command of something.

And yes, she was attracted to him. She *wanted* him. Raieve had never wanted or needed the protection of any man. But if he were to put his arms around her and whisper, "Everything will be fine," she feared that she would listen and believe.

Worse, she feared that she would like it.

How he felt about her, however, was impossible to tell. There had been moments since they'd left Crere Sulace that she'd been certain that he reciprocated her desire, but only moments. He was married, so he'd said. But was he loved, and did he return that love? Somehow she thought not. Intuition told her that a pampered lady from the City Emerald could never be a match for him. Raieve, however, was up to the task.

Most men were so transparent that she might as well have the Fae Gift of Empathy. But she was not Fae, not entirely, and the half of her that carried Fae blood did not carry the Gifts along with it. And so Mauritane remained a knot in her mind, one that she itched to undo.

As night began to fall, they reached a stepped incline over which the stream fell in a small waterfall. Mauritane went ahead, taking Streak lightly up the rise, but then froze and motioned them all to stop. With slow movements, he nudged the horse back down and rejoined them. He dismounted, indicating that they should do the same.

"There's a camp ahead," he whispered. "Six or seven men. Soldiers with mounts."

"Theirs or ours?" asked Silverdun.

"It's hard to say in this light, but my guess would be Unseelie. We're closer to their border than ours, and in all my years in the Guard, I never knew the Seelie Army to send men this far north."

"Things may have changed in your absence," said Silverdun.

"Too much has changed in my absence," Mauritane said.

"Does it matter either way?" Satterly asked. "No matter which side they're on, it's not like we can just walk up to them and say hello, given our . . . peculiar circumstances."

"True," said Mauritane, "but if they are Unseelie, I'll be much less concerned about killing them."

Mave gaped at him. "Will you truly kill Seelie men?"

"Not if I don't have to," said Mauritane.

"So what do we do?" said Satterly. "Do we double back and try to go another way?"

"No," said Mauritane. "We've lost too much time as it is, and there's no guarantee that there's another pass through these mountains anywhere near here. We go through."

Mauritane pulled out his pipe and stared at it, then tucked it away again with an annoyed grimace, looking toward the hill. "But first, let's be certain who we're dealing with. We need someone to reconnoiter. Silverdun, you do possess Poise?"

Silverdun sighed. "Not a shred. I can barely dance a quadrille."

Raieve stood up to her full height. "I don't claim any Gifts, but I damn well know how to move quietly. I spent my entire childhood avoiding Unseelie soldiers."

Mauritane nodded. "Fine. But be careful. And if you're spotted, signal us with a whistle and run."

Raieve smiled, tying back her braids with a bit of string. "If I'm spotted, your signal will be the scream of the first man I kill."

"A whistle will suffice," said Mauritane.

She gave Mauritane a curt salute and started up over the rise. Silverdun hissed after her, "Try not to kill them all before we get there."

Raieve crept along the side of the valley, moving from shadow to shadow. Here the valley narrowed, becoming almost a ravine, and it become more and more difficult to skirt its edge. The valley's bottom here sloped up gently for about thirty feet, then became nearly vertical, its rim at least a hundred feet above her head. As she approached the firelight ahead of her, she felt something akin to nostalgia overtake her. Tracking the Unseelie across dusty terrain, looking for an opportunity to strike; it was just the way she remembered. It was comfortable. It made sense to her.

And they were Unseelie, she could see that clearly now. There were seven of them, light cavalry, in a loose circle around the fire. They'd propped their long lances against a nearby rock. Their mounts stood too far from the fire, too much in the darkness, the reins looped haphazardly over the branches of a tree. In Avalon, Raieve and her friends had regularly stolen horses such as these. The men's boots were off, and they drank and laughed without caution.

One of them stood a desultory watch, but he spent as much time looking over his shoulder at his companions as he did watching the valley. If she timed it right, she could walk right up to him and cut his throat before he even noticed that she was there. Oh, they were Unseelie, all right. Their manner and their accents were proof enough; the markings on their uniforms were simply a confirmation of the obvious.

As she watched, they passed a bottle back and forth, telling jokes whose words she couldn't quite make out. Drunken. Sloppy. Easy prey.

The fingers of her right hand danced along the hilt of her sword. Part of her wanted to draw the blade and run at them, see how many of them she could take before they brought her down. It would be a fine way to die, dragging Unseelie soldiers to hell with her. It would be a death she understood, a death worth dying. Whatever lay at the end of Mauritane's mission was nothing she understood or particularly cared about. So why was she following? She'd given her word, yes, but was it dishonorable to break an oath to a non-Avalona? Or was there more to it than her word?

Grudgingly she let go of the sword and turned back.

"We go in on foot," said Mauritane, kneeling on the ground, drawing in the dust with a stick. "We don't have any ranged weapons, so we'll have to use a simple, direct attack. Raieve, can you move into position behind them without being spotted?"

"Aye," she said. "Easily."

"Good. We'll come within a hundred yards as a group, then you'll come around to the rear and wait. Silverdun, Mave, and I will move quickly, and with any luck we'll take them without a struggle."

"Uh," said Satterly, "what about me?"

"You'll stay behind us," said Mauritane, "twenty-five yards. If any of them flee past us, I'll expect you to make an attempt to stop them."

"Seriously?" said Satterly.

"Now is the time to test your mettle, human," said Mauritane, clapping him on the shoulder. "A man never knows if he can kill until the time comes. Pray to your god that you're able."

"I don't think my god answers prayers like that."

Raieve snorted. "Then what good is he?"

Mauritane ignored her. "Our intent is to capture, not kill. I have no wish to take lives wantonly, and these men may well possess useful information."

Ten minutes later, Raieve was in position. She waited, sword in hand, ready, the welcome rush of adrenaline brightening her senses. Some remnant of sunlight remained in the valley, but the already ubiquitous shadows were slowly spreading everywhere. The sentry, fool that he was, kept turning to his companions to comment on their conversation, looking at their fire each time, apparently unaware that he compromised his night vision every time he did so.

Mauritane leapt from the darkness so quickly it scarcely mattered. He clubbed the sentry viciously on the forehead with the hilt of his saber and the man fell without a sound. Silverdun and Gray Mave appeared in the firelight a moment later, flanking Mauritane.

"Hold!" shouted Mauritane, and even though the order was not directed at her, Raieve could sense the Leadership in his voice, focused into a command that nearly kept her rooted to the spot herself.

To her surprise, one of the Unseelie around the fire immediately sprang to his feet, a long, straight cavalry sword in hand. The insignia on his breast showed him to be a lieutenant. "To arms!" he shouted, and his men rose with admirable speed, each of them flashing hardened silver. Raieve was impressed; at least it would be a fair fight. She ran toward them.

But before the lieutenant could mount a defense, Silverdun made a snapping motion past him and the campfire erupted, spewing flame in every direction. Caught off guard, the Unseelie soldiers lurched away from the fire, and that was all it took. Mauritane managed to disarm two of them before Raieve reached the fight. His blade moved so quickly that it was scarcely visible in the firelight.

The Unseelie lieutenant, however, did not go down as easily. Mauritane engaged him, and the two men began to circle. Raieve's man was small but quick, and she secretly hoped it would become necessary to relieve him of his life before the thing was over. But then Silverdun's man went down, and a moment later the lieutenant called out his surrender.

Raieve took her opponent's sword brusquely and pushed him back toward the fire, which had resumed its former size. Soon all six men were kneeling before it.

In the melee, however, even Mauritane had forgotten about the sentry, who was stunned but not unconscious. He rose and lunged at his nearest opponent, who happened to be Satterly.

Raieve watched helplessly while the sentry rushed the hapless human. Satterly gamely held his sword up, but at the last moment, his arm dropped. Raieve winced, waiting for him to be run through. But instead of flinching away, Satterly leaned forward and rushed at the sentry's midsection. The sentry, expecting a sword thrust, had his sword aloft and Satterly's unexpected attack caught him off guard. The two men collided and Satterly drove the sentry backward. The man tripped and fell, catching the back of his skull on a stone, and was still. Raieve shrugged; all that counted in battle was victory.

Raieve turned back to the fire just in time to see the lieutenant turn his head back to where his horses were tied and shout, *"Cas! Una'ar, cas!"* There was a flash from one of the saddlebags and a tiny winged shape flitted into the air.

"Okay, okay! I'm going as fast as I can!" it shouted.

Mauritane plucked a knife from his belt and flicked it. The knife whirled in the air and bisected the message sprite neatly. It fell to the ground, and Mauritane walked slowly to it and ground it beneath his heel.

"Anything else?" he asked the lieutenant.

Mauritane ordered the Unseelie stripped naked and searched thoroughly, then placed in a line by the fire, on their knees. Their hands were tied behind them. The men acceded glumly, though Raieve did her best to humiliate them as thoroughly as possible. "Your cavalry favors a shorter lance, I see," she said to the unfortunate sentry; even Mauritane chuckled at that before cautioning her against impropriety.

Their search revealed little of note other than a few maps of the Contested Lands; these were probably equal parts cartography and imagination but still better than anything they'd been able to secure in Hawthorne.

Mauritane stood over the lieutenant. "You are in command?" he said.

"I am Lieutenant Ma Denha of the Eagle Regiment," the man answered, eyes forward.

"And I am Mauritane, former Captain of the Seelie Royal Guard."

"I've heard of you," said Ma Denha. "You're a traitor, if I recall correctly."

Mauritane squinted at him. "I've never heard of you, however, so I have no knowledge of the crimes you've been convicted of. But now that we're acquainted, let us speak."

"I am required only to give my name, rank, and posting when captured by the enemy."

"Ah, but we are not enemies, you and I. We are merely travelers who have engaged with you in an unfortunate altercation."

Ma Denha shrugged.

"Ordinarily," said Mauritane, "I would respect your oath of service, and I would not press you further. But I am engaged on a matter that is far out of the ordinary, and I believe that you possess information that may be valuable to me."

Ma Denha's eyes narrowed. "You're bluffing; the Seelie don't torture prisoners. This is common knowledge."

Mauritane moved aside and Raieve stepped forward, running a dagger idly across a whetstone, a tight smile on her face. "You are correct," said Mauritane. "But this woman is not Seelie. In fact, she is not even Fae."

Raieve knelt in front of the lieutenant and touched the dagger to his face. "Mauritane speaks the truth. I'm not Fae. I'm from Avalon. The Heavy Sky Clan."

The man kneeling next to Ma Denha stiffened and swallowed hard.

"You've heard of us?" said Raieve.

"I was stationed near the Heavy Sky territory during the Avalon campaign," the man muttered.

Ma Denha's head snapped toward him. "Be silent, Ensign Miret!"

Miret shook his head. "The Avalona do not consider torture dishonorable, Lieutenant."

"Not against foreigners, no," said Raieve.

Lieutenant Ma Denha sneered at Mauritane. "Your honor allows this?"

Mauritane rocked back on his heels, lighting his pipe. "My honor was stripped from me long ago, as you mentioned. All that remains to me is my duty. Talk and we'll release you. No one but yourselves need ever know. Refuse to talk and I let the woman practice her knife skills."

Ma Denha was silent for what seemed to Raieve a long while, looking into the fire. "Do what you will," he finally said.

Raieve hesitated; Ma Denha was calling her bluff. Despite the rumors the Avalona happily spread among the Unseelie, the clans all abhorred torture. She felt dirty even pretending. If anyone other than Mauritane had asked her to perform this charade, she would have clouted them. She knew for sure then that her feelings were clouding her judgment; she would have to be more careful.

Just as she was about to lower the dagger, Miret spoke out. "I'll speak!" he nearly shouted.

"Miret!" snarled Ma Denha.

"I can't die!" cried Miret. "I can't be tortured. Please!"

Ma Denha struck Miret's face with his shoulder. "Coward! This is treason!"

Mauritane took Miret by the elbow and led him a few feet away from the others, motioning Silverdun to join him. Raieve watched them from the corner of her eye.

"I'll tell you anything you want to know," he said, his voice slurred with fear.

Mauritane puffed on his pipe. "What is your assignment here?"

"We're on a scouting mission. Looking for a safe route through the Contested Lands into Seelie territory."

Mauritane scowled. "To what end?'"

"I don't know," he said. "We were told only to seek the route."

"How wide?" Mauritane asked.

"What?"

"How wide of a route?"

Miret closed his eyes. "Wide enough for two columns."

Mauritane and Silverdun shared a quick glance.

"When is the first incursion planned?"

Miret looked at Mauritane, eyes wide. "I don't know! They wouldn't tell me something like that."

"He's telling the truth," said Silverdun.

"I know," said Mauritane. "I possess Insight as well."

Silverdun snorted. "Is there any Gift you don't have, Mauritane?"

"Describe the lands west of here," Mauritane said to Miret. "What perils are we apt to encounter?"

Miret shook his head. "I don't know that either," he said. We came straight south from the water station at Ce Valon, just on the other side of the mountains. We haven't been west."

"What did you see on the western slopes of the mountains, then?"

"Nothing much. A few bugganes. Some shifting places. Nothing we couldn't avoid."

Silverdun shrugged. "Better than nothing, I suppose."

They asked Miret a few more questions, but it soon became apparent that they'd gleaned from him everything of value. Mauritane dragged him back to the fire, where his fellows refused to even look at him. Raieve felt a sudden pity for Miret that cut through her disgust at his shame. She had done this to him; she had stripped him of his honor.

"What happens now?" said Ma Denha.

Mauritane tamped the tobacco in his pipe. "We'll return your uniforms, leave you enough rations to return to friendly territory. But we'll keep your weapons and your horses. And your boots."

"Captain Mauritane?" Ma Denha began.

"Yes?"

"Would you truly have let the Avalona woman torture us?"

"No," said Mauritane.

"I didn't think so."

There was a choked shriek outside the camp. Raieve looked and saw the Unseelies' horses rearing and straining at their reins. The sound had come from the largest of them, which was kicking at the tree to which it was tied, its teeth bared. The tree bent, then its dry branches snapped, and all seven horses bolted, whinnying fiercely in the echoing canyon. They fled as one to the west, past Raieve.

"What in the hells?" she said.

Then there came a low sound, like thunder. Once, then again. The sound took up a regular rhythm, growing louder each time.

The ground began to shake. The Unseelie men looked to each other nervously. They were naked, weaponless. Helpless.

Raieve unsheathed her own weapon and spun in a slow circle, seeing nothing.

"Do any of you see anything?" said Mauritane, his voice even.

"Nothing," said Silverdun, scrambling up the side of the valley for a better look.

Mauritane handed one of the Unseelie soldiers' swords to Satterly. "Keep an eye on the prisoners. The rest of you, spread out and find the source of this disturbance."

Gray Mave pointed to the southern rim of the valley, his arm shaking. "I don't think that will be necessary," he said.

Raieve looked up. Something was climbing over the precipice at the valley's edge. It was shaped like a man, but much, much larger. In the darkness it was difficult to tell how large. Its hands clawed fingerholds into the solid rock of the cliff face as it descended. It looked over its shoulder and its eyes seemed to lock with hers. The eyes were like twin red suns.

Satterly grabbed Silverdun's arm. "Is that . . . is that the Thule Man?"

Silverdun cleared his throat. "It certainly looks that way."

"You said it was a fairy tale!" Satterly shouted.

"I said it was *probably* a fairy tale."

Thule man

The Thule Man locked eyes with Mauritane. He hung there, fingers dug into the cliff face, then his face twisted into a smile and he let himself drop to the ground. The sound of the impact was like the concussion of a spell-bomb, and the ground shook in its wake.

The Thule Man was not forty feet tall, as the story promised, but still taller and stronger than any man Mauritane had ever seen, and from the sound of his landing, he seemed to be made of stone. His skin certainly looked like stone, rough and pocked. He was covered in dust, the gray hair that sprouted from his head and ears was long and matted with filth, and he was dressed only in a loincloth made of crudely stitched buggane skins. Up close, his eyes blazed bright enough to sting Mauritane's eyes.

"I have come to the appointed time," the Thule Man said. "And I am met." His voice was deep and gravelly, but he spoke in a dialect of High Fae that reminded Mauritane of the oldest historical documents he'd read in the archives at the City Emerald. Mauritane strained to understand him.

"Which of you is Mauritane?"

Mauritane stepped forward. "I am," he answered, also in High Fae. Mauritane chanced a look around. The Unseelie soldiers remained on their knees; Ma Denha was looking desperately at his men's weapons, which lay in a pile out of reach. Satterly stood by Silverdun and Mave, his mouth hanging open. Only Raieve stood at the ready, sword out, ready to do battle.

"This is the instant!" said the Thule Man. "Beyond this I know nothing. I cannot see it. I am at the water's edge." He stared at Mauritane in wonder and fell silent. As the seconds passed, his smile faded and he appeared to grow uneasy.

"What is your business with me?" said Mauritane. "I do not know you."

The Thule Man's jaw clenched and his teeth ground together like stones. Sparks flew from between his lips.

"What's he doing?" Satterly asked.

"What is your business with me?" Mauritane repeated. "Are you indeed the Thule Man?"

"Yes," the Thule Man finally said, through gritted teeth.

"I know you only from a child's story."

The Thule Man's jaw unclenched. "Tell me that story," he said.

Mauritane looked to Silverdun, who shrugged, and to Raieve, who said, "I don't speak his tongue."

The Thule Man slammed a heavy fist into the rock wall behind him. "I have waited long enough for you. If I want the story, you will at least have the courtesy to give it to me."

Mauritane sighed, his mind working furiously. What was this creature after? Was it truly the Thule Man from the book on his father's mantel?

"As I recall," said Mauritane, annoyed at his own confusion, "it was during the Rauane Envedun-e, before the Great Reshaping, before Titania united the kingdom. The Thule Man was a High Magus from the city of . . . Renat, I believe. One of the last true Magi of the Thule Fae."

"No. It was the City Emerald," the Thule Man growled. "Renat was but a village in those days."

"The City Emerald, then," Mauritane continued. "He was an old man who feared death and devoted his studies to the pursuit of immortality. To that end he pushed beyond the boundaries of accepted thaumatics and began to experiment with forbidden things: the Black Arts, Blood Magic, that sort of thing.

"His colleagues cautioned him against that dangerous path, but he ignored them. Then they warned him sternly, but he threatened them. Then one day a serving girl discovered the bodies in his cellar; the victims of his diabolical experiments."

"The story does not mention," the Thule Man interrupted, "that I was by no means the only Magus in those days with bodies in his cellar, nor that the serving girl was directed there by a jealous colleague. But no matter. Pray, continue."

One of the Unseelie soldiers, one who hadn't yet spoken a word in Mauritane's presence, started up from his place by the fire. He ran naked to the stack of weapons and shook a sword from the pile. He shouted his battle cry and ran at the Thule Man, swinging his arm in a powerful arc, aiming for the tendons at the Thule Man's heel.

"Eben, stop!" shouted Ma Denha, but the soldier ignored him.

The blade, however, only struck the skin and recoiled. Eben began hacking furiously at the giant creature, but to no avail.

The Thule Man looked down, irritated, and plucked Eben from the ground. He wrapped his fists around the man's head and squeezed. Mauritane heard an ugly popping crunch and then Eben's body went limp. Blood flecked with gray trickled from the Thule Man's fingers.

"Hold!" shouted Mauritane, mainly to Raieve, who seemed ready to rush the giant herself. "This . . . man has made no move against us, and we are not in battle until I say so."

The Thule Man nodded. "Pray, continue," he said again, wiping his bloody hand upon his thigh.

Mauritane met his gaze for as long as he was able. When he was finally forced to look away, twin spots of red hung in his vision. "When his deeds were made public, the Magi exiled him from their city. From every city he visited thereafter, he was likewise turned away. Finally he came to the Contested Lands and went among the creatures and villains who lived there."

"True enough," muttered the Thule Man.

"Though exiled, however, the Thule Man did not give up his quest for immortality. In desperation, he found one of the shifting places and ate it, hoping it would confer upon him the secrets of time and space.

"But he was wrong. The shifting place proved too powerful for his depraved mind and his perverted *re*. It warped his body, turning him into a giant, and it unhinged his mind.

"And now he lives like a wild thing in the Contested Lands to this day. He finally discovered the secret of immortality, but he paid for it with his soul."

"Is that all?" said the Thule Man.

"No," answered Mauritane. "When I was a child, my mother often added that if I were to misbehave, the Thule Man would come and carry me off to the Contested Lands, where he would eat me."

The Thule Man roared with laughter at this. "It is not enough that I am become a cautionary tale about hubris, but now I am a bogeyman as well." He clapped his hands together in mirth and the shock from it pressed against Mauritane's eardrums.

"What is it that you want with me?" said Mauritane.

"Why do you ask me? Are you not Mauritane? Are you not He Who Clears the Path? Have I not awaited you these many thousands of years?"

Mauritane was baffled. What was he talking about?

"Ah, Mauritane," said Silverdun. "How much do you know about Arcadian mythology?"

"Nothing," said Mauritane.

"He Who Clears the Path is a phrase used in the *Vircest Ana*; it's one of those prophetic works that theologians dither over."

"Then you are mistaken," said Mauritane. "I am no Arcadian. Why do you say it?"

The Thule Man's eyes blazed white hot. "Because that is what I say now. The time quick approaches when my long-held instant ceases. My dying breath is nigh and you must not toy with me, not when I have remembered it for so long. You are the instrument, now give me the reason!"

Mauritane took a step forward. "You speak as if this meeting is preordained, but if that is so then I have no knowledge of it. I am afraid I have no reason to give. And if it is death you expect at my hands, I will not give it unless forced."

"In the dark days," said the Thule Man, his fists clenching and unclenching in a slow rhythm, "during the Unseelie Wars of the Great Reshaping, I did come to these lands, fleeing for my life! I was not afraid but neither would I gladly accept death's embrace. Not then and not ever. The shifting places were fresh then; they were the aftershocks of the most powerful offensive spells ever created. I discovered one that spread across millennia. I took it, shaped it into me. I became it. As you can see, I am quite changed.

"I see those millennia as you look across this mountain range, each season a pinnacle in a view from which I cannot avert my gaze. I have studied their contours, traced their minute gradations. I have found meaning in every hour, signs in the valleys between seconds. This Midwinter is the final peak, this day the foothill, this hour the shore of a dark sea. And at the shore of that sea I have seen you, Mauritane, for years beyond measure, waiting for me with that blade in your hand."

The Thule Man smashed his fist again, this time into the ground at Mauritane's feet. "And you dare to tell me you that you know me not! The past points to you! The years fall at your feet! Now you will tell me the reason for this moment, because I cannot see past it! I cannot see past the water's edge to the land beyond that will point backward and explain these signs! Tell me this and I will lie before you and you may thrust your saber into my eye and finish me!"

"I know nothing of this," Mauritane said, his voice flat.

The Thule Man rushed him then. Mauritane leapt aside, flinging himself to the earth. The creature was strong, but his movements were slow and whatever else he was, he was not a fighter. The Thule Man fell to his knees, then turned in an exaggerated motion and found Mauritane. He lashed out again and missed.

Raieve did not hesitate. She shouted, "Attack!" and ran toward Mauritane.

Silverdun drew his sword, but before he could run, a voice behind him shouted, "Wait!" He turned.

Ma Denha was standing, pointing at his weapons. "Let us fight! That thing killed one of my men and I will have my vengeance!"

Silverdun waved the tip of his sword at the man. "Nobody's stopping you," he answered.

"Can we have our clothes back first?"

Silverdun winced. "I don't think so," and ran at the Thule Man.

Mauritane dodged and stabbed, pushing the point of his saber as deeply into the creature's skin as he could, which wasn't very far. Drops of black blood oozed from the wounds, but not enough to cause any serious damage. His vision narrowed as the Thule Man swung wildly at him. From the corner of his eye, he saw first Raieve, then Silverdun, and then a few of the Unseelie soldiers arraying themselves around the thing, advancing and withdrawing with the Thule Man's movement and stabbing as Mauritane was doing.

Then Mauritane felt something odd. His *re* was slowly ebbing from him. He could almost see it draining into his opponent. The Thule Man inhaled sharply and moaned.

Clearly Mauritane was not alone in the sensation; Silverdun's blade drooped and he stumbled to his knees, just as the Thule Man's leg shot out, catching one of the Unseelie soldiers in the chest, a blow meant for Silverdun.

Mauritane thrust and thrust at the creature's midsection, looking for an opening in the neck or head but not finding one. The Thule Man's heavy fists never caught him full on, but he was kept constantly in motion in order to dodge them. Those fists only made contact once, glancing off Mauritane's shoulder, and the blow was enough to spin Mauritane fully around. And all the while, the *re* continued to drain out of him.

Once full of his adversaries' essence, the Thule Man raised his hands and began the words of a spell, ignoring the blades that plunged into his body all around him. Even as he spoke the first word, the sides of the valley trembled; a low humming sound filled the air. Mauritane felt his skin prickle. Whatever the spell was, it was powerful beyond measure. The Thule Man leaned down to look Mauritane in the eye and Mauritane's vision began to blur with the intensity. He continued speaking the spell, the words spoken in the ancient Thule tongue, so heavily accented that Mauritane could not understand a word. He had no idea what to expect.

But Mauritane never learned what the spell would have been, because before its wording was complete, Mauritane thrust out with his saber, lodging it firmly in the Thule Man's violently flaming right eye. "I can give you no reasons, but I will give you your release," he said.

The creature crumpled and flopped down onto the ground, causing noise but no more thunder. His eyes went orange, then red, then faded to black.

Mauritane shook his head, waiting for his vision to clear. Then he approached the body warily, pulling his sword from the Thule Man's eye socket. It shone a preternatural red in the darkness. He looked around and realized that night had fallen.

Winded, Mauritane staggered back to the fire. The Unseelie lieutenant joined him, still armed, sinking down beside him.

"You're not planning on using that against me, are you?"

"I prefer to fight better armored," said Ma Denha.

Mauritane looked and saw that Ma Denha was, of course, still naked. He stifled a laugh that bubbled up from deep inside him.

"You could have run," said Mauritane. "I appreciate that."

Ma Denha spat. "I wasn't helping you," he said. "I was avenging my man. You're but a Seelie who threatened us with torture and made one of my soldiers dishonor himself." He sneered at Mauritane. "Now it falls to me to slit his throat."

Mauritane nodded. "For what it's worth, I apologize."

Ma Denha stood up. "I'm sure you had your reasons. You appear to be an otherwise honorable man, and I'm not blind enough to think that all Seelie are dogs on sight. But if I weren't sure it would leave my men without a lieutenant, I'd offer you a challenge right here and now."

Mauritane stood as well, his knees shaking with fatigue. "Go then; I have had enough of fighting today as well. If you hurry, you'll probably find your horses a few miles ahead."

"I'm taking my boots with me."

"Whatever you like." Mauritane said.

As the Unseelie soldiers walked away into the night, dragging their dead along with them, Mauritane sat next to Raieve by the fire. Silverdun, Gray Mave, and Satterly were already eating supper from the rations they'd picked up in Estacana. Raieve said, "You're really just going to let them walk away?"

Mauritane looked down. His cloak and his leather chestpiece were covered in dust and blood. "I'm tired," he said.

the vagaries of fair

First Stag dawned gray and misty over the City Emerald, but by evening the clouds dispersed and it was a crystalline sky that Purane-Es beheld as his carriage crossed the Old Bridge into Puorry Lane. From here, looking out over the Emerald Bay from which the city took its name, the sky was the ceiling of a great domed hall, painted black with the tiny flames of witchlit candelabras flickering high overhead.

It was a relief to be back in the city and to be wearing fresh clothes—soft leather boots, silk breeches, and a heavenly cashmere cloak—instead of the all-weather uniform he'd worn to Crere Sulace. Purane-Es ran clean fingers through freshly washed and brushed hair and sighed with pleasure. Facing him in the carriage was a pair of bodyguards and Stilad, his aide. Stilad wore a pair of spectacles high on his nose, and the way the nose protruded from beneath his bald head gave him the mien of a hawk or an eagle. He leaned uncomfortably away from the pair of guards, his small frame comical next to theirs, studying a sheaf of documents he'd produced from a pocket of his voluminous overcoat.

"Does my father know I'm coming?" asked Purane-Es, still peering out the window.

"Yes sir," said Stilad, looking up. "You're expected. I'm told his staff has purchased a case of Eb Elen, twenty years old. He'll probably serve it with dinner."

Purane-Es nodded.

The home of Purane occupied most of a block in an ancient and renowned quarter of the city, where the cobblestones were worn sheer and even the lampposts and sidewalks seemed immutable, eternal. Puorry Lane was the scene of dozens of famous paintings and mestinas; it was the renowned birthplace of a hundred famous lords.

"Welcome, child," said Purane, meeting him at the door. "We have much to discuss."

Standing silhouetted in the doorway, Purane might have been a statue of himself. Still wearing his dress uniform from a troop review earlier in the day, he cut a perfectly clean line, his epaulets glistening gold from the hall lights. Seen in profile, his wide-set eyes and straight edge of a nose might have been a sculptor's gift to a lesser man. The only thing that belied that stony impression was the thick fluid coil of the Century Braid that spilled over his shoulder. The braid was a sign that he'd taken enough lives throughout his career that he no longer bothered to count them.

"Good evening, father," Purane-Es said, pulling off his gloves. "It's good to be back."

Once the proper filial courtesies had been disposed of, Purane ordered supper to be brought and they fell to a sumptuous meal of venison steaks in rose broth, seared stuffed hens, and poppy flowers. They ate in silence.

Finally, Purane pushed his plate away and leaned back in his chair, eyeing his son with a thoughtful frown.

"I trust your mission was a success," he said.

Purane-Es smiled. "As much as it could have been. I delivered my message."

"Don't put on that air of hurt, boy," said Purane. "I still believe this is part of something greater."

"As does Kallmer," Purane-Es said. "He's convinced that he'll get promoted to lieutenant captain once he figures out what that something is."

Purane waved the thought away. "Kallmer is nothing," he said. "You are far more secure than he." He wiped his chin with a silk napkin. "And what of poor Mauritane? How did he appear?"

"With sword in hand, is how he appeared," said Purane-Es. "He disarmed a guard and rushed me when he saw who I was."

Purane laughed out loud. "Incorrigible bastard, that Mauritane. I see you survived. What happened?"

"He's not the swordsman they claim he is. I disarmed him without much of a fight."

The Elder Purane raised an eyebrow. "Really? Prison must not have treated him well."

Purane-Es sat up straight. "Oh, and I suppose it's not possible that I could have bested him unless he were beaten down?"

Purane rolled his eyes. "Relax, son. It wasn't a criticism of you. Mauritane is one of the best fighters I've ever encountered. If he went down easily then he may not be in the best fighting condition. That may bode ill for this . . . whatever it is that the Queen has entrusted to him."

"He appeared to be none the weaker for his imprisonment, father. Perhaps I simply got lucky."

"Enough," said Purane, his voice rising slightly. "What did you learn of his mission? Did he appear to have any prior knowledge of it?"

Purane-Es shook his head. "No, if anything he seemed baffled that the Queen would call upon him."

Purane nodded. "Yes, I expected as much." He ordered wine from a servant and then pointed a finger at Purane-Es. "Whatever you do, don't underestimate Mauritane," he said. "He's a dangerous man. He's brilliant, he's ruthless, and he'll stop at nothing to achieve his goals. He's also utterly devoted to Her Majesty, or at least he was before that business in Beleriand. Make no mistake, child. Mauritane rose to his captaincy through skill alone, and if you take him too lightly, you won't live long to regret it."

Purane-Es allowed the slightest snarl to touch his upper lip. "I'll try to remember that."

"See that you do."

The servant reappeared with a dust-covered bottle and uncorked it before them, pouring two glasses from a crystal serving set on the dining room's mantel.

Purane-Es inhaled the bouquet, swirling the dark purple wine in his glass. "Eb Elen?" he asked, as though guessing.

"Yes," said Purane, grinning at his son's talent. "How old?"

Purane-Es took a sip, swishing it in his mouth. "A guess. Twenty years?"

"There's one thing I will give you credit for, boy, and that's your knowledge of spirits." Purane's mood lightened.

"Speaking of Mauritane," he said, deliberately changing the subject, "I've got a question about the guest list at your latest extravagance."

Purane-Es sighed. "I assume you're referring to one guest in particular?"

"I am," said Purane. "Tell me, son. Why have you invited the Lady Anne? Is she not still married to the man?"

"She is indeed. But she is also noble-born, and he is not. If she wishes to divorce him, she has merely to say it, and it is done."

Purane's eye's widened. "Are you telling me that you intend to court her?"

"I am. And I intend to win her."

"To what end?"

"She was the ideal wife for a Captain of the Guard, father. And someday I hope to inherit that position."

Purane chuckled. "Son, sometimes I don't know whether to praise you or to damn you. You're nothing like your brother was."

Purane-Es's mood drained at the mention of Purane-La. "No, father. I'm nothing like him. Someday, though, I think you'll see that it's a good thing."

The Lady Anne sat primly in the sitting room of Cucu's boutique, pretending that she wasn't being ignored in the same way the Cucu was pretending not to ignore her. When she'd entered the shop, Cucu had shot her an amazed glance, then let her eyes drift past the Lady Anne to another customer. Anne was amazed at the difference a few brief years could make.

As a person of quality, it was tacitly agreed among the patrons and staff at establishments such as this that the Lady Anne should be seen before any merchant's daughter or alderman's wife. She was noble-born, and when she was the wife of the Captain of the Royal Guard, she was given the proper respect. Now she was the wife of a traitor and a criminal, and Cucu could barely countenance her presence.

While she sat, the fluttering that stirred in the Lady Anne's stomach grew to a tremor. She felt ill. Upon receiving the invitation from this Purane-Es, she'd naively thought that her troubles were simply and suddenly behind her. But the sidelong glances from the ladies in Cucu's fitting room spoke volumes against that notion. She wanted to take Purane-Es's invitation from her handbag and show it around the shop, shouting, "See this! I am still one of you! I still exist!" But that wasn't possible. They would all have to wait. And when they saw her at the arm of a Commander in the Royal Guard, a man of unblemished character and noble birth, there would be no cautious looks.

Or would there? Could there be any doubt of her status once she was feted thus? Certainly not. When that day came, just a few nights hence, they would all be smiling at her from behind their fans, asking her to dance in their reels, join in their songs. And then it would be her turn to look sideways. Mauritane be damned.

While she sat, touching her hair with a carefully bred carelessness, a man entered the shop, wearing the uniform of some low office in the Queen's Guard. No soldier, this one wore spectacles and had no braids to adorn his bald head. Someone's aide, no doubt.

The aide strode to Cucu as though he were her master and pulled her aside. They spoke in whispers, every so often glancing in the Lady Anne's direction. Cucu's eyes widened, and she gasped. The man bowed slightly and left as quickly as he'd entered.

"Is that the Lady Anne?" cried Cucu, clutching her hands to her chest. "My darling woman, it's been so long I didn't recognize you. Why didn't you say something?" Cucu took Anne's hands and guided her gently to her feet. "Let me look at you," she said. "Oh, now don't I feel like an idiot?" She clucked her tongue.

The Lady Anne stared blankly at her as she struggled to understand. "The man who was just here, who was he?" she asked, in as haughty a voice as she could manage.

"Oh, him? Just an aide belonging to Purane-Es. A little sprite tells me you're to be the guest of honor at his upcoming fete! I'm so delighted to hear it!" She nearly squealed in what passed for delight. Behind her eyes, Anne read fear and, as much as she hated to admit it, it pleased her.

Anne breathed a sigh of satisfaction. Oh, how they would regret having treated her so poorly. "Think nothing of your oversight, dear Cucu," she said. "I've been hiding out from the witchlight, just waiting for the perfect moment to reappear."

Cucu nodded heartily. "Come, dearie. I've got just the thing for you. Glamoured butterflies, little flowers along the hem that bloom when you dance. It will look perfect on your delightful figure."

The Lady Anne almost said it out loud. Mauritane be damned!

the admiration of the novice/ by the water's edge

"Silverdun! Behind you!"

Mauritane followed his warning cry with a sidelong thrust of his saber. The tip of his blade caught the advancing buggane in the side and it fell to the ground screeching. Silverdun wheeled around, saw that Mauritane had taken it, then continued his spin, planting his dagger in the belly of the creature in front of him.

The bugganes had attacked quickly, without warning. There were perhaps thirty of them. They fell from the treetops, bodkins in hand, their long, sharp teeth bared. They were dressed in tattered rags, with curly, matted hair and lumpy green skin protruding from every seam. Their only sounds were the low grunts of their attacks and the high-pitched squeal of their pain.

When they'd appeared, Mauritane had immediately dismounted and ordered the others to do the same. "Take the horses away from the fighting," he'd called to Satterly, tossing the reins in Satterly's direction as he drew his sword and knife.

From the relative safety of the rim of the small valley where they'd been ambushed, Satterly watched the combat with awe, hardly believing that he might someday take part in such an encounter. With the admiration of the novice, he mentally noted the vast differences in the fighting styles of each of his companions.

Silverdun was a trickster, not so much a swordsman. He would taunt and goad his opponent into a corner from which the creature could not maneuver, then pin him with a short, quick thrust. He cajoled and shouted at the creatures, constantly trying to keep them off balance.

Raieve's chief weapon was her speed. None of the bugganes could touch her; her thin blade whipped and flashed in the morning sun, always finding her enemy's blade before it could find her. She twirled and danced around two of them at once, picking away at them until they fell.

Gray Mave took one buggane at a time, swinging his heavy sword almost like a cudgel. He was slow; but his blows, when they struck, were almost always lethal. His face was blank as he fought, years of martial training as a guard guiding his motions.

Satterly was impressed that Mauritane had somehow assembled what must have been the best team of swordsmen in all of Crere Sulace, not that he was an expert on such matters. How had he known how well their styles would interact? From where he stood, the fight was a foregone conclusion. The bugganes didn't stand a chance. Watching Mauritane, Satterly thought that he might have been able to take on all of the bugganes himself.

He watched Mauritane move, taking on three attackers at once while simultaneously ensuring that his companions were not surrounded or attacked from behind and guiding the melee away from where Satterly stood with the horses. Though it was difficult to see his face for all his movement, Satterly could swear that Mauritane looked almost pleased, as though fighting for him was like breathing for anyone else. He moved without apparent effort, whirling his blades around him with perfect fluid grace, as if he were demonstrating the art of sword fighting, rather than engaging in it.

"Try to remain uphill of them," Mauritane shouted, lashing out with an elbow that caught one of the creatures on the forehead, dropping it to the ground.

Gray Mave cried out, a low guttural sound, as his opponent caught him in the chest with a slash of its thin blade. Mauritane, not able to reach him, took his own attacker by the throat and lifted it off its feet like it was made of straw. He hurled the creature headlong toward where Gray Mave stood clutching his torso. The flying buggane slammed heavily into Mave's adversary. The two creatures' heads crashed together and blood sprayed from between them.

By then, only four of the bugganes remained. At some point, their leader had been slain and they began to fight warily, backing away rather than advancing. They started looking over their shoulders.

"Shall we let them run?" said Raieve, kicking one in the knees.

"No," said Mauritane. "Kill them all."

At that, two of the creatures began to flee. They were surprisingly swift. Silverdun hit one of them between the shoulder blades with his thrown dagger, but the other cut around behind a stand of trees and vanished.

"Streak!" shouted Mauritane. The horse cried out at Satterly's side and ran toward its master. Mauritane caught a stirrup with a raised left leg and swung his body astride the horse before the beast could stop. He kicked Streak forward, shouting, "Go!" He slapped the horse's flank with the flat of his sword.

"What's he doing?" shouted Satterly, as Gray Mave and Raieve finished off the remaining bugganes.

Silverdun shrugged. "I guess they made him angry."

Satterly watched as Mauritane chased the fleet creature, its long thin legs carrying it across the densely packed snow of the valley nearly as fast as Mauritane moved on horseback. Mauritane closed on it, came around slicing with his sword. The creature ducked, stumbled to the ground, and Mauritane fell on it, hacking with his blade.

When he returned, his chest was covered in the thick purplish blood of the thing.

"Why did you chase the creature down?" asked Raieve angrily. "It was retreating."

Mauritane wiped the blade of his sword on one of the fallen creatures' garments. "Bugganes travel in packs of up to a thousand. It wasn't retreating," he said. "It was going for reinforcements." He let the rag fall to the ground. "Gray Mave, how badly are you injured?"

"Not much more than a scratch," said Mave, touching the wound on his chest. "It got beneath the skin, but not by much."

"Put a poultice on it and watch it. The last thing we need is for you to die from an infected wound."

A strange look appeared on Gray Mave's face as he prodded the skin around his cut. "Yes, of course," he said.

"Good then," said Mauritane. "We need to get out of here. Quickly."

Satterly winced, looking to Mave for commiseration. Both of their back-sides were beginning to ache from Mauritane's idea of quickness. They had been two days already in the Contested Lands, and Mauritane had allowed nothing faster than a trot. The gait caused no trouble for the more experienced riders, but Satterly and Gray Mave both had bruises on their thighs from the constant slapping of the saddle. When they complained, Mauritane said only, "Learn to ride properly and it won't be a problem."

Aside from a few bandits, who generally fled at the sight of five armed horsemen, and the current buggane encounter, they had encountered few living things of any kind in the Contested Lands. Their chief enemy, in fact, had been the weather.

"The air in many of the shifting places is much warmer than our current wintry clime," Silverdun had explained as they crossed into the Contested Lands. "That difference creates storms more massive than any you've ever seen."

He had not been exaggerating. The first night saw wind and hail, with stones the size of pebbles striking the tents, bringing Gray Mave's down on top of him. The second day it rained without cease, the storm carried in on a warm, humid breeze from some distant shifting place. The water soaked through even the best-oiled skins leaving their rations, their clothing, even their bedrolls damp. The second night had not been pleasant for anyone.

Now, as they rode away from the small valley, a brisk wind picked up from the south, drying the sweat from their foreheads, and the sun shone through the tangle of clouds overhead, lifting water vapor from every tunic and saddle blanket.

"Tell me again why we have to ride so slowly?" said Satterly, cursing under his breath. "Aren't we in a hurry here?"

Gray Mave nodded sympathetically. "Lord Silverdun must keep watch for the shifting places," he said.

Satterly winced. "I know, Mave. I was just complaining." He groaned. "Do you have anything in your bag for saddle sores?"

"Aye," said Mave. "A concoction my mother taught me the use of. It's effective enough, but it does smell very much like shit."

"I'll pass."

"Suit yourself."

"I don't know about the rest of you," said Raieve, "but I actually feel better. Anticipating an attack from an unknown enemy is worse than the fight itself, in my mind."

Silverdun nodded but said nothing. Since his encounter with Faella, he'd spoken little, hiding his disfigured face behind the hood of his cloak. When asked about it, he would say only, "I can't remove it," and something about that seemed to disturb him deeply.

Finally, Mauritane said, "I agree," though his thoughts seemed to be elsewhere as well.

Later in the afternoon they came upon a rocky outcropping with a flat top that had been kept free of snow and ice by the wind. Though darkness was still more than an hour away, he ordered the others to make camp while he and Silverdun studied the charts.

"I don't see how we can make Sylvan by Fourth Stag at this rate," Silverdun confessed, marking their estimated position on one of the maps. "It's Thirty-first Swan now. That leaves us only five days, and by this chart we're easily seven days out at our current speed."

"I feared as much," said Mauritane, lighting his pipe and drawing on it thoughtfully. "And that's assuming we cross the Contested Lands without further molestation."

"Right. I don't think we have any choice."

"You think we should try the shifting places?"

"I don't see how we can avoid it at this point. It's dangerous, but from the tone of the Chamberlain's letter, it would appear that our lot is even graver if we fail to reach Sylvan in time."

"Do you believe you can find the right places?"

Silverdun nodded slowly, the hood of his cloak hiding his eyes. "It will be difficult, and we'll have to ride even more slowly. But if we come across a suitable patch of torn land, we can make up the time in a few hours."

"Then I believe we have no other viable alternative. Start explaining to Mave and Satterly how to ride into a shifting place while I go for water with Raieve. There is a matter I must discuss with her."

Silverdun raised his head and looked directly at Mauritane. "A matter?" he said, his lip turned up in a mischievous grin.

"Don't be coy, Silverdun," said Mauritane. "It ill suits you."

He rose and called out to Raieve, who had just finished raising her tent. "Come with me, Raieve. Bring the water skins. I believe I saw a stream as we approached." He pointed down a sloping hillside.

When they were away from the camp, he said, "Raieve, there is something we must discuss."

Raieve nodded. "Yes, I've thought so as well."

"Really?" said Mauritane. "We must not be speaking of the same matter. What is yours?"

Raieve bit her lip. "I . . . perhaps now is not the best time. I may have been mistaken."

Mauritane nodded and they walked in silence. He watched her from the corner of his eye. Sharp, proud, beautiful. A part of him ached to watch her.

"Say it anyway," said Mauritane. "Perhaps now is the best time."

Raieve looked at him. "I wanted to ask you. I'm merely curious." She bit her lip again, and Mauritane found that this tiny display of vulnerability on her part warmed his spirit.

"Yes?"

"I've noticed that you seem to be avoiding me. I wondered if perhaps I had done something to displease you."

Mauritane nodded slowly. "I'd like to say I don't know what you're talking about. That would be easier. But it would not be the truth."

It was Raieve's turn to nod. "So I have displeased you in some way."

"No!" said Mauritane, a bit louder than he had intended. "It's not that at all."

"What then?" She brushed her braids away from her face uneasily.

"It's difficult for me to discuss, Raieve, for many reasons. While we're on this mission, I am your captain, not your friend. It's not appropriate to discuss . . . personal matters."

"I think they should be discussed if they interfere with our working relationship, don't you?" Raieve raised an eyebrow.

"What do you want me to say, Raieve?" said Mauritane, stopping and turning to face her. "That I am attracted to you? That I watch you whenever you're not looking? That I wish things were different somehow?"

Raieve looked down. "Would it be so bad if you did say such things? Would it be so bad if I said them as well?" She looked up and their eyes met.

"Such things cannot be said between us," Mauritane finally said. "I have a wife in the City Emerald. I take my vows seriously."

"I know that," she said. "I know that, and I respect you for it. But it does not change how I feel."

"Nor I," Mauritane admitted.

They began walking again. "Then it seems we have reached an impasse," she said.

"It would seem so."

Raieve wiped her eye with the back of her sleeve, though Mauritane could see no tears there.

"What is the matter that you wished to discuss," she said, "since the other matter has so swiftly run its course?"

Mauritane set his jaw. "I believe one of the others is a spy, although which one of them, and for whom, I cannot say."

Raieve looked over her shoulder. "Are you certain? How do you know?"

"Several nights ago, before we crossed the Ebe, someone took a message jar from my saddlebags while we slept. I found the empty jar hidden away from the camp. Last night, another one disappeared. Streak told me that it was a man who had taken them each time, so I knew the spy could not be you."

Raieve snorted. "And here I was beginning to think you might actually trust me."

"I don't have the luxury of trusting anyone, Raieve," said Mauritane.

Raieve must have detected the weariness in his eyes. "No, it was foolish of me to say. I apologize." She began to bite her lip again. She noticed Mauritane's eyes on her and pursed her lips together instead. "Whom do you suspect?" she said.

"For a time I suspected Honeywell," said Mauritane. "He was extremely loyal, but he had a large family, and that could be used against him. After his death, I noticed nothing else unusual until last night."

"It seems unlikely that it would be Mave," Raieve said. "No one knew he was coming with us, him included, until after we'd left Crere Sulace."

Mauritane nodded. They reached the stream and knelt by the water's edge, dipping the first pair of skins into the current. "Of Satterly and Silverdun, I'd be more prone to suspect Silverdun, as much as I am loathe to admit it. He's lost much since his imprisonment and perhaps sees this as a way of restoring some of his former power."

"But what of Satterly?" she countered. "How much do you know about him? He's human, and it's well known that oaths mean nothing to them."

"I've thought about that as well," said Mauritane. The first skin full, he replaced its stopper and draped it on the bank, selecting another. Raieve took it from him and filled it herself.

"I don't trust Satterly at all," said Mauritane, "but I don't think he is the informer. For one, he appears to have had little contact with anyone outside of Crere Sulace, and for another, no one could have suspected that I would select him for this mission." He let the skin sink into the stream. "No, I fear that Silverdun is the one."

"Think of it from the other direction," said Raieve. "Who would place a spy among us?"

"The obvious choice would be Purane-Es," said Mauritane. "He, however, knows as much about this mission as I do. I also think he'd prefer that we fail."

"Perhaps the spy's purpose is to coordinate an ambush by Purane-Es himself?"

Mauritane shook his head. "Not unless he has retainers I don't know about. All of Purane-Es's men that I've seen were once under my command, and I doubt they would have the heart to slay me. Though I would not put it past him to hire mercenaries."

"Who else? The Queen? What about the Unseelie?"

"Honestly, I can't imagine," said Mauritane. "If only I knew why we were here, this would not be so difficult. How can I discern an enemy when I don't even know where I stand?"

He hung his head. "I have tried all my life to live as honorably as I knew how. I trusted those around me. I was loyal to my Queen and my country without question. And now I don't know who or what to trust anymore. After what we did to that Unseelie soldier, making him shame himself, I'm not even sure I trust my own motivations anymore. Where is the line between honor and duty? It used to be so clear to me but I can't see it anymore!"

Raieve touched his arm. "Listen to me," she said. "That Unseelie dog dishonored himself when he opened his mouth and started yapping. None of the others chose to do so. They had honor I never would have given their kind credit for. If a man flees from a battle, is the opposing general to blame for his calumny?"

"It was not a battle, and we deceived him. What bothers me is that I no longer know if my loyalty to my Queen truly justifies it."

"If it means anything, I think you are one of the most honorable men I have known, and your questioning of it only means that you're too wise to be satisfied with following blindly."

"Thank you," he said, his voice hesitant. "But of course now we have reason to believe that the Unseelie may be preparing an offensive. If that happens, then I fear none of this will even matter!"

Raieve's water skin was nearly full. Her hand slipped in the cold water and she let go of it, overbalancing. She began to fall toward the stream.

Mauritane reached out, catching both the water skin and her arm in his strong grip. He pulled her away from the water and they fell backward onto the dry grass. Their faces were only inches apart, their arms and legs touching. They remained motionless that way for a few breaths, their eyes locked and their lips barely apart.

Slowly, he reached out with his other arm and pulled her closer to him.

"Do not be sorry," she said. "Let your worries fall away, just for now." She closed her eyes and leaned forward, brushing her lips against his.

He lacked the strength to fight the current of her. In his confusion she was the only thing that currently made sense. He lowered her to the ground by the water's edge and let his heart take over.

the unusual properties of a shifting place

When morning came, Mauritane and Raieve again found themselves alone while the others slept. From their vantage point, they could see the roughly etched ground that stretched to the horizon in every direction, marked here and there with streams and rock formations and the misty shimmering patches that were the shifting places. From a distance, the shifting places could barely be made out against their surroundings. From the ground, however, they were nearly impossible to spot, and Silverdun had spent the past three days studiously avoiding them. Now, Mauritane was preparing to order his party directly into them, and the thought did nothing for his peace of mind.

"There is much to discuss after last night, don't you think?"

Mauritane sighed. "I suppose there is."

"Ha," Raieve laughed, in the bitter way that Mauritane found attractive. "It's good to know that even as decent a man as you hates to face the consequences of his desires. It speaks well of the others I've encountered in my life."

Mauritane scowled but did not rise to the bait. "I don't know how I feel about what happened last night."

Raieve's laugh dwindled away. "I think I know. You enjoyed yourself, but in the harsh light of day, you find that you regret what came so easily while the sun was set."

"No," he said. "I don't regret what happened. You'll think me a coward or a hypocrite because I don't wish to continue what I started last night. But that's the truth of it. I could offer a dozen excuses but that's all they would be. I won't insult you with them."

"Well," she said ruefully. "That's something then, isn't it?"

"I'm not sorry about what happened," he said.

"No, just loyal to something else."

"Is that wrong?" He glared at her.

"No," she said. "You're a loyal man, perhaps the most loyal I've met. But you should not confuse loyalty and love. I only hope the objects of your loyalty return your favors."

Mauritane changed the subject. "Last night you said you had a plan to catch the informer."

"Yes, but let's discuss it later. I don't think I want to talk to you right now."

Mauritane watched her walk away, knowing in his heart that he'd just let something precious slip through his fingers, knowing also that he wanted her now more than ever.

When they were all awake and ready to ride, Mauritane gathered them on horseback and asked them to pay attention. Raieve showed no trace of her earlier bitterness, and Mauritane felt certain his face was empty of emotion as well.

"I've decided that if we're going to reach Sylvan by Fourth Stag, we must ride into one of the quickened shifting places. Silverdun, explain what I mean."

Silverdun sat proudly on his roan, though he kept the cloak tightly hooded. "There are several different types of shifting place; I studied them extensively in my Academy days. Some are rents in the very stuff of matter. These are lethal, quick moving, and the hardest to spot. Riding into one of them is like riding into a brick wall. Others are fields in which time moves at a different rate from our own. Some are slowed, some are quickened. The quickened places tend to be narrow and stretch for many miles. If we can successfully ride into one of them, a day's ride within might be the equivalent of three or four days' ride at a normal pace."

"Apparent physical impossibilities aside," said Satterly, "it sounds like a great trick. What's the catch?"

"The difficulty is crossing the shifting place's border. If you ride through quickly, at a direction perpendicular to the boundary, you may experience nothing more than a brief headache. Take the crossing too slowly, or at too great an angle, and you could be shredded like a cabbage by the shearing forces of the boundary."

"But we can't even see them," said Satterly. "How do we know to make our approach?"

"I will be your eyes," said Silverdun. "The thing can be done; I've seen it before at the Academy. They have great engines there capable of producing such rifts."

Mauritane nodded. "Ordinarily, on a volunteer mission such as this, I would ask anyone who felt uncomfortable risking his life in such a manner to except himself. Here, though, your chances of survival in the Contested Lands alone are small at best. We ride as one, or we give up now and the rest of you make your escape."

"The rest of us?" said Mave. "Why wouldn't you come with us if we chose not to go?"

"I have my responsibilities," said Mauritane, his eyes on Raieve, who pretended not to notice. "I cannot absolve myself of them. You, however, have not taken the vows that I have."

"Well," said Satterly, "I've come this far. It seems dumb to turn back now."

"For once I agree with the human," said Silverdun. "I'm already receiving bruises; I at least want a chance at the prize."

"I have nothing to return to," said Mave quietly.

"And I have no wish to die alone," said Raieve.

Mauritane frowned. "Fine. It's decided. We ride in five minutes. Be ready."

Silverdun rode far ahead of the rest, carrying a bag of river stones in one hand. He moved slowly, at a walk, whistling out to the left, then to the right, then in front of him. Every so often he would take a stone from the bag and toss it sidearm in the direction of his last whistle. He'd carefully monitor the stone's spinning progress until it landed and fell still, then move on.

After an hour, their campsite was still in plain view behind them. Mauritane sensed that the anticipation of danger was beginning to wear thin, and he continually reminded them to remain alert. Every so often a stiff hot wind would burst forth from some unseen source, or a rain of ice crystals. Some of the shifting places produced eerie sounds, howls and keening wails, some sounding almost Fae or human. Overhead, the sun passed back and forth behind the swiftly moving clouds and the land grew dark and light in strange intervals.

Finally, Silverdun brought his mare to a halt. He threw one stone over his right shoulder, then another.

"This is it," he called back to Mauritane.

Mauritane rode up and stood beside him. He watched Silverdun throw a third stone. It left his hand at a leisurely pace, glinted silver for an instant, then seemed to explode toward the ground at an unbelievable speed. It hopped once, with the same unusual rapidity, then fell to the earth.

"May I?" said Mauritane.

"Be my guest." Silverdun dropped a handful of the water-smoothed stones into Mauritane's palm.

Mauritane threw one, watched the effect repeat, and then tossed the entire handful at once. The stones reached the boundary of the shifting place at minute intervals, and a series of bright silver flashes delineated the periphery of the oblong shifting place.

"It seems to be elongated toward the west," said Silverdun. "Just what we're looking for."

"Good," said Mauritane. "Let's get everyone inside. I'll go first, to show them how it's done and you guide the rest of them."

Silverdun nodded. "Watch closely," he said to the others, whom he waved toward him. "I've got Mauritane aimed precisely perpendicular to where the shifting place will be in a few moments. They don't call them shifting places for nothing, so you must be precise. On my signal, you start moving and I start counting. If you're not in contact with the boundary when I get to three, you're dead." Silverdun threw another stone, so Mauritane could see his target. Mauritane noted the location of the silver flash. He looked forward, seeing nothing, finding it difficult to believe that he was about to risk his life.

"Now," said Silverdun.

Mauritane kicked Streak into motion.

"One," said Silverdun.

He increased his speed, trying to gauge the distance just right.

"Two."

Mauritane realized that he was moving too quickly; he was about to overshoot the mark.

"Thr . . ."

Mauritane heard the beginning of Silverdun's count, but as the word was spoken something hit him in the chest and Silverdun's voice stretched out and fell, lower, lower, lower. Streak reared and nearly turned back; it was all Mauritane could do to force the animal to continue moving.

Then, suddenly, he was safely inside the shifting place. Despite the dull ache in his chest and a sharp pain behind his eyes, he was unharmed. He wheeled Streak around to view the others. Gray Mave was moving forward, his motions protracted, almost comically slow. Silverdun's count seemed to last an eternity. From within the shifting place, he could hear everything outside only as a muted basso roar. Silverdun's voice sounded like the glamoured voices given to dragon puppets in children's theater. Mave moved toward Mauritane at a snail's pace, as though he and his mount were swimming rather than walking.

The forelegs of Mave's gelding entered the shifting place first and for an instant it appeared as though the beast were stretched out along its spine, its forelegs many paces ahead of its hind legs. Gray Mave suddenly winced as though he'd been struck, then he flew into the space alongside Mauritane, traveling finally at a normal speed.

"Are you all right?" asked Mauritane, when Gray Mave's wince did not fade.

"I will be," said Mave. "The buggane's cut did not take the trip well." He held his hand out from his chest and there was fresh blood on his fingertips.

"Have Silverdun look at it when he comes through," said Mauritane. He tried to push out of his mind the thought that the buggane's blade might have been poisoned. "He may know some healing magic for it."

Mave nodded, guiding his horse out of the way for the next traveler.

Raieve was next. Mauritane watched her move, and the slowness of her motions only added to her grace. It was all he could do just to keep his eyes on her. He wanted to ride toward her, pull her up in front of him on Streak's back, and run. Far, far away. But it was not possible. There was a boundary between them that could not be crossed.

She made the crossing without incident, riding a few paces away from

Mauritane to watch Satterly and Silverdun come through. The motions of those outside had a hypnotic effect on those within.

Satterly almost made it but at the last moment pulled back on his reins. Just barely, but it was enough. His horse turned and Satterly hit the boundary at an angle, pitching forward from the beast's back. The horse stumbled in the strange glinting edge and fell onto its side. Satterly was propelled from the saddle, flying through the boundary and landing hard on the ground.

The horse did not make it. It became stuck in the periphery of the shifting place, and they all watched helplessly as the creature's limbs stretched until they broke, the bones shattering, internal organs bursting and spraying their fluids into the maelstrom of the shifting place's edge. The horse shrieked, a high piercing sound that lowered to a toneless rumble one moment, then lifted to the buzzing of an insect the next as the unknown forces that separated the shifting place from the solid world stretched the animal into an impossible shape, then dropped it to the ground, a shuddering sack of meat. Satterly's folded tent rolled out of the mess, completely unscathed, and stopped at Mauritane's feet.

"Oh, God!" shouted Satterly. He tried to stand, then lurched backward and righted himself, finally falling to his knees. He lowered his head and vomited his breakfast onto the soil.

Silverdun rode easily into the shifting place and stood over Satterly, his hideous face red with anger. "Damn you, human!" he hissed. "You could have gotten yourself killed! Why did you rein him back?"

Satterly shuddered. "I got scared!" he shouted. "I got scared and pulled back on accident. It was an accident!"

Silverdun shouted a curse in Elvish that Mauritane had never heard. "Now all of your supplies are gone, and you'll have to double up with someone the rest of the way. That is, unless we happen to stumble onto a horse ranch somewhere out here! I trust you are pleased with yourself?"

"Enough, Silverdun," said Mauritane, dismounting. "Everyone makes mistakes."

"He can ride with me," said Raieve. "I'm no burden on this mount."

Mauritane helped Satterly to his feet. "Are you hurt?" he asked.

Satterly dusted himself off. "Just bruised," he said. "I'll survive."

"Fine, then. You'll double with Raieve for now. Let's move while the shifting place is with us."

"Idiot!" shouted Silverdun, then he fell quiet.

They rode in silence for what seemed like many hours, though it was difficult to tell the duration with any precision. As they rode, the scenery beyond the shifting place moved with a bizarre rapidity, as though they were traveling much faster than Mauritane's other senses told him. The sun, however, barely moved in the sky overhead. The time that passed for them, whether ten hours or twelve, could not have been more than an hour or two in the outside world, for the sun was barely at its zenith when Mauritane's internal clock told him it should be night.

They stopped for a brief dinner. Only necessary words were spoken. It was obvious to Mauritane that the others were still thinking about the sight of Satterly's horse and how easily it could have been one of them. The meal was a grim one.

They mounted and rode again for another seemingly endless stretch. From beyond the shifting place, the sounds of the world were slow and eerie, muffled as though the entire world were buried beneath a pile of blankets.

They stopped again. As the hours wore on and became first one full day, then another, then perhaps a third, the silence among them became overwhelming, as though it were mandated. Each of them seemed lost in thought, pondering the world outside the shifting place as it caromed by in a hazy blur. When they stopped, they watched leaves fall from the trees in slow motion, examined with rapt expressions the fascinating properties of a stream whose waters intersected the shifting place, how it created a bizarre waterfall, the current flowing over some invisible obstacle which, Satterly pointed out in muttered tones, appeared to be the stream's own water.

Mauritane looked into the sky and at some point the sun had moved past its apex and was now nearing the horizon. He felt as though he could not stand another moment in that timeless space. Just ahead in the real world, for so Mauritane had begun to think of it, was a flat, grassy clearing between two dense stands of pine, suitable for a campsite.

"That's enough," he said. "Silverdun, get us out of here."

The relief was evident on every face. "Come along," said Silverdun quietly. "Getting out should be much easier than getting in. Just ride at a quick, steady pace." He pointed to the left. "That way."

Mauritane led Streak out of the shifting place and the world sped up again, taking on its usual sights and sounds. The others followed him out and the shift in their overall mood was palpable. Satterly breathed an audible sigh of release.

"Congratulations," said Mauritane, consulting his charts. "We covered four days' worth of ground in a single day."

"I, for one, felt all four of those days," said Silverdun wearily.

"We'll be in Sylvan ahead of schedule," said Mauritane, attempting to leaven the overall mood.

Only Gray Mave managed a smile. "Well, that's good, isn't it?"

Silverdun slung his tent from behind his saddle and stumbled around it. "It might sound that way after about ten hours of sleep. If anyone asks me to take the first watch, I'll cut his throat."

"I'll take first watch," said Raieve. "Then I plan to sleep for a very, very long time."

"Let's all get some rest," said Mauritane. "Once we've all rested, I want to speak to you. I believe a Hegest is long overdue."

Silverdun nodded soberly. "Yes, Mauritane. You're right. A Hegest would do us all some good."

"What's a Hegest?" said Satterly, his voice slow and tired.

"Wait until tomorrow," said Raieve. "You'll find out."

Mauritane watched her crawl into her tent. She looked back at him for a moment, pursed her lips, then turned and went inside.

hegest

Raieve knelt by the ice-covered poplar and dug her hands into the snow at its base. The previous night's freezing rain had left a clear sheen over everything: the tents, the trees, even the snowy ground. The ice bit into her skin, its jagged edges scoring her already-red hands with white lines. The ground had an empty, wintry smell.

Her hands began to sting. She dug around the base of the poplar's trunk, creating a narrow trench. Just as the needles of cold reached beneath her skin more than she could stand, she found what she was looking for.

The mushrooms were tiny, lavender in color, with wide, flat heads and narrow stems. Icthula. She collected them in her aching palm and brushed them into a jar. The icthula was the final ingredient, joining the spittle, bitter herbs, and radish seed already inside. She scooped a handful of snow into the jar and covered it with a lid, placing it gently on a tiny brazier she'd secreted away from camp.

Above her, at the top of the slope, she could hear Silverdun complaining about his food. She tried to ignore him.

She watched the jar intently until it boiled, holding her hands over the brazier to warm them. As the fire worked the frost from her fingers, they began to sting in a different way, like sharp pinpricks all over her flesh.

She stirred the jar's contents with a stick, watching it bubble, until the mixture turned a purplish color. She lifted the jar using the hem of her cloak and poured it out into another jar with a strip of cloth over the top as a strainer. She let the solid ingredients fall away.

The filtered icthula mixture stank horribly. With a grimace, she lifted it to her lips and drank the whole thing, wincing as the hot liquid scalded her tongue and the roof of her mouth. Almost immediately the drug began to take hold of her, drawing her out of herself until her awareness perched just outside her body, ready to leap out and explore its surroundings.

She stood up, her stomach turning at the dizzying perspective. She climbed the slope awkwardly, cursing herself for her own stupidity. It would have been a lot easier if she had returned to camp first.

The climb seemed to last hours but could not have, because when she returned to camp no one appeared to notice that she'd left.

"It's time," said Mauritane, as she appeared at the crest of the slope. "Have a seat."

Raieve took her place around a new fire, built upon the ashes of the fire from the night before. The flames wriggled and twisted like braids of light.

Mauritane let his eyes rest on her for a moment. The icthula drew her toward him and she held back, forcing herself to remain still for now. She gave him a silent nod and he turned away. The icthula had been her idea; the Hegest his. She'd seen the tiny mushrooms a few nights before and had told Mauritane about them during their ride through the shifting place. It was her mother's recipe she was using.

"Let's begin," said Mauritane.

"Before we start, can someone please tell me what we're doing?" said Satterly, his voice petulant.

Mauritane sighed. "The Hegest is a sharing of stories, but it is not simply words that we share. We speak of our history, our past, our vision for the future. These things bind us, each to the other. They remind us who we are and why we press forward, why we think and act as we do. The Hegest is a Self in words."

Raieve became lost in Mauritane's speech, remembering how he'd whispered into her ear as they made love, remembering the touch of his hand on her thighs and around her waist. The icthula painted the memories as bright as day, depositing her within the circle of his arms by a stream somewhere in the past. She had to shake her head to make the vision vanish.

"So, what do we, uh, do?" said Satterly.

"Watch," said Silverdun. "You'll get the idea."

Mauritane began. He took a handful of some cheap incense Silverdun had bought in Estacana and threw it into the fire.

"I am Mauritane, son of Ticumaura, son of Bael-La, son of Bael, son of Rumorgan, a child of the ancient Thule. On the day of my birth, an egret landed on my father's rooftop. I enlisted in Her Majesty's Royal Guard at the age of twelve. I saw the sun rise over the Plum Mountains on the longest day of the year. I killed an ogre with my bare hands when I was nineteen. I was made an officer in the Guard at the age of thirty, after leading my company to victory against the Unseelie at Midalel. I loved a woman, the Lady Anne, was married in the City Emerald. I was promoted to Captain of the Royal Guard after the death of Secon'anas."

Mauritane took a deep breath. "Now I am again in the Queen's service. That is an achievement I thought impossible only weeks ago. I am honored."

Raieve forced herself to remain calm, while all around her, Mauritane's words tried to draw her back to the stream's edge. She closed her eyes against them.

Silverdun's turn was next. Relying on the icthula to conceal her presence, she moved her awareness forward and into him.

"I am Perrin Alt, Lord Silverdun," he said, and the words were doubled in her mind as she heard them both from her own ears and within Silverdun's head. As he rattled off a list of ancestors that led backward through time toward the very first Lord Silverdun, she let herself ease into the stream of his mind and opened wide her awareness.

Silverdun's eyes were closed; she could see only blackness and splotches of red, tiny tracers of blue. It served as a soft screen against which Silverdun projected the images of his mind's theater, a cast of old, dusty portraits in a hallway, a single face in all of them, perhaps Silverdun's father. In the background of his mind played a repeating string motif that rose and fell in volume, repeating the same few measures over and over. Sometimes the violin was emphasized; sometimes there was a viola next to it, a cello. She recognized the tune as one he'd been whistling all morning.

As he spoke, she concentrated on the pictures displayed on his internal projection screen, like the silhouettes of puppets she'd seen in the markets of her youth. They were changing. Here was a woman holding Silverdun's hand, a mother.

"My mother converted to Arcadianism after I was born," she heard him say. "I was very young, and I remember only the singing."

The violin was silenced and a chorus of singers appeared, chanting a complex aria of love and faith.

"She attempted to raise me in her belief, but my father would have none of it. He feared that Mother's religious predilection would interfere with his popularity at court, and it did. His influence began to wane as stories spread of her evangelism at our country estates."

A hazy vision appeared, Silverdun's mother dressed in court finery, on her knees in a country town square, washing the feet of beggars. Then, Silverdun in his cell at Crere Sulace on his own knees, praying.

"During my last year at the Academy, my father was thrown by his horse and killed. I was the only son, and I was forced to return home to attend to my father's estate and appoint an overseer, for I was still too young to manage everything."

Another sensation, this one of touch, cool hands on Silverdun's shoulders and hair, the sweet, light touch of a mother's love.

"My mother came to me after the funeral and asked me to give all of our family's possessions to the church. I was overwhelmed by my father's death. I thought perhaps I heard Aba's voice in my head telling me it was the correct thing."

Raieve felt Silverdun's anger flow in his veins. "I was now Lord Silverdun and it was my choice to make. Unfortunately, however, my father had two brothers, neither of whom saw me as anything more than an obstacle between themselves and the Lordship. When they heard of my mother's plan, they ran to their friends at court. Some constables and court officials were bribed; a member of the polity gave a judge some friendly advice. I don't know exactly how they did it, but they had me convicted of treason, for what I'm not exactly sure. Only my title saved my life. With me out of the way, they could run the lands as they wished."

The flow of mental images came to a stop. Silverdun breathed deeply. "For years I pretended that I did not care. Lately, though, as I peer at my reflection in my tiny looking glass, I realize that I have allowed my uncles' hatred to make me ugly. Perhaps my mother was simple for believing what she believed. Or perhaps I really did hear the voice of Aba that day. Either way, if I make it out of here alive I'm going to see to it that the Arcadians have my family lands, if for no other reason than to chill the hearts of those thieving bastards." He smiled ruefully. "That is not the story I meant to tell, but I am glad I told it. I am honored."

Raieve pulled herself out of his mind, reeling from the overload of sensations. His thoughts were rapid and overwhelming, full of colors and details, sights and sounds. Her own thoughts were simple and direct by comparison. She took a few deep breaths within her own skin, trying to fight the sensations of the icthula for a moment of clear thought. She found herself unable to ward off the sensory glut and for a moment began to panic, nearly vomiting into the fire.

It was her turn next. She spoke carefully, trying to appear if not calm, then at least sane. "I am Raieve, daughter of Raelin. I am a daughter of the Heavy Sky Clan of Avalon. Our clan is one of the few remaining matriarchal clans on the steppes. I've been called a mongrel and half-breed all my life and shamed for it. I've done everything I can to prove myself a pure-hearted Avalona, if not pure in blood. Was it my mother's fault that an Unseelie soldier wrested her innocence from her when she was merely a girl? Was she any less of a woman for that? Am I?"

She realized she was getting carried away, the force of the icthula dragging her emotions upward and outward, like a cloud of anger. She told the rest of her story through gritted teeth, of the Unseelie invasion and the chaos of their withdrawal. She told of her failed voyage to the Seelie Kingdom to recruit men and purchase supplies for her clan's bid for peace. And she told of her murder of the Seelie official and her arrest.

When she was finished, she heard Satterly whisper, "This is supposed to make us feel better?" She almost laughed.

It was Gray Mave's turn next. She sent out her awareness and nestled around him, searching for a path inward to his mind's core. She found her way in through his eyes and as soon as she was inside, she could tell something was very wrong.

Inside Mave's mind there was a single word repeating over and over, like the sound of a windmill or waterwheel. The word was "Why?" It tumbled through every thought. "Why, why, why, why, why?"

As he leaned forward to begin his story, he clutched at his chest. Raieve could feel the burning soreness of the wound, the deep hot ache of it. The buggane's sword had been poisoned. Gray Mave was dying and he knew it. "I deserve this," he thought to himself.

A memory appeared in his mind, growing slowly from the blankness of his empty stare. Superimposed over the blurred image of the fire there came a creature, a hideous snaking thing that was translucent, nearly transparent, with pale leathery wings and sharp teeth. It called itself Bacamar.

"Look down," said Bacamar in the memory. Mave's internal viewpoint tilted downward and he stared into the mouth of something beyond death. It was the size of a world, the mouth, with lips like continents, red and burning. It had teeth, millions of them, and the teeth had eyes. The eyes were thick with mucous, scaly and green. They peered longingly toward Gray Mave.

"Do something for me," said Bacamar, "and I will let you live again."

Gray Mave swam toward Bacamar in the ice-cold ether of death and nodded. "Yes, anything, only do not let me fall into the mouth."

In the miasma of memory, Raieve could not hear the words that Bacamar spoke as the creature led Mave back down to the world of familiar things, back into himself, where he regained consciousness. He was lying on the floor of his home in Hawthorne with a terrible pain in his throat and Mauritane standing over him with a noose in his hands.

Raieve cried out, and it sounded strange to hear her own voice from across a campfire. Gray Mave's eyes turned to meet hers and she found herself suddenly back in her own body, staring back at him.

His eyes widened. He clutched at his head, clawing at his hair, then stood. She could see him wince from the pain in his chest.

"I'm sorry," he said. Then he ran.

Raieve said something to Mauritane, she was not sure what. But it resulted in Mauritane and Silverdun leaping to their feet and drawing their swords. So it made sense, whatever she'd said. They hurried after Mave, down the steep slope beyond which she'd found the icthula.

"What happened?" said Satterly.

Raieve ignored him. She leaned backward and looked at the sky, fascinated by the shapes of clouds and the brightness of the sun. They all seemed to be saying something to her, but their words were just beyond her vocabulary.

gray mave

Mauritane rushed after Mave, Silverdun at his side, down the snow-clad slope to the north where a wide river bowed across the valley below. Gray Mave ran ahead of them, clutching his chest either from lack of breath or from the sting of the buggane's wound. He stumbled on the root of a giant oak, fell to his knees, then pitched face forward into the snow. The morning sun glinted from the blade of his sword, the weapon lying useless at his feet.

"Is it a trick?" said Silverdun as they sidestepped down the slope.

"I don't know," said Mauritane. "Keep your weapon drawn anyway."

Gray Mave lay on his wide chest, huffing miserably, his face buried in the snow. "I'm sorry," he whimpered. When he lifted his face, a line of mucous dribbled from his nose onto the ground. He was sobbing.

Silverdun, his cloak wrapped around his head like a shawl, prodded the man with his sword. "Hold, Mave. Mauritane, what is the meaning of all this?"

Mauritane took one of the empty message jars from the pocket of his cloak and held it out to Silverdun. "Someone's been stealing these from my saddlebags at night. Raieve and I came up with a plan to catch him during our ride through the shifting place yesterday."

Silverdun eyed the jar suspiciously. "Who's been receiving these messages and to what end?"

"That's what we're about to find out. Sit up, Mave." Mauritane grabbed Mave's shoulder and tugged. Gray Mave winced at the pain in his chest and stood slowly, resting his hands on his knees halfway up.

"The wound from the buggane's sword," he chuffed, out of breath. "I think it's done me in. It's what I deserve, at least."

"Come back to camp, Mave," said Mauritane, without inflection. "We'll talk there."

Silverdun scowled behind his hood. "Why did you and Raieve not include me in your spy hunt?"

Mauritane looked at him. "Why do you think?" He pushed Mave forward and they began marching uphill.

Silverdun thought, then nodded. "Of course. You thought I might be the spy. What about Raieve, then? Did you not think to suspect her? Or did your cock already do a thorough enough examination?"

Mauritane stopped, then turned to Silverdun. "What did you say?"

"Nothing more than what you said to me when I bedded Faella on the Estacana road." He stood his ground. "Or did you think no one noticed your little tryst?"

Mauritane spat. "Fine, Silverdun. You've had your touché. Will there be anything else?"

Silverdun opened his mouth, but Mauritane's look silenced him.

With one of Silverdun's poultices applied to the wound, Gray Mave was able to rest by the fire, although his weeping had not slowed in the interim.

"I'm sorry," he continued to mutter. "I had no choice."

Mauritane knelt in front of him, gripping his sword by the forte, drawing in the snow with its tip. "I need answers, Mave," he said. "Will you tell me what I need to know?"

"All is lost," said Mave. "I am finished."

Mauritane took Mave by the chin. "Answers, Mave! Tell me!"

Gray Mave read the anger on Mauritane's face and began to speak, haltingly.

"I blamed you, Mauritane," he said. "I lost my position at the prison because of your stunt, attacking Purane-Es with my sword. Jem Alan laughed at me. He had me put out on the back road like a servant. I had twenty years service, Mauritane. Twenty years."

"I'm sorry for that," said Mauritane.

Gray Mave's lips drew down in a feeble snarl. "I had only ten years left before I started my pension."

He sat up, struggling against the wound in his chest. His shirt was undone, and blood had already soaked through Silverdun's dressings.

"Jem Alan refused me my wages, and the fee for my cottage was due the next day! He told me I should jump on the nearest fishing boat and go back to what Hawthorners do best."

Gray Mave sniffled. "But I could not go on a fishing boat. I'm terrified of the water, you see. Every time I go near the sea I have terrible premonitions of death. This Gift of Foresight is no gift to me. It's a curse!" He spat, and what landed on the snow was marbled red.

"So I did the only honorable thing. I made a noose and I stepped into it."

"And that is when I arrived," said Mauritane.

"No, no," said Mave, staring into the fire. "Much happened between those events.

"I . . . shuffled out of my body and I rose upward. Up, up, into the sky, like a bird. The air around me grew dark as night and the stars came out. There was something swimming between the stars. Something awful, like a snake made of water, with a dragon's wings! It was hideous, this thing. And then it spoke to me in a woman's voice.

"She said I could not go on yet, said that she wanted me to do things. And she said if I did not do them, then I would be sent somewhere . . . somewhere evil. She showed me the place. I cannot describe it. Like a mouth, a great mouth. With eyes."

Gray Mave looked at Mauritane and his eyes were glazed and unfocused. "I agreed," he said, sobbing again. "I agreed. Anything to avoid that mouth, those dripping eyes. She said you were coming to find me and that I should go with you. She said that I was to report to her master of our progress, our plans. She said if I gave you over to her master, she would let my spirit ride past the evil place."

He sniffled. The sound was a quiet roar. "It was your fault, don't you see? It was your fault to begin with. I said yes. I agreed. And that is how I have betrayed you."

Mauritane's jaw was set. "To whom have you betrayed us? Who is the creature's master?"

Mave covered his eyes with his hands. "He is Hy Pezho, Black Artist of the city of Mab!"

"Traitor!" Mauritane shouted. He drew back his sword and held it over Mave's head.

"Yes. Please," said Mave. "Please do it."

Mauritane hesitated. He looked across the campfire to Raieve, who was beginning to recover from her icthula trance. He thought he saw something in her face like pity. He lowered the weapon, deferring to her better nature.

"I cannot kill you, Mave," he said. "You have dishonored yourself, but not of your own accord. Besides, there is nothing to be done about it now. Silverdun tells me you will be dead of your wounds in a few days. Perhaps you can make peace with yourself before then."

Gray Mave fell backward onto the rocky ledge by the fire and rolled into a fetal position, cradling his bloody chest within his arms.

They rode on, Mauritane holding Mave's reins while Silverdun continued his watch for dangerous shifting places along the road. The sun overhead was bleached white, distant.

Past the river valley, the land grew more level. Mountains appeared in the distance, purple and indistinct.

"Those are the Western Mountains," said Silverdun. "We're close. We should be at Sylvan with time to spare."

Mauritane nodded. He divided his attentions between Gray Mave and Raieve. Mave rode slumped in the saddle, looking as though he might lose consciousness and fall to the ground at any moment. Raieve looked little better, though she did seem to be improving, however slowly. She swayed unsteadily in her seat, a faraway look in her eyes. Every few minutes she looked at Mauritane, her face flashing recognition, then looked away again.

The path they followed skirted the same broad river they'd seen earlier in the day, following its bends across the land. Though the road was more level, the growth of trees and brush became denser and they made no better time than before.

As the sun bent toward the west, something appeared ahead of them, a small figure seated atop a huge spherical boulder at the side of the path. They rode closer and Mauritane could see that it was a young Fae girl, perhaps eleven or twelve years of age. She was sitting on the rock with her legs drawn up to her chest, her arms wrapped tightly around them. She wore loose-fitting garments of a pliable, smooth fabric: a pair of long blue breeches fell to her feet, holes torn in the knees, and her cloak was shiny and puffy, like a burgundy cloud.

She spoke a greeting to them in a language unfamiliar to Mauritane's ears, waving shyly in their direction. When they were nearly upon her, she stepped down off of the rock and stood in the road. She spoke again, the same greeting. From here, Mauritane could see that the tips of her ears were badly injured; on either side of her head were tight-fitting bandages soaked through with blood, and the high points of the ears were missing entirely; they stopped well below the top of her head.

To Mauritane's surprise, Satterly started and rode forward, speaking in what appeared to be the same tongue. The girl laughed, said something back. The two of them held a brief, rapid conversation, smiling and pointing both at the other riders and down a narrow trail that angled from the main path into the woods.

"This is amazing," Satterly finally said, turning away from the girl. "She's human," he laughed. "And she's not alone. There's a settlement . . ."

Satterly was cut off by the sound of several resolute clicks that emanated from the brush.

"Don't move!" a voice bellowed in halting Common. Three human men stepped from the brush, dressed in a similar fashion as the girl, who now ran away giggling down the path. The men carried weapons of some kind, long metal tubes affixed to bases that resembled the wooden stocks of crossbows. "These weapons spit fire!" shouted one of the men, again in Common Fae. "So beware!" He was tall and lean, with a thin red beard and long hair tied back in a ponytail.

Satterly spoke out again in the human tongue. It was fast and incomprehensible, slurred syllables that ran into one another making each sentence sound like a single improbable word. The man responded with a lengthy tirade, pointing toward the Fae members of the party with a dark look on his face.

Satterly swallowed. He turned to Mauritane and said, "He says his name is Jim Broward, that we're all under arrest, and that you'd all better say your prayers."

the familiar

H y Pezho was enjoying tea in his new accommodations when the second sprite arrived. The tiny creature buzzed in through the thick damask drapes, drawing a line of sunshine across the splayed antique Thule rugs on the wooden floor. Hy Pezho's sitting room looked out over the violet hangings of the Royal Complex. From where he sat waiting for the sprite, he surveyed one of the most desirable fore views in the entire city, second only, perhaps, to Mab's. It was a fine thing.

"A message I have," sang the sprite, when it was in speaking range. It continued singing, off key, "a message I have for Hy Pezho! For Hy Pezho— that's the person who gets this note! A message, a message, it's my job to deliver it. Hey, Hy Pezho, don't say no!" The sprite finished its song with a tiny flourish, landing on the huge oak table in front of Hy Pezho. A bowl of fruit sat on the table; the sprite did a back flip onto a pear and sat.

Hy Pezho looked around carefully, then leaned toward the sprite. "Speak," he said.

"This message is full of names and dates and things. I should probably have some of that tea to settle my little brain first."

Hy Pezho reached into a pocket in his tunic and pulled out the tiny dried body of the first sprite the Awakened One had sent. He tossed the remains on the table.

"Ay-yi-yi!" said the sprite. "Looks like she got on your bad side. What did she do?"

"She kept asking for things and wouldn't shut up."

The sprite bit its tiny lip. "So, just the message then?"

Hy Pezho nodded.

"This message is from the Awakened One. He says that he has confirmed that a meeting will take place between the one called Mauritane and a Seelie Guard called Kallmer in the Rye Grove of Sylvan. Highsun. Fourth Stag. He doesn't know yet what the purpose of the meeting is, nor does Mauritane. He does say that interesting secrets will be revealed about the cuteness of sprites!" The sprite winced. "That last bit may have been a tiny embellishment on my part."

"Is that all?"

The sprite looked uncomfortably at the corpse of its former colleague. "Yep. Gotta run!" It took off backward and flitted out the window before Hy Pezho could catch it.

"Bacamar," said Hy Pezho. "Where are you?"

The familiar descended through the overhead canopy. "I was bathing in the sunlight above, master. Do you have need of me?"

"The prison guard suicide has given us what we need. They're meeting one of the Seelie Guard in Sylvan on Fourth Stag."

"The Seelie Queen leads a merry chase," said Bacamar, her lithe tongue extending and receding. "One presumes that a fascinating business will take place on that day."

Hy Pezho nodded absently. "I suppose," he said. "I don't really care, to be honest."

"Nor I," said Bacamar. She glided down to the floor and curled at Hy Pezho's feet. "Master?" she said quietly

"Yes, Bacamar?"

"I do not wish to pester you with my own small wants, but I am eager to be with you in the flesh. Are you not as eager as I?"

"I am," said Hy Pezho.

"It occurs to me," said Bacamar, "that if I am to inhabit the body of Queen Mab, then perhaps you will not be attracted to me. At close range she is an old and withered thing. Could I not possess the shape of a comely lady-in-waiting and live with you as your concubine?"

"In time, certainly." Hy Pezho was amused. "But we walk a very fine line. We will need a Queen who is . . . pliable, in order to execute our ultimate aims. Once I am enthroned, then all things are possible."

"I long to touch you with real flesh, my lord," said Bacamar. She rose up on her leathery wings and looked him in the eye. "And I will not be kept waiting forever."

"I will not keep you waiting, Bacamar." Hy Pezho rose and stroked her long body, his fingertips passing through her diaphanous skin.

"I understand that you are a man and that you have needs," said Bacamar, petulant. "But I do not want the stink of your whores on you when you are mine. Perhaps you might stop bedding them now and save yourself a bath."

"Jealousy does not become you, servant."

"You wound me."

"As you wound me with your mistrust."

They eyed each other. Hy Pezho took his cape from behind his chair and hurried out of the room, whistling the sprite's tune. Bacamar watched him go, her eyes filled with inhuman lust.

Queen Mab spread a chart on the wide oak table of her council chamber. She pointed to a spot on the map, a city poised at the base of a mountain range that occupied the map's western boundary. The city was within the Seelie Kingdom, less than a hair's breadth from that land's border with the Contested Lands.

"The Contested Lands are narrowest near Sylvan," she said. "For years the Seelie have expected an attack from Us there. Regina Titania has historically garrisoned several thousand of the Seelie Army there, along with a phalanx of her Royal Guard. During Midwinter those numbers are increased. Do you see how she gives away a weakness in this manner? In a time when snow and ice would reduce the likelihood of a campaign's success, she fortifies." She looked around. "Laese'am, do you have a question?"

"What weakness does Titania reveal by this?"

Mab smiled. "We do not know. That is what We plan to discover when We take Sylvan on Fourth Stag."

There was a shocked silence in the room, as each of the Prefects looked to the others, gaping. Only Hy Pezho was not surprised. He sat idly in his wide chair nearest the Queen, his arms folded across his chest.

"There are two great enemies to the south, gentlemen," said Mab. "We dealt a crushing blow to one of them when we brought low the city of Gefi. The Arcadian cult will make no further headway with Our subjects this year. But their priests and monks will be planning future incursions even now, and We must take Our war against them to the source.

"Our other foe is far less subtle and far better armed." A nervous chuckle ran through the chamber. "But We will tell you a secret about Regina Titania. When winter comes to the Seelie lands, she is weakened. We know this. We have scrutinized her carefully over the centuries, during our elongated cold war. She grows ever weaker as the season progresses and then one day, suddenly, she is renewed. The sun returns to the City Emerald. The ice cracks on the Ebe. All is well within the Great Seelie Keep. We would pay well to know what it is that rejuvenates her. Hy Pezho?"

Hy Pezho rose and cleared his throat, looking out over the assembled Prefects, those high and mighty who only weeks ago would not have acknowledged his existence. They were all watching him now. It was beautiful.

"My father had many spies within the Seelie Kingdom over the years. He lived a long time, and he had an excellent memory. He began to notice a recurring event that took place during the season the Seelie call Midwinter. The story is this: Titania sends out an emissary to some remote corner of her kingdom. The emissary returns to the City Emerald and within a day, the Queen is restored. The emissary and the location are never the same. Nothing else is known." He leaned forward, stabbing his finger on the map at Sylvan. "But this time we know who the emissary is. And this time we will be there waiting to discover his errand."

"Thank you, Hy Pezho. You have done well." Mab looked around. "You have all served Us well over the years. We do not need to tell you your orders. Go now and prepare for a southward advance and an assault on the Seelie border. Our trials will soon be at an end!"

the promenade route/ butterflies

On the day prior to Purane-Es's fete, the Lady Anne received a program booklet containing the promenade route, the seating chart, and the dance cards of the most prominent guests. She sorted through them happily, recalling the days when doing so was joyfully commonplace and dull. She traced the promenade route with her finger through Southmarket out the city wall to the Villa Diosa.

For days, the name of Purane-Es had plagued her. She knew of a Lord Purane who had replaced Mauritane as Guard Captain. Purane-Es was, of course, his second son. But that was not it. What about the first son, Purane-La? Was that name familiar?

Purane-La.

It was he that Mauritane had murdered, the commander in Beleriand. Of course.

How could she be so foolish? How had she not remembered the name? Two years ago the name of Purane-La had been on many lips, spoken quietly behind waving fans. At her husband's tribunal in the Aeropagus, the elder Purane sat on the side of the kingdom, whispering back and forth with the Queen's solicitor. The high tribunal was a long smear in her memory, three months of shame and horror that culminated in her exile. She had not wanted to remember.

Surely this Purane-Es was not as stupid as she. Certainly he had not forgotten. What, then, was his motivation? Was he an Arcadian convert, inviting her into his villa to offer forgiveness for her husband's act of cruelty? Certainly not. Arcadians did not throw lavish parties at their country villas; they gave away their villas to be used as monasteries and temples.

What did he want with her? She could not be any further humiliated, and her husband was no longer a concern to anyone. So why?

She considered not going, forgetting the whole thing. Then the courier arrived with her new dress from Cucu's and she knew that she would go, and that she would wear the dress, and the consequences be damned.

The Villa Diosa was an heirloom of the Purane lordship, a long graceful structure of white granite with open terraces and marble fountains and vast acreage. It sat astride a hilltop overlooking the city's southern wall. Its facade opened to a vast garden of fruit trees and low shrubs, narrow winding pathways meandering throughout. A staff of a dozen man-sized clockwork rabbits served drinks to the lesser nobility from silver trays; they went on two legs and wore waistcoats and spectacles, their mechanisms whirring as they bowed. The grounds had been spellwarmed at enormous expense, and a botanical mage had been called in to tease the flowers and grasses into temporary livelihood, belying the frigid weather that held outside the villa's gates.

About an hour before sunset, a horn sounded in the city below. From a garden overlook, a frail girl in pink clapped her hands and pointed down toward the city. The high noble promenade was beginning.

The Lady Anne sat in her sedan chair, her dress arranged perfectly around her with a white fur throw covering her against the cold. Her two carriers stood by at attention, awaiting the signal to lift her and begin the procession. She was third in line, following only after the Elder Purane and his current Lady, he astride a white cavalry stallion and she in a gold filigreed palanquin borne by eunuchs. Anne could not have asked to be placed more prominently in the riding order, but she felt conspicuous in spite of herself and sat low in her chair, feigning a dignified aloofness.

A horn sounded and the promenade began, to the applause and whistles of the assembled peasantry and merchant families. Standard-bearers in uniform plied the streets of Southmarket, conveying the emblems of the high nobility in attendance at the fete, walking in martial stride. Behind them came the flower girls in their petticoats and gaily colored bows, their cheeks red in the wintry air. The musicians followed, horns braying and tambourines crashing, performing popular songs so the assembled onlookers could sing along. Only when the musicians and crowd had finished a chorus of "Cir

Laeana, Titania" did the nobles begin moving. By then, the Lady Anne was shivering beneath her throw, doing her best to keep her public smile in place around chattering teeth.

> *Cir laeana, Titania,*
> *Tesede far'ara tila!*
> *Cir laeana, Titania,*
> *Tesede far'ara tila pi stel!*

The crowd cheered again as the song came to an end and the musicians launched into something new that Anne didn't know. Seeing the rapt attention in the faces she passed—especially the wide-eyed little girls, the daughters of merchants and street vendors clamoring for a glimpse of her gown— she began to experience anew the feeling of nobility, the essence that she once took for granted and now had to struggle to remember. It was like being reborn. She inhaled the brisk air and beamed nobly, having found the smile of a lady hiding not so far beneath the surface of her as she'd feared.

The promenade wound through the streets of Southmarket, past the market stalls themselves, and then out through one of the southern gates, the soldiers there standing at attention as the parade went by. Outside the city, the wide Nest Pirsil Road had been decorated with paper lanterns that glowed with pink and blue witchlight in honor of the family Purane. The lanterns marked their way up the hill to Villa Diosa, and the members of the promenade experienced the evening's "perfect moment" with a simultaneous sigh of approval. Just as the sun came to rest on the western horizon, painting the sky scarlet and orange, a vast collection of colored birds was released from hidden cages near the villa. Their wings caught the fading sunlight and they glowed in its warm radiance, beating out across the Emerald Bay and away.

In the comfort of the spellwarmed garden, the Lady Anne sipped a drink from a tall glass, wondering where she ought to stand in order to appear both indomitable and inconspicuous. She touched her hair lightly and felt around it to make sure the butterflies were still there.

Her dress was, as in days past, a Cucu original, a one-of-a-kind floor-length gown of deep royal blue silk, with a tastefully dipping neckline and a tight waist that accentuated her hips. Periwinkle and lavender glamoured butterflies dipped and swayed across the fabric of the gown, their motions carefully subdued to avoid distracting the gaze from the gown's wearer. They plied the two-dimensional sky of the dress slowly and gracefully, passing beneath her arms and twirling together at the skirt's hem. Cucu had added a floral comb to the ensemble, complete with a pair of its own butterflies that swooped around her head, remaining graciously out of her line of sight.

"Good evening, Lady," said a voice behind her. She turned and saw a man approaching her, tall and lean, wearing the dress uniform of a commander in the Royal Guard. He was young, with fair skin and glossy black hair that fell in a comely tangle of victory braids over his left shoulder. His face was serious as he bowed, but his eyes lit up and he smiled when their eyes met. "It is unkind of you to deprive the rest of us of your company. Such beauty must be shared; I cannot let you remain alone a moment longer." He took her hand and brushed his lips across it.

She looked around quickly, suppressing a smile. "There is no one convenient to introduce us formally," she whispered, looking past him.

"Then we must be bold," he said, copying her gaze, "and introduce ourselves."

She drew herself up to her full height, hesitating before she spoke. If her presence here was merely an exercise in cruelty, then the lovely young man would blanch and turn away when she spoke her name. Now was the time to find out, before she began to enjoy his company too much.

"I am the Lady Anne," she said regally, "daughter of Corwin." She studied his eyes for a trace of horror and found none. Instead, he grinned.

"Lady, I am honored," he said, bowing lower. "I am your host, Purane-Es."

She started. This was Purane-Es? She had expected something different, someone more military and detached, like his father. What game was this?

"It is I who am honored," she said. "The deeds of your family are well known, and your father has carried that tradition well."

He nodded. "You are gracious as well as beautiful, Lady. But come, the musicians are anxious, and it is our turn to dance." He held out his hand, and she reached out slowly, her own hand shaking though there was no chill, and took it.

Whatever else he was, Purane-Es was the most excellent dancer she'd ever encountered. He moved her effortlessly across the terrace in front of the bandstand, dipping and spinning her as though they were choreographed. The other couples on the floor paused and watched them move, awash in the music and the joy of their motion. As they danced, he held her waist firmly, his palm pressed against the small of her back. She felt the warmth in his fingers and experienced a sensation she hadn't felt in years: she felt safe, protected from what was unsure and fleeting, happily cocooned in the arms of another.

When the music finished, she was flushed from the exertion, her breathing a bit heavy. The other dancers applauded politely, smiling in their direction. It was joyous.

"Would you care for some refreshment?" said Purane-Es. She nodded, letting him lead her by the hand in her excitement.

The mechanical rabbits brought out trays of sparkling wines and Purane-Es took two glasses, handing her one. "I did not know that noble-born girls could dance as well as the traveling show waifs," he said, teasing her gently.

She pretended shock, then confided, "Perhaps I am no lady at all; you have not checked my credentials."

"In that case, I should have you thrown out. But," he said, shrugging, "you're making such an impression that I may wait for a while."

Other couples joined them. Purane-Es stood and talked happily for a long while, then realized he had several ladies remaining on his dance card and bowed out gracefully. Anne stood chatting with a trio of ladies-in-waiting to the Queen who giggled and asked to touch the butterflies in her hair. They knew her name; they must have known her past.

Prestige covers many wrinkles, her father would say. She was still noble-born. She was still desirable, even with Mauritane's weight hanging from her neck. It was even possible that Purane-Es knew her past and did not care, saw only her. Perhaps he had even spied her during the tribunal and loved her from afar, awaiting just this time to begin wooing her. It was possible, certainly. It was possible.

She drank more, danced more. She whispered with the ladies as they fanned themselves by the bandstand. She let herself become lost in merriment, as she once had in happier times, as she once had even with Mauritane, long ago.

The night sped past, a swirl of music, dancing, and wine. Finally the musicians packed up their instruments and the clockwork rabbits were retired. The guests disappeared in twos and threes and fours, their laughter carrying up from the road as they vanished into the night. She and Purane-Es were locked in conversation, talking of music and dancing and poetry and the intrigues of the court. When she looked up, she realized that they were alone on the huge terrace. The torches in the lawn had begun to burn out, one by one, and now only a few remained, casting long stuttering shadows on the far wall of the terrace.

"They've all gone," she said sadly.

"Perhaps," he said. "But you are still here, and that is all that matters."

"You've decided not to have me turned out after all?"

"No, I would not do such a foolish thing."

The Lady Anne suddenly felt too close, nervous. She took a step backward. "I must admit," she began carefully, "I was surprised to receive your invitation. We have never met, and . . ."

"And you wondered why I would invite the wife of my brother's murderer to a party. Is that what you meant to say?" Purane-Es leaned in, his arms folded across his chest.

"Well . . . I suppose so. Yes."

"I have a confession to make," he said. "I do not know how or why, but I feel as though I can trust you with anything. This evening we've spent together is unlike anything I've ever experienced. Do you feel the same?"

Astoundingly, she did. "I . . . yes." She looked away.

"The truth is that I lured you here under false pretenses," he said. "I brought you here hoping I could ply you with wine and music and make love to you and in some way exact revenge on Mauritane for what he did to my brother."

She gasped, holding her hand to her mouth. "You didn't!"

He nodded. "I did. At least, that was my plan." He balled his hands into fists and held them at his side. "I tell you this because I want you to believe what I say next. I have never met anyone like you. I find that, despite my prior motive, I am moved to strong emotions toward you. I find I want to pursue you in the courtly ways of love, write sonnets for you, sing ballads beneath your window. Those are the things I was made for. Not revenge. Not malice. I only want to be with you and the rest be damned. Vengeance be damned. Hatred be damned!"

"Mauritane be damned," she whispered.

"What?"

"Mauritane be damned," she said. "I am still his wife, and I still suffer his shame. I don't know if I can believe you. I want to, but I cannot."

"My lady," he said. "I am yours. Only let me prove it and I will." He was fearful, plaintive. He put his hands on her shoulders and kissed her, pressing his mouth against hers. She kissed back, searching for the truth of his words in his touch. If there was deceit in him, it was hidden from his hands and his mouth.

"If you want me," she said, "then marry me. That is how you shall prove your love."

Purane-Es released her and stood back. "Are you serious?" he said.

"I am, if you are. Marry me tomorrow and we will let all else pass away."

"I would give anything that it be so. But your marriage to Mauritane . . ."

"He is not of noble birth. I have only to say it and that marriage is over. Have a witness brought forth and I will say it before him. Then let us never speak that name again."

Purane-Es wrapped her in his arms. "Can this be?" he said. "That out of such anger can come such love?"

"Let it be so, darling," said the Lady Anne. "Let it be so."

She fell into his arms and they stayed that way, clinging to one another, until the sun returned and cast out the remaining shadows.

a matter of perspective

Satterly was unable to judge his emotional response. Amid the dread of being led single file at gunpoint toward an unknown destination, he felt a peculiar elation, the comfort of human voices and faces, almost a feeling of kinship. Only the red-haired man, Broward, spoke. The other two men and the young girl with the bandaged ears walked in silence through the wood. The girl, who had introduced herself to Satterly as Rachel, skipped ahead of them, seemingly oblivious to the gravity of the situation.

"Tell your friends that the first one of them that makes a sudden move gets buckshot in his face," said Broward. "Tell them that if anyone moves their hands funny or reaches for a weapon, or starts to chant or anything like that, we shoot first. Tell them."

Satterly repeated Broward's words to the others in Common, translating awkwardly.

"Where are they taking us?" asked Mauritane, his face grave.

"He hasn't said." Satterly turned and spoke to Broward in English. "Where are we going?" he asked.

"You'll find out," said Broward, urging him forward with the barrel of his shotgun.

Satterly turned back to Mauritane and shrugged. "He won't say."

"Are those weapons dangerous?" said Mauritane.

"Very. One shot at this range would take off your head."

Raieve walked beside Gray Mave, letting him put weight on her shoulder. "How are you, Mave?" she asked.

"I'll manage," he said, but his face was pale and he'd begun to breathe in ragged, wet puffs.

"He can't take much more of this," Raieve said.

Mauritane looked back at her and said nothing.

Silverdun walked at the front of the line, his eyes downcast.

After two or three hours of marching, the forest trail opened onto a clearing at the base of a tree-lined hill. Inside the clearing was a row of three small wooden huts, with simple open windows and roofs of thatch. A large fire pit was in the center; several more humans sat around it, one of them turning food on a spit. The clearing was empty of snow, floored with packed earth, and was surrounded by a fence made of dark, corrugated metal rods bound together with some kind of rope. One of the humans, a boy scarcely out of his teens, ran forward and pulled open a wide gate constructed of the same materials.

Behind the huts was a low structure, again of the corrugated metal rods, that reminded Satterly of the lion's cage in the circus. Taking the place of the lion, however, was a solitary Fae man, dressed in the robes of a scholar, seated in meditation at the cage's center.

Something in the clearing caught Satterly's eye. It was a machine; a short, wheeled contraption with a metal bar that rose from the chassis to make a handle. It was covered in rust. Satterly racked his brain trying to figure out what the thing could be, his mind settling on the single, narrow point of reference rather than try and comprehend the situation at large. He'd seen the thing before, or something very like it. A long time ago. What was it? He pondered the problem for the space of a few breaths, utterly confused. Then the answer hit him with an almost physical force.

It was a lawn mower.

Satterly stood in the center of the noise and activity around him, trying to take in the scene at once and failing. The girl Rachel was one of three children, all girls, all about the same age of nine or ten. All three of the children wore the same bandages on their ears. Everyone Satterly could see was dressed in a bizarre combination of tattered human clothing, animal skins, and cheap Fae cloaks and boots.

The woman talking to him, Linda, was in her fifties and had long curling gray hair tied loosely behind her head.

Linda walked alongside them as they were led past the huts toward the low metal cage. "We don't mean you any harm," she said. "At least, not most of us, anyway." She tried a weak smile. "Hopefully if everything goes as planned, we'll be out of your way and you guys can just go on with your lives."

"But what are we here for?" said Satterly. "What do you want with us?"

"You'll find out," she said. "Soon enough."

One of the men, the one who'd led the horses, now crossed in front of them and opened the cage's door. There was no lock, just a simple latching mechanism that worked from the outside.

"Oh, shit!" said Satterly. "The bars! Don't touch the bars!"

Silverdun, who had been reaching toward the side of the cage to steady himself, withdrew his hand. "Why not?" he said.

"This stuff that the cage is made of," said Satterly. "It's called rebar. It's made of steel. Steel is made of iron. You guys shouldn't go anywhere near it."

At the mention of the word "iron," all four of the Fae shrank back from the bars.

Once the cage door was shut, the Fae scholar raised his head and looked up at them as though he hadn't noticed anything prior to that moment.

"Hello," he said. "Welcome to hell."

"You'll forgive me," said the Unseelie scholar, who introduced himself as Hereg. "So many months surrounded by these bars have weakened me. I no longer know what year it is, I have trouble remembering. Is it Midwinter in the Seelie lands?"

Mauritane nodded. "Firstcome eludes us for awhile yet."

Hereg shook his head slowly. "I'm afraid it's my fault that you all have been brought here. For whatever is to happen, I am to blame."

"What is to happen, Hereg?" said Mauritane.

Hereg smiled. "In a cage, even the sons of Mab and the sons of Titania may comfort one another," he said. "Perhaps more of us ought to be in cages, eh?"

"We must bend to circumstances," said Mauritane. "But answer the question."

"Have any of you trained in the magical arts?" he asked.

"I have," said Silverdun, the hood finally pushed back, his hair flowing. "I studied Elements at Queensbridge."

"Ah," said Hereg, rocking forward and back on his knees. "A man of the

Elements. Just so, just so. You are, perhaps, aware of the Unseelie master of Spatial Thaumatics, Beozho? His *Works*?"

"I know of it," said Silverdun.

"Beozho teaches that the spaces between spaces may be enlarged and contracted. He describes the four axes of spatial harmony and gives manipulation keys for each." Hereg rocked forward and drew in the dirt with his finger, making a crude picture of a cube. "Using a premonitive resonator," he said, "the frequency of the space within a space may be tuned to achieve sufficient stability for passage, creating a doorway." He drew lines placing the cube upon a planar surface, then rubbed them out and altered the perspective with new lines. Depending on how Mauritane looked at the cube, it appeared to be either extended away from the plane or sinking into it.

"I cast runes to find one who is premonitively gifted," said Hereg, looking from Silverdun, to Mauritane, to Raieve, to Gray Mave. His eyes stopped on Mave and he pointed. "He is the one. He is to be my resonator."

"What does all this mean?" said Mauritane.

"I know what it means," said Silverdun. "He wants to use Gray Mave as a crowbar. Except instead of a packing crate, he's going to open a space between two worlds."

blue sky of earth

Night fell. Hereg continued to speak, sometimes veering into heavily accented High Fae that Satterly could not decipher. Eventually, he gave up listening and wandered to the edge of the enclosure. As much as he hated to admit it, none of it made sense to him. The nuts and bolts of Fae magic sounded more like an alien differential calculus than the storybook finger twiddling he'd once imagined. And it always came back to the equally alien concept of *re*, the magical essence, or sense, or power, or whatever it was that let the Fae do what they did. Trying to understand how Fae magic worked without being able to sense *re* was like trying to understand music theory without being able to hear.

It was unspoken among his fellows, but obvious, that the presence of iron in the bars was beginning to affect them unfavorably. It was bad luck even to speak of iron, so no one said it, but no one needed to. The mere proximity of it seemed to act as a depressant, dulling even Mauritane's reactions almost to the point of stupor.

Satterly stood at the edge of the cage and looked at the guard. He was a young man, no more than thirty, his long greasy hair tied back into a ponytail. He was so tall he had a tendency to hunch forward; his head was permanently angled outward like a turtle's. He leaned against the back of one of the huts, a shotgun within easy reach.

"How'd you get mixed up with them?" the man asked, out of nowhere.

"Me?" said Satterly, surprised. "Oh, well, it's a long story. My name's Brian Satterly."

"So y'all are all together? Like, you're friendly?"

Satterly puffed out his cheeks in thought. "Well, we're not enemies, but

I wouldn't go as far as to call us friends, either. Let's say we're joined by circumstance."

"Joined by circumstance," the man repeated, enunciating each word. "Huh."

Satterly frowned and changed the subject. "So, uh, what are all you people doing here? How did you get to this world?"

The man laughed. "We drove," he said.

The woman named Linda skirted around the huts and joined the guard at his post. Back near the fire, some of the children peered in their direction, but most of the adults looked studiously away, as though trying to ignore them. Linda whispered quietly with the guard for a few seconds, pointing and gesturing.

She stuffed her hands in the pockets of a pair of threadbare jeans and approached the cage. "You," she said, pointing at Satterly. "What's your name?"

"Brian Satterly," he said. "I just went through this with your friend."

"My name is Linda Grossman," she said. "I want to apologize for all of this."

"I'd feel better about that if I knew what 'all of this' was," said Satterly.

"Come on out," she said. "Just you, none of the others. We'll talk."

Satterly glanced back at Mauritane, who'd noticed Linda's approach and now was staring hard in her direction. "She says she wants me to go with her," said Satterly.

Mauritane's face was cold. "Go, find out what you can," he said. "We're having a bad time of it. I don't know how Hereg has survived so long in this cell."

Satterly nodded.

"Just reach around and undo the latch," Linda said, backing up. She turned to the young man. "Give me the Browning," she said. He scowled but reached into his coat and handed her a pistol without protest.

Satterly reached around and unhooked the latch, stepping carefully into the open clearing. Moonlight dyed the night a pale blue; it reflected from the snow at the forest's edge and caught in Linda's dark eyes.

"Come on," she said. "Let's talk."

She led him past the huts and continued walking, past the clearing and into the forest.

"See that hill over there?" she pointed.

Satterly nodded.

"That's where we're headed."

They walked in silence for a few seconds. Despite his confusion, Satterly felt comforted by Linda's presence. She was *normal*. She was a bridge back to the world he assumed he'd never see again. He imagined that if he were to lean in and smell her neck, he might begin to cry.

"I was elected to talk to you," she said, walking with her hands in the pockets of a too-large brown cloak. The butt of the pistol protruded alongside her right wrist. "I need you to understand a few things, and I want to know some things about you."

"Okay," Satterly said.

"Mainly, I want you to understand that we don't mean you any harm, not really. All we want is to get home. No one's going to get hurt if I have anything to say about it."

"That's fine, depending on how much say you have."

"I have almost enough." She scowled. "I need to know if you're willing to help us."

"I might be under different circumstances," Satterly said. "I don't appreciate being held prisoner. And my friends aren't doing so well in that cage of yours."

"We didn't . . . well, I didn't mean for that to happen. So, they are your friends then?"

"Why does everyone keep asking me that?"

"You're human, and you speak their language. We could use you to help us get back, and in return we'd be willing to take you with us. We just want to know what side you're on."

Satterly stopped short. "So you really have a way out of here?"

"Yes."

"I . . . I don't know. Most of the time I'm not even sure what I'm doing with those guys. I mean, I've been through a lot already with them, but . . . I don't know. Sometimes I don't even think they want me around."

"So you'll help us?"

Satterly thought. "I have to think. I said I'd go with them; we're on a mission, sort of."

"I can't tell you what to do," said Linda. "But we're leaving this place tomorrow, one way or the other. Like I said, I just don't want anyone to get hurt. If you help us, you can do whatever you want. Come with us, ride off with your Fae friends. I don't care. But I do know this: if you don't cooperate, Jim will force you. And I can't control him."

"I have a question," said Satterly. "Why didn't you just ask? Maybe we would have helped anyway. I don't understand why I would even need to choose sides."

"I guess Hereg hasn't explained the spell to you yet."

"No, not to me."

"The way I understand it, in order to create the way out, he needs the full premonition essence from a catalyst Fae. I have no idea what that means, but whatever it is, it's apparently quite painful."

"I see."

"Do you?" said Linda. She folded her arms across her chest. "Understand, Mister Satterly. Your companion might very well die tomorrow. There's nothing you can do about it. I didn't want it to happen this way, but there it is."

Satterly raised his voice. "You keep saying that things aren't the way you want them, so why don't you do something about it instead of forcing it all on me?"

"Because I was outvoted, Mister Satterly. I have children, and the people who outvoted me have guns. And they don't really like me very much as it is. That's my reality."

He followed her up a steep wooded trail. Halfway up the hillside, she stopped and walked away from the trail, beckoning him to follow. Something metal glinted in the filtered moonlight. A truck.

"What the hell?" said Satterly. It was a flatbed truck, mostly buried in drifting snow but recognizable. The bed of the truck held a number of open containers filled with metal rods in varying quantities.

"That explains the rebar everywhere," Satterly said.

"This stuff has saved our lives a dozen times," she said. "It's strong, it's durable, and the Fae avoid it like the plague."

"How did this thing get here?" said Satterly, baffled.

"I'm getting to that," said Linda.

They continued up the hill. Farther along, a yellow tow truck was wrapped around the trunk of a stout pine, its exposed edges mottled with old rust.

"We never found out what that guy's name was," said Linda, pointing at the truck. "No wallet." She shrugged. "When we buried him, we called him Joe, because that's what it said on the side of the truck, but he didn't look like a Joe to me."

Satterly said nothing, only goggled at the truck as he walked past it.

"This is my car," she said, pointing. A Volvo station wagon rested on its end in a ravine, its taillights pointing skyward. From where Satterly stood, he could reach out and touch the rear bumper.

"You're from Georgia," he said stupidly, pointing to the license plate. Then he noticed the registration tag on the plate. It had expired in June of 1994.

"How long have you been here?" he said, turning toward her.

"Fifteen years," she muttered. "We've been here fifteen years."

As they neared the top of the hill, Satterly began to notice a light emanating from there, steady and blue. It cast long shadows through the tree trunks. Glancing to the left, Satterly noticed that the ravine that held Linda's Volvo continued up the hillside, carving an ever-narrower depression into the earth. Curiously, as the ravine neared the top of the hill, it grew more rounded, more regular, smaller, until Satterly would have sworn it was a drainage ditch, something man-made. The source of the light was at the top of the ravine.

It was a blue sphere of light embedded in the ground, the size of a softball. It glowed with its own radiance, its makeup uncertain. Satterly took a step back and tried to comprehend what he was seeing.

The ravine narrowed even further, becoming shallower as it ascended the slope, finally diminishing in size to a perfectly rounded trench the size and shape of the blue patch of light. The glowing circle was nestled at the top of the depression, as though someone had been rolling it through the mud, leaving the ravine in its wake.

"There it is," said Linda simply. Satterly reached forward to touch the circle and she grabbed his hand. "Careful of the boundary," she said. "It's sharp; it'll take off your finger if you're not careful."

"What the hell is this thing?" said Satterly, kneeling and peering into the circle. He looked back at the ravine. "Did this little thing dig out that huge hole?"

She nodded. "It used to be much bigger," she said.

"What is it?"

"That, Mr. Satterly, is the blue sky of the planet Earth," said Linda. She knelt next to him, laying the pistol across her knees. "Or at least what you can see of it from here."

convertible

"Why couldn't you just walk back through?" said Satterly, gazing into the blue orb. "When it was bigger, I mean."

"I'll show you," she said. She picked up a stick from the ground, illuminated by the sphere's light. She poked the end of the stick into the light and they watched as it was torn to splinters by an unseen force.

"According to Hereg," she said, "the same force that's causing it to contract is distorting the membrane between the worlds. His spell is going to enlarge and smooth out the boundary." She dropped the stick and wiped her hands on her pant legs. "That's what he says, anyway. Who knows how much of it is true?"

"He's been in that cage a long time, I gather."

"Yes, we caught him trying to steal food from us about eighteen months ago. We'd built the cage to hold some of our more precious belongings, but with the storms and the cold weather, we had to move them. Again, locking him up like that wasn't my choice, but without him, we'd probably be dead by now."

"I gather that you and Jim Broward don't always see eye to eye," said Satterly, turning away from the light.

"You gather correctly," she said. "I don't think he's a bad man, we're just . . . very different. He's got his people, his son Chris, who was guarding you just now, and Meyer and Jenny, they're a younger couple. My son and I, we tend to see things differently from them."

"Sounds like it's been a long fifteen years," said Satterly.

"You can't even begin to imagine. There have been bad times. My husband was . . . he died in an argument with Jim about five years ago. Sometimes the Fae come; there's a city about a day's ride from here, you know. A place called Sylvan, in Seelie territory."

"Yes," said Satterly. "That's where we're headed."

"And the girls, the children." She bit her lip. "I worry about the children, the ones that were born here. All the time."

"Why do the girls all have bandages on their ears?" Satterly asked.

"I don't want to talk about that," said Linda.

"Tell me how you got here," said Satterly.

"It's a long story," she said. "Ancient history now."

"Up to you."

She leaned back on the ground, her hands stretched out behind her. "It was June," she said. "My husband and I were driving our son Jamie to camp in Tallulah Falls, Georgia. We'd just moved to Atlanta from Rochester, New York. We thought maybe Jamie would meet some other kids, you know. Do some archery, whatever kids do at those places. He was thirteen, it was an awkward age for him." She stopped and peered at Satterly in the darkness. "Why are you smiling?"

"I'm sorry," he said. "It's just that I haven't seen another human being or spoken English in so long, it actually seems more strange than my life does now. It's just bizarre, that's all."

"Anyway," she continued. "We got lost heading out to the camp. My husband was driving. We were following the signs out to Lake Rabun, just like the directions said, then we hit a fork that wasn't on the map. We went the wrong way, we doubled back, got lost. Next thing I knew we were on this little dirt road and I was afraid the Volvo was going to bottom out any second.

"I don't know what happened next. One second, we were on a tiny dirt road near Tallulah Falls, Georgia. The next second, there was no road. It just disappeared. Like that." She snapped her fingers. "The trees changed, the goddamn mountains changed. All around us. All at once. David lost control of the wheel and we pitched into that big ditch.

"In those days, the hole was huge. Big enough for Paul to drive a semi through, at least. He was the first one through, or at least the first one who stuck around. He'd been here almost a year when we showed up. He was on his way to a construction site, just minding his own business, then boom! He crashed his truck, landed in some godforsaken alternate dimension or whatever the hell this place is, and he was alone. For a year. I don't know how he survived, I honestly don't.

"When we got here, Paul kept trying to convince us that we somehow weren't in Georgia anymore. I mean, as far as we knew, we'd just taken a really wrong turn. We couldn't figure out why this truck driver had been living in a lean-to for a year when he could have just walked down to the interstate and hitched a ride. I was never a Girl Scout, but even I know that if you walk in one direction long enough, you're gonna hit road sooner or later."

"But there was no road," said Satterly.

"No, there was no road. Just the path you were coming along when they . . . you know."

"Yeah." Satterly scratched his nose. "They call them shifting places," he said. "They spring up spontaneously; they do all kinds of weird things."

Linda stood suddenly, wiping the dirt from her back. "None of that matters anymore," she said. "Let's get back."

Satterly walked in front of her back the way they'd come. Neither of them spoke. When they passed the huge fire in the center of the encampment on their way to the cage, all the humans sitting there watched them pass. The girls, their eyes glinting in the firelight, looked on somberly as they walked by.

"Think about it," said Linda. "If you want to come with us, we could use the help."

Satterly sat in the cage, leaning against the bars. They were cold to the touch. In the center, his friends huddled together, sleeping fitfully. Were they his friends? Satterly closed his eyes and thought about home.

The next morning dawned bright and crisp. A breeze blew in from the north, raising the temperature to something approximating comfort. Satterly awoke to the sounds of breakfast being cooked around the fire. He knelt by Mauritane and gently shook him awake. Mauritane's eyes were bloodshot, underlined with dark circles. Wordlessly, the two of them roused Raieve, Silverdun, and Gray Mave. Mave's wound had come open again during the night, and Mauritane tore off another length of his cloak to use as a bandage. Mave refused to stand and would not eat when food was finally brought to

them. Satterly helped replace Mave's bandages. He was beginning to understand how Mave was able to do what he'd done to them, and the thought
chilled him to his bones.

Jim Broward came and rattled the cage. "Well, Satterly, are you with us?"

Satterly stood, his stomach clenching in his chest. He walked to the bars
and nodded. "I'm with you," he said.

Broward nodded and opened the door of the cage.

From outside, the cave was invisible. Over time, the humans had encouraged trees and shrubs to grow over the opening, giving no indication that the
opening existed. Its mouth was low, no more than six feet high, overhung
with damp rock and fuzzy moss. Inside, though, the space was enormous;
their torches glinted off far walls and slowly filled the cavernous room with
light. There were two dark shapes huddled in the back of the space, black
oblongs that were oddly familiar to Satterly as they entered the cave.

Meyer Schrabe was about Satterly's age, somewhere in his thirties; he had
long, curly hair and a prominent nose that looked either broken or permanently swollen. According to Linda, he was on Jim Broward's side of things,
though to Satterly he seemed like a perfectly decent person, all things considered. The two girls, Polly and Jasmine, were his. They tagged along beside
the men while their mother, Jenny, lagged, talking with Linda and Linda's
daughter Rachel.

There were torches evenly spaced along the wall, set into sconces fashioned from the omnipresent rebar. Meyer left Satterly with the girls to go
light them.

"That's our daddy," said Polly, the older of the two. She watched her
father, a sweet loving look on her face.

"We love our daddy," said Jasmine. "We'll miss him."

Satterly kneeled next to Jasmine. "Why will you miss him?" he said,
humoring her. "Aren't you going with us?"

"No," said Jasmine. "We're not going anywhere."

"Says who?" Satterly frowned.

Polly looked at Jasmine. "Quiet, stupid," she said. "He doesn't know
things."

"Voila!" shouted Meyer. He stood by one of the oblongs in the cave's rear.

He reached for the edge of a tarpaulin and pulled, revealing a sight that nearly brought tears to Satterly's eyes.

It was a red convertible, big, wide. Human. A 1971 Pontiac LeMans.

"This is the greatest automobile ever made," said Meyer, brushing over the paint with his fingertips. "A wolf in sheep's clothing. A '71 LeMans Sport, with an extremely rare 355 horsepower, 455 cubic inch V8. Aluminum intake manifold. Four-barreled carb. Four on the floor, with a power top, Rally wheels, and an AM motherfucking eight-track stereo in the dash."

"Just ignore him," said Linda, coming up behind them. "Once he starts talking about that thing there's no stopping him."

Meyer rolled his eyes. "It's only the greatest car ever made," he said.

Satterly was shocked. "But it looks so good. There's no way this car's been here for fifteen years."

"Time goes slower in the cave; it's great for the cars, but every minute we spend back here is more like twenty outside. So get back there and start pushing."

"A shifting place," said Satterly. "Okay, but why are we doing this exactly?"

A few feet away, Jim Broward took the other tarp off of his own vehicle, a mideighties Chevy pickup that was badly dented on the passenger side.

"Linda take you out to see the Hole?" asked Meyer, pushing the Pontiac from the driver's side, holding the wheel through the window.

Satterly grunted a yes.

"Well, it's been climbing that hill for years now. Problem is that it's now about fifty feet off the ground in our world." He leaned into his work. "We have to bring it down to earth."

Satterly wiped his forehead. "Mind telling me why we can't just drive out of here?"

"Batteries won't hold a charge in this place," said Meyer. "We have to roll them down the hill."

Broward stood by his truck, scowling. "Hey, you two. Stop screwing around and push."

It was backbreaking work pushing the two automobiles up the sloped floor of the cavern and into the sunlight. Satterly looked out across the hilltop and could see what looked like spires protruding from the mist in the distance. Past the hilltop the ground grew level; only baked earth and lonely trees separated them from the veiled city.

"What's that?" he said, pointing.

"Fae city," said Meyer. "Sylvan. We don't go there."

In the other direction lay the blue sphere, or the Hole, as the humans called it. By day it wasn't particularly remarkable, just a swatch of color in the dirt. From the mouth of the cave, the ground sloped downward to where the Hole lay in its ditch.

"When we're ready, we'll start the cars rolling, pop the clutches, and put the cars in place running," said Meyer.

Paul, the former truck driver, reached into the back of Broward's pickup and pulled out a length of chain that rattled metallically against the truck bed. At its end was a menacing steel hook.

"Is it strong enough?" said Broward.

"How the hell should I know?" said Paul, tugging on the chain.

Broward nodded. "Let's go get Hereg."

Satterly felt a tug on his shirtsleeve. It was Rachel, Linda's daughter, her hair done up in pigtails.

"Mister," she said, her face grim. "Once they all leave, can we go with you to Sylvan?"

Satterly frowned. "No, honey, we're all going home together." She made him uncomfortable; it was a discomfort he'd experienced before but couldn't place.

Rachel shook her head. "I am home," she said. She reached for the bandages around her ears and tugged. They came off, revealing ragged wounds dried to the color of rust, sliced across the tops of her ears. Despite having been cut, however, Satterly could see the beginnings of two perfect points sprouting from the raw flesh. The points were perfectly formed, perfectly Fae.

"See," said Rachel. "I am home." She pointed at Satterly. "You don't know it yet, but so are you."

homecoming

Satterly stood in front of the cage, feeling like a traitor.

"Mauritane, can I talk to you?"

Mauritane seemed to take a moment to recognize him. The influence of the steel bars was worsening. "What?" he said, keeping his distance from Satterly and the bars.

"It's just that these people have found a way back to my world," said Satterly, looking into the dirt. "And that's all I wanted, was to go home. And also, you know, I was never much help to you anyway. It seemed like I was always getting in the way or getting yelled at or laughed at by somebody. So, I think I'm going to go ahead and leave with these people. Back to my world."

Satterly looked up at Mauritane. Mauritane's face was tired. The lines in his face were deeper and the number of gray hairs in his head seemed to have doubled since they'd met.

"You betray me as well?" said Mauritane. "I should have expected it from you. I never trusted you. I trusted Mave."

"This isn't easy for me," said Satterly. "If that's any consolation."

Mauritane laughed and staggered away, his right hand constantly reaching for a sword that was not there.

"Come on!" said Chris Broward. "We don't have all day!"

Chris and Meyer Schrabe opened the gate to the cage, shotguns at the ready. No one in the cage moved. Raieve glared out of the bars at Satterly and spat into the dirt.

The two men took Gray Mave beneath the arms and dragged him out of the enclosure, his boots making double lines in the muddy ground.

"God, this guy is heavy," said Meyer. "We should have brought my car around."

Satterly waved, awkwardly. "Bye," he said. "I'm sorry."

Only Raieve watched him leave. Silverdun and Mauritane sat with their eyes cast downward, their fingers drawing idly in the dirt.

Hereg had been painting symbols all morning long. He carried a handful of brushes, painting on every available surface in blue, green, and black. Meyer's wife, Jenny, followed him around with a collection of earthenware jars, each containing a different color of ink. Slowly, methodically, he worked. By midday he'd covered most of the small clearing with Fae runes, their multicolored angles and curves covering the stone ground, the rocks, the tree trunks. Even the flowers of the magnolia tree at the top of the hill had been painted. Meyer complained when Hereg began applying paint to the LeMans but relented after a withering stare from Broward.

As the day wore on, Satterly helped push the cars into place and attach the chains to the makeshift harness that Paul had built for the Hole. When sent down the hill to retrieve something from the huts, he studiously avoided his former companions in their cage. Several times he stopped and spoke with Linda. She was flushed and nervous; she continuously moved her hands. Satterly understood how she felt. As Hereg's spell came closer and closer to being cast, Satterly found himself remembering his own home, his own past. He started opening doors in his mind he'd long assumed shut for good.

"Do you know what?" he said to Linda. "I can't remember my phone number. I can remember my locker combination from tenth grade, but I'll be damned if I can remember my phone number. Can you?"

Linda thought long and hard and eventually gave up. "It started with a three. I'm pretty sure of that. But we'd just moved, so that's hardly my fault."

Satterly laughed. He threw his arms around Linda and hugged her. She hugged him back. What the hell? They were going home.

Hereg finished lighting his candles and approached Satterly, plucking bits of dried wax from his fingertips. "Your companions will survive," he said in halting English. "I will release them once you have gone."

"Thank you," said Satterly in Common. "I would hate for anything to happen to them because of me. I don't know how you survived so long in there."

"I am schooled in the mind and body art of meditation," Hereg said. "I taught them a few lessons. It should keep them."

"You seem much improved," said Satterly.

"One thing," said Hereg, still in English. "The children. Will your companions take them once you are gone? I know nothing of children, and they would not be welcome in the Unseelie lands."

Satterly squinted at the tired scholar. "Why do you say that? The children said the same thing. Aren't they coming with us?"

Hereg smiled, a broken, wasted gesture. "You'll see."

"The thing begins now!" he suddenly shouted. "Bring the wagons! Pray to your gods. The thing begins now!" He swept his robe around him and began chanting in an ancient dialect of High Fae. *"Kho felas she annas! Kho fel ess biret! Kho felas ammar!"*

Hereg walked to the ravine, where the blue sky of Earth glittered like a sapphire. He knelt before the sphere, where it rested in the center of his runic scrawl. Satterly tried in vain to follow what Hereg said. Something about naming the axes of motion, calling out for the true names of something, a plea to something deep within. Satterly could not understand it.

Satterly looked up to the hill's highest point, where the LeMans and the pickup waited. Meyer was behind the wheel of the convertible, and Jim Broward was in the truck. At a signal from Hereg, they both released their brakes and began rolling slowly down the hill. Dried leaves and twigs crackled beneath their tires. Broward's truck stuttered in its motion. The engine coughed and sputtered to life, lurching the truck forward. Broward revved the engine and dropped the truck into a higher gear.

Meyer's first shot at popping the clutch failed. The LeMans growled once, twice, then died, continuing its slow roll down the slope. Meyer, his hair blowing in the slight breeze of the car's motion, froze. The car continued to roll forward, now halfway down the slope. In a few moments he would be at the level of the ravine.

Broward honked his horn. Hereg jumped, frightened by the sudden noise. Meyer started, nodded furiously. He jerked the gearshift and leaned backward. The car coughed again and the engine caught, nearly bottoming out on the slope.

"Give it gas!" Broward shouted through his open window. Meyer closed his eyes, wincing. The LeMans eased slowly to life, idling with a steady roar.

"Let's go!" shouted Broward. "We don't have much time!"

They drove the rest of the way down the slope without incident, stopping at the level of the sphere. Their camp was at the far bottom of the hill, where the ravine expanded and leveled out into the forest.

Satterly felt a hand on his shoulder and turned. It was Linda. "Can you believe it?" she said. "It's really happening."

Satterly nodded. He looked to Hereg's left, where Gray Mave lay, tiny runic markings covering his entire naked body.

"Satterly!" cried Mave, catching his gaze. It came out as a whisper.

"Uh, I'll be back," Satterly said to Linda. He approached Gray Mave.

"I can already feel it beginning," said Mave. "I can feel him pulling the life out of me. He's channeling my Gift, pressing it into something larger. More focused. It's beautiful."

"You're going to be okay, Mave," said Satterly, kneeling beside him.

Mave shook his head and coughed. "I'm beyond that now, Satterly. Look." He ran his hands over his chest wound. The skin there was black and rotting. "Those bugganes really got me. It was all I deserved."

"No, Mave. You didn't deserve it. You did what you thought was right."

Mave reached out and took Satterly's hand in his. It was surprisingly soft and warm. "I always knew what I was doing was wrong," he said. "Now, at least I can atone for it."

"Dammit," said Satterly. "It's not true. You don't deserve to die."

Mave tried to sigh but only produced an ugly wet cough. "Satterly, don't cheapen my death. Let me be noble for once."

Satterly sat down hard on the hard ground. Somewhere, a hot wind began to blow.

"Move away," said Hereg, taking Satterly roughly by the shoulder. "Get out of the way."

Satterly stood up and stumbled backward, toward Linda.

Hereg turned to face the sphere and called out a few more phrases in his ancient dialect. The sphere began to shimmer, clouding over.

The wind Satterly had felt on the ground now grew to a gust, racing over his skin like the Santa Ana he'd felt once in Los Angeles, a wall of hot air. The trees around them began to shake and sway, their few brown leaves scattering and swirling in the wind.

Hereg cried out something unintelligible and the sphere began to grow. The wind intensified, and Satterly felt Linda holding on to him for balance. The whisper of the floating leaves grew to a roar as the trees for dozens of yards in every direction started to bow crazily, shaking loose entire branches that dropped to the earth with ugly thuds.

Satterly inhaled a mouthful of old dust, rotten ice, and dirt. The sphere was getting larger, now the size of Hereg, continuing to expand.

The sphere sat precariously now at the top of the ravine. Directly before it stood Hereg, the wind blowing his robes around him. Behind him, Mave lay on the ground, his body beginning to shake. His eyes were closed. Behind Mave, Meyer and Broward were backing their vehicles into position on either side of Mave's prostrate form.

Paul stood alongside holding a length of chain in each hand. When Meyer and Broward were in position, he ran behind the cars, clipping his chains to their frames. He walked along the chains' length, checking their position, allowing them to flow through his hands as he circumnavigated the sphere. When his circuit was complete, he nodded to Hereg, handing him a loop of heavy wire that terminated one of the chains. Hereg's skin crackled when it came into contact with the steel of the wire, but if he felt pain he did not show it.

"*Avi ke'ele!*" called Hereg. From what little he understood of Fae thaumatics, Satterly recognized the call to a triggered memory spell, a keyword that launched a previously spoken bit of magic. The sphere changed colors, sparked; electric flashes shimmered inside its depths. It became completely opaque, darkening to black.

"Now," said Hereg. "I have placed a solid skin around it. It can be moved now. But it must be done quickly!" He stepped quickly to the side, dragging Gray Mave's limp form with him.

Paul signaled to the men in the cars. He ran and stood behind the sphere, taking a coil of the chain, the one Satterly had seen earlier with the hook at the end, and hurling it over the black shape. Hereg caught his throw clumsily and fastened the hook to the loop that he held. He waved to the drivers again and leapt out of the way.

Both Broward and Meyer gunned their engines, dropping into first gear. Both autos lurched forward and stopped short as the chains pulled tight against the hard surface of the sphere. There was a sharp grinding sound, the chains grating against the unnatural black exterior of the Hole. For a few seconds, nothing happened. Then, slowly, the giant shape began to move.

They drove downhill, along the path that Linda had led Satterly up the night before. They passed the unknown dead man's tow truck, Linda's Volvo, Paul's semi. The Hole continued to expand, growing to the height of the tallest trees. It radiated waves of energy, like a hot road on a summer's day. The wind continued, boring its way through Satterly's clothes, stinging his eyes. He helped Hereg drag Gray Mave down the long hillside.

When they reached the bottom of the slope, the LeMans died. The sphere's progress halted instantly and Broward shut off his truck, leaping out of the cab.

"Let's go!" he shouted. "Let's go!"

"I need the blood now!" Hereg cried over the wind. He held a long curved knife.

"Take mine," shouted Broward. He held out his hand.

"What about the children?" Hereg shouted back.

"We share the same blood, all of us! They're our kids! They're human!"

Hereg shook his head. Broward took the knife from his hand and sliced across his own palm, letting his blood seep onto the ground.

"The blood of life calls its people homeward!" Hereg called, his voice suddenly grown louder, stronger. "Make straight the path!"

The sphere responded with a brilliant white flash. Suddenly, within its confines, a paved street appeared, lined with low brick homes. Young trees were dotted over freshly mowed lawns. Minivans and late-model sedans were parked in the driveways. It was dusk there.

For a few breaths, no one moved. No one spoke. Satterly only heard the sound of the wind rushing through him, saw only the vision of home. Hereg broke the tableau.

"It will only hold for a few minutes. You must go now!"

Broward threw up his hands. "You heard him! Go!" He pushed Paul toward the sphere. Paul took a deep breath and stepped across the threshold. The light coming across the border refracted his silhouette; for an instant he appeared in double. Then he was standing on the street. Tears were streaming down his eyes. He screamed soundlessly, his fist to the skies, laughing. One porch light snapped on, then another. Doors opened and young men in blue jeans and women with babies at their hips stepped onto their concrete porches. Paul sank to his knees, weeping.

"Let's go!" said Broward. He pushed his own son. "Go!"

Chris stepped through the Hole, much to the shock of the suburban audience. Satterly tried to imagine the lean, scraggly Chris Broward materializing from nowhere onto their master-planned street. He laughed out loud.

Meyer and Jenny each took one of their daughters' hands, and they walked toward the sphere, the four of them in a line. "Welcome home, girls!" shouted Meyer. They stepped across the boundary of the sphere.

The two parents doubled and passed through to Earth. The girls, however, simply walked through the Hole as though it were not there. When they had passed all the way through the mass of it, they stepped out the far side, their faces solemn.

Meyer and Jenny turned around, bewildered, looking for their children. They stepped backward toward the sphere, but when they reached its edge, they did not reappear. Instead, they disappeared from view entirely.

"They can't come back," whispered Satterly.

"Damn you, Hereg!" cried Broward. "Damn you to hell!" Broward pulled a pistol from his vest and leveled it at Hereg, his face red. "Send those girls through, right now!"

Hereg shouted back. "I told you I cannot. The children are Fae. They are children of the land, whether you wish it or not."

"Mother fucker," Broward roared. He pulled the trigger and Hereg's head snapped backward. He fell to the ground in a spray of red.

"Fucker!" shouted Broward. He stepped through the sphere, screaming.

Only six people remained on the Fae side of the sphere. The two Schrabe girls knelt on the ground, their faces buried in the dirt. Linda clutched her daughter Rachel to her chest, looking horrified toward the sphere. Her son,

Jamie stood by her, his hands clenched into fists. Satterly was riveted to the ground.

"Mom, what do we do?" said Jamie. It was the first time Satterly had heard him speak. "What do we do?"

"Go through, Jamie. Go through. We'll figure it out."

"What about Rachel?"

"Go!" she shouted. Jamie winced and ran, slurring through the Hole and onto the street.

Framed by the sphere, a small crowd was forming in the deceptively near street. Homeowners were pouring into the street to watch, jaws hanging, as filthy, long-haired people kept appearing from nowhere. Meyer and Jenny were shouting something from the other side that couldn't be heard. Paul had Meyer by the shoulders, holding him back. Jenny stumbled and fell to the ground.

"Go through, Rachel," Linda said, through tears, pleading. "Please, go through."

Rachel stepped forward, reaching out with her hands, her feet moving slowly. Her fingers penetrated the barrier of the Hole and she stepped through. She did not reappear on the street. Instead, she passed through the sphere just as Polly and Jasmine had and stood forlorn on the other side.

Linda shrieked. She sank to her knees, uttering unintelligible sounds. Flecks of Hereg's blood were smeared on her face.

Satterly looked from her to the Hole. It was beginning to dim, to fade slightly around the edges. For an instant he considered just leaving, stepping through that strange doorway and back into the world that he knew and that knew him. He almost took a step toward it but at the last second turned backward and looked toward the now-empty settlement. Mauritane was the only one of the three in the cage standing. His arms were crossed over his chest, his face was pale, his expression grim.

Satterly looked at Mauritane. They regarded each other across the distance. Satterly let his gaze fall to Linda. He knelt beside her and cradled her to his chest. She sank into him, sobbing uncontrollably. The Hole fluttered and sparked, shrinking rapidly until it became a mere pinhole of light against the battered snow.

Part Three

The High Priest: Let us begin our discussion with the topic of the Gifts, as you call them. If they are gifts, who has given them? And if not, then from where do they come?

Alpaurle: You seek to trap me in an answer, as do all those who claim to provide answers rather than seek them. The truth is not a fish that can be caught. It is the ocean in which we swim. Is a gift not a gift if the giver is unknown?

The High Priest: You seek to tangle me in words.

Alpaurle: No, I seek to unravel you with them.

The High Priest: What, then, is the nature of a Gift?

Alpaurle: I will ask you this question: when a man rides a horse up a mountain, do we say that he has climbed the mountain?

The High Priest: Of course. That is obvious.

Alpaurle: And yet the man has done nothing. The horse has climbed the mountain.

The High Priest: Again, your words grow out of your mouth like weeds strangling the sunlight.

Alpaurle: But is this not exactly how we speak when we speak of the Gifts? Do we not say that Stilzho has turned water into beer, when what we really mean is that Stilzho's Gift of Elements has done this thing?

[*A weak analogy here, Alpaurle's line of reasoning is supported more thoroughly in* The Magus, *Canto II, Verse 4.*]

The High Priest: How can you say that the Gift and the man are separate?

Alpaurle: I speak the words, but you cannot hear them. What is the man? What is the Gift? If a man uses a Gift, then how can he also be the Gift?

The High Priest: A man may use his arm, but we do not say that the man and the arm are separate.

Alpaurle: No, you are correct. We do not say that. Let me ask you another question, since you are so wise in matters of the body. If a man's arm is cut off, he is still a man, is he not?

The High Priest: Of course. That is a foolish question.

Alpaurle: And by your reasoning, the severed arm is also a man. Am I correct?

[*Alpaurle here has committed an error in logic, first noted by Raema of Ves in the Fourteenth Stag in Lamb. The error is known as the false-converse nature of attributes.*]

The High Priest: Anyone can see that what you say is false.

Alpaurle: And so is your suggestion that the man and the Gift are one.

The High Priest: Again you have tricked me with your quick tongue.

Alpaurle: You have tricked yourself, because I have only asked these questions of you for my own learning.

The High Priest: Fine, then man and Gift are not the same, as the followers of Aba have claimed. And yet do the Arcadians not speak falsely when they claim that the Gifts must be sanctified in their use?

Alpaurle: You must tell me the argument. Why do they claim the Gifts must be sanctified?

The High Priest: They claim that the Gifts are from Aba, and that whatever comes from Aba must be used to serve Aba.

Alpaurle: They claim also that Aba is the embodiment of the Good, do they not?

The High Priest: They do.

Alpaurle: Let us assume that they are correct for the moment. [*The remainder of the argument begs the question.*] If something contains only goodness, then nothing but good can issue from it, correct?

The High Priest: It seems obvious, but I suspect another trick.

Alpaurle: Then if the Gifts have come from Aba, must they not also be good?

The High Priest: That follows from your previous assertion.

Alpaurle: I have not asserted anything, but I think I understand your meaning. Will you not also say that what is good and what is holy are the same?

The High Priest: I had not thought of it, but it seems obvious as well, for that which is holy must always be good.

Alpaurle: And do we not sanctify what is holy?

The High Priest: Of course.

Alpaurle: So, by your reasoning, one can do nothing else than sanctify the Gifts! As you have said, that which comes from Aba must only be good, and therefore holy, and therefore sanctified.

The High Priest: You have deceived me again!

Alpaurle: Certainly it cannot be so, since you have made the assertions yourself. I merely asked questions of you . . .

Alpaurle
from *Conversations with the High Priest of Ulet, Conversation XXI*
Edited by Feven IV of the City Emerald

sylvan

Sylvan is the only city in all of the Seelie Kingdom that remains green in Midwinter. Beneath the snow, their slow motions hampered by hanging threads of ice, the grass continues to grow and the trees retain their leaves throughout that dark season. In rooftop gardens and tiny courtyards, delicate flowers of jasmine and honeysuckle exhale their fragile breath into the gauzy morning air. Hot springs lace the air with steam; mist roils in the city streets, warring with the cold, bathing the cobblestones and lampposts in milky white.

In Sylvan, only the Temple Aba-e stands above the mist. From its foundation on the Mount of Oak and Thorn, the grand edifice rises in three massive stone tiers. The bottom tier covers the entire mountaintop, its sides blackened by thousands of years of dirt and grime, the carts and hovels of the peasantry pressed against it. Its face is dappled with thousands of white dots, the prayers of commoners written for a few coppers by bored scribes, folded and pressed into cracks in the stone. The second tier is open to the air, composed only of columns and archways of stone, massive clear glass windows. A bridge leads from the Common Road to a gallery on this tier, where Fae from every station come and stand in the shade during hot summer days, gazing into their reflections in the dim silent pools, contemplating the statuary crafted by innumerable generations of Arcadian coenobites.

The third tier, that one is a mystery. Permanently shrouded in clouds, its shape is difficult to discern. Sometimes, at odd points during the day, a laboring farmer or strolling alderman will look up and see the clouds pierced by a shaft of golden light and, for an instant, he will see the Temple Aba-e in its entirety. But those moments are rare and unpredictable and have yet to yield a reliable account of the complete structure.

The rest of Sylvan bends toward the temple like flowers toward the sunlight. The Mountain of Oak and Thorn describes the city's western boundary, beyond which are the barren wastes where nothing survives. Sylvan nestles in a valley at the base of the mountain, her stained-glass spires and dizzying cobblestone streets winding up the hillside toward the temple. The garden villas and castles of the nobility line the rim of the valley's bowl, and the accommodations descend in rank proportional to their altitude. At the valley's floor, where the fog is thickest, the lowborn and outcast of Fae society mix in poverty and anonymity. The streets are narrow there, and the inns and bordellos display no signs or markings of any kind. From the City Center it is a long way to the silver-shrouded peak of Oak and Thorn, though they reside in the same city, and the one is but a few hours walk from the other.

On Peacock Lane, in the heart of the City Center, Fourth Stag dawned beneath a gray shroud that hid the temple from view. Evelyn Yeoh watched the dim smudge of sun climb above her back courtyard, drinking coffee while the children clambered out of bed upstairs. Morning was her only quiet time. The coffee, black and heavily sugared, was one of the few indulgences she allowed herself, and she exacted the maximum enjoyment possible from it.

She'd nearly finished her coffee when she heard a light tapping at the door. She approached the front room warily, longing for a world with door chains.

"Who is it?" she said.

"Brian Satterly," said a familiar voice from the other side of the door. "Is that you, Evelyn?"

Evelyn pulled the door wide and rushed to embrace him. She pulled back, holding his hands and looked at him. Could this be the same Brian Satterly that she'd sent from the real world just two years ago? He was tanned and thin, his hair worn long in the Fae fashion, dressed in the winter clothes of an Eastern merchant. You'd have to look twice at him to tell he was a human.

"Oh God, Brian," she said, hugging him close, "I didn't think I'd ever see you again! When they took you, I was horrified. But there was nothing I could do. You must understand . . ."

Satterly stopped her. "It's okay, Evelyn. I knew there was nothing you could do. I just need to know. Did Leila make it?"

Evelyn looked at him sadly; he'd never known, for all this time. "Yes!"

she cried. "Oh, yes! I visited your sister after you were . . . you know. She was devastated, of course, but little Leila is just fine. I don't think she remembers a thing."

"Thank God," said Satterly, his shoulders slumping in relief. "Oh, thank God!"

Looking over his shoulder, she noticed the woman and three children standing behind him. "My, you've been busy," she said, eyeing the children.

Satterly looked around and smiled wanly. "Very funny. Can we come in? I need to talk to you."

"Of course! What a silly question. Come in, come in." She pointed to the garden gate, where a strong Fae man stood with a sour expression. "Is your bodyguard coming, too?"

Satterly looked back. "Mauritane? I think it's best if he wait out there."

"If you say so." She blinked. "Come on upstairs. You can talk to me while I help the kids get ready. We can probably find some snacks for these three."

Evelyn knelt and looked at the girls. They were Fae children, dressed in rags, undernourished. "And what are your names?"

"I'm Rachel," said the tallest of the three. "And that's Jasmine and that's Polly."

Evelyn stood. "Human names," she said sadly. She let them all in and shut the door.

"That's kind of what I wanted to talk to you about," said Satterly. The woman still hadn't said anything. "This is Linda," he added.

Evelyn shook the woman's hand; she muttered a quiet hello.

They went upstairs. The kids, both human and changeling Fae, were in various stages of morning readiness. Some were still in bed, some were wrestling on the floor. The oldest children sat in the southern window seat reading books. The Fae children tended to be more sluggish in the morning; since they outnumbered the humans nearly two to one, the humans tended to rise early to have some time to themselves.

"Leala," Evelyn said, calling over one of the older Fae girls who was mostly awake. "Please take these darlings and get them something to eat, would you?"

"Yes, Miss Evelyn," said Leala, curtsying. "Come, we've got some wonderful peonies left over."

The girl named Rachel looked at the human woman for permission, but the woman was staring into space and didn't acknowledge her. Hesitantly, she followed Leala, as did the other girls.

"Brian, come over here," Evelyn said. "Tell me what's going on. How did you get here? I thought you were in prison for life."

"Here's the *Reader's Digest* version," said Satterly, scratching the three-day beard growth on his cheek. "I was in for life. But I got out in order to go on a kind of secret mission. I can't really talk about it. If we're successful, then we get pardoned. Or so they say, anyway. I don't even really know what the mission is."

"But it has something to do with this woman and her kids?"

Satterly sighed. "No, we picked them up along the way. They don't have anywhere to go, and I thought maybe you could help them."

Evelyn laughed. "What do you think this is, a boarding house?"

"Could you please just do it? For me?"

Evelyn blew out a puff of air. "I don't know, Brian. I suppose, for a little bit. The kids aren't a problem, but we'll have to find a place for your friend Linda. But I'm afraid I've got some bad news for her."

Satterly half smiled. "What's going on with them? They act Fae; they even look Fae."

"Were they born in Faerie?" she asked.

Satterly nodded. "I think so, yes."

"Human children born here are a very special case. It's happened before, and your friend isn't going to like what I tell her." She sighed, chuffing the hair out of her face with a heavy breath. "They can never go to our world, Brian. It would be dangerous . . . for everyone."

Evelyn and Satterly stared at each other. "How's she going to react when I tell her that?" Evelyn asked.

"I don't know. She was here with some people who had come to Faerie through a shifting place. She doesn't really know what's going on."

"I'll take care of her for you. I suppose that's the least I can do. But what about you?"

"I have to go with that guy, Mauritane."

"On your mission."

"Exactly."

"I see. Will you come back?"

"I don't know." Satterly frowned. "If I survive, I think so."

"You think so. Well, I suppose that's something."

The inn was smoky and dark; it smelled of urine and cheap wine. A pair of musicians leaned in the corner, banging out sounds that were barely musical but created enough noise to mask conversation. Mauritane and Raieve shared a bench across a worn table from Satterly and Silverdun.

"We meet Kallmer in the Rye Grove in two hours," said Mauritane. "We don't know what to expect, save that we are expected. I have never trusted Kallmer, though."

"And we know nothing of his orders," said Raieve.

Silverdun shook his head. "The Chamberlain's letter implied that he would be the source of whatever item we are to ferry to the City Emerald."

Raieve frowned. "So why not simply use this Kallmer to retrieve the item, whatever it is? Why are we involved?"

"Two possibilities," said Mauritane. "One is that we are being used as a decoy for some larger purpose."

"And the other," said Raieve, "is that Her Majesty needed a courier who wouldn't be missed."

"I don't believe so," said Silverdun. "I've been thinking about your experience at Crere Sulace, Mauritane."

"In the South Tower?" said Mauritane.

"Surely it was no coincidence that you had such an odd encounter on the eve of our adventure. The two must be related somehow."

Mauritane narrowed his eyes. "You think that the Queen is after me personally?"

"I don't know. You were Guard Captain for years. Certainly that puts you well within her sphere."

Mauritane shook his head. "I've never met Her Majesty personally, if that's what you mean."

"You were the Captain of her Guard and you never met her?"

"I'm not of noble blood. All of my instructions and briefings came through the Chamberlain."

"Could the Chamberlain be involved somehow?" said Silverdun. "Perhaps he's blamed something on you and this is his method of eliminating the evidence."

Mauritane stiffened. "I've never met a more loyal man than Marcuse. He is above reproach."

Silverdun nodded. "But is he above bribery? Is he above fault?"

"He is not involved. He would never be so bold."

"Enough of this," said Raieve, annoyed. "How are we to approach this Kallmer? What do we do if he's arranged an ambush?"

"You'll retreat. I'll remain and parlay with him. I am obligated to do so, regardless of the circumstances. You are not."

"I'm not leaving you," said Raieve.

"Nor I," said Silverdun.

Mauritane looked at Satterly, who was listening with his mouth drawn down in a deep frown.

"It's time to discuss what happened among the humans," said Mauritane.

Satterly nodded.

"You tried to escape. I told you I would kill you if you did."

Satterly nodded again. He looked at Mauritane, a tear forming in his left eye. "I know that's what you said. You have to do what you have to do. But I didn't leave. I could have, and I didn't. I stayed because I knew you all would have rotted in that cell if I hadn't. That has to count for something."

"You were, however, prepared to abandon our mission, when it was convenient for you to do so."

Satterly sighed. "I suppose I was."

Raieve cleared her throat. "If you're going to kill him, you should kill me as well. I would have done the same thing in his place."

Mauritane slammed his fist on the table. "Does a man's word mean nothing anywhere but here?" he shouted.

"I don't know," said Raieve. "I'm not a man."

"You know what I mean," said Mauritane.

"I do," said Raieve. "But I also know that there are some things that mean more than a promise. A promise, at its heart, is only words, Mauritane. Some things, like home, are far more powerful than any words."

"The question is academic," said Mauritane. "I'm not going to kill Satterly. We need him. Though it seems more foolish with each passing day, I
still think he is going to prove his value before this task is complete. We each
have a point of view on the matter of his guilt. When we are sipping brandies
around a fire someday, we can debate the subject. For now, let us move on."

They entered the Rye Grove from the south, just as the blurred sun
reached its zenith in the sky. The grove was in the northwest quadrant of the
city, in the shadow of the Temple Aba-e. The air was cold here, the icicles
long and thick on the eaves of gazebos and the branches of trees. The great
stones around which the grove was built were obsidian, ancient and rough.
They stood in a circle at the grove's center, each the height of two men, the
Sylvan altar in their center.

A man in the uniform of a Royal Guard Commander stood at the altar,
making an offering of wheat. He stood and brushed his gloved hands on his
trousers.

"Ho, Mauritane!" he called. His voice was strong and deep.

"Kallmer," said Mauritane.

"Welcome to Sylvan." Kallmer made a sweeping motion with his arm.

At the signal, dozens of soldiers stepped from their hiding places behind
the stones, the trees, even the grove's gates. Each one held a crossbow leveled
at Mauritane's head.

"They tell me you can catch crossbow bolts with your bare hands," called
Kallmer, approaching him. "But I do not think you can catch sixty."

He looked at Mauritane. "You can't, can you?"

what there was of commitment

Purane-Es embraced the Lady Anne at his father's gate. Puorry Lane was a swirl of snow, tiny dry flakes that moved in random directions and dusted their hair and shoulders. He kissed Anne and her lips were cold, but her mouth was warm.

"Be strong," she said. "Do not falter, love."

"I won't falter. There's nothing he can say to change my mind."

"Then let us go in," she said. "It's so cold out today."

A servant opened the door and led them to Purane's sitting room, where a merry fire burned in the grate. Drinks were waiting on a silver tray next to the settee. Lord Purane and his wife sat in matching chairs by the fire.

"Welcome!" said Purane, rising. "A toast to the newly married couple!" He smiled broadly.

Purane-Es drank the toast and put the glass down a bit too hard. He was neither accustomed nor inclined to defying his father, and he had no doubt it would be unpleasant.

After a few more formalities, Purane-Es interrupted. "Sir, there is an urgent matter I would discuss with you."

Purane regarded his son, taking his measure. "Yes, I was about to say the same thing."

Purane-Es swallowed hard and followed his father into the study, leaving the ladies to make polite conversation. Where the sitting room had been warm and inviting, the study was large, oppressive. The floor here was hard stone.

"There's been a development in the northwest," began Purane, drawing a map from a set of tall slots in the study wall. "It could not fit our plans more perfectly."

Purane-Es winced. "Our plans are the reason for my visit, sir."

Purane took a long look at his son, his eyes cool. "Speak, then."

"You know, father, that I did not choose a martial life for myself. That was Purane-La's goal, not mine."

"Go on."

"Anne is a revelation to me. She reminds me of what I have always wanted. She encourages me. I've sung for her some of my poems and ballads and she believes . . ."

Purane laughed out loud. "Poems? Ballads? What nonsense is this?"

"Perhaps you hadn't noticed that before Purane-La's death I was one of the most highly regarded balladeers at court. Given time I could be the best."

"Rubbish."

"It's not rubbish. It's what I want."

Purane laughed even louder. "What you want? What *you* want?" He sat at his desk and placed his hands carefully on the dark surface. "Son, I see that I have not communicated clearly. Your desires do not enter into my thoughts at all."

"Father!"

"Quiet, boy! Do you think I've worked all of these years building up the name Purane just so you could piss it away with your fancy new bride? If so, you're an even greater fool than I thought. I'd sooner see you dead than waste everything I've built."

"And you don't care that it means nothing to me?"

"I believe I've made myself clear on that point. We have a great opportunity here, to ensure our position at court, in the military, with the Queen Herself. When you arrive at the palace with the object of Her Majesty's desires, whatever in hell it may be, and Mauritane's traitorous head on a stake, our places will be secure. Secure, perhaps, for all time."

Purane-Es sat in a high-backed wooden chair. "And if I refuse?"

His father reached into a desk drawer and laid a sealed letter on the desk. "This comes from the Chamberlain," he said. "It's for you."

Purane-Es took the letter warily and opened it. "This is a set of orders," he said. "I've been called to Sylvan."

Purane nodded.

"Why is the Queen sending me where you want me to go? It makes no sense."

"If you'd been paying attention to current events instead of mooning over your new love, you might know why." He leaned back in his chair. "Our spies have sent word that Mab is moving south at her top speed. We believe she's massing forces at the border."

Purane-Es stared. "But it's been years since the last engagement at Midalel. Anyway, what's that to do with me? Is the Seelie Army no longer charged with protecting our borders?"

Purane shook his head. "You have no military sense, boy. Think! When the Seelie Army begins to concentrate along the border, they will quarter in Sylvan. And what will happen then?"

"The Beleriand rebels. They'll go mad."

"Exactly. Any concentration of force there will be construed as an offensive by the rebels. You're being sent to Sylvan to maintain the peace."

"But the rebels know my face. They despise me because of Mauritane. My presence will only incite them further."

Purane nodded.

"And that's exactly what you want, isn't it? You want to start a civil war!"

"The Beleriands and their Gossamer Rebellion are the only thing that stands between us and total control of the Kingdom. Mab is no threat during Midwinter. Her forces wouldn't make it to Midalel now, even if the border troops let them walk past. What better time to take care of the rebel problem?"

"And if the rebels attack first, then the Queen is not the aggressor and Her hands are clean in the eyes of the Arcadians."

"Precisely. Maybe you aren't as stupid as I thought." Purane paused while his son rolled his eyes. "And while all of this is going on, you will 'discover' Mauritane at large in Sylvan, wrest his prize from him, and present it to the Queen along with the heads of every Beleriand leader you can muster."

"And you will have orchestrated everything, behind the scenes, no doubt taking full credit for all. I won't do it."

"How childish you are! You are not my only remaining son. If you care not for your reputation, think of your younger brothers."

"I'm sorry, father. I won't do it."

"You won't do it."

"No."

Purane leaned back as far as his chair would allow and gazed at the ceiling. "Son, who sent the order for Purane-La to reduce the town of Stilbel to ashes?"

Purane-Es moved backward as if he'd been slapped. "What kind of question is that?"

"An important one. Who sent the order?"

"Mauritane sent the order."

Purane stood and edged around the table. "Mauritane sent no such order, and you know it. I was there, Purane-Es. I saw the look on Mauritane's face when he came upon the two of you. Had I been him, I might have slain your brother myself. He was enjoying himself a bit much for such a loathsome task."

"What are you suggesting, Father?"

"Only one person could have forged those orders. Only one person was in a position to do so."

Purane-Es lowered his head. "How long have you known it was I?"

Purane's lips pursed. He leaned close into his son's face, and Purane-Es could smell the wine on his breath. "I did not know it for certain until this very moment."

"I only wanted to cause trouble for Purane-La. I wanted everyone . . . you, to see how cruel he'd become. If I had known how much trouble it would have caused I would never have done it."

With a speed that belied his age, the Elder Purane lashed out at Purane-Es with the back of his hand, sending the younger man sprawling backward onto the floor. "Why would you go out of your way to shame your own brother?"

Purane-Es pulled himself up onto his elbows. "I hated Purane-La. With every bit of me, I despised him. I wanted to hurt him. I regret it now. Not a day goes by that I do not think of it."

"How nice," said Purane. "And all it cost was the life of your brother and the career of one of our finest Guard Captains."

Purane-Es stood, shaking with rage. "I see that you have not suffered overmuch as a result," he sneered.

"I made the best of an ugly situation. As I am doing now. If you are not in Sylvan in four days, I will go to the Queen Herself and tell her what I know about you and our dear Mauritane."

"You wouldn't! You'd be ruined along with me."

"Anything less than complete success *is* ruin, son. Your brother knew that, if nothing else. Before you had him killed." Purane stood and adjusted his long coat. "Now, will you go break the news to your lovely new wife, or shall I?"

Purane-Es swiped a tear away with his sleeve. "I'm glad Purane-La is dead," he snapped.

Purane brushed past him to open the door. "I can't tell you, boy," he whispered, "how many times I've wished it had been you instead."

the number of interpretations/
a relative's commendation

The Castle Laco straddled the rim of Sylvan's valley. From its southern terraces, the Temple Aba-e and the mountains beyond created a lavish backdrop to the city below. To the north, at the edge of vision, was the outpost of Selafae. Beyond it lay the Unseelie lands. Mauritane glimpsed both views as they were marched through the palace and into its cellars.

In centuries past, the palace had served for a time as headquarters for the Seelie Army's western division. An ancient wine cellar had been converted into a stockade and it was here that Kallmer's men led Mauritane, Raieve, Silverdun, and Satterly, prodding them into a wide cell with the tips of their lances. The far wall was packed earth, the bars narrowly set and of polished hardened silver.

Kallmer stood outside the cell clucking his tongue while a pair of soldiers removed the prisoners' manacles and withdrew, locking the door behind them.

"Who would have believed this tableau three years ago, eh, Captain?" said Kallmer. He laced his fingers behind his back and began to pace. "I, the—how did you put it in your review?—the undisciplined and unreliable lieutenant, now promoted to Commander of the Sylvan region, standing watch over you, now fugitive and traitor. The Arcadians say that Aba's will is rarely what we predict, and I am tempted to believe them."

Mauritane strode forward and took the bars in his hands, furious at being thus imprisoned twice in a week. "Are these your orders, Kallmer? Or are you writing your own?"

Kallmer smiled. "As one's distance from the City Emerald increases, so does the number of interpretations one may discover in his orders. I believe I may have been instructed simply to send you on your merry way, but there was no provision against detaining you briefly for a chat, was there?" He stopped pacing. "Anyway, my position is a self-auditing one, so if I feel I have made a breach of conduct, you can be certain that I will chastise myself appropriately once all is said and done."

Mauritane loosened his grip on the bars with some effort. "What do you want?" he said. "I have orders as well, and mine are less open to interpretation."

Kallmer nodded slowly. "Yes, I've been told as much. And that's exactly why we're here, dear Captain. You see, I can't help but feel a bit left out of this happy business. My orders were cryptic and brief, though they came from the Chamberlain himself. It's a failing on my part, I'll be the first to admit, but I detest being used as a pawn in someone else's game. If there is an advantage I can press, why, I will press it."

"What do you want?" repeated Mauritane.

Kallmer continued, ignoring him. "All I've been told is that I was to meet you in the Rye Grove, ensure that you were properly provisioned, and then send you on your way to the City Emerald. Now imagine my surprise upon receiving such orders! My former captain, convicted of treason and imprisoned, is to show up at my door with his band of companions, and I am to kiss him on the cheek and cheer him southward. Odd, no? I think there's more to it than that." He spun on his heel. "I did a bit of investigation. I had a brief chat with a mutual friend: Purane-Es. Remember him? He's not the brightest star in the sky, Aba bless him, and he came to me, trying to find out what I knew. He managed to let slip that you might be conveying something of great value to Our Beloved Lady." He picked up a scabbarded sword from a simple wooden table in the corner and rapped it on the bars in time with his words. "I. Just. Had. To. Know. More!"

A tall man in distinguished middle age descended the staircase at the far end of the room. A train of scribes and pages followed him.

"Commander Kallmer," said the man. "Is all well?"

"My Lord," said Kallmer, bowing low enough to scrape his fingers on the dirty stone floor. "I had only just begun."

Mauritane recognized the speaker as Baron Geracy of Sylvan Major, the highest titled man in the region. The Palace Laco was his country estate.

"Mauritane," said Geracy, brushing a mane of gray hair from his lined face. "You have disappointed me twice. Once as a traitor and again as a fugitive. I am astonished that I once trusted you with my life."

Mauritane nodded back. "I apologize for that, Lord. I would that you might one day learn my point of view on those matters."

"Hm," said the baron. He turned for the stairs. "Kallmer, carry on. And remember, when Lord Purane shows up, tell him what a favor I've done for you, loaning out my cellar, and invite him for dinner."

Kallmer winced. "My apologies, Baron. Purane is not coming himself. He's sent Purane-Es."

"Oh," said Geracy. "Forget it, then." Geracy started up the stairs, his boots thudding on the old wood. One of the scribes, a waifish girl in an overlarge robe, made eye contact with Mauritane from the base of the staircase. She gazed at him for an instant, waited until Kallmer turned his back, and then mouthed the words "Fear not." She turned and quickly ascended the steps with her fellows.

Mauritane cocked his head to watch her go. He was certain he'd never seen her before.

"Do you know what I think, Mauritane?" said Kallmer. "I think you've got something valuable. I think you're Her Majesty's courier and that whatever it is you're carrying is something she doesn't want anyone to know a thing about. Hence all the secrecy and skullduggery." He stepped toward Mauritane. "Here's a deal: give me what you've got and I'll kill you quickly. Blades across the throat, crossbow quarrels through your eyes, your choice. Don't give me what I want, and we'll see if the baron's old torture machines still work. We'll start with the human, since I know he'll want to talk quickly. The baron has one device, lots of pulleys and levers, I don't even know what it's for. I think it would be fun to find out though, wouldn't it?"

He glanced at Raieve. "Next, I'll take care of your little bit on the side there. I assume the Lady Anne doesn't know about her? Of course not, and more power to you, I say. I almost hope she *doesn't* talk, because it will be so much fun trying to convince her."

"If you lay a finger on me," said Raieve, "I will depart this life with your balls between my teeth. I swear it."

Kallmer laughed. "That would be a lot of fun," he said. "But before I do any of that, I want you to have dinner with the baron and me. You can enjoy a delicious meal, your last, and ponder the terms of my offer. When dinner is over, I'll expect your decision."

"You can have my decision now," said Mauritane. "I don't have what you want. I don't even know what it is."

Smiling, Kallmer headed for the staircase. "Whatever you say, Captain. I'll see you at dinner."

Mauritane stared at the roasted boar on his plate, unable to eat, a deep sullenness welling within him. Too many things had wrested control from him of late. He was finally out of prison but could not seem to avoid seeing the world through the bars of a cage.

They dined on one of the southern terraces. Geracy sat at the head of the table, drinking too much wine and talking loudly. Kallmer sat next to Mauritane, gnawing on a piece of meat. Across the table sat the Lady Geracy and her daughter Elice, both sitting uncomfortably silent in the presence of a known traitor. A few paces away, four of Kallmer's guardsmen stood with crossbows at the ready.

Mauritane looked up at the daughter, whose attention was fixed on her nearly empty plate. Behind her, the fog-clad summit of Oak and Thorn made a halo around her head, her golden hair glinting in the fading sunlight.

"I think it's important to expose a young girl to many things," Geracy was saying to Kallmer, indicating his daughter with the point of his dinner knife. "The children of today ought to be aware of things. They must grow up too fast nowadays."

"I'm sure you're correct, Baron," said Kallmer. He'd had a few glasses of wine himself and had spent the entire meal making eyes at the girl, who seemed to Mauritane barely out of puberty.

"Given any thought to my deal, Mauritane?" said Kallmer, as though asking about the weather. He leaned in and whispered. "I'd hate for you to have to watch your friends suffer. Especially that tempting half-breed girl. My, my." Kallmer wiped his mouth with a thick cloth napkin.

Mauritane said nothing. He pushed his plate away, inadvertently spilling a glass of wine onto the tablecloth.

"You always were a difficult son of a whore," said Kallmer.

A bell rang somewhere in the house. A few moments later, an armor-clad courier stepped out onto the terrace bearing a tiny parcel. He bowed deeply, his breath heavy beneath his closed helmet.

"I am for Mauritane," he said.

Kallmer twisted in his chair, looking at the baron with surprise. "Since when is his mail being delivered here?" He rose. "I'll take that," he said.

"Apologies, sir," said the courier, his voice tinny behind his faceplate. "I am for Mauritane only."

The baron scowled. "This is most irregular, Kallmer," he said. "No one is supposed to know he's here. Whom have you told?"

"I've told no one!" said Kallmer, defensively. "Who sent you?"

The courier bowed. "I come from the Chamberlain Marcuse himself, sir, in the City Emerald."

Kallmer had no response.

"Get on with it, then," said the baron. He fidgeted uncomfortably in his chair.

Mauritane rose slowly and accepted the package. He took a pen from the courier and affixed his signature to a paper receipt.

"What are you waiting for?" said Kallmer, when the courier did not leave. "A gratuity?"

The courier was impassive. "I am to wait until the package is opened by Captain Mauritane."

Mauritane sat at the table, confused. The parcel was small, no wider than the palm of his hand, wrapped in rough paper and tied with twine. He undid the knot and tore the wrapping away, revealing a small wooden box, inlaid with diamonds and painted with a bright blue lacquer. The box had no latch and opened easily. Inside was a smaller velvet box and a note. The note read, "This belonged to a relative of yours. Your Queen now asks that you earn one for yourself, after the same fashion." It was signed and sealed by the Chamberlain Marcuse.

Mauritane opened the tiny velvet box. Inside, nestled on a padded cushion, was a bronze medal, black with age. He recognized it immediately; the blue striped ribbon and bronze star were the hallmarks of a Special Commendation from the Seelie Royal Guard. Mauritane had himself awarded dozens of them. He turned the medal over and read the inscription on the back. It was faded but legible: "To Bersoen, son of Berwan, for distinguished service."

Mauritane raised his head. His eyes caught those of the girl, Elice. Like everyone else at the table, she was gawking at him, only hers was a look of . . . was it anticipation?

"I saw this in a dream," Elice whispered to Mauritane over the table. "I thought I recognized you . . ."

"Silence, child!" shouted the baron. "You'll speak when spoken to." He stood and turned on the courier. "Your man has opened his bauble. I suggest that you now be on your way."

The courier nodded and made for the wide double doors, making no reply.

Kallmer tore the box and the medal from Mauritane's hands. "What is this about?" he said. He handed the items to the baron. "What is this about?"

The baron scanned the note and dangled the medal in front of his eyes. "I can make no sense of it." He pursed his lips. "I do not like the looks of this, Kallmer. I fear you may have gone too far . . ."

The baron's words were cut short by a cry from inside the palace. A moment later, the courier staggered back onto the terrace, a knife's hilt protruding from his belly just beneath the chest plate of his armor.

"You are under attack," the courier groaned. He sank to one knee, clutching his stomach, then fell face forward onto the tiles.

Five men, dressed in thin gray cloaks, raced out of the house with long knives in hand. They overwhelmed the already-surprised guards, subduing all four of them in a matter of seconds.

Kallmer drew his sword and stood. The baron clutched his dinner knife like a dagger. "How dare you!" shouted Kallmer.

One of the cloaked men stepped forward, lowering the hood of his cloak. He was a young man; a wisp of a beard stood out from his chin. "I would not recommend that, Commander," he said. Twelve more men stepped onto the terrace wearing similar cloaks, dragging the bodies of Kallmer's personal guard with them.

"What is the meaning of this?" said the baron, his face purple. He crossed the table to stand behind his wife and daughter, both of whom where shaking with fright.

"I mean you no harm, Baron," said the man. His hair was cut close, no braids, and his eyes were the color of slate. "At least, no more than usual. I am here to liberate Captain Mauritane."

"You'll do no such thing," said Kallmer. He leapt at the man, his sword flashing.

"*Ko ve anan*," the man said, making a circular gesture with his hands. Kallmer sat down hard on the ground, his face twitching, then slumped sideways, leaning against a table leg.

"Who are you?" said Mauritane. He felt instinctively for his own sword and cursed silently when he remembered it had been taken.

"My name is Eloquet," the man said. "I am a cell leader in the Beleriand Resistance. We've been watching you since you entered Sylvan."

"Why did you come for me?" Mauritane asked.

"You are a hero to my people for slaying the butcher Purane-La. You have suffered much for that sacrifice. Now Aba has brought you to us and it is our duty to aid you."

Mauritane shook his head. "I don't believe in Aba."

Eloquet shrugged. "I do not think He minds."

Suddenly Mauritane understood. "The page in the cellar. She was one of you."

"Our eyes are many," said Eloquet, nodding. "We must go. More troops will come."

"What of my companions?" said Mauritane. He reached for Kallmer's sword, fastening it to his own belt. "And Kallmer. Is he dead?"

"No, the commander's time has not yet come. Your companions have already been freed. Now come quickly."

"Wait," said Mauritane. "We need to take her as well." He pointed at Elice.

"Absolutely not!" said the baron. "You'll take my daughter over my corpse!"

"Will you come willingly?" said Eloquet, pointing his blade at Elice.

The girl nodded, her face unreadable. She stood from the table, dropping her napkin. The Lady Geracy fainted.

"Come back here with my daughter!" shouted the baron, but Eloquet had already whisked her off the terrace.

"Thank you for your hospitality, Baron Geracy," Mauritane said without a hint of sarcasm. "The meal was delicious."

black art, black artist

Mab sat in Her throne room, surrounded by butterflies. The tinkling music of chimes, the smoke of glowing braziers, the steady hum of the city flowing through the Unseelie sky.

"Bring me Wennet," she said, to no one in particular. A pair of servants hurried from the room.

One of them returned a moment later. "On his way, Majesty."

Mab leaned back on her throne, consulting a map of the Seelie lands in her head. First she would have Selafae, then Sylvan. From that well-fortified spot, she could take her time, moving slowly southward until the City Emerald lay in her grasp and she set her dogs loose in the Seelie Grove to piss all over Regina Titania's potted plants. She had only to find the man named Mauritane and all else would fall into place.

Wennet, Master of the Chambers of Elements and Motion, stepped quietly into the throne room, squeezing his cloth skullcap tightly in his fists. Beads of sweat stood out from his red forehead.

"What is your status?" said Mab.

"Majesty, we have redoubled our efforts in order to accede to thy orders. We are at full sail and pushing the limits of the load-bearing struts and the plinth courses, according to the Chamber of Structure."

"Ignore Fulgan," said Mab. "He is always complaining about his precious structures. We'll break more than one plank by the time this has ended."

"Yes, Majesty."

"Are you fully staffed? Is your supply of understudies ample?"

"Yes, Majesty."

"Be sure you have enough. This journey will take a toll on them. Don't spare your men, Wennet. Push them until they drop and then replace them. Make heroes."

"Yes, Majesty."

"We are to be on top of Selafae by dawn. You are dismissed."

Wennet backed slowly from the throne room, nearly walking into a column in the process. One of the servants took him by the elbow and guided him out.

Mab waved her fingers in the air and slinked into a glamour that made her appear as she had when she was very young and very beautiful. The butterflies shimmered and changed colors to match her dress. She took one of them on her finger and brushed it against her nose. "Come, darlings," she whispered. "We have an appointment with a gentleman."

At the forward end of the Royal Complex was a small pleasure garden that Mab tended with her own hands, in the few idle moments she allowed herself during the day. Servants, ladies-in-waiting, and members of the Prefecture were strictly forbidden. Only one other held a key to the place, and as she entered the garden he was there, lying in the grass, his head propped on a pillow.

"Good afternoon, Hy Pezho," said Mab.

"Majesty," he said, rising to his knees. "Thy glamour is radiant."

"Do you like it?" she said. "Is it what you might call . . . attractive?"

"Only if the petals of the rose are but attractive. Only if the flight of the dove is merely pretty."

Mab let out a gay laugh and sat beside him. "You are clever, Hy Pezho. We enjoy cleverness at times."

"Whatever pleases thee," said Pezho, pouring her a glass of wine from a bottle at his knee.

"Do not stand on ceremony here, darling. Save the proper forms of address for out there." She waved her hand toward the towering spires of the Royal Complex.

"I am honored to speak to . . . you thus." Hy Pezho smiled lazily.

"Come, kiss me," she said.

"First, drink a toast." He touched his glass to hers. "To the Unseelie."

"I will drink to that," she said. She lifted her glass and drank.

Once she had drunk, Hy Pezho stood, tossing his glass on the ground. He began to chant in ancient Thule Fae, his throat growling with the gutturals of the language.

"Whatever are you doing, love?" said Mab, unconcerned.

"I am exacting my revenge," said Hy Pezho, breaking his chant. He spat on the ground and made a sweeping motion with his arms. "*A fel-ala!*" he cried.

There was a deep croaking sound beneath the floor as thick beams beneath their feet began to move. A whisper grew, rising in pitch and volume, like a fierce wind through a forest of trees. It became a rush, then a howl.

The garden soil split wide in an ugly crack, dirt spilling into the darkness. Beneath the imported earth, the city's lumber cracked and separated, creating a dark chasm that stretched along the length of the garden.

Mab did not move.

"*A fel-ala em!*" shouted Hy Pezho. He glared at Mab, goading her. She refused to move.

"Will you not even put up a fight?" he called over the noise.

Mab only smiled.

Inky tentacles appeared from the dark rift, spilling out into the verdant space. They were wet and irregular, like black sausages. One of them reached toward Mab and licked across her exposed ankle.

Something began to hoist itself from the abyss. It was black and misshapen, covered about its body with stiff red hairs that waved in the breeze. A single orifice masticated slowly, revealing uneven lines of sharp teeth.

The tentacles were everywhere, upending planters, splashing in the fishpond, crawling up the rose trellises. Soon the garden was full of them. They surrounded Mab like fingers and tightened against her flesh.

"I assume you have a speech prepared," said Mab. She flattened her long skirt as much as she was able.

Hy Pezho was unnerved by her calm. He stuttered. "I . . . I have come as the instrument of my father's vengeance," he said. "You had him murdered in his sleep. I have been waiting for this day for a very long time."

Mab sighed. "It's a shame you didn't know your father as well as I did.

Perhaps you would not have bothered. Still, vengeance is an act with which I have a passing familiarity. Proceed."

Hy Pezho stamped his foot. "Must you always be so damnably composed? Can you never show a hint of fear, even as you are moments away from eternal torment in the belly of the fel-ala?"

"No, I would not give you that pleasure, even if it were the case." Mab stood, and the tentacles fell away from her.

"How . . . the fel-ala is my personal wraith, my creation!" Hy Pezho called upon it again, but the creature refused to budge. Its glassy eyes moved back and forth between Mab and Hy Pezho.

"A bit of advice," said Mab, closing the distance between them. She stood before him as though she were about to kiss his lips. "When you seek to lure your enemy down a dark alley, it's best to inquire who owns the buildings on either side."

With a wordless command, she set the fel-ala upon Hy Pezho. She watched as the tentacles embraced him, digging their tiny, sharp spines into his flesh and drawing out the blood and the animating spirit within.

"Bacamar!" called Hy Pezho, with the last of his breath. "Save me!"

Bacamar floated down and alighted on Mab's shoulder.

"I have but one thing to say to you," hissed Bacamar.

"Please," gasped Hy Pezho. "I cannot . . . the pain." The color leached from his face and hands, turning them a dull gray.

Bacamar whispered, "It is never wise to keep a lady waiting."

They watched until he was dragged beneath the ground, through the chasm and into the nameless place where the wraiths make their home. Mab spoke a few words of Motion and the garden floor healed itself, coming together into a rough seam.

"Boys," said Mab.

beneath sylvan

Mauritane was reunited with Raieve, Satterly, and Silverdun at the rear gate of Geracy's palace, but the renewal of their acquaintance was a brief one.

"Get in," said Eloquet, pointing at a covered delivery wagon parked at an angle in the alley. Mauritane helped Elice into the rear of the vehicle and the others followed him, including several of Eloquet's men. The remainder faded into the lush greenery that surrounded all of the homes at the valley's rim. Eloquet ordered one of his followers into the driver's seat, then hopped in the back himself. The wagon began to move with a lurch.

"There are Seelie Army posts everywhere," said Eloquet. "We can only assume that the Queen has prepared another offensive against us."

Mauritane shook his head. "Unless Her Majesty's opinion has changed on the subject, I doubt it. During my tenure as Captain of the Guard, she avoided the issue entirely."

Eloquet nodded. "She does not wish to anger those among the nobility who support our cause."

Mauritane shrugged. "In my experience, the Queen does not care whom she angers."

"He's right, Mauritane." It was Silverdun who had spoken. Mauritane looked at him, wondering when he had last heard the man speak. The cart jolted unsteadily with its heavy burden of Fae.

"He's right," Silverdun repeated. "Sympathy for the Arcadians and those in the Western Valley has grown steadily over the years as they find more and more converts among the highborn. My mother was one of them."

"And you believe Her Majesty bows before their influence?"

Silverdun shrugged. "I believe She wishes to avoid a conflict, that is all."

"Through all this, I remain a servant of my Queen, Silverdun." Mauritane scowled. "It does us no good to speculate. Large enough numbers of the nobility, especially in this region, despise the Arcadians. And, as Kallmer implied, they have a great deal of leeway at such a distance from the capital."

Raieve, pressed tight against the baron's daughter, brushed a strand of the girl's golden hair from her mouth and said, "Pardon me for interrupting, but what's going on here? And who is she?" She nodded in Elice's direction.

"They are of the Beleriand rebels," said Mauritane, indicating the men squeezed into the cart. "Apparently, the Seelie Army is preparing another offensive against them."

Raieve nodded. "And why have they rescued us from Geracy?"

"While I was Captain of the Queen's Guard I made no secret of my distaste for these offensives. Even to the point of slaying a man I should perhaps not have slain."

"The butcher Purane-La?" barked Eloquet. "If ever a man deserved to die it was he. He burned the town of Stilbel to the ground. He . . . he trapped the townspeople in their homes and laughed as they were consumed. They say it was you, Mauritane, who gave the order and that he was only following you, but we know that it is not true."

Mauritane's face fell. "The Aeropagus determined otherwise."

"But you did not give the order!" shouted Eloquet.

"No," said Mauritane. "I did not."

"But if you did not give the order," said Raieve, "who did?"

"You've met him," said Mauritane. "He was the man I tried to kill that evening at Crere Sulace."

"Purane-Es."

Mauritane nodded. "The very same. It was he who sent the order, forging my name on the documents. He was one of my personal lieutenants. Purane-La was his elder brother. Whether Purane-Es was out to ruin me or only his brother, I do not know. He got both for the price of one."

"Were there ever harsh words between you and Purane-Es?" said Raieve. Now that the subject had finally been broached, she was ready for an explanation, regardless of its poor timing.

"Many," said Mauritane, sighing. He peered out the wagon's flap. "Are we near our destination?" he asked Eloquet.

"A few more minutes," Eloquet said.

"Purane-Es was fervently opposed to my policies regarding the Beleriand rebels and to Arcadianism in general. He often insisted that we ought to bring to bear all of our forces against them and wipe them out entirely."

Eloquet laughed ruefully. "He is, unfortunately, not alone in that sentiment."

"It appears he got his wish, at least partially," said Mauritane. "By causing Stilbel to be destroyed, tensions soared to their highest since the days of the original Gossamer Rebellion. And by putting my name on such dangerous documents, by bringing me to Stilbel just as Purane-La finished his work, knowing how I might respond, Purane-Es guaranteed my tribunal and subsequent replacement by his father. The order, on its own, might have caused nothing more than a scandal. But taking the life of Lord Purane's heir was unforgivable in the eyes of the nobility."

Raieve was shocked. "Surely there were witnesses? Did no one speak in your defense?"

"No one who ranked as high as Purane-Es," said Mauritane.

"So," said Satterly. "What's everyone so upset at the Arcadians for, anyway? After being in this country for two years I still haven't figured it out."

"It is a matter of the Fae Gifts," said Silverdun. "The Arcadians believe that the Gifts are from Aba and should be used in his service alone."

"And that brought all this about?"

"Not by itself," continued Silverdun. "The Western Valley, where Beleriand is located, lies within the mountains to the west of here. Its people are vastly different from the majority of the Fae you have met. They don't use glamours; they are against illusion in all its forms.

"The original Gossamer Rebellion was an abortive attempt by Beleriand to secede from the Seelie Kingdom altogether. In those days, Beleriand was ruled by a baron named Pellings, a truly brutal fellow who was almost universally loathed, both in and out of the Western Valley. Once the baron was removed, the problem subsided for a while, but it was only a matter of time before the trouble started again.

"Now, of course, the Arcadian faith has swept outward and there are many in the nobility who see the Arcadians as a threat to the Seelie way of life." He chuckled. "Whatever that is supposed to mean."

"But that's not enough of a reason to send armed forces into a region. There must be more to it than that," Satterly said.

Eloquet answered him. "It was not enough to decry us in public. Some of the more reactionary lords here in the west, Geracy among them, believed that it was necessary to stem the tide of Arcadianism at its source. They began targeted assassinations . . ."

"That has not been proven," interrupted Mauritane.

"Please, Mauritane!" said Eloquet. "You disappoint me. Shall I list the names for you, the causes of death?"

"I speak as an official of the Seelie Court."

"Look around you," said Eloquet. "You are no longer in the Seelie Court. The assassinations took place, and we retaliated."

Mauritane said nothing in response. An uncomfortable silence reigned for a few breaths.

It was Elice, the baron's daughter, who broke the silence. "I hate to be the voice of dissent," she said, uncertainly. "But my father does have a point about the Arcadians. They've done awful things, caused millions in property damage, defacing public glamours and things, and they've hurt people, too."

Eloquet laughed out loud. "What wonders from the mouth of a child!" he said. "Young lady, an agent of your father murdered my wife in front of me, garroted her with a harp string. And you speak of defacing property as though it matters!"

Elice sat up straight. "My father would never do such a thing."

"No, you're right about that," said Eloquet. "He'd hire someone else to do it."

"Would someone please tell me what she's doing here?" said Raieve, looking ready to slap the girl in the face.

Mauritane looked at the girl, for some reason his opinion of her softening. "She is the object of our quest. She is what we have come here for."

"What?" said Silverdun, Satterly, and Raieve, in unison.

The wagon came to a sudden stop.

"There's trouble ahead," said the driver. "Roadblocks."

"Stay here," said Eloquet. He leapt from the wagon.

"What's going on?" said Satterly.

Eloquet returned. "The Royal Guard has set up roadblocks at the City Center entrances. They must be looking for us. Come on."

"I'm not going anywhere," said Elice. "I think I made a mistake."

"Quiet, girl," Raieve said, a knife instantly at the girl's throat. "If you whine your regrets too loudly, you could get us all killed."

"Come on!" whispered Eloquet.

They climbed from the rear of the wagon, Raieve holding Elice at knifepoint. Their wagon was in a line of similar conveyances on a wide cobblestone road. The road passed through tall housing blocks as it descended to the City Center district. At an archway ahead, eight or ten soldiers of the Seelie Army were stopping and inspecting each cart. Mounted cavalrymen passed through the archway and peered down into the vehicles in line.

Eloquet led them silently through an alley and into a side street. They clung to doorways and dark alleyways as much as possible, Eloquet and his men consulting at each corner.

After a few tense minutes they seemed to find what they were looking for. It was a square grate set into the cobblestones, an arm's length across. One of Eloquet's men produced a hardened silver bar from his cloak and set about prying off the grate. A fetid odor of stagnation and urine emanated from the grate.

"Is that what I think it is?" said Satterly.

"Only if you think it's a sewer," said the man with the prying bar.

Elice reared back in Raieve's grip. "I am *not* going down there," she said.

"Have you ever had one of your fingers cut off?" Raieve asked her.

The girl shook her head, tears forming in the corners of her eyes.

"If you'd like to keep it that way, I suggest you remain silent from now on."

They descended into the sewer, lowering themselves through the grate. They dropped into a wide rounded tunnel, large enough that they were able to walk double file. There was a low rush and a cold breeze that followed the course of the frigid, ankle-deep water in the passage.

"Where are we going?" asked Mauritane. "If the City Center is cordoned, it would seem foolish to go there of our own accord."

"We're not going to the City Center," said Eloquet, but he would say nothing else.

The tunnel began to seem endless. It was broken every hundred paces or so by grates identical to the one they'd crawled through. Every so often, a pail of refuse was thrown through a grate, falling on one or more of them. They trudged farther and farther, always descending, following the current. Walking in water, even as shallow as it was, was tiring, and within minutes even the most fit among them were huffing.

Finally the tunnel leveled off, and the flow of water was diverted down a smaller opening. Grateful, they walked along a dry channel for what seemed like hours but was probably not more than half of one. Their footsteps echoed sharply in the corridor; that and their breathing were the only sounds. Mauritane felt, and assumed the others felt, that it would be somehow dangerous to speak here, even though there was probably not much danger from the Seelie Army by now.

The tunnel began to climb again, and a new flow of water began; now they climbed against it. The smooth walls of the tunnel disappeared and they began walking through what looked like a natural cave. Icy water dripped from the walls and the ceilings, and the air was colder by several degrees. Once they passed the final grate in the artificial tunnel, the light faded to blackness.

"Did anyone think to bring a torch?" came Silverdun's voice. "I'd use witchlight, but the troops up there could be using sniffers."

As if in answer to his question, sparks of flint against silver chimed in the darkness, revealing Eloquet, crouching against the breeze with a tiny lamp cradled in his arms.

Eloquet managed to light his lamp. He was rising when the tunnel floor suddenly jerked out of the earth and slammed back into place. Only Mauritane remained standing; everyone else was pitched to the floor of the tunnel as a grinding roar filled their ears, passing over them like a physical force. Mauritane could feel the shaking in his teeth and his gut. Somehow Eloquet's lamp remained lit throughout, and the cave was a flickering scene of confusion as the wall of sound passed over them, the sides and floor of the passage shuddering in its wake.

"What's going on?" cried the girl.

"Earthquake," said Raieve.

"We don't have earthquakes this far north," said Eloquet.

"What then?"

"I don't know," he said. "But I no longer trust this passageway. Let us be on our way, and quickly."

Except for a bit of fallen debris and a great deal of dust, they managed the remainder of the tunnel without incident. It rose ever more steeply until it reached a grate the height of a man, set in a square opening cut into the rock. Water poured out through the grate in a steady rush.

"What now?" said Raieve.

Eloquet knelt and felt for something on the floor of the tunnel, his hands reaching down into the black water of the cave. He found something and tugged. A thick chain lifted out of the water and a wooden hatch followed, covered in loose stones and muck. It rose at an angle to the flow of the water, and the diverted stream found its way through the hatch and below.

"We go down," said Eloquet.

There was a ladder of bronze set into the walls of a vertical shaft. Eloquet went first, and the rest of them followed, with Eloquet's soldiers taking up the rear. Elice squealed when the water poured over her face but said nothing.

Another natural chamber lay below. The water from the hatch above, stemmed once the hatch was closed, broke into rivulets and disappeared among the rocks. At the top of the inclined floor of the chamber, a pair of heavy doors was set into the wall.

As they approached, the door opened. A tiny man wearing a pink robe stepped into view. His head was shaved bald and he wore a long beard that trailed beneath his shoulders.

"Greetings," he said. "My name is Vestar, and I am the abbot here. Welcome to the Temple Aba-e."

above sylvan

"Come in quickly," said the abbot. "Your arrival coincides with a great turmoil."

"What was that shaking?" said Eloquet. "What happened?"

"We do not know," the abbot said. "Please, quickly."

They were led through a series of passageways, all filled with men and women in pink and white robes, moving quickly, their eyes down. No one spoke, but there was great industry and efficiency in their motions. The passageways were high and wide, generous light given off by kerosene sconces set at regular intervals. They passed an enormous kitchen, pouring out steam and cooking smells. Beyond that was a chapel and halls filled with what appeared to be sleeping quarters.

"My cell is small," said the abbot. "Eloquet and Mauritane, come with me. The rest of you wait here, please." He indicated a large sitting room for Eloquet's men and Mauritane's companions and led the two men down a side hallway. He stopped at a door that looked like any of the others.

Inside there were only a small cot, a pair of simple chairs, a bureau, and a wooden writing desk holding a gas lamp and some papers.

"You know me," Mauritane said to the abbot.

"I've known of you for some time," said Vestar, his eyes cool. "You are a hero among Aba's children."

When Mauritane did not respond, the abbot continued. "An unwilling one, no doubt, but the hero is a creation of the beholder, not the beheld."

"What's happening outside, Vestar?" said Eloquet. "When we descended, there were patrols surrounding the City Center. And now this great shaking."

"Polthus has been sent up to determine the answer to your question. I expect him any moment. Please, won't you two have a seat?"

Vestar sat on the edge of the cot, his hands in his lap. Mauritane and Eloquet took the chairs.

"They are preparing another offensive," said Eloquet.

Vestar nodded. "I believe so as well, but we must not make hasty assumptions. Aba always allows for redemption, even among the Fae nobility." He smiled. "I am only teasing."

"What next?" said Mauritane.

Vestar regarded him silently, the calmness of his gaze soothing Mauritane's nerves. "That depends on you," he said. "What is your purpose in Sylvan?"

"I am on an errand for Her Majesty."

Vestar nodded. "You remain loyal to the crown. Loyalty can be an admirable trait. You should not, however, confuse loyalty with faith."

Mauritane's eyes widened. "I once had an instructor who said the same thing about loyalty and trust."

"True," said Vestar, smiling. "They are not the same. Trust, loyalty, and faith. They are all different. But which is most valuable?"

They were interrupted by a knock on the cell door. "Enter," said Vestar.

A pudgy boy with a clubfoot opened the door and bowed toward the abbot. "The news is not good, abbot. The earthquake has caused a lot of damage in the city below. There are fires in the City Center. Some of the people have begun to riot against the Seelie soldiers and Royal Guardsmen."

Vestar closed his eyes, his fingers reaching for the prayer beads around his neck. "Is there a way in which peace may be restored?"

Mauritane stood and paced. "With Kallmer in charge of the Guardsmen, anything is possible. He's reckless and won't see anything wrong with using excessive force to subdue the populace. Who is the Seelie Army commander here?"

"Prae-Alan," said Eloquet, spitting the name like a curse.

Mauritane nodded. "A harsh man but an intelligent one as well. He'll remain calm during this. Kallmer, though, may panic."

"Mauritane," said Eloquet, "there are over thirty rebel cells out there. They are all prepared for aggression. If the soldiers begin firing on the crowd, they will defend Sylvan."

"How many in each cell?"

"They range from eighty to a hundred men and women."

Mauritane did the math. "And the Seelie contingent?"

"The last count was a thousand men, but they are far better armed. New forces seem to arrive with each passing day."

"This is odd," said Mauritane. "When I was arrested, there were no plans to wage an offensive of any kind against the rebels. Such campaigns take months to plan. Why now? What has changed?"

"There have been several visible Arcadian converts within the City Emerald," said Vestar. "Would that be enough to provoke this?"

"Arcadianism does not necessarily imply support for the rebels."

"True."

"I think there is more to it than that," said Mauritane finally. "Something else is going on here."

"Perhaps we should go above and see for ourselves," said Eloquet.

"Let's do that," Vestar said.

They stood in one of the great archways of the temple's open tier. From the archway the entire city was visible, a great bowl of mayhem. Fires had spread in three different places in the city. At the outskirts of the City Center, the Seelie Army waged an unsuccessful attempt to rout a throng of peasants that crowded the streets, hanging from windows and lampposts. Their shouts reached as high as the temple. Elsewhere, once-tall buildings lay in ruins, ant-sized Fae climbing over the wreckage.

"I am touched by a deep sadness," said Vestar. "Eloquet, is there nothing that can be done? Will your people work with the Seelie to restore peace to our city?"

Eloquet frowned, lines crossing his forehead. "I could order my own men to do so, but the cells are decentralized. There is no hierarchy of leadership. They all act independently, as we do."

As they spoke, a column of mounted men in gray cloaks appeared on a bluff just below the bridge that led to the temple. They were positioned at the flank of the Seelie soldiers who fought to contain the chaos in the City Center.

Eloquet strained to recognize them. "I can't see who it is. Perhaps Melnan's cell. I can't tell."

The riders began to descend the bluff; an instant later their battle cries reached the ears of Mauritane, Eloquet, and the abbot. The Seelie were caught utterly unprepared. The rebels swarmed into their ranks, hacking and slashing with a ferocity that was visible even from such a great distance. Within a few moments, most of the Seelie had been slaughtered. The few remaining attempted to retreat into the crowd.

Mauritane was unsure which side he ought to be cheering for. Either way, he was deeply concerned. Something had just begun that could not easily be undone.

"Are you and your people safe here?" asked Mauritane.

"It is difficult to say," said the abbot. "Do you think the fighting will come to the temple?"

"Better to plan for rain and remain dry either way," said Mauritane.

Vestar said, "I will leave such things to you and to Eloquet. I ask only that you do what you can to prevent a full-scale war; that is more important even than the safety of the temple. As the prophet says, no war is holy."

"But, Vestar. The temple . . ." Eloquet began.

"Is only a building. And we are only servants."

"You are the chief abbot for the entire region. You are irreplaceable!"

"No, it only means that I am chief custodian. It is a job anyone can do. But we have gotten ahead of ourselves. We do not even know if our friend Mauritane will assist us."

Mauritane was confused. "Why wouldn't I?"

"You have pressing business elsewhere. Your duty to your Queen."

"If I can help here, then I am doing my duty to my Queen."

Vestar nodded. "Even if your mission fails?"

Mauritane thought back to the Chamberlain's letter. "Failure is death," it had read. He had no doubt what would become of him if he were not in the City Emerald on time.

"Many of the men down there were once under my command," he said. "I still feel responsible for them. And at the same time, the lives of my three companions are at stake if my mission does not succeed. Which lives are more important? I cannot decide that. All I know is to throw my shoulder where it will do the most work."

"Well spoken," said the abbot. "Do what you can."

"What if," said Eloquet, "you are asked to choose between those men you so love in the Royal Guard and the men under *my* command? What then?"

Mauritane looked at him. "We will have to make sure that does not happen."

"I might argue that it's happening even as we speak." Eloquet pointed down toward the City Center. Another company of Seelie Army soldiers had advanced toward the location of the rout, finding the rebels there tending to their wounded. The army officer wasted no time with a parlay; the men attacked on sight. Caught off guard, the rebels were unready for the assault. Half of them were slain before a single one of their weapons was drawn. The sounds of battle drifted up toward the temple, the clash of metal on metal and the screams of dying men.

"We must stop this. Eloquet, I must speak to my companions, explain the situation to them."

"Of course."

"Then, I suggest you and I ride out to speak with Commander Kallmer of the Royal Guard. Perhaps together we can sway his judgment."

Before Eloquet could answer, a young woman in the pink robe of the temple appeared in an archway, running toward them. She stopped, her hands on her knees, out of breath from running upstairs. She was also crying, terrified.

"We've just had word," she managed. "That . . . was no earthquake." She tried to catch her breath, struggling with the words. "It was . . . an explosion. The Unseelie have crossed the border. They destroyed Selafae. Messages are pouring in now. A great column of fire, it incinerated the entire city. In seconds, just gone. A column of fire."

Eloquet led the girl to a stone bench. She sat and collected herself. "They think . . . it is the city of Mab herself. And it is now heading directly for us."

Mauritane looked toward the northern horizon, where nothing unusual could be seen. "It's true then," he said. "The Unseelie have been preparing for a war."

He turned to Eloquet. "How far is it to Selafae from here?"

"Two days' ride on horseback," said Eloquet. "How long for Mab's city to reach us?"

"Depending on the wind, less than a day. Maybe a bit more. Certainly the army has received the same news and is preparing." A light flashed on in Mauritane's head. "Wait! Now I understand," he said.

"What?" said Eloquet.

"The Seelie Army's presence here. There isn't any offensive brewing against the rebels. They're here because of the Unseelie! The soldiers we discovered in the Contested Lands can't have been the only ones; our spies would have seen this invasion coming for days." He scratched his head. "Come, Eloquet. We must talk to Kallmer now more than ever."

"What are you thinking, Mauritane?"

"I have no doubt now that we can prevent a civil war. But I don't think you'll prefer the alternative."

Vestar had fallen to his knees. He pulled his prayer beads from inside his robe and began to whisper prayers, weeping for the lost children of Selafae.

duty interferes/ someone else to blame

"Things have changed," said Mauritane.

Silverdun, Raieve, and Satterly sat around a low table eating rice and fish. From the looks on their faces, they had heard nothing of recent events. The girl Elice sat sullenly in a corner, facing the wall.

"What's happening?" said Silverdun. "No one has said a word to us."

"The Unseelie have detonated something, a powerful spell weapon, on Selafae. The entire city has been destroyed. They are advancing on Sylvan as we speak."

"The Unseelie!" said Satterly. "Then the earthquake we felt . . ."

"An effect of the explosion. The quake has taken its toll here in Sylvan. The rebels have begun attacking the Seelie forces openly in the wake of its destruction. The city is in chaos."

"What are we going to do?" asked Raieve.

"I've decided to stay and help defend the Seelie Kingdom. Regardless of what happens here, our mission is . . . in grave danger of failure. You all knew what failure meant when you agreed to join me. Therefore, I release you from your service; you are all free to go and take your chances on your own."

They were stunned. "I don't know what to say," Satterly began.

"If we survive the Unseelie onslaught, I will make a plea before the Chamberlain that your lives be spared in exchange for my own. I wish I could offer you better. You deserve better."

"That's very kind of you," said Silverdun. "But . . . this is all too unexpected."

Raieve said, "What are the consequences of occupation by the Unseelie?"

Mauritane looked away. "We've been at war many times in the past. Whenever the Unseelie have taken Seelie lands, the people have suffered under their yoke. They are made slaves or worse."

"I will stay, then, and fight," said Raieve. "In my culture, there is no greater honor than to die in the service of one's people."

Silverdun sighed. "If the Unseelie overtake Sylvan, they will destroy this temple. My family lands are not far from here; they will go as well. What, then, would I have to escape to?"

All eyes turned to Satterly. He fidgeted in his chair. "What are you guys looking at me for?" he said, uncomfortably.

"You are under no obligation to stay," said Mauritane.

"Well, I guess I'd be asshole of the year if I left now," he muttered. "I don't know what I can do, but I'll pitch in where I can."

"Do not agree so lightly," said Mauritane to all of them. "Honor is generally only beautiful when viewed from a distance. There is a good chance that none of us will survive."

"And what chance had we before?" said Silverdun. "We all knew going into this that there was little hope for survival. I just didn't want to die in that damnable prison."

"In that case," said Mauritane, "let us be more than fellow travelers from now on. Let us call each other friend as well."

"Mauritane," said Raieve, "may I speak with you for a moment? Alone?"

Satterly and Silverdun took the cue. They stood and ambled off down the hallway, carrying the empty dinner dishes with them.

"Yes?" said Mauritane, once they were alone.

"I wanted to tell you. That morning, after we made love, I was unfair to you. I knew you were married and that you would not have been unfaithful had things been different. I was as much to blame as you. I'm sorry."

"You have nothing to apologize for," he said. "Nothing."

"Mauritane," said Raieve, taking his hand. "That's not all."

He leaned into her and placed his hand gently on her shoulder. "Tell me."

"I am in love with you," she said. "I started loving you the day we met. You speak of commitment, and duty, but none of those things matter to love. I cannot apologize for how I feel." She looked up, into his eyes.

Mauritane backed away from her, slowly. "I don't know what to say," he started, his frustration welling to the surface. "I wish . . . it seems my duty interferes with me at every turn. I can never seem to avoid it!"

"I know how you feel in your heart," said Raieve, her softness dissolving. "That you deny it is where you are always going wrong." She turned and ran down the hallway, wiping her sleeve roughly across her eyes.

The Royal Guard forces had seized a hotel in the Mid City earlier in the day, and terrified guests were still flowing out into the chaotic night under the watchful eye of a dozen guardsmen. No efforts were being made, however, to unload the equipment and ammunition that sat in carts on the far side of the lobby. In fact, it appeared that some of the carts were actually being loaded for travel.

Kallmer had acknowledged the parlay flag, ordering his men to lower their weapons. A pair of them escorted Mauritane, Eloquet, and the abbot to the center of the wide formal dining hall. Kallmer had appropriated the room for his field office. He was seated at a long table of dark mahogany, papers spread everywhere across it.

"You realize, of course," began Kallmer, "that if you were not accompanied by the temple's abbot, I would have shot you on sight."

"That is why I have come," said the abbot.

"Technically," said Kallmer, "one cannot even ask for parlay unless there is a war going on. Are we at war with one another?"

"That is what we are here to avoid," said Mauritane. "Certainly you have heard the same news we have from Selafae."

"Any such information would be classified," said Kallmer.

"Then you know that Mab is on her way here, even now. The figures are not difficult, Kallmer. If we are divided, fighting amongst one another, the Unseelie will roll over us. But if we are united, we have a chance against them."

Kallmer smiled. "You are proposing an alliance? With the Seelie Army and the Royal Guard on one side and a band of terrorists on the other?"

Eloquet spoke up. "Many of our men were once Seelie Army officers themselves."

"I've no doubt," said Kallmer, unimpressed. "It's an intriguing notion, Mauritane, but irrelevant. We're pulling out of Sylvan."

"What?" said Mauritane. "Why?"

"That is also classified information. But I will tell you this: based on what our scouts reported from Selafae, if you have any interest in saving your skin, I suggest you get as far away from Sylvan as possible. I tell you this," he waved his arms beneficently, "for the sake of our long-lost camaraderie."

"Before I go, however, I'd like to make some kind of arrangement for Geracy's daughter. What is it you want for her? Gold? Weapons? If it's something we can spare, I'll give it to you just to get Geracy off my back."

"You can assure Geracy that she will come to no harm."

Kallmer shrugged. "Fine! I no longer care. This is all to do with your secret mission, isn't it? You're lucky, Mauritane. Earlier today, I would have killed you to learn that secret. Now, it seems I have more pressing matters to attend to." He reached for an overcoat that hung on the chair next to him. "Are we finished, then? I have important business elsewhere."

"To where will you fall back?" said Mauritane. "Paura?"

"Classified," said Kallmer. "I really must be going now."

"You can't have had orders from Purane already. If this is your own decision, it's a poor one. Purane will have your head for it."

Kallmer stood. "Mauritane, the city of Mab sails ever closer as we speak, bearing a weapon of mass destruction whose properties we can't even begin to understand. We've lost nearly a quarter of our combined troops to your rebel friends in the past four hours alone. Retreat is not just the sensible option, it's the only option."

"Sylvan has never been occupied by the Unseelie, Kallmer. Never! Do you want to be the first commander in history to let that happen? The Queen herself will hang you. You must know that."

Kallmer seemed to break down before their eyes. "And what do you recommend, Mauritane?" he said, his voice rising an octave. "That I simply sit here and wait for my own death?"

"Working together, we can stop Mab before she comes within range of

Sylvan. Then we'll have only ground troops to contend with, and we are far more skilled than the Unseelie on the ground."

"And how do you propose to stop Mab?" said Kallmer, still skeptical but no longer shrugging into his coat.

"We have a plan," said Mauritane. "But we need the schematics of the city of Mab that the Royal Guard intelligence has developed."

"I can't confirm the existence of any such documents."

"I can," Mauritane said. "I helped draw them."

Kallmer scowled. "What is this plan?"

"That information is classified," Mauritane said.

Kallmer laughed, but it was not a happy sound. "What are its chances for success?"

"Good enough."

Kallmer paced behind his desk. "I will have to discuss the matter with Prae-Alan. He will not be pleased."

"If the Royal Guard and rebels unite against the Unseelie, Prae-Alan would be a fool to balk at that alliance. And he is not a fool. If you tell him the arrangement already exists, the Seelie Army will have no choice but to agree to it. Unless, of course, he values his life even less than you do."

"What is your motivation behind all of this, Mauritane? You are no longer Captain of the Guard. Why risk your own neck?"

Mauritane took a long look at Kallmer and saw only fear there. "If you have to ask," he said, "then you know nothing about loyalty."

Kallmer pursed his lips but made no reply. Instead, he changed the subject. "How long will it take to execute your plan?"

"If we go now, we will see success by this time tomorrow."

"Isn't that cutting things awfully close?"

"If the winds are with us, we should have plenty of time."

Kallmer blanched. "And if they are not?"

"Then we will have to hurry," said Mauritane, a cold smile on his lips.

Kallmer reflected for a moment, presumably contemplating the various avenues by which death had recently suggested itself to him. "I have one question before I agree."

"Ask."

"Did you send the order for Purane-La to destroy Stilbel?"

"No," Mauritane said simply.

Kallmer nodded. "No, somehow I didn't really think so." He thought a bit longer. "Fine," he finally said, "we'll do it your way. At least then I'll have someone else to blame while I'm waiting for the ax to fall."

Mauritane nodded. "Good. Get me the plans."

Kallmer dispatched a lieutenant to the records wagon. "When this is over, Mauritane, I expect you to tell me what this mission of yours was all about. It's the least you can do."

"If we are both still alive, I will tell you."

"That," sighed Kallmer, "is fair."

deals

The Mechesyl Road was wide and flat, its grassy median and broad hexagonal stones extending all the way from the Travel Guild Center outside the City Emerald to Sylvan's southeast gate. Purane-Es's troops rode in columns five wide, filling the entire road. The troops forced the merchants and travelers to the shoulders, where they waited impatiently for the hundred or so men on horseback to pass.

Purane-Es rode ahead of the formation, only the standard-bearer preceding him. He let his gaze fall on the snow-clad trees in the median, watching them drift past his field of vision in the predawn light. Anything to mitigate the sight of the horse's hindquarters he'd been staring at for the past seven days.

The Lady Anne had not been pleased. She'd called him a spineless fool and worse. And yet, despite her anger, he still felt her love reaching him from somewhere behind her eyes. He persisted, she relented. He explained to her as best he could his relationship with Father, how brutal he'd been to them as children, how brutal Purane-La had been to him in return. He made noises about the Unseelie threat. He avoided mentioning Mauritane and his damned orders for Stilbel. She wept and begged him not to leave. But there was nothing he could do. Lord Purane had a crossbow to his head, and the bolt was one he could never share with her.

She said she no longer loved Mauritane, that she loved only him. What would she do if she found out what had really happened? Purane-Es's stomach churned. How long would he be forced to pay for that one error in judgment? He'd never meant for things to go so far. He'd certainly never meant for his brother to be killed.

Or had he?

Sometimes, Purane-Es admitted to himself, he had wished La dead. Purane-La, the firstborn son, the one who could do no wrong in his father's eyes. La was Father's great achievement, and Es was merely his backup. Purane-Es had spent his entire life as an understudy, waiting in the wings for his father to notice him in any other way than to point out his failings. "You are wasting your life, Purane-Es," he'd often said. "You're not half the man your brother is," was another favorite. Sometimes, when the old man had had a few too many drinks, he would quietly admit that he wished Es had never been born. "You're useless," he'd observe, as though talking about a hen that didn't lay. Fortunately, by the time Purane-Es had left for University, he'd learned to shut such things out. He no longer heard them.

Regardless, being runner-up to Purane-La was paradise compared to being his replacement. Since La's death, Purane-Es had come to hate his father in an entirely new way, in the manner that men despise other men, and not just the simple loathing of a son for an aloof parent.

What kind of man blackmailed his own son?

Could Purane-Es really be blamed for any of this? All he'd ever wanted was to lounge beneath the shady trees at court, singing songs and stealing kisses in the moonlight. He'd never wanted this. Not any of it.

A scout from the messaging post in Paura interrupted his reverie. The boy ran out of the guardhouse, calling his name.

"Purane-Es! Are you Purane-Es?" called the boy.

Purane-Es nodded, taking the boy's hastily scrawled message, which had arrived via message sprite. He read Kallmer's report of the earthquake, and the subsequent news from Selafae and the riots in the City Center.

"What am I riding into?" he mused out loud. He tore up the message and rode on, his personal troubles momentarily forgotten.

The Rye Grove was teeming with activity. Seelie Army soldiers drilled alongside members of the Royal Guard. Battle mages tested their spell-weapons, creating clouds of green and blue smoke over the trees. From the farrier's tent, the sound of hammers and the smell of the silver-hardening vats drifted out over the field. The morning mist was thick but had already begun to burn away beneath an unusually warm sun.

Purane-Es sat high in the saddle, curious about the figures he saw coming and going in gray and brown cloaks. They looked like peasants; most had no braids, and none of them was clean shaven. Even the Royal Guardsmen he saw looked a bit ragged, their uniforms not to regulation, their braids casually slung over their shoulders. It was depressing to see.

Kallmer came to greet them; he'd been leading a drill and was drenched in sweat, despite the cold. "Commander Purane-Es," he said, his voice guarded. "Your presence coincides with events both wondrous and fearsome."

"We need to talk," said Purane-Es, refusing the offer of cordiality.

"Of course, Commander," said Kallmer, emphasizing the rank to remind Purane-Es that his was equivalent. "I've set up a temporary headquarters in a hotel just up the street."

Purane-Es handed his reins to a groom, and they walked the short distance to the hotel. The streets were quiet, save for the activities of the military in the grove.

"Your message indicated riots," said Purane-Es. "If there is rioting here, it's being performed by an exceedingly polite mob."

"We've . . . gotten that situation under control since that message was sent. I apologize; there hasn't been time for a follow-up."

Purane-Es quickened his pace. "So we only need to concern ourselves with the earthquakes, advancing armies, and columns of flame. Is that correct?"

"More or less," said Kallmer.

"You've got new orders," said Purane-Es. "I want you to gather your men and prepare to pull out of Sylvan. If what you're saying is true—and I do plan to verify every word of it—then we should fall back until reinforcements arrive. We did not think they would cross the border so soon, or so spectacularly."

"Who gives this order?"

"The order will come from my father once I speak with him."

"But he has not yet spoken."

"That does not matter. We are of one mind on this matter."

"Show me an order from Purane and I'll prepare my men. Until then, I retain command, and I give the orders."

They reached the hotel, and Kallmer pushed into the lobby, Purane-Es following him. "I can have you stripped to graveyard walker, Kallmer. You are walking a gossamer thread."

"Save it, Purane-Es," said Kallmer. "Why don't you go back to the City Emerald and write a love song? I have work to do."

Purane-Es stopped in the lobby, unable to believe what he'd just heard.

"Pardon me?" he said, his hands in fists.

"You heard me," said Kallmer. "Run along to your daddy."

"I'll have your head for this! Do you have any idea who you're speaking to?" said Purane-Es.

"Yes, I do. I know quite a bit about you, in fact. And if you try to get in my way, I'm fully prepared to spread that knowledge around."

"What do you think . . ." began Purane-Es, but he was cut off by a tall, aging lord who waved his hands for Kallmer's attention.

"Commander Kallmer!" shouted the man. "I have been waiting for hours!"

Kallmer bowed stiffly to the man. "Lord Geracy, we are doing everything we can to locate your daughter. As soon as I know more . . ."

"I don't have time for your equivocation, Kallmer," the man shouted. "I am leaving Sylvan in ten hours and if my daughter isn't with me, I'll speak to the Queen herself about this! I'll see that you and that cursed Mauritane are hanged from the same branch!"

"You're the third person to threaten me with death in the past twenty-eight hours," said Kallmer dryly. "The threat is losing its edge."

"Mauritane?" said Purane-Es, his interest piqued.

"Yes!" shouted Geracy. "Kallmer had that fiend imprisoned at my palace. But he allowed the man to escape from under our very noses, with my only daughter as a hostage."

Purane-Es looked askance at Kallmer. "Why, Commander! Your report did not mention anything of the sort. Have you grown forgetful?"

"It's nothing to do with my orders," said Kallmer, fuming.

"Quite the contrary, I think it has everything to do with your orders." Purane-Es smiled with mock politeness.

"Forgive my ignorance, but whom do I have the pleasure of addressing?" Geracy said, somewhat calmed by Purane-Es's presence.

"I am Purane-Es, of the City Emerald." Purane-Es gave a brief bow.

"You're Purane's boy!" the man said. "I am Geracy. Your father and I hunted together once or twice."

"Yes, he's spoken of you," said Purane-Es, although he'd never heard the man's name in his life. "If you'll pardon me," he said to Geracy, "I believe I can straighten this matter out with my fellow officer and have your daughter back in no time."

"Finally!" said Geracy. "Perhaps you can convince him not to pursue this dangerous alliance as well!"

"Alliance? Oh, we must speak in private," said Purane-Es.

Kallmer sat at his makeshift desk, peering across its wide expanse at Purane-Es, who paced furiously before him. A pair of sergeants tended to paperwork at another table, ignored. Otherwise, the room was empty. Kallmer poured drinks and laid out the previous day's events in brief, leaving out anything to do with the escape and kidnapping Geracy had complained about.

"Amazing," said Purane-Es, when the story was finished. "But where is Mauritane now, if not here? If you have created an alliance, why do your troops not train together?"

Kallmer nodded. "Well, Mauritane is at the Temple Aba-e. He's working on some plan of his own devising right now. As to the troops, we thought it would be a bit much to place them side by side. We're going to deploy them separately, under joint orders from me, through Mauritane. He's the only person who both sides will follow. So the rebel troops are assembling in a grove near the City Center, and . . ."

"Mauritane will lead the troops!" Purane-Es shouted. "Mauritane is a convicted traitor, a murderer, and a madman. Have you lost your mind?"

Kallmer took a moment to compose his thoughts. "Do you think me stupid, Purane-Es? All I've done is allow Mauritane to do my job for me. If he fails, there will still be time to evacuate. But if he is successful, then credit goes to us." He leaned back in his chair, making a steeple with his fingers. "Again, there is nothing you can do about it."

Purane-Es drew his sword with a smooth motion. "Do not be so sure, Kallmer."

"Don't threaten me, you pompous ass," said Kallmer. "I know what happened at Stilbel. I know it was you who gave the order, not Mauritane."

"That is not a lie you ought to be spreading," said Purane-Es. "Such talk could get you hurt."

"And it could get you hanged," said Kallmer. "You lied under oath at the tribunal, and I can prove it. Perjury by a nobleman is a capital offense."

"You can prove nothing."

"Oh, but you're wrong," said Kallmer. "I was there."

Kallmer allowed that to sink in. "I was an aide for the commander at Beleriand, and I was transferred briefly to Mauritane's command while you and your brother were out slaughtering villagers. I know he did not write the order, because I transcribed the order that he *did* write. I still have a copy."

"If you are so familiar with the facts, then you know that Mauritane amended his original orders. The order to secure Stilbel was an amendment. What you claim to have proves nothing."

"I assume you never read the original order, then," laughed Kallmer. "It states, and I quote, 'whatever means you take to secure the valley east of the river, you will by no means harm any of the civilians along its length.' That would make for quite an amendment."

"You're lying," said Purane-Es.

"Don't you wish that I was?" said Kallmer. "I've been holding on to that little tidbit for years, just waiting for the moment it might come in most handy. And now that I know it was you, I also know who to blame for not speaking out all this time. I'll tell them that you threatened my life, as you did just a few moments ago outside, in front of witnesses."

"You wouldn't."

"Try me, Purane-Es. I beg you."

Purane-Es lowered his sword. "Fine!" he said. "Fine! You win. If you want to die here attempting heroics, be my guest. I'll return to the City Emerald and speak with my father. Once the Unseelie are defeated, assuming you yet live, I'm sure we can come to some kind of . . . arrangement. Assuming that an arrangement is what you're seeking from all this."

"An arrangement would be delightful," said Kallmer. "I believe a new assignment will be in order for me, closer to home, and perhaps a promotion to lieutenant captain."

"We shall see," said Purane-Es, his rage barely contained.

"Yes, we shall."

"Just one more thing," said Purane-Es. He moved as though to sheath his sword, raising the hilt over his head. Rather than stow the blade, however, he leaped quickly forward and thrust across the table, driving his point home through Kallmer's eye socket. Kallmer jerked, his hands grasping at his face, then slumped backward into his chair, dead.

The two sergeants looked up from their work. Purane-Es wiped his sword on Kallmer's cloak. "I was forced to kill him in self-defense," he said. "And if you know what's good for you, you'll agree with me, now and forever."

elements and motion

"How are all five of us going to fit in that thing?" asked Raieve, uncertain. It was not possible to her that the fragile Unseelie flyer could leave the ground at all, much less with five armed occupants. It was shallow and seemed held together with nothing but string and optimism.

Here at the top of the Temple Aba-e, the mist was like a second covering of snow over the city. A chill wind howled through the stark archways at the building's summit. The flyer rested at an angle on the rooftop, looking to Raieve like a lost sailboat. The abbot knelt by them, saying more prayers. Raieve could not understand the words that he prayed, but she was glad that someone was doing it. Some of the pink-robed monks stood by, watching the scene unfold.

"Eloquet will take the controls," said Mauritane. "Satterly will sit next to him in front, since he's the tallest. Silverdun and I will ride in back, with you sitting in one of our laps."

"That hardly seems dignified," said Raieve.

"Dignity is not the goal. We are to be drunken revelers returned late from the city of Gejel. That is why we do not know the current passphrases."

"And you really believe this . . . thing . . . will fly?" said Raieve.

"A friend of mine died so that you could fly in this 'thing,' woman," said Eloquet. "Marar Envacoro was one of the bravest men I've ever known."

"It was not my wish to offend," said Raieve, blushing. "I do not mean to diminish the sacrifice of your friend."

"And you're certain we'll have clearance to get into the city with it?" asked Mauritane.

"I think so," said Eloquet. "In peacetime, they do not even check the passphrases. Marar was able to come and go as he pleased, and he visited us here often, coordinating the church's Unseelie operations. The flier was spell-worked to return to the temple upon his death, so it escaped detection even unmanned. Now that they are at war, however, I suspect they'll be a bit pickier about who gets in. Marar and I spoke often about this contingency and he believed it would work."

"What happened to him?" said Satterly.

"Mab's legionnaires cut his throat. His name has joined the list of martyrs."

Satterly nodded and didn't say anything.

"Are we ready then?" said Mauritane.

"I think so," said Eloquet. "Vestar?"

"A simple prayer, I think," said the old man, rising to his feet. "Aba, pro-tect these of your children as they embark on a mission whose goal is peace. Let them commit only what is necessary of bloodshed, and spread your pro-tection like a blanket over them, for they act in your name."

"The girl Elice is safe, the baron's daughter?" Mauritane asked Eloquet.

"My men are watching over her. She will come to no harm. I do wish you'd tell me why we're keeping her, though. Perhaps I'd feel more comfort-able about it."

"I wish I could tell you," Mauritane said.

Eloquet looked around. "Right, cut the moorings. We're off!"

One of Eloquet's men swung an ax, and the ropes holding the flyer in place snapped, sending the craft lurching forward into the sky.

"How does this thing work?" Satterly shouted over the wind.

"Its power comes from the city itself. It can't operate very long away from the city's power source, but it should be just enough to get us back when we're done."

The city of Mab had appeared on the horizon in the early morning, a wide charcoal shadow against the northern skyline. Its approach was ponderous, seemingly infinite, but whenever Raieve looked up, its bulk seemed closer. Now she was almost glad to be flying directly toward it, if only to end the waiting. It grew in size and definition as they flew; she tried to make out the details of the city, keeping her mind full in order to block out the cold and fear.

They passed over the northern outskirts of Sylvan and sailed across the forest to the north. Somewhere in that direction lay the still-burning wreckage of Selafae. According to witnesses, the city had been incinerated in a matter of seconds by a tiny projectile. The ones who'd seen it and lived swore the missile was no larger than a man's head.

As they approached the city of Mab, Eloquet veered to the east, keeping the flyer low to the ground. They would make a wide circle and approach the city from the northeast to make their cover story more believable.

Already they could see the troop transports beginning to ferry their cargo to the ground. The wide, flat vessels detached from the city's ragged underbelly, each carrying a hundred or more men in tight formation, as well as horses, weapons, and supplies. Soldiers on the ground hurriedly felled trees so the transports could land in greater numbers.

"Why are they landing troops so far away from Sylvan?" asked Silverdun.

"These are only the backup infantry and cavalry," said Eloquet. "The primary column will remain in the city until it lands. These soldiers will secure the surrounding villages and clean up the mess when it's all over."

"They have more backups than we have troops!" shouted Satterly.

"Not quite," said Eloquet, "but enough to make me uncomfortable."

Once they'd reached a sufficient distance to make a plausible approach vector, Eloquet brought the flyer about and they glided toward the city of Mab. Now they were running with the wind, and Raieve realized that the flyer itself made no sound whatsoever.

"Check your costumes," ordered Mauritane. "And keep to yourselves. We don't want to start a fight before we even reach the city."

The city grew to take up half the sky, and it kept growing. Raieve had to admit she was impressed. From the outside, the city of Mab was one of the most beautiful things she'd ever seen. Enormous masts rose into the heavens bearing multicolored sails. Long streamers of purple and red flew from posts all over the rails and from the rigging as well. Though the structure had obviously been amended heavily over the years, its basic shape was that of a pear sliced in half along its length. The top deck was mostly flat, and the hull underneath was smooth and rounded. From the flat expanse rose a number of towers and spires; they mingled with the sails, their solidity complementing the constant rippling of the sheets.

It was not until she could see individual Fae crawling in the rigging and scurrying about on the decks that she was able to assimilate the scale of the sight before her. The city of Mab was more massive than anything she'd yet seen made by Fae hands. It would take half an hour to ride the length of it at a gallop. And it flew.

A pair of guards standing along the wall hailed them with the blast of a horn. Eloquet reached for the flags at his feet and shuffled through them. "I certainly hope this works," he said. He held up the flags in the order Marar Envacoro had specified in his final message. Green, then blue, then yellow, then green again.

The horn blew again, twice.

"That's not good," Eloquet said. "That's a signal to hold position."

"What do we do?" said Satterly, nervous.

"Don't do anything yet," said Mauritane. "We gain nothing by panicking."

One of the guards disappeared from the wall, and within seconds a flyer twice the size of theirs was in the sky, sailing toward them.

"That's a military patrol flyer," said Eloquet.

"Keep still," said Mauritane. Raieve looked down and noticed Mauritane's grip tighten on his sword. She wished she were in a less vulnerable position.

The patrol ship pulled alongside theirs and the single officer glanced over at them.

"Those are last month's flags," he said. "Do you have the new ones?"

Eloquet leaned out over the abyss, a huge grin on his face. "I must apologize, sir. I do not. We've been away at the Palm Festival in Gejel for the past twenty days."

"Do you have your identification with you?"

Eloquet reached into his tunic and withdrew a folded set of papers.

"Envacoro, eh? Tax collectors get twenty-day holidays now?"

"It was a special bonus." Eloquet continued to grin.

Raieve almost let go a sigh of relief. Then the guard looked over Eloquet's shoulder and seemed to notice them for the first time. "The rest of you, let's see your papers."

Sitting on Mauritane's lap, Raieve could feel his legs tensing to leap at the guard.

"I've got them," said Silverdun, rising awkwardly from his seat. He handed the guard a torn piece of cloth from his cloak.

"What's this?" said the guard.

"Why, our papers, of course," said Silverdun. His words were slow and singsong. "All perfectly in order, too."

The guard turned the cloth over in his hand. "Yes, that looks about right," he said. He handed Silverdun back the brown strip as though it were a thick stack of documents. "Carry on. Hope you had a good time, because we're at war now, and you're tethered for the interim."

After the guard had flown, Satterly said, "What just happened?"

Silverdun smiled, the first time Raieve had seen him do so in weeks. "My mestinal training finally pays off," he said. "I showed him the documentation he wished to see, plucked from his own memories."

"Good work," said Mauritane. Only then did Raieve feel his muscles relax beneath her. "Let's go, Eloquet."

Eloquet nodded. "I'm letting the flyer take us to its accustomed mooring," he said. "Marar's home is in a deliberately inconspicuous part of the city."

When they were close enough to see the faces and hear the shouts of the people of Mab, Raieve began to have second thoughts about their endeavor. In her previous life, the grudges and vendettas had all been personal. She knew none of these Unseelie people. How many innocents would die? It was not right, but she did not know what would be better.

Eloquet let the craft steer itself into a bay, between a pair of much larger and more opulent flying machines. They stole from the flyer quickly, trying to remain silent and yet appear as natural as possible to any passersby. Fortunately, there were none.

"We made it," breathed Eloquet.

"Don't start celebrating yet," said Mauritane. "We may not have impressed that guard as much as we thought."

The area in which they'd landed appeared to be a small marina, although that was certainly not the appropriate word here. Raieve wondered what the correct word for such a place was. Worn piers of mottled gray wood jutted out from the edge of the city's grand deck; instead of water, however, beneath them was only empty sky and the black and white of snow on rock beneath them.

They passed through the piers and into a narrow alley surrounded on either side by square structures of dull yellow. The walls were woven from a rough cloth and they fluttered in the wind. Only a few people stirred in the alley, most of them clutching thin garments to themselves, unprepared for the sudden cold.

"Drop your cloaks," said Mauritane.

"What?" Silverdun pulled his own cloak tighter. "It's freezing out here."

"This city spends almost all of its time in much warmer climes," said Mauritane. "We'll stick out like boggarts in a henhouse."

"What about our swords? Won't those be conspicuous?"

Mauritane sucked in his cheeks thoughtfully. "I don't suppose you've spent much time with the Unseelie," he said.

As if to explain his point, a cluster of five or six citizens rounded the corner, beer steins in hand. Each of them wore a sword or dagger at his belt. They passed by, ignoring the band of trespassers entirely.

"At least we know we fit in," said Eloquet.

"Let's go," said Mauritane.

Mauritane walked quickly, with a sense of purpose. He made no attempt to appear inconspicuous as they crossed through the jumbled maze that was the city of Mab. That was his way, of course. He went wherever he chose, and he did not seem to worry about the consequences. But, of course, he always did worry. He just never showed it. Raieve sighed and followed him, trying to keep up.

Had the city actually been a ship, the Tower of Sail could have been its mizzenmast, positioned as it was behind the soaring Royal Complex. From the main deck, the Tower of Sail rose up through a number of levels, passing vertically through open galleries and dark curtains. It was surrounded by open air for at least ten paces in every direction, leaving only one access point, a set of low double doors at the tower's base. A quartet of guards stood tired watch over the portal, two on one side and two on the other. It was easy to imagine that no one had ever attempted to lay siege to the building, so well was it protected by the mass of the city itself.

"Is everybody ready?" said Mauritane in a whisper. They stood in a cluster near a piece of abstract statuary, waiting for the tower's courtyard to clear. When the number of passersby had been reduced to two, Mauritane nodded, and they began.

"My honor, sir!" Satterly shouted at Eloquet. "That is what you have insulted."

Eloquet wheeled on him. "You have no honor to insult, peasant!"

Satterly leapt at Eloquet, catching him about the shoulders and pummeling him to the ground, where they hit the wooden floor with a crash. For an instant, the ground swayed unsteadily. Satterly rose to his knees and pounded Eloquet repeatedly with his fists.

Once they'd gotten the attention of everyone in the courtyard, Mauritane and Raieve broke off from the group. Silverdun remained, ostensibly trying to separate the fighting men.

Raieve approached the two onlookers, trying to look frenzied. "Please help!" she cried, taking the hand of the one of them. They were young men, drunken university students perhaps, and both of them seemed to notice her appreciatively at the same time.

"What's going on?" asked one of them.

"Which one is your lover?" asked the other.

"They'll kill each other," Raieve sobbed. "Please help me."

"What's in it for us, darling?" asked the first.

"Oh, please help!" She took them both by the wrist and started dragging them toward the struggle. While she pulled on their wrists, she chanced a look at Mauritane.

In a glance, she saw this: Mauritane approached the four guards, his hands outstretched, as if pleading for help. He motioned to Satterly and Eloquet. She heard him say, "Would you please . . . " While he was speaking, his right hand went for his sword. The guards, looking over his shoulder, had their eyes on the fight and not Mauritane. It was all the time he needed. He leaned into his first thrust, catching the guard on the right in the chest. With the blade still embedded, Mauritane pivoted gracefully to the left, his body flowing beneath his sword hand. He pulled the blade out, drawing the killing edge backhanded against the neck of the second guard, who'd taken a moment to look down at his fallen comrade. Continuing the motion, Mauritane bounded across the doorway to the second pair of guards. He rammed the first one with the pommel of his sword, pushing him up against the tower's wall, while the other reached for his weapon. The first man fell, gasping for breath. Mauritane, still holding his sword pommel-forward, spun around to the right. His blade entered the second guard's belly; Mauritane twisted the hilt and the man collapsed.

It had all taken less than the space of a breath, and the two young students had seen nothing, compelled as they were by Raieve's plight.

"Now!" shouted Raieve. She grasped the boys' wrists more firmly and jerked them forward. The smaller of the two stumbled and fell to his knees. The other managed to remain on his feet, only to be decked by a blow from Eloquet, who'd managed to run up behind Raieve and tackle him.

In a few more breaths, all four guards and the two boys were safely inside the tower's anteroom. It was a small, undecorated circular space with a staircase leading up to the left and a small door on the right. Silverdun quickly bound the two boys and the single living guard with spellwire before they gained the presence of mind to protest. He wove layer upon layer of the sticky, translucent gel from his fingertips, coating their mouths, arms, and legs.

Meanwhile, Mauritane helped Satterly and Eloquet undress the dead guards. Raieve stripped unselfconsciously in front of them; she could not help, though, but glance at Mauritane while she pulled her leather leggings down over her calves. He was watching her. At least that was something.

Mauritane, Raieve, and Eloquet donned the guards' uniforms, leaving Satterly and Silverdun to guard the door. Silverdun would be able to keep the door magically locked for a while if there was trouble, and Satterly . . . Raieve supposed he could throw himself against the latch or something, if it came to that.

Mauritane had memorized the plans of the building. Their target was three flights up and they ran toward it, taking the steps two at a time. Sooner or later they would be discovered; every second counted.

They reached the top of the stairs safely. They exited the staircase, stepping into a whirlwind of activity where, dressed as guards, they were completely unnoticed. Scholars hurried past in the wide hallway, dodging each other as they consulted long scrolls, whispering to each other as they consulted enormous books resting on podiums along the length of the corridor. At the far end of the passage, an archway led into darkness; the only illumination beyond was sparse candlelight that flickered in ghoulish shadows on the walls.

"Is that it?" whispered Raieve.

"Yes," said Mauritane, in a normal speaking voice. He motioned upward with his chin, indicating that she should speak normally as well.

"Fine then," said Raieve, at full volume.

Eloquet touched the prayer beads beneath his tunic. "It's time," he said.

"Yes," said Mauritane.

They strode toward the darkened archway. One of the passing scholars, a pitifully thin man, noticed them approaching and moved to block their path. "You can't go in there," he hissed, annoyed. He held up a bony finger. "This is a critical time."

"Shut up." Eloquet shoved the tiny man sideways against the stone wall of the hall, where his skull struck with an ugly crack. Heads turned across the length of the corridor, watching as the scholar slumped against the wall.

"Aba forgive me," said Eloquet.

They drew their swords and ran through the archway. Candlelight danced on the faces of monsters. The sight was so unexpected that all three of them stopped short.

The things were arrayed in a wide circle, easily ten paces across, sitting nearly elbow to elbow. They were not Fae, at least not entirely. They had been mixed somehow with birds, it seemed, although the hybrid was neither beautiful nor graceful. Hideous, deformed wings grew all over their bodies; their tiny eyes gleamed from within enormous bald heads. Instead of mouths they had flopping black beaks that dripped with saliva and foam. When they noticed the intruders, their heads tipped back and some of them made quiet gurgling sounds.

"These are the masters of Elements and Motion?" said Eloquet, gasping in fear.

Mauritane caught himself first. He shoved Eloquet and Raieve into action. "Don't think. Move!"

Raieve went for the one closest to her and started slashing. The thing did not move to defend itself. It simply sat there, the bubbling noise coming from its throat. The force of Raieve's shocked thrust nearly cut the creature in two. It fell backward with a single, wet cry, dropping into a puddle of blood and tiny black feathers.

"What are these things?" she wondered aloud, sweeping her braids back with her free hand. "Are they Fae?" She stepped sideways and struck out at another one. Like the first, it did nothing to save itself.

"They're bred magically with eagles," said Mauritane evenly. "It improves their inner sight. That is how they move the city through space." His sword twirled in his hands, felling one after the other of the creatures, all of whom succumbed with nothing more than a plaintive wail.

Raieve looked out toward the archway. The scholars stood at the threshold, horrified. Some of them covered their mouths with their hands. Raieve couldn't help herself. She smiled at them, licking her lips. One of them fell over sideways.

A few moments later, all of the bird-things were dead or dying, their blood beginning to puddle on the floor. As the last one fell, the room seemed to dip and sway, like a seagoing vessel cresting a giant wave.

"Let's go!" shouted Mauritane. He barreled toward the door. The scholars, already petrified, fell back at his approach.

They reached the door to the stairwell just as it burst open. Silverdun backed out of the doorway, followed quickly by Satterly. The stairwell was teeming with guardsmen in chain mail. They carried vicious-looking curved swords and thin daggers.

"How many?" shouted Mauritane, slamming the door shut before any of the guards could reach it.

"I didn't stop to count," said Silverdun, drawing his sword now that he had room. "I'd guess a dozen. More coming. Held them off as long as I could."

"You did well, Silverdun."

"I'm scared all to piss," Silverdun said.

"So am I," said Mauritane.

The door crashed open again.

Raieve lost sight of her companions. She ran towards one of the guards, crashing into him with her sword aimed at his groin. Blood spattered onto her fingers. The man beneath her grunted, his face red. She rolled off of him, tripping another who bent down to grasp at her legs. Her sword flashed out at a pair of exposed ankles, severing the tendons of each.

The floor swayed again, this time more violently, and several of the men around her fell onto their knees. She whipped her blade around, slashing into the face of the man next to her. He screamed like a child.

Something was dripping down her neck. Standing, she reached up, touched her head, felt a deep cut there. She had no idea when it had happened.

Another guard came at her. This one moved in low and fast, grabbing her around the waist. Raieve leaned forward and bit down on the man's ear, tearing it slowly from his head. He jerked backward, and they toppled to the floor together.

It seemed to go on forever in this way; as soon as she pried one of them off of her, another one was upon her. She strained against them, her sword arm aching, but none of them managed to touch her with a blade. She blessed her good fortune and kept swinging.

When Raieve stood up, it was already over. Mauritane stood with his feet planted, casting his body back and forth for new foes. Easily a dozen bodies lay on the floor. Silverdun was on his knees, holding his stomach. Eloquet and Satterly leaned against the wall, breathing hard.

Satisfied that the stairway had been cleared, Mauritane took a deep breath. "Let's go," he said. He turned and saw Silverdun kneeling. "Are you all right?" he said.

"I'll survive," Silverdun said. "Took one in the family heirlooms."

"We're all alive," said Raieve, shocked. "Five against . . . eighteen, and we all survived. How?"

All eyes turned to Mauritane. It was Eloquet who said, "You possess all twelve Gifts, don't you? No normal man can fight like that."

Mauritane didn't answer. "Time is running short," he muttered.

"It's true, though. Isn't it? The man who possesses all Gifts in equal strength cannot be beaten by any foe. I saw you. You watched over each of us, protected us while you fought." Eloquet pressed.

"Enough," said Mauritane. "Now go or I'll cut you down myself!"

Eloquet knelt before him. "You are He Who Clears the Path," he said. "Only the one who comes after you is more holy."

Mauritane dragged Eloquet up by his collar. "Not again!" He pulled the man close. "I won't have any of that. Move! Now!"

They ran for the stairs, now silent.

Outside, a phalanx of soldiers waited in the courtyard, their shields close. Behind the ranks of shield-bearers stood a row of bowmen. Mauritane ran headlong into the courtyard and stopped short, the others right behind him.

"Hold fire!" cried a voice from behind the shields. Raieve turned to back away but found the great double doors of the tower were now pushing themselves closed.

A tiny woman, ancient in appearance, perfect in poise and elegance, pressed through the soldiers. Her hands were raised toward the doors, and she beckoned them toward her. When they had closed completely, she dropped her hands and regarded Mauritane.

"Titania's messenger," she said. "What have you done?"

"Death to Queen Mab!" shouted Eloquet. A knife sailed from his fingers, aimed at the woman. "This is for Marar Envacoro!"

The dagger caught in her chest and she sank to the ground. "Who?" she managed.

"That . . . is Queen Mab?" whispered Raieve.

Mauritane nodded.

Mab stood again and pulled the knife from her flesh as though pulling a pin from a pincushion. She looked at Eloquet, her face serene. "You are about to die; very painfully, I might add. If you think your god Aba can save you, I suggest you call on him now." She took a step forward. "Guards, take them."

Mauritane ran directly toward her, his sword raised high. He shouted to the heavens, a war cry from a faraway place.

The archers raised their crossbows and aimed them at his breast. The order came to fire.

Then the world fell away.

Raieve felt herself pitch forward. She reached out to stop her descent and kept falling. The floor seemed to drop away from her as she continued downward.

She hit something hard, a wooden wall perhaps. When she opened her eyes, the world had turned sideways. Wind sang in her ears. Her stomach tried to leave through her mouth. All around her, men were shouting at the tops of their lungs. Somewhere, in the midst of it, she heard Eloquet's voice, speaking the spell words that had brought Envacoro's flyer to the Mountain of Oak and Thorn.

She was praising him for his presence of mind when a wooden spar came about fast and cracked into her forehead. The sunlight dimmed and she pitched forward onto her face.

When she awoke, she was aboard the flyer, sprawled across the laps of Mauritane and Silverdun.

"What happened?" she said.

"You got hit by a flying hunk of wood," said Satterly. "Are you okay?"

"We got out?" she said.

"Look behind you," said Eloquet. She raised her head painfully and looked backward.

The city of Mab was split down the middle in two jagged halves. From within the wrecked hull, geysers of water from torn plumbing lines sprayed into the afternoon sky. A swirling fire spread across the massive main deck of the city, sending up tongues of flame along the cloth sails and the rigging.

"Look," said Satterly. "It's falling out of the sky."

It was true. The entire city had begun to dip toward the earth. Entire sections of its architecture began to split off and hurtle toward the ground. Fliers sprang from every part of the city's walls, some so loaded with Fae that they themselves tipped and spiraled to the ground.

With a peal like thunder, the two halves of the city separated. The forward half, that containing the Royal Complex, remained aloft while the rear half lost all buoyancy and plummeted. Whatever screams might have been heard were lost in the rush of wind and the cry of metal and wood tearing and breaking, a symphony of destruction.

As Raieve watched, the remaining half of the city lurched once, then twice, then it listed to the side and began to fall, tumbling end over end.

The two halves struck the forested ground within seconds of each other. There was a flash of light from the ground, then an enormous billowing of dust. Then the sound of the explosion reached them, screaming like the roar of death that it embodied.

In the confusion, no one bothered to follow them as they sped away.

"We made it," said Eloquet. "We did it! We did it!"

Mauritane looked wearily at him. "There is no cause to celebrate what happened here," he said. "We just murdered thousands of innocent Fae."

"We saved Sylvan," said Eloquet, his eyes searching.

"Yes," said Mauritane. "I suppose that's one way of feeling better about it." He turned his eyes away from Eloquet's.

Raieve chose to remain silent. She ran her brown-stained fingers through sticky hair, remembering her clan's practical adage that blood and conversation do not mix.

"Look!" said Silverdun, pointing at the ground. "We weren't as successful as we might have hoped."

In the light of the burning city, Raieve saw troopships on the ground, ranks of Unseelie soldiers still filing out of them. There were hundreds of them, perhaps even thousands. As she watched, the soldiers began rushing toward the city's wreckage, fighting the heat of the blast to reach it.

"No," said Mauritane. "And we failed to achieve our primary purpose. See the barge there in the center of the ships? With the gold and purple banners?"

Raieve nodded. The barge was surrounded by soldiers; a curtained palanquin was just visible on its decks.

"That," said Mauritane, "is Queen Mab's."

Hours later, when the damaged flyer finally returned to the temple's roof, it was dark. The round disk of moon bathed the world in a rich indigo glow. No one was waiting to greet them.

Confused, they hurried down the many flights of stairs that led to the middle tier, where the massive stone columns cast shadows in the moonlight.

"Look," said Silverdun, pointing.

Raieve looked down the bridge, where Eloquet and his men had built a barricade against the turmoil in the streets below. The barricade had been demolished.

"Let's go downstairs," said Eloquet, his voice shaking.

Before they reached the great room, they knew. It was too quiet; the rooms and halls were vacant, devoid of sound and movement.

In the great room, where the temple's worship services were held, a massive fire had been set in the central fireplace. Surrounding the fire were twisted bodies in pink robes, some of them badly burned, others bathed in blood. The bodies were piled on top of each other, dozens and dozens of them. Raieve had never seen anything like it.

Looking away, Raieve saw movement from the corner of her eye. On the steps leading up to the dais, a tiny figure sat, cradling someone in her arms.

"Someone's alive," said Raieve, pointing.

They approached the figure on the steps. It was a young girl, dressed in the white robe of a novice. She cradled the still form of the abbot Vestar to her, holding his head in her lap. She stroked his bald head gently, kissing his hand, whispering prayers into his ears.

"Are you Mauritane?" the girl said, not looking up. Her voice was flat.

"I am," said Mauritane.

"The man said I should give you this when you came. He took the girl with him, the baron's daughter. He said it was about her." She handed him a rolled note from within her robe, her eyes on the abbot's face.

Mauritane unrolled the note and read it. It simply said, "I win," and was signed by Purane-Es.

the battle of sylvan

Many of Eloquet's men had fallen alongside the residents of the Temple Aba-e, their corpses mixed indiscriminately with those of the coenobites. A hasty search revealed no survivors except the girl holding the abbot's lifeless head; the girl herself was deeply in shock and could tell them little else about what had happened.

During the search, a group of soldiers from Eloquet's cell returned from the city; they walked into a tableau of agonized silence. Satterly paced slowly by the fire; Raieve knelt by the dazed girl. Silverdun sat with his head in his hands, staring forward.

Mauritane was deep in thought when the soldiers returned, barely noticing them. It would be tempting, he imagined, to chase Purane-Es down and beat him to death slowly with a tree branch. He imagined the scene graphically. But it was no use. There was no punishment for Purane-Es that would compare to the tragedy the fool had evoked. And for what? Revenge? Envy? Simple malice? Mauritane could not understand Purane-Es's mind, and it troubled him.

Regardless, the destruction of Mab's city had not prevented a war, it had only evened the odds. Seeing the expressions of horror on the faces of Eloquet's men, Mauritane realized that Purane-Es had fouled things up even more than he'd thought.

"The Royal Guard Commander did this?" said one of the men. "And with our backs turned! They lied! We trusted them and they lied!"

"I knew we should never have allied with them," cursed another.

Eloquet attempted to calm them. "The Unseelie are still coming," he said. "If we turn against the Seelie now we will all die, as surely as anything I know to be true."

"What difference does it make?" said a blond boy, reeling at the sight of the bodies. "We're all dead anyway."

Eloquet swallowed. "No. When I tell you what I'm about to tell you, I think you'll believe differently." Eloquet related to them the story of Mauritane's fight aboard the city of Mab, how his battle cry had split the city in two.

Mauritane didn't say anything, although he knew his cry had done nothing to tear the city apart. The great ship, without its Masters of Elements and Motion to hold it together, had flown apart from its own weight.

"I'm telling you, Mauritane is He Who Clears the Path," Eloquet said. "He is the one who prepares the way for She Who Will Come."

Mauritane thought back to what the Thule Man had said and shivered, but said nothing for fear of encouraging Eloquet. Whatever mantle was being thrust upon him, he wanted no part of it.

"And you think," said Silverdun bitterly, "that these murders are the sacrifices spoken of in the Rauad Faehar? 'And you will know him by the great surrender that comes around him, when the blood will pool at his feet.'"

"That is what I believe," said Eloquet.

"If that makes you feel better, then so be it."

Some of Eloquet's men glared at Silverdun.

"Don't be so blind, Silverdun," said Eloquet. "When our people hear what's happened here and who caused it, the alliance we worked so hard to create will crumble in an instant. Aba could not have wanted this; the Rauad also says that Aba will redeem for good all that is evil. Aba will take back pain and suffering from the Usurper and the Adversary and sanctify them."

Silverdun grimaced. He looked at Eloquet for a long time, then nodded. "I suppose anything is possible," he said.

Mauritane touched Eloquet's shoulder. "Eloquet, you are a good and brave man. I don't believe what you're saying about me, but I respect your belief. I also think if enough of your people believe it, it will sustain our alliance. Will you speak to the other cell leaders on my behalf, telling them what you've just said, even though I don't believe it?"

"I don't care if you believe it or not; it's the truth." Eloquet forced a smile. "It will be difficult, though. I only know three names. Those three know only three names as well. It will take time."

"Do what you have to do. Time is not one of the Gifts."

Eloquet took a number of his men and ran from the great hall, barking orders as he left. He returned a few moments later, though, carrying a set of reins in his hand. He led a tall stallion into the room; the animal shied away from the fire, making a quiet noise in its throat.

"One of my men found him," said Eloquet. "He's been asking for you all over the city."

"Streak!" said Mauritane. He ran to the horse and touched its shoulder. "I was afraid I'd lost you."

"It pleases me to see the Master again," said Streak, his speaking voice as always hoarse yet eager. "Will we ride again soon?"

"Very soon," said Mauritane, patting the creature's neck.

"You wanted to see me?" Satterly stepped into the great hall, now appropriated by Mauritane as his command center. The bodies had been removed quickly and with respect; one of Eloquet's men had gone down into the City Center from the long bridge and asked the peasants for help. None of them had complained while they dragged the bodies from the room.

"Yes," said Mauritane. He lit his pipe and took a quick puff before speaking. "I've decided I don't want you to fight," he said.

Satterly nodded. "I didn't do very well up there in the city of Mab," he said.

Mauritane shook his head. "It's not that. I want you to use your scientific education to work on a problem."

Satterly nodded. "If I can help, I will."

Satterly listened to Mauritane's concerns and then walked out of the great hall, unsure how to proceed. He wandered for most of an hour, watching his shadow twist and turn in the light of the oil lamps. He stood at a corner and watched the tiny flame move back and forth.

"Oh my God," said Satterly. "That's it!"

Eloquet's young blond lieutenant was busy loading supplies onto a wagon when the human Satterly stopped him with a tap on the shoulder.

"Excuse me," Satterly said. "Can you tell me where you buy your kerosene?"

Mauritane and Prae-Alan, the leader of the Seelie Army forces in Sylvan, met Eloquet and the leaders of twelve other cells in the Rye Grove just before midnight.

"What is their answer?" said Mauritane.

"They will continue to fight," said Eloquet. "Not all of them, but almost all. The ones who will not fight alongside the Seelie will at least do nothing to aid the forces of Mab. They will withhold their vengeance until the Unseelie have been repelled."

"You are all agreed on this?" asked Prae-Alan.

"We are," said one of the cell leaders, a stocky man with long ears and short braids. "But only if He Who Clears the Path leads us."

"Fine," said Prae-Alan. The matter had already been discussed, and Prae-Alan was simply glad that his own countrymen wouldn't be trying to kill him while he defended their borders. He didn't really care about anything else.

"But we will not forget this," said another cell leader. "We will not forget, and our reprisal, when it comes, will make you long for the days when Queen Mab was your chief concern."

Raieve was sharpening her sword on a snakestone when Mauritane came for her. "It's time," he said. "Our scouts tell us the Unseelie will be in place by dawn."

Raieve nodded, running her thumb along the blade. "There's no way we'll be in the City Emerald by First Lamb, even if we survive. This entire mission has been a waste of time for us." She continued sharpening her blade.

"No," said Mauritane, "it brought us where we needed to be, when we needed to be there. And it's not First Lamb yet. Anything is yet possible."

Raieve looked up at him. "I can't say I agree with you," she said.

The North Valley sat just north of Sylvan; its southern rim was a narrow strip that descended into the city on the far side. To the north, the Unseelie were waiting, hidden by the thick forest and the mist that spilled out from Sylvan. The predawn light glowed blue across the faces of the combined Seelie forces. The entire southern rim was a cacophony of shouted orders, neighing horses, and the chanting of the battle mages preparing their spells. Silver ground against sharpening stones and quarrels clicked into the notches of hundreds of crossbows.

Finally, the order to stand ready came, and the soldiers fell into place.

The first line was cavalry; each man on the line had been chosen from his company by the drawing of lots. Men from each division—chosen from the Seelie Army, the Royal Guard, and the rebels—stood at the ready.

Behind them were the battle mages. They stood slightly higher on the valley's edge, their spellcasting components surrounding them like miniature cities. The defensive mages had already begun chanting their shields, creating waves of purple light above the heads of the front line.

Next were the ground forces, the infantry. There were not enough swords to go around, so some of the men, mostly the rebels, carried axes, sledgehammers and clubs. Among them stood the crossbow archers, who would charge into battle among the infantry, their weapons effective only at very close range.

The longbowmen stood at the crest of the hill, the final wave of defense. There were no spell shields above their heads, which gave them room to fire but also left them vulnerable to overhead attack. They did not carry swords; if the battle were ever to reach them, it would already be over.

Mauritane, riding Streak, faced his army. Prae-Alan was at his left, Eloquet at his right, both on horseback.

"There are some who will say," Mauritane began, "that our shared desire for survival is all that brings us together here." His voice was loud and strong; it carried all the way back to the archers. "I believe that is only a small part of the truth. Within each of us is the heart of the Seelie; that great soul that gives action to our limbs, quickness to our minds, and the *re* to our magic. The heart of the Seelie was once pure. It can be pure again. Whether Aba judges us now in his heavenly chariot, or whether a man is alone with his own conscience in this life, we do not all agree. So be it. History will not judge us based on what we believed but rather how we acted when put to the test. So it is with Aba. So it is also with our conscience. This valley is not simply a battlefield; it is a crucible in which the heart of the Seelie will be placed under the pestle and ground beneath a heavy weight. If the Seelie heart is pure, it will not shatter or crumble. Instead, it will shatter the crucible, crumble the pestle that attempts to grind it."

The men cheered, raising their swords to the sky.

"We shall take the day, not because we are stronger, though we are. Not because we are faster, or better trained, though those things are true as well. No, we shall take the day because we know that what lies to the south of this valley is worth defending. And what are we defending, exactly? Not the cities, for those will someday fall to the ground! Not the rocks, for those will erode over the centuries! Not even our own children or the children of our neighbors! They too will pass away and become dust. But the Seelie heart shall remain! It is eternal! And woe be unto those who think to squeeze it in their grasp. For what is eternal can never be crushed, can never die!"

The men cheered again with renewed vigor. Mauritane knew they would follow him into the jaws of death, and he was both infinitely grateful and infinitely sad that it was true.

"Now I give you your battle cry. The Seelie Heart!"

"The Seelie Heart!" they shouted back. "The Seelie Heart!"

Across the valley there came a flash and a dull roar. The battle had begun. The Unseelie forces began to pour out of the woods, making their lines along the northern rim of the valley. Queen Mab rode before them, giving the army her benediction.

The battle mages cast their long-range missiles and wards, meeting the defenses and the magic-seeking projectiles of the Unseelie. Deafening explosions rocked the valley. Great clouds of green and blue mixed with the milky-white fog. Bolts of silver lightning flashed back and forth so quickly that none but the mages could comprehend it. As they fought in the skies, the mages also battled in their minds, some of them falling to the ground, clutching their heads or their bellies, some of them bursting into flame.

The battle in the skies was decided in seconds. The Seelie had taken their first piece of the victory. The remote seers divined fifty Unseelie mages destroyed out of a potential hundred, whereas the Seelie had lost only twenty, and all of their defensive wards remained in place after the altercation.

Mauritane wheeled Streak and rode to the cavalry commander. "Prepare your men. We ride at my signal!" He rode to the front of the line. In seconds the commander flashed the ready sign at him. Mauritane took a deep breath. "Aba," he whispered. "If you are there, please be on our side."

Mauritane held his sword aloft. The Seelie army fell silent. For a few seconds all that could be heard were the dying fires from the magic conflagration below and the rustle of impatient hooves.

Mauritane dropped the sword. "The Seelie Heart!" he cried. They charged.

The fighting raged through the morning. Mauritane's archers took out fewer of the Unseelie cavalry than he'd hoped, and the mounted Seelie were forced to make up the difference in close combat. Swords flashed and crossbows cracked. As it had done so often before in battle, time disappeared for Mauritane. His mind entered a different place, where all he could see was the field around him. All he could hear were the reports of his subordinates. All he could think was strategy, motion, attack, withdraw, hold, advance. Faces blurred together; motions simplified and became geometric. Mauritane moved through the chaos, applying his blade when necessary, mostly giving orders.

There would be no retreat. If the Unseelie were to cross the valley into Sylvan, then they could launch their projectile bomb where there were no battle mages to pluck it from the sky. Mauritane had to assume that the weapon had survived the city's destruction—it would be foolish to assume otherwise.

As the sun moved across the valley, the Seelie forces advanced, inching across the basin's floor. Mauritane brooked no retreat, would not back down from the enemy. He led charge after charge into the thickest wedge of Unseelie troops, striking for the heart of their command. The Unseelie officers of the center column were forced to call continually for reinforcements, preventing their wings from flanking the Seelie either to the east or the west.

Mauritane fought, slashing and slashing, taking cuts and bruises, and once even a deep bite, forcing out the pain, keeping his thoughts only on forward motion. An Unseelie general fought near him for a while. They eyed each other over the riot of bodies and horses and blades. Soon they were face to face.

Mauritane watched the general come at him, placing a barrier of his own men between himself and Mauritane's remaining cavalry. They squared off. Mauritane glared at the man, passion and anger searing his mind.

The general raised his sword as if to charge. Mauritane steadied himself. Instead, though, the general produced a dagger in his left hand and whipped it not at Mauritane but at Streak. Mauritane felt the beast tense beneath him, then falter and fall to his side, nearly crushing Mauritane's leg. Mauritane rolled off of the animal and looked up, anticipating the general's next attack.

But the attack never came. The general had sheathed his weapon, laughing at Mauritane, and was now riding back behind the lines.

Mauritane found himself suddenly behind his own infantry as they rushed forward to take the next hill. The few remaining cavalrymen had mounted another assault on the small rise at the valley's base.

Mauritane examined Streak's knife wound. The blade had gone in between the shoulders, and the horse appeared to have trouble breathing.

"I have failed you, master," said Streak, struggling for breath.

Mauritane stroked the horse's head. "No, Streak. You served me well."

"I do not wish to leave you."

"I do not wish for you to go." Mauritane put his arms around Streak's neck and squeezed gently. "You are a good horse," he said. Streak took a final breath and collapsed on the harrowed ground.

The fighting continued well into the night. Those of the battle mages who were wounded pitched in by sending up fiery balls of witchlight to illuminate the valley. The sky above became a swirling incandescent palette of pinks and blues and greens, casting harsh black shadows on the icy ground as the soldiers continued their struggle.

While Mauritane's men continued their relentless assault against the central concentration of Unseelie forces, the Seelie cavalry on the valley's western edge began to weaken. Behind the front lines, four divisions of Unseelie infantry peeled off from the main wedge and went for the weak spot.

It was the mistake that cost them the battle.

The thin cavalry line had been a feint; when they were finally penetrated, two companies of Seelie archers arose behind them. Their arrows felled row after row of Mab's infantrymen until their officers realized the error and tried to withdraw. But it was too late. Mauritane took advantage of the momentary weakness and sent everything he had down the middle of the Unseelie front. They held position, briefly, and Mauritane lost what was left of his cavalry. But they could not hold forever. Finally, the Unseelie line broke. Mauritane's infantry poured through the gap, cutting a wide swath through the no-longer-protected battle mages. The sky above the Unseelie grew dark, and the Royal Guard's mages went to work with a different kind of witchlight, directing beams of intense and focused brightness at the Unseelie soldiers. Blinded, they fell back even farther.

Thus pierced, the invading army was now cut off from its commanders. Their foot soldiers spun, confused, unable to discern where the Seelie attacks were coming from. From there, it was simply a matter of time.

One of the Unseelie generals broke rank and fled, taking his companies with him. The Seelie raced to fill the gap. What remained of Mab's army—confused, tired, disheartened—turned and fled to the north, bearing Queen Mab to safety on a palanquin of silver and gold.

Mauritane fell back against a stone, his sword arm numb, his senses reeling. Around him the smell of blood and death mingled with that of the frozen earth and old snow. The witchlight began to fade, one by one, until only torches remained to give light. It was time to withdraw, to collect the dead, and to sleep.

Word came that Seelie Army reinforcements were now a day out of Sylvan. It was over. There would be no further attempts at invasion. Lacking surprise, there was little Queen Mab could do now but escape with her life.

Eloquet, staggering across the field, helped Mauritane to his feet.

"We've got a few fresh reserves," he breathed. "We're setting up sentries all across the valley's edge. You should go rest."

Mauritane stood unsteadily, wiping his hands on the front of his tunic. "Yes, I think you're right." He took two steps and collapsed to the ground.

When Mauritane awoke, it was late afternoon. He found himself in a plush four-poster bed with satin sheets and more pillows than he could count. Fresh clothes lay on a chair beside him.

He dressed and washed his face in the basin by the bed. Stepping out of the room, he now felt every cut, every scrape, every bruise. He limped down a flight of stairs into a wide hall, where a family of strangers sat eating.

"You're just in time for supper," said the man at the head of the table. He rose, introducing himself as Thura, an eel importer.

"Taking you in was the least I could do," the man offered. "Eloquet is an old friend of mine."

"An eel trader, eh?" said Mauritane, sitting and filling his plate. "I used to be one of those."

There were parades and celebrations planned in Sylvan all night long. Mauritane made himself as scarce as possible, spending most of the evening trying to round up his companions. Finally, near midnight, after a long succession of speeches given by city officials and noblemen, Mauritane was left alone with Silverdun and Raieve in Thura's study.

"How do you fare?" said Mauritane, looking both of them over.

Raieve's leg was immobilized in spellwire. "I got trampled during the Unseelie retreat," she said. "I broke almost every bone in my foot, but I will survive."

Silverdun's face was badly cut; he wore a bandage that covered his left eye and most of the left side of his face. "I suppose I can't get much uglier," he said, shrugging.

"What of Satterly?" said Raieve. "Where is he?"

Mauritane sighed. "I was hoping he'd be back by now."

"We've lost two more days," said Silverdun. "First Lamb is four days away. It's at least six days to the City Emerald riding hard, and we don't even have the girl."

Mauritane nodded. "That's true," he said.

"I don't regret it," said Raieve.

"Thank you," Mauritane said. He raised his eyes and looked at her. She met his gaze and they sat that way until Silverdun grew uncomfortable and changed the subject.

"Mauritane, wake up." It was Silverdun, standing over him. Mauritane was in Thura's bed again, although this time he remembered how he got there.

"What's going on?" he said. Looking out the window, he could see that it was still night.

"There's something in front of the house you should see."

Mauritane stood and followed Silverdun out onto the terrace. There was a low rumbling noise coming from the road below. Mauritane looked down and nodded with approval.

Meyer Schrabe's 1971 Pontiac LeMans sat in front of the house, its engine producing a steady purr. Satterly, behind the wheel, was grinning from ear to ear.

"Time to go," said Mauritane, walking inside and reaching for his clothes. "We're not done yet."

steel

Mauritane had never dreamed that anything, especially a huge metal wagon, could go so fast. The speed at which they flew along the Mechesyl road was awe inspiring. Satterly, he noticed, had never looked as comfortable as he did now, guiding the vehicle with his wrist over the steering wheel.

"We could go faster," Satterly shouted over the rush of wind, "but if there's ice on the road we'd be in big trouble."

Mauritane nodded, thankful that this was as fast as it got.

Satterly had thoughtfully provided a number of thick blankets to drape over the steel parts of the car, but even so Silverdun had managed to burn himself on a mirror housing. He'd forgotten the thing was steel and not silver, the former being virtually unknown to him, and had rested his hand on it by mistake. Mauritane had seen steel before, in a demonstration of human swordsmithing at the academy, and had never forgotten the fiery slickness of those polished blades.

"How did you find fuel for this thing?" Mauritane asked. Part of him wished that the moveable covering for the automobile were not broken—the wind at this speed was fierce and relentless—but another part was glad for the distraction and embraced the briskness of it.

"I was looking at one of those kerosene lamps in the temple," Satterly said. "And I remembered reading that the first automobiles in my world were run on kerosene. But it didn't work very well. There was another by-product of the kerosene-making process that they'd been mostly throwing away, until they realized it was perfect for an automotive fuel. I asked one of Eloquet's men where they got their kerosene, and he pointed me to the Lamplighters Guild in Sylvan."

Satterly pumped his feet, moving the lever at his right in rhythm. The car lurched and roared even louder as they started up an incline.

"It turns out that the Lamplighters Guild keeps a lot of this stuff around—there isn't even a word for it in Common—and they use it as a solvent. It's good at getting grease off of your hands. I paid them four silver khoums for about forty gallons of it. That'll be more than enough to get us to the City Emerald."

The roaring of the engine dropped suddenly in pitch, and a low staccato rumble seemed to envelop them. Mauritane jumped in his seat.

"Sorry!" said Satterly. "The fuel I bought is very different from what this car is used to running on. I had to make a couple of adjustments to the . . . power-thing-that-makes-it-go . . . and I didn't have the tools or the time or the experience to do a very good job."

The car made another series of rumbles and then dropped into a smooth rhythm again.

They met the Seelie Army reinforcements coming the other way on the road. At first the soldiers were wary of the loud machine, but the news of the Seelie victory had already gotten back to them on the wings of multiple message sprites, and when Mauritane was recognized in the passenger seat, the soldiers mobbed the car and cheered. He waved and nodded at them, but he could not bring himself to smile.

After leaving Sylvan in the dark of night, they'd driven through most of the day, stopping only for latrine breaks and refueling. It was nearly impossible to speak while driving, and so for the most part all four of them—Satterly, Mauritane, Raieve, and Silverdun—were left to their own thoughts. Raieve mostly sat watching the scenery fly by, while Silverdun stared blankly ahead, clutching his stomach as though he felt ill.

When they stopped for the night, Mauritane asked him, "Silverdun, are you unwell?"

"Riding in that thing makes me damned queasy," he said.

Satterly laughed. "You're carsick," he said. "It's very common where I come from. Nothing to be ashamed of."

"Who said I was ashamed?" Silverdun grumbled.

They'd stopped near a grove of trees, still preferring to remain away from towns and cities, though they were harder to avoid the farther south they drove. They sat around a campfire and continued not to speak. The silence of the drive seemed to have overwhelmed them.

As he sat looking at his friends, Mauritane snapped out of his own concerns long enough to realize that none of them had any idea what the future held. The City Emerald was near; at this speed there would be time to catch up with Purane-Es and still make it by First Lamb. All of Mauritane's concentration was focused on his upcoming confrontation with Purane-Es, and he hadn't stopped to consider what might lie beyond, after the successful completion of their mission.

Prison had a way of dulling one's sense of the future. The days slouched by, one by one, each more or less the same. During his two years at Crere Sulace, Mauritane had almost learned to stop thinking about the road ahead entirely. A man with a life sentence had no business thinking about what lay beyond today.

This mission had been in most ways the direct opposite of imprisonment, and yet he'd still managed to avoid thinking beyond its single tangible goal. Go to Sylvan, get the girl, be in the City Emerald by First Lamb. While it had been going on, First Lamb had seemed very distant indeed. But now, First Lamb was not so far off. It was the day after tomorrow. And it was only upon thinking it, as he peered into the yellow twists of campfire in front of him, that Mauritane himself began to wonder what might happen after that.

The next morning, the car would not start. It had snowed a bit during the night, and though they'd covered it with a heavy tarpaulin, there was still a gleaming of ice on the machine's front window. Satterly sat in the driver's seat, performing a complex and noisy starting ritual that produced slow, choking sounds, but not the growl of its active state.

"What's the matter?" Silverdun said, standing by the car's door and clapping his hands together against the morning chill.

"Thing-that-makes-it-go is too cold," he said. "It doesn't want to start."

"Would it help if it were warmer?" Silverdun asked.

"Well, yes," said Satterly. "But . . ."

"All you had to do was ask," said Silverdun. He walked around and placed his hands above the sloping metal front of the car, careful not to touch it. He drew the rune for spellwarmth in the air over the hood and closed his eyes, taking a deep breath.

Within seconds, the ice crystals spread across the front glass were replaced with rivulets and vapor.

"Is this enough?" asked Silverdun.

Satterly performed the starting ritual again. The car made a few sneezing sounds, then a quicker sound like call of a heron, and then the machine sprang into life.

"That'll do it!" said Satterly. "Let's go!"

The hills of the far western reaches were replaced by the wide plains of the Low Country that lay northwest of the City Emerald. Farm after farm blurred past them, all smothered under a layer of snow, the fields barren. The going became easier once they passed into these arable lands; there were fewer towns, and the army detachments were all behind them now.

Each time they approached a trader or a coach headed in their direction, Mauritane steadied himself in case it was Purane-Es. And with each traveler that proved not to be his prey, Mauritane felt more and more uneasy.

When they passed the Paracala Bridge, Mauritane began to listen to his deepest fears. From the bridge to the City Emerald was no more than eight hours' ride. If Purane-Es had been riding at top speed, he might have reached the city by now. And then what? Would he take the girl to the palace and claim that Mauritane had turned traitor once again, spinning some wild tale for the Chamberlain? Or had he already ditched the girl and was just hurrying home to watch the public spectacle of Mauritane's failure? However Mauritane looked at it, Purane-Es reaching the city before him was bad news.

An hour later, they found him.

There was a group of riders blocking the road, several dozen of them, sporting the caparisons of the Royal Guard. They were resting their horses in the lee of a stone wall that ran alongside the road. A young woman in a thick fur cloak stood at the center of the group, her hands tied before her. As the car approached, a few of the guardsmen turned their heads at the sound and, seeing what was coming toward them, ran at it with their swords out.

"Stop the car," said Mauritane.

Satterly slowed the vehicle to a stop, and they climbed out onto the road.

"What is all this?" said one of the approaching guardsmen.

"Who's the commander you're riding with?" said Mauritane, his hand on his sword.

"Purane-Es," the man said.

"I have business with him."

"Who are you?"

"Mauritane."

The guardsman choked back a gasp. "Mauritane?" he said, his eyes wide. "You . . . the hero of Sylvan!" The rest of the guardsmen dropped their reins and ran toward the car, awed whispers spreading throughout their ranks.

"That man is no hero." Purane-Es strode between his men, pushing the guardsman aside. "He is a criminal, a traitor, and an escaped convict."

Mauritane ran toward him, his sword out before anyone could move. Purane-Es, his weapon already drawn, barely managed to parry Mauritane's lunge, the blade coming within an inch of his face. Mauritane grabbed at his shirt collar and dragged him down face forward onto the cobblestones.

"Get him off me!" shouted Purane-Es. None of the guardsmen moved.

Purane-Es clawed at Mauritane's eyes, anything to get away from him. Mauritane pulled back, swearing. Purane-Es used the advantage to rise to his knees and elbow Mauritane in the groin. With a grunt, Mauritane fell back, rolling to the side and back onto his feet.

Purane-Es stood and attacked, a low thrust that skittered off of Mauritane's blade. Mauritane's riposte was quick; the tip of his sword lashed across Purane-Es's forehead, drawing blood.

They closed. Purane-Es drew a dagger and came in low with sword out and knife high. He lunged and missed. Mauritane followed the motion of the attack and thrust, his blade slicing deep into Purane-Es's belly.

Purane-Es staggered forward a few more steps and fell.

"Someone get him away from me!" shouted Purane-Es.

Mauritane raised his sword.

"Wait," said Purane-Es. "There's something you should know."

The blade wavered in the air. "Speak quickly."

Purane-Es looked up at him, one hand across his bloodstained tunic. "The Lady Anne is my wife now. She divorced you." His eyes were narrow, and he winced from the deep wound.

"That is a lie," said Mauritane.

"No," said Purane-Es. "I brought the wedding certificate to show you in Sylvan. I'll show it to you."

"No," said Mauritane. He raised the blade again.

Purane-Es reached into the side pocket of his tunic and withdrew a scrolled piece of parchment, tied with a red ribbon. "Check the seal," hissed Purane-Es, his eyes rolling back in his head. "It's authentic." He turned to his side, clutching his belly.

Mauritane took the scroll from him and unfurled it. He scanned the print several times.

"She never loved you," said Purane-Es. "She loves me. Only me."

Mauritane sank to his knees and looked Purane-Es in the eye. "Is this true?"

Purane-Es nodded. "I win."

Leaning forward, Mauritane took Purane-Es by the lapels of his cloak and jerked him off the ground, then slammed his head onto the cobblestones. Purane-Es cried out in pain.

Mauritane screamed. He pistoned his arms roughly back and forth, smashing Purane-Es's life out onto the Mechesyl Road. He kept screaming.

transformations

auritane stood on a high platform at the edge of the Great Outer Court, overlooking what appeared to be the entire population of the City Emerald. All but one, anyway. The Lady Anne was not among them, not anywhere that he'd looked. He continued to search the crowd, scanning over the thousands of faces and seeing none of them.

The Lord Chamberlain Marcuse was at the podium, giving a carefully worded speech about Mauritane's heroism. Despite his ancient appearance he had no difficulty orating to the enormous court, his voice low and rumbling. He sketched the details of Mauritane's life, skipping gracefully over Mauritane's conviction for treason and alleged prison break, implying subtly that the former Guard Captain had spent the past two years on some kind of elaborate undercover operation.

Mauritane sighed and waved a pageboy over, asking for the third time if anyone had seen his wife.

"No answer at her home, sir," whispered the page.

Surely she had not already moved their things out of the house on Boulevard Laurwelana. That would take weeks, and the marriage certificate was dated only ten days ago. Could she be hiding? If all that Purane-Es had said was true, then she would not be eager to see him. It occurred to Mauritane that perhaps she had, in fact, been receiving his letters over the past two years and had simply been ignoring them. How had she become such a stranger to him?

Lord Purane was trotted out, bearing the Guard Captain's cloak. "We of Her Majesty's Royal Guard welcome you back, Captain Mauritane," he said. Always the politician, Purane had agreed without protest to the Chamberlain's suggestion that Purane-Es had died in combat at Sylvan. Returning the captaincy to

Mauritane appeared to be his grand gesture to the public as the mourning father and elder statesman. In reality, however, it was the price he paid to keep Purane-Es's name clean. Mauritane had had nothing to do with any of it; the machinations had all taken place during their brief drive to the city following Purane-Es's death, moving at the speed of politics and message sprites.

Mauritane rose as Purane walked on stage, tacitly accepting his part in the melodrama.

"We welcome you, Mauritane," Purane announced, placing the cloak around Mauritane's shoulders. "I trust you will find the Guard as able as you left it."

"I am honored," Mauritane responded. He locked eyes with the man, wondering what kind of father he had been to his sons that they would turn out as they had. Purane-Es's blood was still sticky between Mauritane's fingers. That Lord Purane knew it and was still able to pretend courtesy was a kind of hypocrisy that Mauritane could only pity and never understand.

"Get ready to greet your public," the Chamberlain said. He turned to the crowd and shouted, "I give you Mauritane, the hero of Sylvan and Captain of Her Majesty's Royal Guard!"

Mauritane stepped forward and cheers burst forth in the square. Shopkeepers and message boys threw their caps in the air. The ladies-in-waiting on the grandstands blew bubbles and whistled down at him.

The Chamberlain had Silverdun brought forward next. Silverdun managed to smile and wave. He even made eyes at a few of the ladies in the stands, despite his new face. None of the ladies seemed to mind.

Satterly and Raieve came next. They both received cheers as well, but nothing compared to what Mauritane got when the Chamberlain said his name one last time.

"Maur-i-tane!" the crowd cried in unison. "Maur-i-tane!"

For a moment, Mauritane looked over the crowd and was suddenly aware of who they were and what they represented. They were the blood of the Seelie Heart, and they mattered more than what Purane-Es had done, or what the Lady Anne had done, or even what Mauritane himself had done. This was a moment of pure joy for the Seelie people and he would share it with them.

He raised his eyes to the sky and the blue of it stung his heart. Over the

Seelie Grove, a single puffy cloud made its slow way across the sky, golden and shining. The smell of salt from the Emerald Bay was in the afternoon air; it was a different smell entirely from the dank Channel Sea waters that pervaded the air at Crere Sulace. The Emerald Bay smelled like childhood and friendship, simplicity and love.

The Pontiac was still parked in front of the stage; some event-planning functionary had thought it good theater to have them drive out of the square in it, not realizing that the crowd would mob the car, touching its sides and injuring themselves in the process. A line of Guardsmen was dispatched, and they were able to leave without further incident.

Outside the square, the Chamberlain approached with a trio of huge guards. "Come," he said briskly, his effusive public demeanor gone. "Your Queen wishes to greet you."

Mauritane froze. "Me?" he said.

"All of you."

"But my wife . . ." Mauritane began.

The Chamberlain looked at him. "There will be time for that."

They were led through the Inner Court, where the nightingales on their perches trilled and the troubadours and skalds sang and danced. Already, someone had composed a ballad of Sylvan, and it was performed throughout the palace grounds

The ancient palace rose before them in the Inner Court, its stones worn to their essential shapes, its towers dark and shrouded in the past. The blue and gold flag of Titania flew outside the gates, fluttering in a gentle breeze.

They were admitted to the palace via a seldom-used side entrance, although it was one Mauritane knew well, since it was convenient to his old office. Walking through the corridors there, he experienced a feast of emotions, not all of them painful.

The throne room was plain, compared to the rest of the palace. The walls were mostly bare, and the thrones themselves were simple, high-backed stone chairs that were built of the same material as the palace. To Mauritane, who had never been allowed here before, the sight was an awesome one regardless. The trio of guards led them into the room and left, closing the door behind them.

Only one of the thrones was currently occupied. King Auberon sat slumped in his chair, his eyes open but vacant, his fingers drumming a slow rhythm against the arm of his throne. He neither moved nor looked at them as they entered.

Momentarily, a small door behind the Queen's throne opened and Regina Titania swept into the room, leading Elice, daughter of Geracy, by the hand. The Queen's appearance belied her many thousands of years; if Mauritane had to guess he would say she was too young even to be a grandmother, and yet the children to whom she had given birth had lived so long ago that they had spoken a different language. She was tall, very tall, her movements precise and sinuous. Her face was open but fierce, all proud angles and lines of concern. Her violet eyes, about which many poems had been written, were at once gay and serious. She wore a simple white gown that flowed to her bare feet, and the Seelie Crown rested lightly over her close-cropped hair.

Mauritane had not seen Elice since that morning. After Purane-Es's death, Raieve had dragged her, kicking and screaming, into the automobile. She'd calmed down a bit once in the Pontiac but had not spoken a word. She remained silent and agitated even when they arrived in the city amidst a hail of trumpet calls and confetti, and she was whisked away by the Chamberlain and his men. Now she was calm, and her hair had been cropped short to match the Queen's.

The Queen let go of Elice's hand and ascended her throne, sparing a quick glance at her husband. Elice sat at the Queen's side, looking down at them, an odd smile on her face.

"Welcome home, Captain," said the Queen. "We are honored to have your in Our service."

Mauritane bowed low. "The honor, Majesty, is mine. I am . . . it is my greatest joy in life to have served thee."

Regina Titania smiled briefly, showing a line of perfect white teeth. Her smile was that of a gently scolding mother. "It pleases Us to hear it, although We are aware that the road has been difficult."

She leaned forward, resting her chin in her hands. "You do not know it, Mauritane," she said, "but you are a hero in more ways than one. In more ways than you can possibly imagine, in fact. And for that you shall be both rewarded and reviled in your time. But today, you are a hero to Us and to Our people."

Mauritane bowed again. "It is my pleasure to serve thee, Majesty."

"Bring your companions forward, let me look at them," she said.

Satterly came first. She stood and took his face in her hands, peering into his eyes. "You are human. Do you wish to return to the world of your birth?"

"May I stay instead?" said Satterly. "I have a friend in Sylvan that I'd like to see again."

"As you wish," said the Queen. "I am feeling generous of spirit today. And those who engage in the changeling trade are no friends of the kingdom."

She waved Raieve forward. "You are Raieve, of the Heavy Sky Clan of Avalon."

Raieve nodded.

"You do not care much for the Seelie Fae."

"I am from a different place," said Raieve, unafraid.

The Queen smiled again. "Indeed. What boon may I grant you?"

"I wish only to return to my homeland. I came to this world for assistance in bringing peace to Avalon. I was arrested and imprisoned for my trouble."

"You will be provided with what is necessary," said the Queen. "Though your experience may show otherwise, We sympathize with the plight of our neighbor world and wish her peace and prosperity. You may speak with my Guard Captain about the matter after I am through with him."

The Queen looked over her shoulder at Silverdun, who stood still at attention. "Are you Lord Silverdun?" she asked. "You are altered."

Silverdun bowed. "I am, Highness."

"Come forward."

The Queen rose and examined Silverdun's ruined face with great care. "There is no glamour here," she said, sadly.

"No, it will not come off."

"Do you know what this is?" she said.

Silverdun shook his head.

"This is the work of the thirteenth Gift. The Gift of Change Magic. It has not been seen since the Great Reshaping."

Silverdun touched his face. "Change Magic? But it was only a girl that did this to me."

"We were once only a girl, Lord Silverdun, and look what We have accomplished." She looked away, sadly. "All of these things are coming to pass as We have always known they would." She leaned in toward him and spoke quietly. "You have been marked, Lord Silverdun, by the one who will eventually unseat Us, though that day is far from today."

"Unseat Your Highness?" said Silverdun. "Impossible."

"Hear me, Lord Silverdun," the Queen whispered in his ear. "In your lifetime, the magic will go out of the world, and the one who did this to you will be the cause of it. When that time comes, We will no longer be fit to rule. You must be prepared for that day, for I will call on you by name. This is for your ears alone."

The Queen gently stroked Silverdun's face with her fingertips. As she touched him, the lines of his face stretched and rearranged themselves. When she moved her hands away, he was nearer to the old Silverdun, recognizable at least, and no longer misshapen. But he was not the same.

"I've restored your face as much as I'm able," said the Queen. "Some of the changes wreaked upon you are more than skin deep, and not all of them were caused by the one who cast that spell upon you. Wear this, your third and final face, with pride. It suits you."

"Your majesty," said Silverdun, bowing.

"What boon will you take, Lord?"

"Only that I be allowed leave to help restore the Temple Aba-e in Sylvan."

"You go with my blessing," said the Queen. "The followers of Aba are no enemies of Ours, any more than the north wind is at war with the south wind. Sometimes they meet and cause a storm, but neither despises the other for what it is."

"You are most gracious, Majesty."

"Enough," said the Queen. She nodded to the Chamberlain. "Take these away and find them suitable quarters in the guest wing. Have a meal prepared for the high court and the lambs slain. Leave Mauritane here with Us."

Silverdun, Satterly, and Raieve filed out of the throne room following the Chamberlain.

The Queen returned to her throne and knelt before it, taking the hand of Geracy's daughter. Together they rose and approached the center of the throne room.

"As my honored servant," the Queen said to Mauritane, "We offer you the only gift We have that is worth what you have given Us. Our secret."

Mauritane did not understand.

"You risked everything to bring this young woman to Us, and you never asked the reason."

"It is not necessary for me to know the reason," said Mauritane.

Again, the Queen smiled. "Your loyalty borders on faith, Mauritane. Listen, and We will tell you a story."

The Queen led Elice down to the floor of the throne room and they sat opposite each other, the Queen on the left, Elice on the right. They locked eyes, and the Queen reached up and took the crown from her head, placing it gently on Elice's unlined brow.

"When I was a girl," she said, switching to the first person, "I was innocent and brave. I was one of the most powerful of those who dwelt here during the time of the Great Reshaping. I could bend the entire world to my will if I so desired. I wanted only what was best for the Faerie Kingdom, and in my innocence I believed that I could provide it. I tricked the son of Aba into becoming my husband. There he sits." She cast a tender glance at Auberon, still staring blankly into the distance. "If he remains in that body, I do not know. I removed the power of speech from him so long ago."

She returned her eyes to Elice. The air around the two of them seemed to shift and move, as though they sat in a desert mirage. "All of the magic that went into the Great Reshaping was locked into the forms it created. I realized too late that this magic was irretrievable and that there was no more to replace it when it was gone. There were some who would have used up all of the magic in this world and made it a place without miracles and wonder. I believed that was wrong. I wanted the Faerie lands as I knew them, so I gathered my strength and I struck the magic of change from my people. I wrestled the power to destroy my kingdom from their grasp. I was devoted, you understand, to securing the future of my land."

The air continued to shimmer. Mauritane thought he could see the shapes of the two women begin to shift around them.

"After a hundred years had passed, the Seelie lands were mine. Mab was the only one powerful enough to stand against me, and either I or Aba removed her from my sight. She went north to make a place in her own image, and I remained in mine. But all was not well here. In my singleness of purpose, owning the land as I did, the warmth began to flow from it. The birds stopped singing, and the hot winds ceased to blow from the west. The land of summer's twilight began to grow cold, and snow began to fall, blowing down from the northern wastes. The River Ebe froze in its course."

Mauritane blinked, trying to follow what was going on before him. The light in the room had gone funny, and his eyes were playing tricks on him.

"That was the first winter. I consulted my wizards and my philosophers, and none of them knew why it had happened. They suggested sacrifices and spells and dances to the long-dead gods of the sun and the winds. Deep in my heart, though, I knew the answer. I had failed my land and my people. In my devotion, I had lost my vision of what it was I had sworn to uphold. I had become corrupt, just as anyone with power is corrupted. I realized I was no different or better than anyone else; I was just more powerful."

Mauritane tried to focus his eyes on the two women before him and found himself unable. They seemed to be at a distance from him that his eyes could not register. Suddenly his perspective shifted and he could see that the Queen's lips were no longer moving. Her voice was coming from the girl, Elice.

"Desperate, I begged Aba for the answer. I called him down from his palace in the sky and I asked him what to do. And what he told me is something I have never forgotten. 'All that is flesh is corruptible,' he told me. 'All that is in order will one day decay.'

"It was not the answer I wanted. My people loved me, needed me. Or so I thought. And in my desperation I came upon a solution, one that only I could provide. I searched the kingdom for an innocent soul that hearkened back to my own. I found her, finally, in the far east. She was the daughter of a baron whose name I once swore never to forget but have long since forgotten. The epitome of innocence and ambition, just as I had been. I brought her to me."

The shimmering of the air began to recede. Mauritane looked again, and it appeared now as though the Queen were sitting to the right of Elice, though he had not seen them change position.

"I brought to bear the magic of change upon her and upon me. I gave her my memories and my desires, and I took hers into me. I gave her my face, my form, my voice, and in return I took my leave from the cage I'd built around myself. Regina Titania walked from the throne room on that day, and Laura Crere Sulace ruled in her place. Her fresh spirit allowed the rivers to melt and the warm breezes to blow again. Summer returned to the land, and all was well.

"At least, it was for a time."

The two women rose. The motion of the air was gone, and now it was indeed Elice who stood on the left and Queen Titania who stood on the right.

"Her reign lasted one hundred years. And when her heart faded, winter returned. She cast her net for a replacement and found one, just as Regina Titania had done.

"As the centuries continued, a new heart was brought to bear on the kingdom every hundred years. And that secret became the most treasured and most dangerous of all. For if anyone were to discover that Titania no longer ruled in the City Emerald, the Seelie Kingdom would fall away like sand. Mab could press her ancient claim to the throne, and an age of darkness would come to the Seelie Fae. And I am not yet prepared to let that happen. Soon, but not yet.

"So," said the new Queen, "you understand that the secrecy and the deceit that accompanied your errand were of unfortunate necessity.

She smiled. "That is my story, and the moral of it I leave for you to discern. I trust you will take your lesson where you can find it."

The Queen returned to her throne, and Elice stepped slowly down to where Mauritane stood. The girl took his hand and kissed him lightly on the cheek. "Thank you," she whispered.

"What boon do you ask, Mauritane?" the Queen said. "Anything in my power to provide I will give you."

Mauritane struggled for words. "All I want I have," he said. "Only now I would like to go see my wife."

The Queen's face was somber. "You have served Us well, Mauritane. We will hold your boon in abeyance."

Mauritane nodded.

"Is there something else?"

He paused. "Something yet troubles me."

"Speak."

"Twice during this mission I have been called 'He Who Clears the Path,' once by the Thule Man and again by an Arcadian."

"Ah, the Thule Man. We knew him once, when we were both much younger. And you wish to know what this means."

"I do."

Titania leaned forward in her throne and rested her chin in her hands. It was a girlish posture for a Queen.

"It is a prophecy, nothing more; prophecies surround Us like gnats. But We see that it troubles you."

"I do not wish to be the slave of fate," said Mauritane.

The Queen giggled. "We are all slaves," she said. "Not to fate, though, but to our own hearts. Not even your Queen is exempt from that."

"But if a prophet sets a path for me, then my own honor means nothing. I am a puppet."

"No, you misunderstand. The Prophet sees, yes. *But to see is not to cause.* The title of 'He Who Clears the Path,' like any other such, is simply a pedestal upon which your own choices have placed you. Had you opted to be a coward or a fool, someone else would eventually have stood there."

She gestured him closer and almost whispered. "It is one thing you and I have in common. Greatness casts a long shadow; cast forward by the sun and backward by the moon."

"I still do not understand," said Mauritane looking down.

The Queen smiled gently, taking his chin in her hand. "It makes no difference to Us."

He met Raieve in the hallway outside the main dining hall. She, Satterly, and Silverdun were being feted there, the standard complement of nobility and would-be nobility hanging on their every word, laughing at their jokes and racing to fill their cups.

"I had to get away from them all," she said. "I want nothing more to do with this place."

"I was coming to find you," he said. "I'm about to go home."

"I see," she said flatly.

"I wanted to say goodbye."

She raised an eyebrow. "You haven't yet arranged my escort back to Avalon."

"Come to my office in the morning," Mauritane said, slowly. "I'll have someone there take care of you."

"Oh." She turned away.

"Raieve . . ."

"What? What do you want from me?"

"I just want you to know that I am glad to have known you."

She looked at him, and he looked back.

"I won't forget you," he said.

She nodded. "I . . ." she began, struggling with the words. "I'm sorry about everything."

"There's nothing to be sorry about," he whispered. He put his arms around her and clutched her to him.

"If you're ever in Avalon . . ." she began, but tears began to come, and she pushed him away. "You know how I feel." She ran off down the hallway and disappeared.

Silverdun walked with Mauritane to his home on the Boulevard Laurwelana. "I've spoken with Satterly," he said. "We're returning to Sylvan in the morning. There's much to be done there."

"You spoke of the temple," said Mauritane. "Have you become an Arcadian then?"

"I don't know," Silverdun said. "Let us say that I have reopened the option. For Satterly's part, I don't know if he's more excited about looking after lost changelings or the lost human woman he left there." He smiled briefly. "What will you do, Mauritane?"

"I'm going home," Mauritane said. "I'm going to talk to my wife, try to pick up the pieces of our marriage. There may yet be some love for me in her heart."

"Purane-Es was a liar and a fool," said Silverdun. "You mustn't take anything he said too seriously."

"We'll find out, won't we?" said Mauritane. They were at the door of Mauritane's building. "I am glad you were with me, Silverdun. I knew I could count on you, and you never disappointed me."

"If I recall correctly, you threatened to kill me if I did."

Mauritane nodded. "That's true," he said.

They embraced. "Come visit us up in Sylvan when you get the chance," he said.

"I'll do that. Goodbye, Silverdun."

"Goodbye."

Silverdun watched him go in and turned away from the building. The sun overhead was warm and bright, and he felt truly blessed for the first time in memory. He looked out over the Seelie Grove, its lush vegetation buried under a carpet of snow, and watched amazed as the first tiny patches of snow there began to melt, dripping away in tiny rivulets. It was beautiful.

Mauritane's keys had been taken from him years ago. He rang the bell, and when only a servant answered, his heart fell from his chest into his stomach. The steward made him wait in his own parlor. He sat uncomfortably in a high-backed chair. The furniture was different—he felt like a stranger here.

After too long of a wait, Lady Anne made her entrance, dressed neck to toe in black.

"Captain Mauritane," she said, curtseying. "Your unexpected presence is a pleasure."

Mauritane stood and dismissed the servant.

"Wait a moment," the Lady Anne called after the steward. "Captain Mauritane and I require an escort."

The servant glanced between Mauritane and the Lady Anne and cowered in a corner.

Mauritane reached for her hand. She pulled it gently from his grasp, her pleasant smile never moving.

"What is this? An escort? And you in widow's weeds?" he said.

The smile faltered a bit. "If you're here to pay your respects for my husband, there will be a formal ceremony in the Ash Grove tomorrow."

Mauritane's strength left him and he fell into the chair. "I am your husband," he said. "I am."

"Not any more," said the Lady Anne. "I am the wife of Purane-Es, and I am in mourning. So if you would please excuse me, I have much to do."

"You can't mean this," he whispered, his voice shaking.

"It was good of you to come, Captain. I will pass your respects along to my husband's family."

Mauritane stared at her, unable to move.

"Is there something else?" Her eyes and lips were as delicately positioned as her gown and her jewelry. She was a mask, impenetrable.

He said nothing.

"I see," she said. "Goodbye, then." She spun, her black skirts swirling around her, and hurried from the room.

Mauritane remained in the chair, staring at nothing, until the servant regained his composure and finally asked him to leave. As he stepped out of his home for the last time, he felt a splash on his shoulder. Looking up, he saw water dripping from the icicles above the door.

the city of mab

Queen Mab reclined on a floating platform overlooking the construction site of her new city. The platform was covered and decorated with flowers; a hundred different varieties. She plucked a purple foxglove from its stem and chewed it thoughtfully. Behind the chaise where she lay a servant fanned her in a steady rhythm.

The scene below pleased her. The new city of Mab would be larger than the last. Her architects had arrived at a design that was both pleasing to the eye and also more imposing, better to send forth into battle and easier to defend. Her apartments were now being installed over the superstructure. From them she could peer over the battlements, calling out orders to her troops below, the clouds near enough to touch.

All was on schedule; the base of the city would be finished before the summer quakes came to topple it. She would fly again soon.

Some of her ministers could still not understand why she preferred her flying cities. They were children; they whispered behind her back as if she could not hear every word spoken and they plotted as if their schemes were not as transparent as gossamer. But they were easy to manipulate and that was all that mattered.

They prattled on and on about finding new lands on which they could settle and build their staid villas. They wanted metropolises that would stand for millennia, never moving, testaments to the builders. Long ago she had tried to explain to them that nothing was ever built that did not one day fall to ruin. They pointed to the Great Seelie Keep in response and she only smiled behind her hand. That too, she told them, would one day fall, and the sound of its falling would be heard across many worlds. She would see to it.

But she was a gracious empress, was she not? She allowed them their invasion of Avalon, let them see for themselves what a trouble it was. She sent only the worst commanders, certainly, and purposefully gave them conflicting orders so that it all came to nothing. It had taken many years and many lives for them to see their folly, but that was so often what was required. It was a lesson that every generation needed to learn.

She'd come to understand that there was no idea so foolish that each new age could not revive it.

Soon the Chambers of Elements and Motion would come to life again. She had cast her net far and wide across her empire for the best masters and this new crop was every bit the equal of the one she'd lost to the Seelie. This time the Chambers would be better protected; she would not be beaten the same way twice. And in the Secret City, high in the clouds, so high that land could not even be seen from its decks, her Magi were turning out Hy Pezho's weapons by the scores. Building them required blood and death and innocence, but it was worth the price. That which would bring Regina Titania to her knees was worth whatever she paid for it. In the end, humbling the Stone Queen was all that truly mattered. Everything else fell away; everything else was transient. Only She remained, and only Her abasement would be meaningful.

As for Hy Pezho himself, well, he had been a piece of work. So much like his father. And he had come to the same end. This was another cycle that repeated across the centuries; the men who believed they could best her. Had any of them bothered to lift their noses from their red-inked books of thaumatics and instead perused a work of history, they would have discovered that there were reasons that Mab had ruled for as long as she had. But they never learned. It grew so very, very tiresome.

Ah, but there was something else coming, wasn't there? For the first time in many, many years, Mab had begun to have those special dreams, the dreams of foretelling. As always with powerful things, the dreams were both insistent and vague. Someone was coming. Someone would come to her.

And everything would change.

But that was later; there was no use putting this in the hands of her court seers. They would only equivocate and argue and pen endless discourses that amounted to nothing. She'd once split a prophet down the middle with a

THE CITY OF MAB 341

wave of her finger to alleviate the boredom of him. The others had been more careful after that, but not for long enough. Never anything for long enough!

But this city before her would last awhile, and that was good. And beyond it another, and another, and another.

One Year Later

The road Mauritane walked along was lined with wild strawberries and raspberry bushes. He stopped from time to time and picked a few of the tart, pink strawberries and washed them down with water from the stream beyond. Up the road, a tiny village stood at the bank of a wide river, smoke from their cooking fires rising from the houses and disappearing into the blue sky.

He shifted his pack to his left shoulder and continued walking, conscious of the absence of the military sword at his waist. He closed his eyes and smelled the honeysuckle, opened them and looked up again at the potent blue of the sky.

After leaving Sylvan a month ago, though, it was hard to imagine any place more beautiful. Sylvan during Firstcome was a sight to behold. With the coating of dirty snow gone, the city had come once more into its own. The mists were lifted and the valley was cleansed by the rains of Firstcome that poured over the temple and the city below, washing away the grime of the cold season that had passed, washing away the ashes and the bloodstains of last year's bitter struggle. All was still not well in the west and perhaps never would be. One battle would not solve anything, and the rancor between the Arcadians and the nobility there would not be washed away as easily as the remains of the battle.

And yet, strides had been made. Eloquet had, at Mauritane's relentless urging, consented to join the Royal Guard. He'd risen quickly in the ranks over the last year, thanks in part to his reputation from the Battle of Sylvan, and in greater measure to his skills as a leader and his love of country. He would someone make a fine replacement. An Arcadian as Captain of the Guard. That would be something.

Looking ahead, Mauritane could see a figure kneeling in a garden outside one of the houses. He changed his course and left the road, angling toward the lone gardener.

At the temple in Sylvan, he'd shared a bottle of wine with Satterly and Silverdun. They'd spent a few languorous hours renewing their acquaintance. They told stories from their days at Crere Sulace and talked about their lives now and how things had changed. They compared scars and relived old wounds. They remembered lost friends. It had been good.

Mauritane crunched through a litter of leaves from the oak trees overhead. A small field of wheat was all that separated him from the village now. The woman kneeling in her garden looked up at him and froze. She stood, slowly, dusting her hands off on her long dress. Shading her eyes with her hand, she looked across the swaying stalks of grain and called out his name. She leaped out of the garden and sprinted toward him.

The sky overhead was so blue; Mauritane thought his heart might break. Across the river, the bright sun of Avalon began to angle downward toward the mountains. Mauritane let his pack fall to the ground and ran across the field to meet her.

About the Author

MATTHEW STURGES has written several books for DC Comics, including *House of Mystery*, *Salvation Run*, *Blue Beetle*, and the Eisner-nominated *Jack of Fables* (with Bill Willingham). *Midwinter* is his first novel.

He lives in Austin, Texas, with his wife, Stacy, and their two daughters, Millie and Mercy.

Visit him online at http://www.matthewsturges.com.